ABOUT THE AUTHOR

Simon Whitworth was born in Watford, England. He
finished writing *Jessie Granton and the Invisible Steps*
after he moved to the Isle of Wight.

He is now working on the sequel.

JESSIE GRANTON

AND THE
INVISIBLE STEPS

SIMON WHITWORTH

Matador
Unit E2 Airfield Business Park
Harrison Road, Market Harborough
Leicestershire LE16 7UL
Tel: 0116 279 2299
Email: books@troubador.co.uk
Web: www.troubador.co.uk/matador

www.theinvisiblesteps.com

ISBN 978-1-80514-037-5

British Library Cataloguing in Publication Data.
A catalogue record for this book is available from the British Library.

Printed and bound in Great Britain by 4edge Limited
Typeset in 11pt Adobe Garamond Pro by Troubador Publishing Ltd, Leicester, UK

Matador is an imprint of Troubador Publishing Ltd

Contents

CHAPTER 1

A Little About Me

My name is Jessie Granton, and these words are true, but you will decide whether you believe them or not. I am slight in build, very short, with green eyes and long brown hair. People say I'm beautiful, but I can't see it. To me, beauty is in nature, not in me. I don't look at myself like that.

I was born in the spring of 1992, at home at Granton Manor, and into the Granton fortune. I should feel lucky to have lived in such a magnificent house, deep in the heart of the Kent countryside. The countryside and the wildlife, I loved; they felt like home. The house, less so. It was huge and stately, with echoing wood-panelled rooms and dark corridors. The height of the ceilings and the size of the building were overwhelming, and there were parts of it that were never even used. Multiple members of domestic staff floated in and out on their daily chores, and yet it always felt empty. Surrounding us were acres of manicured lawns and neatly pruned borders, also tended to by solemn-looking workers.

Every opportunity I could, I would run outside with my beloved Tansy, a tan and white collie, delving into the furthest parts of the grounds and the woodlands just beyond them. It was in these that Tansy and I spent our time, lying amongst the mass of bluebells, thousands of them, a candy store of nature at its most beautiful. When the bluebells retreated, the daisies were our favourites. Nothing else would matter once we were amongst them. We would pick a spot to sit where the sun would make its way through the canopy of branches and warm our faces and bodies, and we were absorbed into the landscape like welcome friends. Sometimes I would dangle from a branch, swinging gently as Tansy stared up at me, and I down to her. I could dangle there for hours, just thinking.

I didn't go to school; instead I was tutored at home by my mother, who was strict but fair, and kind in her own way. She understood, I think, that I preferred the company of animals to humans and to spend my time hanging from trees, rather than meeting other children or going on excursions. I heard mutterings, mostly from the staff, that I was 'different' or 'peculiar', but I didn't care. When I had to be with people, if I wanted to gaze and stare, which I did a lot, then why shouldn't I? That's how Tansy and I communicated, for the most part. We didn't need so many words – our connection was closer than that.

My father – who they say I'm the most like – was short like me, but commanding nonetheless. He was spare with his words, and often preoccupied, though when he did talk and play with me, it was a delicious jolt of pure joy that surprised me every time. When I reached about ten years old, he decided to teach me how to fly. I was apprehensive at first, but the sky seemed to welcome me, and I loved it. The speed, the power.

2

I could go into the outside world without ever really going there. Although it was just a two-seater light aircraft that we would take off and land in the grounds of Granton Manor, to me it was the biggest and best plane ever made.

Within no time at all I was flying as well as my father. It turned out I was a natural, just like him. When I did my first landing, he helped me down from the plane and spun me round and round.

"You are the cleverest girl in the world," he said, "the cleverest girl ever born."

I had never seen him look so jubilant. My heart took hours to slow down after that. I just couldn't contain my happiness, and tossed and turned in bed that night, overflowing with excitement and pride.

It was the last time I would feel that way for a very, very long time.

CHAPTER 2

Without a Trace

Two days later my world was crushed. My parents left Granton Manor in the light aircraft, for what purpose I never knew. But wherever their destination was to have been, they failed to arrive. Neither my parents nor their plane were found. They simply disappeared without a trace. In the four years since that day, not one search had brought up anything. Not a thing. And so I lived with the hope, probably foolishly, that one day they would come home to me. Apologetic, of course, with a truly lavish reason for their disappearance. I took to watching the sky, hoping for a glimpse of their plane, and then when that didn't present itself, just letting the clouds cushion me and the gentle blue of the sky soothe my heart.

How quickly my life had changed, from having my parents with me and living as we pleased, to becoming an orphan, with domestic staff charged with my care yet I didn't care for them at all. I didn't find them kind towards me; it was like I was an inconvenience. My only friend was Tansy. Sweet, silky Tansy, whose eyes bored into mine as though she understood my every thought and feeling. I think she really did understand. She and I roamed the grounds as before, and lay in our bluebell haven, but it wasn't the same. The one question that flooded my head was: Why? Why did this have to happen? And why my parents? Why me?

I learned to block out the question after a while and to shut out the sadness too. If bad things had happened, they must have happened for a reason. I just didn't know what that was yet. I didn't know what to do with myself either, as the tutoring had disappeared along with my mother. The housekeeper, the sharp-faced Mrs Talbot, had employed a tutor to spend afternoons with me, but I just refused to speak to her. At all. She soon gave up, and I was left to my own devices. Tansy and I spent all day outside, whatever the weather, taking nature books with us from Daddy's library. I learned the names of every flower, every bush, every creature I saw, and even learned how to whistle like a song thrush and call out to the blackbirds. I made friends with a muntjac deer and helped her with her kid when it got injured. And Tansy was always by my side, sensing when to stay quiet and still and when to protect me. But even that wasn't to last.

Shortly before my eleventh birthday, about a year after my parents' disappearance, the decision was made to send me to boarding school. The staff claimed they could no longer look after me and that I couldn't go without an education any longer. I was furious.

They organised a funeral for my parents, even though there was no evidence they were even dead; 'presumed dead' was apparently enough. What few relatives I had left were not interested – or not that I could tell, anyway. Those who made it to the funeral seemed far more interested in my parents' money that was left behind than in the child now living without a mother or father – me.

And worst of all was being separated from Tansy. I was not allowed to take her to boarding school, no matter how much I pleaded. I could have handled anything if Tansy had been with me. But it wasn't to be, and they had to prize her off me on the day I left home, my trunk stuffed with nature books and very little else. I had a small framed photograph of my beautiful girl, which I put up beside my bunk as soon as I got to the school, much to the sniggers of the other girls there. But what did they know? Not one of them could ever surely be as loyal, loving and true as my beloved Tansy. Her brown eyes fixed me morning and night as I stared, ignoring the snide whispers and titters that reverberated around the dorm as the girls poked fun at my height, my way of talking – or lack of, and my passion for nature. Tansy would have treated them with disdain, I'm sure of it, and would have snarled her best snarls, baring her yellow teeth and making them feel sorry for ever uttering a word against me.

CHAPTER 3

Green Girl

.

The less said about my time at boarding school, the better. I found a way to get along with people and stop them from bullying me. In fact, I rather excelled at standing my ground, after practice, until I gained the nickname 'The Tiny Terror', owing to my deadly staring, my 'impertinence' and my obstinacy. I was also known as 'Green Girl' because of the amount of time I spent either in the school meadow or pinning up posters about animal cruelty and the environment, which led to much eye-rolling from students and staff alike. And because of my piercing green eyes.

But school bored and frustrated me, in particular the elocution lessons which we all had to endure. Mrs Perryman, who carefully enunciated every word, had already told me I spoke beautifully, with the diction of a lady many years older than myself, reinforcing to me the pointless nature of the lessons. So I made frequent attempts to escape from Wolfsons, which never actually worked. I longed for Tansy and the woodlands and the freedom to do as I pleased. The school holidays were good but not long enough. The staff at home had diminished to Mrs Talbot, two gardeners and a couple of cleaners, so if I dodged Mrs Talbot, I could lead a pleasant enough life, feeling the pull of nature from the moment I woke up to the moment I flopped, exhausted, into bed.

I put up with Mrs Talbot's sneers whilst I was at home, and her gruff phone calls whilst at school, until one day I received the second most devastating news I had ever had: Tansy was dead.

Not only was my poor girl dead, but the staff had neglected to tell me for two whole weeks. And not even with a phone call to the school, just a letter. Written by Mrs Talbot and completely lacking in sympathy, she curtly informed me in her mean, spidery writing that Tansy had strayed into a neighbouring farm several times and been caught rounding up their rather sleepy sheep. On getting no assurances from the Granton staff that it would not happen again, the farmer took it upon himself to shoot Tansy. Dead. For doing no more than that which ran through her veins – to herd sheep in her sweet, skilful and gentle way, no doubt. The horrible, hateful man.

As for Mrs Talbot and the staff, I couldn't begin to contain the rage I felt at the injustice of it all. My loyal, wonderful friend shot because of neglectful humans who couldn't care for the most obedient, undemanding dog you could meet.

My mind was made up.

I could not allow the staff at Granton Manor to continue working there. I had to find a way to get rid of them, at least for a while, while I figured out a plan. And I could not tolerate a single second more of being trapped at Wolfsons Girls.

So I didn't.

CHAPTER 4

Freedom Awaits

Mrs Talbot's letter had informed me that she and the rest of the staff were taking the opportunity, now that no one needed to be there for Tansy, or for me until the February half term, to take some time off by way of a holiday. A holiday – after what they did! Or didn't do…

This was my chance.

I spent hours after dark in bed, plotting my escape route. This time it would work because it had to. And this time there was no coming back to Wolfsons.

***

It was surprisingly easy once I'd thought it all through. From the pilfered door key, to lies that got me access to the sick bay, to the middle-of-the-night dash when the school nurse had nodded off. With the help of Josephine Linley's make-up bag (unbeknown to her), I made a pretty good impression of a young woman way older than my fourteen years, and after hiding outside the nearby train station in the shadows for four hours, I hopped on the 5.45am to Higham without anyone batting an eyelid. Not that there were many eyelids or humans belonging to them at that time in the morning.

On approaching Granton Manor, the sun burst through the clouds in an almost comedic flourish, as if the earth and sky themselves were welcoming me back home, ready for Jessie Granton to take her rightful place as heiress and owner of the Manor and all of its grounds. Especially its grounds.

***

And so it was, that aged fourteen and twelve days, I stood in my father's library, plans laid out across the antique oak reading table, my mind buzzing. Scraps of paper bearing my determined attempts at forged signatures fluttered to the floor, piles of legal-looking documents teetered, and maps adorned the nearby wall. My plans to despatch the Granton staff and take over the Manor were coming together. I just had to disappear for long enough that when I returned, Granton Manor would be legally mine. The documents I had faked looked really impressive, if I say so myself. Wolfsons had been informed that I had left the school with immediate effect, with the Granton staff's approval. The Granton staff had been informed that they were no longer required owing to a long-lost uncle who had been located and nominated (by a fake newly discovered will, of course) to take over the estate until I reached eighteen. Naturally, no such uncle existed but my forged solicitor signatures were extremely convincing. All I needed to do now was to disappear.

Before that, I needed to practise.

My means of temporary escape this time, was not a humble train but a plane. Because, of course, I could fly and was actually rather good at it.

Since Daddy's plane was now gone, the only aircraft I had at my disposal was my great-grandfather's de Havilland, which he had flown in the First World War. It was in perfect working order, as were his leather flying jacket and goggles. These I would reverently don for every practice session I embarked on, despite the jacket drowning my still-tiny frame. When flying in a piece of history itself, I felt, one should wear the correct attire.

The aircraft was nicknamed 'The Flying Coffin' as its huge fuel tank was positioned between the pilot and the jump seat. Unsurprisingly, this didn't feel like such a witty joke as when my parents first told me, years ago, as a wide-eyed five-year-old. I had to fight the rising nausea the first couple of times I got in, taking deep breaths and repeating to myself 'Remember the plan. Do it for the plan'. As the de Havilland thundered along the lawn and then roared into the sky, a surge of excitement would take over, and once airborne, I would feel a deep sense of peace. Here, my mind would ease and my thoughts would become clear, though I always had to return to Granton Manor, with the bump of the aircraft, back to earth and reality.

Until the fifth time, when that didn't quite happen.

CHAPTER 5

What Secrets the Sky Has to Offer (Pleased to Meet You)

The fog lay heavy around the grounds as dawn broke on that chilly spring day.

I fired the de Havilland up once more. By now I was almost smug at my skills at taking off and landing neatly, though the dense mist was a bit of a worry. With my shoulders hunched forward, my hand gripping the joystick, I managed to raise the plane's nose by sheer instinct, feeling my way through the murk until I was puttering jerkily across the small woodland at the furthest edge of the estate. Without the visual aid of the ground below to help me level the plane, I just kept it soaring up, the freezing fog making me gasp for breath as I raised the craft even higher.

Eventually, in danger of my engine cutting out, I levelled the plane. It responded well, and the engine thanked me by settling down to a steady murmur. Although I wore my usual flying attire – leather jacket and goggles – I had on a favourite

12

floaty dress underneath. I had been utterly fooled by the sunset the night before and believed today was to be a mild, sunny day. It was not what a young lady should be flying a plane in, no doubt, but the freezing fog around my exposed legs kept me, thankfully, from drifting into sleep.

It did now dawn on me that I had no way of landing this plane. Unless the sun could break through to burn the fog away, I really was in trouble. Beginning to panic, I held the controls tight, pushed my knees together and stared directly ahead. I was still very good at staring even after they'd tried to stop me doing it at boarding school, which, of course, I simply ignored. Just as when I was younger, I felt very strongly that if I stared hard enough, I would soon see what I needed to see. Right there in that plane, things would become clear. Because the staring was not just about looking and gazing; it was about seeing. As in, really seeing.

And I was right. As the sun emerged, and the fog fell aside, my de Havilland and I were haring across open countryside just feet above the ground. Once again, I tightened my body, leant forward and peered over the tiny windshield. I tried to raise her, but the wheels clipped a small hedgerow, pulling the left wing towards the ground. As the tip touched down, we spun helplessly out of control.

I couldn't believe I was crashing down. How had I managed to smash the plane like this?

As my body was jerked back and forth, time managed to slow down and stall. As if watching from above, I saw my beautiful plane tossed high before crashing down for the final time, with me a crumpled heap inside.

At last, everything was still. The engine had died, and I now sat in the ruined carcass of this once-great flying machine.

A strong smell of fuel brought me rapidly to my senses. I remembered that I was sharing this confined space with gallons of petrol. I removed my goggles, unfastened myself and jumped the short distance to safety. Once out of danger and far enough away, I sat, using a tree for support, and stared back at the wreckage. My great-grandfather had taken this plane to war and returned with not a mark on it. I had flown it up to the stars – or so it felt – and still managed to hit the ground.

I pushed my head back, giving a sorrowful sigh and examined my wounds. My head was throbbing a little and my hands were bruised where they had been flung against the cockpit equipment, shielding my face in the crash. But I was conscious and not bleeding, just a little shaken and shocked.

The sun had all but totally removed the fog and, as it had done on so many occasions, warmed my face as I closed my eyes and began to feel dozy in the hazy heat. Wiggling my toes as I rested, I felt a wave of sorrow at how much my life had changed since I was little. Images of playing outside in the forest with Tansy filled my mind, running through the undergrowth, so carefree… For the first time since my parents' death, I felt emotion well uncontrollably inside me in a way I had never allowed before. A single tear made its way out and fell onto my hand. It was followed rapidly by several more and then I held my face in my hands and cried and cried. For how long, I am not sure, but it felt so good as each tear lightened the burden. I couldn't stop, or didn't want to.

"You'll feel better soon," a small voice said.

I blinked, and decided that the knock to my head had perhaps caused a little confusion or a spot of hallucination.

I felt a slight tickle on my big toe. I opened my fingers and stared down once more at my feet. I sniffed hard and then continued crying.

The tickle continued and then began to feel as if something was tightening around my toe.

Then I heard the tiny voice again. "Crying is good for you."

OK, so now I had gone officially mad, not just the kind of 'crazy' they used to call me at school, before they stopped daring to.

The yanking on my toe continued.

Had I broken it, or pulled it out of its socket?

The voice was still talking. "The tears will wash away your pain and then you will feel peace and calm, sweet thing…"

My sobs had turned into slightly panicked yelps as I squinted down through my swimming eyes.

Then I felt on my hands a slight gripping sensation, warm and gentle, and it slowly but surely pulled my bruised fingers away from my face.

And there he was.

He was standing to my side and held his small face inches away from mine. He twitched his nose and blinked the loveliest pair of big brown eyes I had ever seen.

"Please stop crying now," he said.

I sniffed once more and wiped my face and eyes. If I was hallucinating or dreaming, this was a very pleasant dream and I hadn't the energy to resist it. So I blinked several times and then focused on this tiny creature who stood only a foot or so high right beside me. His hair was shoulder-length, blonde and curly. He had a round face which was covered in very fine fur, and a cheeky smile which ran from ear to ear. The boots he wore were hard leather with laces which were knotted, maybe in an attempt to be bowed. He was dressed in a very smart brown waistcoat, but scruffy old trousers which didn't quite meet his boots, and then finally a big green parka coat which brushed the ground behind him.

"Who and what are you?" I asked. I wasn't afraid of him; how could I be? He was so gentle.

"I am Oakleigh, a Bella," he replied, so pleased with himself that he hopped from side to side.

"A what?" I stammered. "One of the angels' helpers?" An obvious thought had just struck me: "Does this mean I am dead?" In fact, on uttering the question, I realised I wasn't as afraid as I might have been. If this was the afterlife, it really wasn't that bad at all.

"No, no," Oakleigh replied, "you are very much alive."

This took some time to digest.

CAKLEIGH

"So," I then ventured, "who or what is a Bella?"

"That's what I am," he replied, still dancing from foot to foot. "Would you like to meet Willoughby?"

"Yes, of course," I said, without really thinking. Who was Willoughby?

"Come with me, then," said Oakleigh, already attempting to pull me to my feet and leading me across the grassy field. I refrained from asking too many questions as

I followed the creature, who was remarkably swift at crossing the ground on his diminutive legs, marching forwards, with his paw-like hands swishing the longer grass stalks out of the way as he went. We seemed to be heading to what looked like woodland, at the far end of the field, stretching out ahead of us.

Once in the woodland, the sun flickered through the trees intermittently, highlighting, to my pleasure, rows and rows of bluebells – thousands of them.

Oakleigh marched on, apparently having the speed and energy of a creature twice his size, across moss-covered ground and past lichen-caked trees, all accompanied by birdsong quite unlike any other I had heard before. The birds sang not individually, but as a choir, their sound bouncing off branches, forming the next chord for their beautiful melodies to build upon again and again.

As we emerged from the darkness of the clearing, my eyes adjusted to the bright sunlight, now so strong it felt like a spotlight just on us. I was thankful for a slight breeze, which rolled the bluebells within the clearing to stroke one another, and warmed my face.

WILLOUGHBY

"Willoughby, are you there? Willoughby, it's me, Oakleigh, and Jessie," my new companion said, smiling up at me.

Had I told him my name?

17

Before my very eyes, a small cluster of bluebells began to separate and from beneath them a grubby, circular felt object began to appear as if sprouting up through the earth. As I continued to watch, a little aghast, the object grew some more until the full length of what turned out to be a tiny top hat protruded from the soil, a flash of black hair visible beneath it.

I staggered back a little, but Oakleigh grabbed onto me and held me fast, his arms clamped firmly around my knees. The hat progressed slowly upwards, now revealing long, straight black hair beneath it and a fringe that covered a small, ruddy face. The figure continued to grow until it reached a foot or so, pushed a cane out in front of it and brushed the fringe away from its face. This creature, too, had startling big brown eyes, but his expression was sterner than Oakleigh's and he didn't smile. He just stared up, watching my face for the slightest reaction. Then he spoke. "You look tired, Jessie."

"How do you both know my name?" I asked, trying not show anger, but with a little force. It confused me, and my right foot rose an inch or two to stamp the ground. But in return they both blinked sweetly, unperturbed by my outburst.

After a pause, in which they remained calmly gazing up at me, I took a deep breath and reluctantly answered: "Yes, I feel shattered. This morning has been a bit... unexpected. I really do feel very tired and quite dizzy."

I raised my hand to the cold sweat that had formed on my brow, and felt myself floating down as my mind and body gave way.

CHAPTER 6

So I'm a Relayer

I woke with a jolt. Sitting up quickly, I squeezed my hands into the blanket that covered me. My heart raced as I scanned around, with no memory of my new surroundings. Once again, my hands squeezed on the blanket, pulling it high to my chin.

"How did I get here?" I whispered, remembering my dream of Oakleigh and Willoughby. Fear rose and fell within me. It never stayed long, as curiosity always took over. So I let the blanket rest on my lap and continued to study the room. Where was I and how did I get here?

It was a log cabin. But it felt crude to call it that, as it had been constructed with great skill from the finest hardwood. There wasn't much in the room. One table, three chairs, all beautifully made, though very small, and a lone cupboard fitted neatly into the far corner by the door that led to who knows where. A half-burnt candle sat within a pool of wax in the centre of the table, extinguished. The bed on which I sat was large in proportion to the rest of the furniture and

19

surprisingly comfy. And the blanket? Well, to cover myself with the softness of a thousand woven feathers was such a treat that I pulled it over my shoulders before I stood up. I pushed my arms outwards, feeling myself with these fine feathers to be a bird.

A little voice came from outside. "Jessie, Jessie, are you awake?"

"Yes, I am," I replied tentatively, wondering who on earth it could be. I cleared my sleepy throat. "Can I help you?"

"It's me, Willoughby."

"And me, Oakleigh."

I gasped. Surely they weren't real? Was I still asleep?

"Oh my word!" I stammered. "I thought that you were just a dream."

"Can we come in?"

I shook my head and touched the wooden wall behind me; it was real, and I did seem to be awake.

"I suppose so," I said, peering at the doorway in the corner.

"Well, let us in then," Oakleigh asked, with a tap, tap on the window behind me.

I spun my head round and stared at the two little faces, each occupying a small pane of glass.

"Oh, sorry," I said, springing over to open it. "I thought you would come through the door."

"That's all right," Oakleigh replied, shrugging his shoulders and stretching his little booted leg over the frame and then falling onto the bed.

Willoughby followed in the same manner and laughed as he fell onto Oakleigh.

"Why didn't you use the door?" I clamoured as the two creatures wriggled about on the pillow.

"Oh, that," Willoughby answered, replacing his top hat to a tilt and still laughing at Oakleigh. "It's quicker for us to climb up the side of the tree than use the steps."

"Up the tree? Am I up a tree?" I said in a shrill of disbelief. I bounced across the bed to look for myself, only to be halted by Willoughby's firm arm and his cane tapping on my ankles.

He looked solemn as he responded: "That is a normal place for a Relayer."

"Okaaay," I replied, sitting back down. I felt a little told off, and pulled my knees up to my chin. "What is a Relayer?"

"I'll explain that," Oakleigh said, whilst jumping off the bed and landing with his two oversized boots on the hardwood floor. He made quite a thud for a creature standing only one foot tall. He walked enthusiastically over to the small cupboard, twitched, and then disappeared.

"Where's he gone, Willoughby?" I asked, concerned that something awful had happened to him.

"He hasn't gone anywhere. He has just changed size to get your telescope."

"My telescope?" I replied, becoming confused again.

"Yes, Jessie, your telescope. How else would you relay messages back to us?"

"I'm sorry, Willoughby, but this is making no sense to me at all."

"Jessie, I too am sorry. But you must ignore your confused state of mind and learn from now on to accept everything that happens."

I stared at the spot where Oakleigh had just stood. As quickly as he had disappeared, he returned into view with a grin that was almost too big for his face. With outstretched arms he balanced a crystal tube easily twice the size of him. As it rocked precariously from side to side, the sunlight sparkled off the tube and bounced off Oakleigh's kindly eyes. They remained fixed on me, as did his grin, which was now pushing his ears together at the back of his head.

Willoughby seemed oblivious to Oakleigh's presentation. He was more interested in rethreading his bootlace back through the top hole of his boot. It seemed to be causing him some distress, as his little paws struggled to pick the threaded ends through the hole.

"There we go," he said with some relief as he finally managed it. I turned back to Oakleigh, who had moved forward and now had a strong hold on the tube.

"Take it, then," he said, looking a little disappointed that I wasn't as enthusiastic as he was.

"Yes, of course. Sorry, Oakleigh." I held my hands open to receive the crystal telescope. In truth, I was terrified of dropping it. But once it was within my hold, I experienced an immense urge to hurl it across the room, just as you feel when looking down from a great height that you may just lean a little too far forward and simply drop.

"What's wrong?" Willoughby asked, squinting and frowning. He held his gaze on me as if he were feeling and understanding my thoughts. "Just do as your heart is telling you."

"But I can't, it's wrong," I said, now holding the tube with fear.

Willoughby gave me a reassuring smile. "Just follow your feelings. How do you know it's wrong? It might be absolutely right."

So I did. I clasped the tube with a firm grip and – *whoosh* – it flew with such power out of my hand that it slammed into the wall, rebounded, and flew out of the window.

The two of them rushed over, stood on tiptoe and stared out. I could see the backs of their little heads following the descent of the tube. I now joined them and saw its spectacular demise on a fallen tree. It broke into a thousand pieces.

"Oh, Willoughby, that wasn't supposed to happen," said Oakleigh.

Willoughby pushed the rim of his hat with his cane.

"No." He paused. "It wasn't." He sounded quite stunned.

"She threw it," Oakleigh said, dispersing any blame from himself by waving his little paw back towards me.

I wasn't sure how bad the consequences of this madness would be, but I knew I had done something ludicrously stupid, especially when, from nowhere, more small creatures appeared and gathered around the broken remains of the crystal telescope. A handful at first, then twenty, then hundreds, all clambering out of the bluebells and growing to size. They were Bellas – all of them, I realised. Like Oakleigh and Willoughby, but with different features and hair, and very different clothing. As I looked more closely, I realised their clothes were all from different periods in history, some Roman, some medieval, some Victorian, right up to the present.

"Why did you do that?" Oakleigh said, bringing me back to what had just happened.

"You two said follow my heart," I faltered. "And I didn't know what it was or why you were giving it to me. I've always felt the urge to break fragile things – they make me anxious."

Oakleigh glared at me.

"Can't we just get another one?" I pleaded. I knew this was feeble, but I really didn't know what else to say. "I thought you could read my mind and that's why I threw the tube. I

23

thought it would release some kind of magic. It all happened so quickly."

"Magic?" Willoughby replied in an almost inaudible sound. "We're not magic. Yes, we can live forever – well, until we go back to our natural form – and yes, we can go small and then big. But there is nothing magic here. It is just not normal to you. I did say that you would have to open your mind."

"That's easy for you to say, Willoughby," I retorted. "But I am standing here, in a place I've never been to before, not even knowing whether I'm alive or dead, or dreaming, or hallucinating…"

"Calm yourself, my girl," said Willoughby, placing a soft paw on my leg and fixing me with his knowing eyes. "I see you are distressed but we will figure this out and you will learn how to just trust us and open up that mind of yours. You'll see."

Oakleigh tugged on Willoughby's coat and said nervously, "We had better go down." He pulled himself out of the window, getting tangled with Willoughby again, and they both made their way down the tree at lightning speed.

"Can I come down?" I shouted after them.

Willoughby's faded voice echoed through the thick mass of branches. "Yes, I think you had better."

"Should I follow you?" I shouted back, not thinking for one minute that I could descend the tree as they had done.

"No, follow your heart and jump," Oakleigh shouted up, now standing at the bottom.

A few minutes earlier I would have done, but now I had enough sense to use the door.

I opened it, and found that from this side of the cabin

there were no treetops, just blue sky. My eyes followed the steps which spiralled endlessly around the tree into a cushion of clouds. There was no handrail, so I hugged the tree as I spiralled round and round and round. I was thankful for my years of tree climbing and dangling. The bark felt strong and protective against my skin as I leant my weight against it and felt my way down.

After a few minutes I came to a platform where a natural hole in the tree trunk had been formed, maybe from a fallen branch, but this was big, easily big enough for me to climb through. I entered the passage, squinting to see where it led. The natural light faded after a few feet and I held my hands out in front of me. Feeling the smooth wood reminded me of pebbles that had been shaped and polished by the sea. I was just about to turn around when my leading hand brushed against my next surprise.

"Oi, what are you doing?" a voice shouted. It had a similar ring to Willoughby's and Oakleigh's, but a much higher pitch.

I jumped back towards the light as the sound of scampering feet grew close, and then I saw her.

I couldn't put into words why this little creature caught my heart.

LEANNDI

It was just the way she stood there, shuffling from side to side, smiling with her eyes wide. Her hair was in a ponytail, brushed up maybe in an effort to make herself look taller. Her eyes were as velvety brown as Willoughby's and Oakleigh's, but they seemed in some way bigger. As I moved towards her, she stood still and arched her head back, never losing eye contact. The closer I got, the more her head leant back.

"Who are you?" I said quietly.

"Who are *you*?" she replied in a somewhat stubborn tone.

"I'm Jessie."

"Well, I am cross," she said, looking up at me as a cat would when it demanded attention.

"I've never heard that name before."

"It's not my name, stupid. My name's Leanndi and I am cross with you. I was asleep in there and you made me jump awake."

"Sorry, Leanndi, I was trying to get through to the clearing and I wasn't sure if this tunnel was the way. To be honest, walking around the tree with no handrail to stop me falling was not at all nice, so I am already very unsettled."

She tilted her head to one side, and held her tiny paw to her mouth.

"Mmm, okay, I forgive you." She moved forward, holding her arm upwards to clasp my little finger. Her paw wrapped around it and we were off back into the darkness of the tunnel.

"You must be our new Relayer," she said as she pulled me along.

"Yes, I have been told that I am," I replied, putting total trust in the direction I was being pulled in.

"Who told you that you are, then?" she asked as we increased speed.

"Willoughby and Oakleigh," I said, holding my other hand out in front of me as a natural precaution against the darkness. But she didn't answer. Instead her little paw tightened around my finger as she pulled us to a halt, whilst quite aggressively kicking open a small door, which thankfully led us back into the light.

"Wait, Leanndi. I have to crawl through that." I dropped down quickly as she and her enthusiasm continued dragging me like a rag doll behind her.

"I wonder what's happened over there," she said as we entered the clearing where the Bellas and my broken telescope were.

"Unfortunately, Leanndi, that was something to do with me," I replied, whilst squeezing the last of my body through the door.

"Okay, let's go and fix this." She marched forward.

I found it comforting that she didn't even ask how it had happened, just said that she would fix it. So I quickly brushed the dry mud from my knees and hurried to catch her.

We made our way to the gathering and swiftly moved to the front. Although Leanndi seemed even smaller than the others, she had an immense determination and moved them aside, some with a high-pitched "Move!", some with a paw in the back. When we got to the front, she looked up at me and blinked.

"I don't really like crowds. I can't see anything," she said, sounding quite rattled.

Instinctively, I leant down to her and she scampered into my arms. I put her to one side and she balanced herself in my right arm. Instantly, she had her air of importance back and she looked around.

"What are they doing?" I whispered.

As Leanndi turned to answer me, her ponytail tickled the bottom of my chin. She stared at me with her eyes wide. "Be quiet," she whispered. "I will tell you in a minute."

Not wanting to make another mistake, I did as she said.

"Got one!" Oakleigh screamed, and began doing a funny little shuffle on the spot.

"Stand still, Oakleigh," Willoughby growled, and rested his cane firmly on Oakleigh's shoulder.

Oakleigh froze on the spot and Willoughby thrust his top hat towards him. Oakleigh carefully slid a circular piece of glass off his paw and into the hat.

"Now keep looking," Willoughby said sternly, with his head back down, scouring the area. Oakleigh dropped on all fours and continued to search. We all looked on until a soft voice broke the silence.

"Leanndi, bring your new friend to me." Her little head spun around, looking back over her shoulder, then back to me. She scampered down from my arm, firmly held my little finger and pulled me through the variety of Bellas.

I broke my silence. "Who's that?"

"That's Grandad," she replied, marching forward. "You will like him. He is very kind and knows so much about everything. He sorts us out and he will sort you out too. Look up there." She pointed with her free paw up towards the treetops, whilst still marching forward. "Can you see it?"

"What am I looking for, Leanndi?"

"Your house. That's your house up there. Can you see it?"

She pointed so far upwards, she lifted herself off the ground.

"Oh yes, I can," I replied, wishing that it wasn't so high.

"I like it up there," she said. "You can see the whole world – that's why you're up there."

I had so many questions to ask about it, but I also wanted to know who this 'Grandad' was, so I bit my tongue.

Leanndi must have sensed my questions because she frowned briefly but then said happily, "Grandad will explain all about it, and when you've spoken to Grandad, Bluebell will show you the rest of the Land. She's Grandad's closest voice."

CHAPTER 7

The Wisdom of Grandad

We approached a hedgerow with a human-sized arch, and Leanndi let go of my finger. "He's the other side of that, just go through." I thanked Leanndi and walked onwards, unsure of what I was expecting on the other side. Was Grandad another Bella, but an elderly one? Or a human, in his own private dwelling?

Somehow I sensed that on the other side of the arch would be something very special, bringing to mind images of rainbows, glitter and shooting stars, however corny that felt. Even I, with my renowned disdain for TV, had watched the odd Disney movie in my time. But what I beheld before me was even more beautiful and true than anything like that. It was more like a Victorian orchard. It smelled fresh and clean, just as if a summer shower had knocked the natural fragrance of apple and pear trees into the air. Water droplets sat on every petal and leaf. A fine mist shared itself with every new bud and filled my lungs with a purity they had never felt before. I stood there drinking it in, feeling the tranquillity engulf me.

I noticed a man tending the fine soil of a flowerbed. He knelt on a tartan blanket and, whilst he trawled for weeds, he steadied himself with a walking stick. This ordinary sight brought back a temporary moment of sanity.

"Hello, I'm Jessie. I was beginning to think I'd never see another person again." I paused, and then asked, "Are you Grandad?", praying for a normal response, because I hadn't yet seen his face. But he chuckled and pulled himself slowly to his feet using the walking stick, and turned to face me.

What a relief… he was human! What a lovely face he had, too, beautifully lined. He smiled at me, showing weathered, rosy cheeks. His light blue eyes sparkled, as if he were still in his youth. They complemented his silver hair, which flopped stylishly forward. He wore an old checked shirt, heavily frayed at the collar and cuffs, and a thick, warm woollen cardigan, which hung off his frail frame. His faded grey cord trousers were worn almost through at the knees. But I recognised the boots he wore, because they were exactly the same as the ones the Bellas wore: big, chunky leather, made to stand the test of time. I wasn't sure if it was possible for Bellas to have a human grandad, but he had a very comforting grandfatherly way about him, so perhaps they called him 'Grandad' because he felt like one. He certainly instantly felt like one to me, at any rate, even down to the floppy silver hair my own grandpa had had, and a particular elegance despite the comfy clothes.

"Hello, Jessie, you're looking better," he said, in such a familiar tone that it seemed as if I had known him forever.

"Thank you. I am so much better than I was yesterday. Actually, I do feel really very good." I shocked myself with the realisation that I felt incredibly well despite the crash and the events of the last few hours.

"Come over here and sit with me. I know that you must have many questions you want answering." He moved towards an old wooden bench under an arched trellis overhung with scented wisteria.

I walked by his side.

Before we had even sat down, I had to ask, "Is all this real? Am I dead? Where the hell am I?"

He steadied himself with my arm as he eased onto the bench, breathed a sigh, paused, and then continued.

"No, you are not dead, but you would have been had you not landed here. You see, this woodland and surrounding fields are not on Earth as such. This place floats above and within the clouds, as it has done for many thousands of years. It is – how can I put it – a watchtower. A very large one, around twenty miles in circumference. It's not the only one of its kind; there are four in total, evenly placed around the world. We have communication between the Lands but travelling to and fro is challenging. As you can imagine, the distances between us are great. We just try to do our best from our own Land here. From here we can monitor the good and the bad, man's destruction of the planet, and also his futile efforts to restore it."

I was screaming to ask so many questions that I started to speak, but he raised his finger and I knew that I should listen.

"The Bellas, some of whom you have met, are a tiny woodland creature unique to the Floating Lands. At their full height they stand at no more than one foot, but they can reduce down to nothing. They can all be recognised by their large boots and parkas, but they adopt their own individual styles and accessories to reflect their inner spirit."

Grandad sparkled as he went on: "Their visual form lies dormant within the bud of a flower – in our case in the bell of the bluebell – until a spirit of kindness leaves the Earth below who has more to offer, or a wrong to put right. The free spirit is then placed by an angel into the heart of the Bella, bringing it to life. They then have a second chance to make a difference to a world that needs reminding of simple kindness."

"How lovely," I said. "So, when a kind person dies, their spirit lives on and can enter into a Bella? And who are these angels?" It was a lot for me to take in.

"Slow down, Jessie – all will become clear. You see, Bellas were created to undertake quests on earth, to help out humans and bring good deeds and love into the world or to right some wrongs. But not all of their quests are successful. This was made to be deliberately so, in order to ensure that Bellas truly valued life and strove to achieve success in their quests wherever possible. Because if their quests are a failure, Bellas can die. Not as a human being or animal does, but by letting their spirits leave. What was unforeseen, however, was that allowing Bellas' spirits to leave would make it possible for darkness to enter instead. Rather than a kind spirit entering a Bella, darkness can now enter, in the form of a brutal enemy. Created as an evil version of Bellas, essentially, these enemies are known as the Malissols. Each one can only be harmed by one of their own kind. Quests are now failing frequently on Earth, so evil is taking the upper hand, and the Malissols' number has grown greatly."

"Oh my goodness," I exclaimed. "That all sounds awful." Then I dared to ask, "And me? How do I fit into this, and how am I to help?"

"Ah." Grandad raised his finger again to shush me. "You see, we Relayers – and you will be able to do this too – can see twenty-four hours into the future, a premonition."

I breathed deeply and hurried my question out.

"How will I do that?"

"Please let me finish, Jessie," Grandad said firmly. "It is not possible to stop all disasters, disease, pain and hurt. But it is our, and your, duty to do what we can to help – not just humans, but every living thing. Bellas have many different sides and gifts. You know how a child who is lonely and hurting inside often has an invisible friend? Well, these are not imaginary. They are in fact a Bella making itself known to that child. Or how a disaster is narrowly averted? Once again, that would be the work of the Bellas.

"You must understand, Jessie, that we cannot help everyone and everything. But the decision to allocate the Bellas to what you feel is preventable will be in your hands. Remember always that if the quest ends in failure, Bellas will die of a broken heart as their spirits leave. Nothing you say or do will change this process." Grandad looked deeply into my eyes. "So, Jessie, it is for you to decide if a quest and the outcome you desire are achievable."

"But how would I know?"

I couldn't bear the thought of anything at all happening to my new little friends, least of all for them to let their spirits leave because I had sent them on a quest of certain failure.

"Jessie," Grandad said, not loosening his grip on my arm, "you came to us for a reason, and, trust me, you will know, because when you send them out on a quest, you are sending your heart with them. Besides, at first you will be working with Willoughby, Oakleigh and Leanndi, whom you have met already, and Bluebell, whom you will be meeting shortly. They are truly magnificent creatures, each with their own skills.

"Willoughby is a great leader and fighter. No one can match his bravery, and he takes it on himself to bring back the others. Thank God he hasn't failed yet!

"Oakleigh, although he tends to be over-enthusiastic, has a gift for fixing almost anything with the few little tools he carries with him.

"Bluebell is so intelligent. Her talent is to think one step ahead, and calmly defuse the situation. And she remains elegant, carrying herself with such grace that it still leaves me breathless. She has been by my side from the very beginning and we almost think as one. I don't know what I would do without her!" Grandad said this with such love that it almost seemed to leave him quite sad.

"And what of Leanndi?"

Grandad's face instantly broke into a smile, and he chuckled.

"Leanndi was once an invisible friend, but she got too attached and did not want to leave the child as he grew stronger. So we brought her home, and now she's a fine little scout for the other three. She does like to be at the forefront of everything."

He still smiled at the thought.

"I noticed, Grandad, that the other Bellas were wearing different periods of clothing. Why is that?"

"Oh that! That's quite simple. It's from the time period that they were most active in helping. Each of them holds a true account of history. No more speculating or elaborate guessing. You can talk to history itself through these marvellous time capsules. But now many of them have retired from the field, and they carry on with different duties here at Bluebell Wood. Don't get me wrong, they worked for many hundreds of years before they chose to retire. You see, it is very demanding looking after humans and the planet!"

I raised my courage to ask another question, the one I was still embarrassed by.

"I'm sorry I broke your telescope. Why do you think I did that? I just couldn't help myself."

I was now feeling stupid and somewhat sorry for myself again.

Grandad held my arm tightly, as he had before, and said, "Don't worry, it wasn't yours to use. You will fashion your own way of relaying messages. Anyway, it is the lenses of the scope that hold the power to see a day ahead, not the casing. The lenses are incredible things, Jessie. They will not only enable you to see events in the future, but also things in the present that are happening elsewhere. You will be able to guide the Bellas on their quests on Earth without even being there yourself. You have much to learn, young Jessie, but I have complete faith in you. Willoughby and Oakleigh will bring the lenses to you as soon as they have found them both."

My mind was racing, my emotions rushing to keep up with it all. The darkness I had felt when Grandad spoke of the Malissols was penetrating. This was rapidly becoming my battle too.

I wanted to ask so much more, but we were interrupted by a sleek white horse being led through the mist of the orchard.

"Grandfather," a little voice said as it came close. Grandad loosened his grip on my arm and gently tapped me.

"Let me introduce you to Bluebell."

The little Bella continued forward, leading the magnificent horse by her side. Its mane flowed along its neck like an ocean

wave, never ending, beginning from its
ears down to its shoulders, with each
step creating a new wave. Its eyes
shone blue-black, and it towered
over its little handler. On its back was
a Victorian lady's side-saddle and it
wore a bridle so highly polished that
any of the Queen's cavalry would
have been proud of it.

Bluebell herself was dressed very
differently to any of the others. Her
posture and the way she moved were
like those of a young lady who had
just graduated from a high-class
finishing school.

She seemed to float
alongside her magnificent
steed, holding herself beautifully straight
and not once looking at the ground. She wore a bright
yellow 1920s-style riding dress, and a riding hat laden with
feathers.

"Bluebell, this is Jessie."

She smiled and moved forwards, holding out her little
gloved paw.

"Pleased to meet you, Jessie."

"It's lovely to meet you, Bluebell. Grandad speaks so
highly of you," I said as I took her tiny hand.

She held her smile, and cast her beautiful eyes towards
Grandad.

"And so he should. I think he'd be quite lost without
me! I suppose he would like me to show you the rest of our

treasured Land. The best way to do that is on horseback, and there is no finer horse than my boy, Daniel!"

She let go of my hand and whispered, "Down, boy."

Obediently, Daniel dropped his head and she walked elegantly along his nose to stand between his ears. He raised his head and, like a perfectly rehearsed circus trick, dropped his nose again and flicked it back. Keeping her perfect form, she spun twice in the air and landed effortlessly on the saddle. Of course, she sat as a lady would have done, with both legs to the side of the horse, back straight, and totally unruffled.

"Hop on, then," she said.

I wasn't at all sure that I liked the idea of getting on Daniel's back. I adored all animals, of course, but had never actually ridden a horse before or even sat on one.

"Come on," Bluebell said. "We'll look after you. Just hold onto the back of the saddle and pull yourself up."

Hesitantly, I moved closer and took a firm hold of the saddle, trying to pull myself over. I counted to one, two and then on three gave a small jump. I had managed to lift myself about six inches off the ground, but it didn't matter, because Bluebell leant right over and pulled with extraordinary strength on the shoulder strap of my dress and I flew off the ground and landed with a bump behind her.

I could hear Grandad laughing as Bluebell spun Daniel on a sixpence, and we galloped off into the mist of the orchard.

"You'd best hold onto my waist," she said over her shoulder. "We are just going to do a small jump to leave the orchard. Hold on tight and go with me."

I didn't believe that holding onto Bluebell's waist, or any part of this one-foot-tall Bella, would prevent me from falling off. However, I'm glad I did, because it wasn't a small jump at all. The hedgerow that we soared above had to be at least six feet high. I screamed and closed my eyes as we hit the other side, and now had my arms wrapped around her, with my nose buried in the top of her fine feathered hat.

"You can loosen your grip now!" she said, sounding a touch disgruntled.

I raised my face as we galloped onwards, and the mist that lay heavily in the orchard was soon behind us.

CHAPTER 8

Turbulence Shocks

As each stride of our splendid steed carried us into open fields, it struck me that this countryside had been totally untouched by mankind. Nature certainly held the upper hand here. Butterflies floated from the long grass, carried by the turbulent breeze of Daniel's effortless power.

Within no time we had reached the top of one of the many rolling hills, and Bluebell pulled Daniel to a stand and turned him side on. We looked back at Bluebell Wood.

To our right, further down the hill, ran a river dividing the land. Its ripples hit the sunlight in shimmering golden flashes.

"Where does that run to, Bluebell?"

"It runs to the end of the Floating Land and off the edge, to join the clouds, and will turn into raindrops. It will never run dry. How could it, when we spend a lot of our time within the clouds? I'll show you." She turned Daniel again, to gallop down to the river as it snaked through the fields and the occasional spinney of trees.

I was now enjoying the experience so much that I had managed to loosen my grip on Bluebell, and was relishing the spray of pure water that flew up from around Daniel's hooves. The landscape was so simply balanced, from the silent cluster of colour on a bed of lush green, to the vibrant reds and yellows, which appeared randomly dabbed yet too precisely positioned to have been left to chance. I felt unfaithful to the fine grounds at Granton Manor as I longed now for other images of nature beyond those I had left behind.

All at once, noises like claps of thunder broke my daydreaming. One bang after another shot through the air. Bluebell shouted to hold on and turned Daniel away from the river and up a steep hill.

"What is it, Bluebell?" I shouted, as I held on for dear life, but she said nothing.

We reached the summit of the hill and hit the flatlands on top at speed. I'd had no idea a horse could go that fast. Bluebell leant forwards and repeatedly urged, "Come on, Daniel!"

I could hear his breathing over the sound of his hooves as he pushed himself to the limit. For us the ride was smooth, but our poor horse was struggling, though I knew that for Bluebell he would not relent until she gave her next command.

We turned sharply to our right and headed straight for a ridiculously huge oak tree that seemed to stand alone, dwarfing all around it.

The thunderous sounds continued in hits of three. We reached the oak, and Bluebell pulled Daniel to a standstill.

"Hurry, Jessie," she said as we dismounted, "get in the tree." She took hold of my finger with one paw, whilst leading Daniel with the other. "Come," she said, "there's no time."

I now noticed an opening in the tree, so large that all three of us were able to clamber in and hide.

"They've missed one," she said, pointing out of the hole. "Look out there!"

I didn't know what I was looking for, but whatever it was made the ground shake. Then, just above the trees, travelling at great speed, a jumbo jet passed over. The noise was deafening. Branches and smaller trees crashed to the ground, and vapour coated everything in its path.

It was all over very quickly, and all that remained was the smell of aviation fuel and the devastation left behind.

"Oh my word, Bluebell, that was terrifying," I gasped.

"Yes, it is when they miss one," she replied, backing Daniel out and beckoning for me to follow. "See there." She pointed into the far distance. "Those big wooden turrets hold cannons. We fire very powerful shots of air into the sky, pushing the planes off course. You would know this as turbulence when you are in the plane, but for us, it's survival."

I couldn't quite believe it. "So, you Bellas cause the turbulence? You can blow big aeroplanes away? That's amazing! But why don't they see your Floating Land?"

"Humans see only what they expect to see and nothing else," she replied, already sitting again, unruffled in her little saddle.

I clumsily mounted our tired but resilient steed and we slowly made our way back to the river. Just minutes ago, this beautiful Land had been exuberant with colour, with wildlife going about its natural business. Now the stench of fuel and the aftermath of the hideous flying monster left nothing but broken trees, damaged flowers, and pollution. I didn't say anything to Bluebell, but I was terribly embarrassed to be human, especially knowing that all the Bellas wanted to do was to help us. I could tell by her body language that she was upset, but like me, she said nothing.

After Daniel had taken a well-deserved drink, we trotted for twenty or so minutes along the river.

Once out of the flight path, the countryside seemed undisturbed, lifting both Bluebell's spirits and mine. The river slowly widened and we came to a large lake, edged with reeds and willow trees that swayed gently in the breeze. It was a haven for birds, which were landing and taking off in their hundreds. Clearly, this was a well-known place of rest in the bird community. They seemed very organised in their arrivals and departures, never overcrowding the lake, just politely moving on to let the next flock in.

To our left was a small rock face where the wavelets of the lake continuously lapped, and sitting there with their feet dangling over the edge were six old Bellas. Some sat smoking what seemed like ancient clay pipes. Others held musical instruments, none of which I had ever seen before, but they made a sound that filled the air with soothing and melodious chord structures which made every beat of the birds' wings even more magical.

Another of them was gently placing oak leaves on the water. As he did so, he whispered, "Farewell. Our eyes will follow you; our hearts are with you. Remember your quest. I pray I will see you tomorrow."

We dismounted and walked towards them.

"Hello," Bluebell said, as we joined them on the rock face. "This is Jessie, our new Relayer. Jessie, meet some of our Elders."

They acknowledged us by simply nodding, and continued with their business.

Bluebell tugged me forward, and whispered in my ear, "The Elders are very wise old Bellas who perform important duties. Look carefully at the leaves."

I leant forward and watched one of the elderly creatures place them gently into the lake. On each leaf, sat four tiny little Bellas all in a row, facing the far side of the lake. The current took them forward into the mist, and they were gone.

"Where are they going?" I whispered into Bluebell's soft ear.

"They are going on their quest," she replied quietly as we watched them disappear, then she pulled my arm and jumped up. "Come on, I'll show you." She hurried me off the rock and around the edge of the lake.

As we approached the far side, I could hear the rushing water, and then we came across a small wall made of flint. Bluebell let go of my hand and, with one jump, landed on top of the wall and looked down.

"Come closer," she said, looking back at me and then down again. I moved forwards and gazed downward. At first it looked like nothing more than a small waterfall flowing off the cliff, but after a few moments, the thick mist that blocked our view below cleared and, for the first time, I could see directly down to Earth.

Instinctively, I grabbed Bluebell and jumped back. A cold sweat came over me and, apart from the wriggling of Bluebell trying to loosen my grip on her, I felt nothing. For a few moments afterwards, I didn't even breathe.

Still holding Bluebell tight to my chest, much to her dismay, I slowly edged backwards away from the wall. I felt her twitch, just as Oakleigh had done, as she reduced in size and dropped free.

I was still holding my arms as if she were there. Then she appeared in front of me.

"Thank you for your concern, Jessie, but there is nothing to be frightened of – just don't fall over the side. Come and look again," she said, adjusting her fine clothes and hat.

I really didn't want to, but she pulled me back against the wall and I nervously stared over the top and watched the little ones flow with the water off the lake and vaporise into a cloud that passed beneath us, blocking our view of Earth.

"See there, Jessie?" Bluebell said. "They will go down to Earth in a raindrop or on a snowflake, or sometimes they'll just float all the way on a breeze. It's a really nice part of being a Bella. Anyway," she continued, jumping to the ground, "let's take you back to Grandad. I'm sure you've seen enough today."

I didn't answer, and didn't move at first, just gazing at the direction the Bellas had gone in, thinking of their tiny bodies floating downwards, all that way. But Bluebell strode forward determinedly and so I followed. We were soon heading towards Bluebell Wood, with Daniel in full stride.

Thankfully, on the return trip, we went around the orchards and not over the high hedgerow. Although my confidence was somewhat greater than before, I did not relish the thought of jumping such a height again. Bluebell pulled Daniel into a slow walk as we entered the clearing, where some hours earlier all had gathered to watch Willoughby and Oakleigh search for the lenses. But now it was empty and, apart from the sound of Daniel's heavy breaths and clops, softened by the fallen leaves and foliage, all was still.

I dismounted next to the small door through which I had entered the clearing earlier. I said my goodbyes to Bluebell, shaking her little gloved paw, gave Daniel a pat on his sweaty neck, and watched them trot off into the woods.

It was good to be back to the closest thing I had to familiar surroundings and to be on my own two feet. It even felt a relief to be in the hollow tunnel of the tree. This time I left the small door open for light, though I still had to feel my way again along the smooth wood, at least until the light of the larger opening welcomed me home. Tentatively, I made my way up the spiral steps, hugging the tree as I had before, no longer fearful of the fading sunlight. Darkness began to cover Bluebell Wood.

I entered my cabin, looking forward to my bed, remembering how safe and comfortable it had felt earlier that morning, though also realising that I had not eaten. But there on the table, lit by the remainder of the candle, was a wooden bowl filled with fruit. Beside it were a loaf of bread and a big slab of cheese. My hunger increased tenfold as I pulled the chair out and tucked in. The bread was still warm. I ripped off one end and pawed it into my mouth, squeezing a lump of cheese into the corner as well. This was such basic food, but I did not remember anything ever tasting this good. I was so preoccupied with my feast that it took me a minute or so before I felt three little sets of eyes staring at me.

In a row on the edge of my bed sat Willoughby, Oakleigh and Leanndi. The feather blanket was too thick for their legs to hang over freely, forcing them to sit with the soles of their big boots facing me, almost covering their small bodies from view. I felt awkward as they stared at me and I stared back at them with my cheeks filled with bread and cheese.

"Is that nice?" Leanndi said, fixing her gaze on my swollen face.

I chewed ferociously and swallowed hard before answering her. "Yes, lovely."

"I'm glad that you like it," Willoughby joined in. "We don't eat meat, as that would be a bit strange, to help every human and creature, and then to eat them."

I didn't answer as I had once again filled my mouth, so I nodded in agreement, but could not stop eating.

Oakleigh jumped off the bed with an oversized thud and joined me at the table. He sat first on the chair and stared at me, then on the table, edging himself ever closer. He now sat a few inches away from me and his eyes left mine and stared at the fruit.

"Grandad is in there and he wants to see you when you have finished eating, and can I have that apple?" he said in a single breath.

"Yes, please help yourself. Where is Grandad?"

I stared around the room.

Oakleigh, already eating the apple, pointed to the wall. "In there," he mumbled.

Willoughby jumped off the bed with a thump and walked to the wall nearest the door. He raised his cane, stood on tiptoe, and pushed the top of one of the logs which formed the wall. He hopped back, and six of the logs swung, like a door, towards him. There, looking into a telescope and then back to a large map laid out in front of him, stood Grandad.

He appeared to be talking to himself, giving directional instructions. Stunned by what I had seen, but still unknowingly pushing food in my mouth, I just stared into a huge room.

Grandad finished talking to himself. "That's a great job, now come home."

Willoughby entered the room, followed by Oakleigh,

who had tumbled off the table, throwing his apple core out of the open window. Leanndi rushed over to me, took my little finger in her paw and led me, still eating, after them.

Grandad carefully folded the map and placed it in a leather sleeve, which he in turn placed in the bookcase beside what appeared to be thousands of other such sleeves.

"Hello, everyone," Grandad said, smiling at us all. "What do you think of your new watchtower, Jessie? This is where it all happens."

"It looks smashing," I replied, "but what do I do in here?" I gaped at the vastness of what to me looked like a grand library. A rush of memories of my father's library washed over me, filled with the nature books I used to devour.

The three Bellas sat in a row, but this time on the table where Grandad had laid his map. Their eyes were fixed not on me but on Grandad.

"Do you have the lenses, Willoughby?" Grandad asked, as usual ignoring my question.

Willoughby tilted his head. His top hat rolled down his arm and was caught neatly in his paw. Grandad placed his hand inside and, like a lucky dip, pulled out two lenses.

"Now, Jessie," he continued, "these are now yours to use. Any ideas about your casing?"

All eyes were back on me and I wanted for once to think quickly. And then it came to me: my flying goggles, the ones I had worn yesterday, and now my only family heirloom.

"Yes, I do," I replied excitedly. "In my plane there are some old flying goggles. Shall I go and get them?"

"I'll go," Leanndi said, already jumping off the table and running into the other room, onto my bed and bouncing out of the window.

Grandad turned to the array of beautifully bound leather books. He ran his long, fragile finger over the spine of one book that, even I could see, stood out by its age.

"Some of these books, Jessie, go back to the beginning of intelligent man. Not all have words. Some are stories illustrated in picture form, but nevertheless they are still records of times and places. And here" – Grandad pointed to where he had placed the map – "there is a map of every town, city, river and sea in the world. It is from here that you will guide and send the relevant information to the Bellas in the field."

I hated myself for my next question, already knowing what the answer would be: "Grandad, couldn't you just use the internet for all this? Wouldn't it all be on there?"

Grandad balked, as I had predicted, and then stared at me. "Jessie, I think you must have realised that we do not use electricity in Bluebell Wood or endless technical devices as you do on Earth. We couldn't rely on technology, but we can rely on each other. I'm surprised that you – Green Girl – should ask this."

I jolted at my former nickname, flushed bright red and felt anything but green at that moment.

Bluebell then entered the room gracefully but slightly out of breath.

"Sorry I am late, Grandad. I had to wash Daniel down and rug him up for the night. He has had a very busy day."

"That's okay, Bluebell. We will just wait for Leanndi to return, and then we can start. Would anyone like some tea?"

"Yes please, Grandad," I rushed out, desperate right then for the comfort of a nice cup of tea.

Bluebell stepped forward, offered to make it, and

disappeared into the other room. Before she returned, Leanndi appeared, running joyfully in to join us. She was trying to wear the goggles, but her little face was only covered by one half of them and she stared through it, steaming up the glass like an old-fashioned diver. Willoughby removed them from her head with his cane and slid them down to me.

"Does anyone have a knife?" I asked, and Oakleigh jumped forward.

"Yes, I do," he said, rummaging around in his bag. "Here you go."

I took the knife and felt its weight in my hand. It was very small but sharp. I slid it between the glass lens and the leather that held it in place and, like a tossed coin, it spun away. I repeated this with the other side and took the new lenses from Grandad. Amazingly, they looked just the right size for my goggles.

I stared at Grandad. Had he known all along about my goggles and been way ahead of me on this? He gave me the briefest of winks, almost more of an eye twitch, but enough to confirm my suspicions.

I reversed the process with the lenses, but this time taking great care not to scratch the glass. It was a bit tricky, like putting a bike tyre onto a wheel, but once I had one piece in place, the rest followed. There was a breathless silence in the room as I held the modified goggles in my hand. Grandad moved closer and put his arm around my shoulder.

"Jessie, when you put these on, it will all start. But don't worry; I will be here to guide you through. But first, tea."

CHAPTER 9

Lightning Strike
(My First Quest)

Bluebell had returned with six steaming mugs of tea – two human-sized – which she managed to balance on a teetering tray with her outstretched arms. We chatted for a while about trivial matters, which almost took my mind off what was to happen next. The four little Bellas sat facing me on the table and I couldn't get the thought out of my head that their survival lay in my hands. But they didn't seem unduly concerned. They laughed about their times together on previous adventures.

When we had finished our drinks, Bluebell stood up on the table and called me over. I moved forward to be at eye level with her, and she placed her graceful paws on my shoulder. "Good luck," she said. "You will be fine."

Then she smiled, squinted, picked up the tray of empty cups, and disappeared with it to the next room. The other three stood and wished me luck: Oakleigh with a hug, Leanndi jumping into my arms and holding tight, and Willoughby with a very firm paw-shake.

Grandad and I were now alone. "Okay, Jessie, put them on." My hands were slightly damp and my stomach churned with nervous excitement.

I laced the goggle straps over the back of my head and slowly pulled them over my eyes. At first the room was normal.

Then a darkness fell and the images, small at first, started moving towards me. Slowly, and then faster and faster, hundreds of different images appeared. I stood uneasily as they flew at me, people crying, cars crashed, animals trapped, so many terrible events. I wanted it all to stop, but I couldn't raise my arms.

Then one image flew past the others and faced me alone. At first it made no sense at all, but as it became clearer, I could see a small house: a very beautiful place in the countryside, surrounded by trees. There was a sign on the door, 'Rosemary Cottage'. It appeared to be evening time, and there was a light on downstairs, with a man writing at a desk, and another lit room upstairs, with a woman putting a child to bed. It all looked very normal, idyllic. I knew that I wasn't there, but I still felt as though I was invading their privacy. I tried to raise my hands to remove the goggles, but my arms stuck fast to my sides. I watched the woman turn the lamp out in the child's room, flick the stairwell lights on and make her way downstairs. I was just about to say to Grandad that nothing was wrong, and ask if I should try again.

Then a flash of lightning filled the image, pushing me back across the library, and a thunderous clap of noise that felt as if it had split me in two.

I couldn't see. My eyes burned with excruciating pain as

I stumbled around the library. Then as quickly as it had hit, it flew away from me, leaving the image of the beautiful little house ablaze. There was no sign of the family. Another clap of thunder shattered the air and torrential rain began to fall. My arms were free to move and I ripped the goggles off.

"Bloody hell, Grandad, you could have warned me!" I said angrily, but also pleased to be in one piece. "What the hell was that?"

"Well, by the way you jumped around the room, I would say that you have just witnessed lightning." Grandad moved to the door and called the others back in. "But remember, it hasn't happened yet. That was a vision from the future."

"You said the telescope lenses can show me the present too, though, Grandad. How do you know it was from the future?"

Grandad smiled. "A very good question. Whenever you look through the lenses, you will see a bright flash before any images from the present but no flashing light for images from the future. In this instance, there was no flash – I would have seen it bouncing off your goggles. So, this was something that hasn't happened yet."

I gazed at my goggles, somewhat stunned by the power in those lenses.

As before, the Bellas sat in a row above the table.

"Well, what did you see?" Bluebell asked, eager to know immediately.

"Lightning, that's what I saw – lightning," I replied, still wide-eyed and feeling a touch uneasy on my feet.

"You are not sounding very compassionate, Jessie," Oakleigh said, with a displeased look on his face.

I realised instantly that I had not given a second thought

to the family in the house, and I felt sick that I could be so selfish and stupid.

"I am so sorry, everyone. I could not see the family after the lightning. All the lights were out and the house was on fire."

"You must have seen *something*," Willoughby said, impatiently tapping his cane.

"Only the name of the house, 'Rosemary Cottage'." I was breathing hard, my heart still beating too fast.

"Well, that's a start," Grandad said, then turned to Leanndi and whispered something in her ear. She happily trotted out of the room, bounced off the bed in the bedroom and went out of the window.

"Where's Leanndi going?" I asked, not wanting any more surprises.

"She has gone to get the Weatherman," Grandad replied.

Who was the Weatherman? I was in too much of a state to ask, so I just stood there, holding onto a chair to steady myself.

The library was quiet as we waited. It seemed to me to be an age, but it could only have been a few minutes before Leanndi returned, this time not through the window, but through the door.

She was followed by a Bella, the eldest by far whom I had met. His hair was long and grey and he wore a three-quarter-length suit jacket which reached the top of his boots. Around his neck was a pendant, half of which depicted the sun, the other half the moon. He had more facial hair than the others, and it was also totally grey. His eyes were a strange silver-blue which, for a Bella, lacked emotion. Held out in front of him he carried a number of books and charts.

"Evening, Grandad," he said, then coughed deeply and cleared his throat. Grandad did not answer, but just patted him on his round shoulders. The Weatherman raised his arms above his head, sliding his books and charts onto the table. He followed them onto the table with one extraordinary leap, and turned to Grandad. "How can I help?"

"Well, we have had a lightning strike, but all we have to go on is the name of a house," Grandad said on my behalf.

"That's okay," the Weatherman said. "It is the time of the strike that is important. So, what time did you see it?"

His eyes flared open, catching the candle's glow and becoming totally silver in colour, fixed not towards Grandad, but towards me.

I stammered my words, as – I must be honest – this old Bella scared me a bit, despite his diminutive size.

I looked at the clock. "Well, just a few minutes ago, so – about nine o'clock."

"That's good enough," he replied, instantly relieving the tension from me. He disregarded all of his books and charts except one book, which he laid open in front of him. He knelt down and, with his furry grey paw, started scrolling down the pages.

"Times, times, times," he repeated to himself. "These are all of tomorrow's hits of lightning, the ones that I have foreseen. You say you saw the strike today at nine o'clock, so twenty-four hours away would be nine o'clock tomorrow night. So, the strike to Earth at nine o'clock will be in a village called Upper Chine in the south of England. Six hours beforehand, luckily for you all, there will be a rainstorm that your travellers, Grandad, can use to fall directly onto this area. I thank you all for listening. Nice to see you, Grandad."

And with that, he gathered his belongings, hopped off the table and left.

Leanndi and Oakleigh giggled to themselves as soon as the Weatherman had left the room as if they found him somewhat amusing.

"Come on." Grandad clapped his hands. "We have work to do: to think how to stop the lightning hitting the house."

We all pondered this for a while. I racked my brain for memories of the geography lessons I had sat through at Wolfsons Girls with the useless Miss Jennings. Though she didn't teach us much, I did recall a National Geographic programme she had shown us about extreme weather…

And then it came to me. Not how to do it, but what we had to do.

"Re-route it," I said. "We have to re-route it."

Leanndi flashed a smile at Grandad then gently touched my hand in encouragement. "You are catching on so quickly, Jessie. That is the right answer!" she replied.

"Okay," Grandad said, showing me a slight smile. "I think we need to go to the workshop."

As I glanced between the four Bellas and Grandad, I realised, to my embarrassment, that they had all known already that the lightning needed to be redirected. They had just been pretending to mull it over while I came to the solution myself.

I followed them out onto the winding steps, around the tree, not into the passageway I'd been through earlier, but further down. It was hard for me to keep up. This was tough enough in daylight, but now in the dark it was almost impossible.

We entered another passageway which was, thankfully, lit

with hundreds of candles. Row upon row of Bellas worked on their individual tables, sewing, welding and shaping a variety of objects.

"Arkley!" Grandad called, and one head lifted while the others continued their work.

"Grandad," he replied. He turned his welding torch off and raised his mask. He was huge for a Bella, with perfectly formed, muscular arms visible to all in his dungarees. He moved with accentuated hips and threw his arms high to enhance each word. "What can I do for you?"

Grandad smiled before answering, then gave a small cough. "Well, we need to divert some lightning away from a family and their home in England." He paused, tilted his head towards me, then asked, "How could we do that, do you think?"

Arkley looked surprised, then glanced at me and back at Grandad. "Ah, he said, his eyebrows raised. "Ah, yes, how indeed…" He tapped his forefinger to his upper lip and emitted a somewhat exaggerated "Hmmm" before disappearing off, with tiny quick steps, talking to himself as he went. Grandad laughed. "Good old Arkley!" he said.

I stared after him, slightly bemused.

We all waited for ten or so minutes before Arkley returned with a sketchbook and a sample of fabric.

"Look at this fabric," he said. He tossed it in the air, and it flew high to the ceiling and opened up. It caught the slightest breeze and hovered above us, rippling and enchanting, as it slowly made its way down. It was the purest white and, even by candlelight, it seemed to reflect light and glow as if it held a magical illumination of its own.

I held my hands aloft as it gently caressed my fingertips and melted around them. I had never felt anything so soft.

"Where does this fabric come from?"

Like water, it slipped through my grasp.

Arkley smiled at me. "It is for the angels. We make their robes here."

The angels. I had forgotten about them. "Grandad, who are these angels? When can I meet them?"

Grandad shook his head gently and nodded me back in the direction of Arkley.

"Sorry, Arkley," I stumbled, "I just have so many questions... This stuff is beautiful." I gazed at the shiny material in its elegant heap on the floor.

"Right, Grandad," Arkley continued, "this is what I propose to make. His left eyelid half-closed in what I could have sworn was a wink.

"First," Arkley said, "there will be a kite made from this fabric, under which there will be a wicker basket. Your travellers can glide from Bluebell Wood down to Earth, but they will have to be full-size. With this fabric they will rise up, not down, unless we have their full weight. Once they near their destination, they will pull on four copper strings that will turn their kite into a balloon."

"Good, Arkley, good," Grandad said. "But won't it need to be made of metal to attract the lightning? Isn't that right, Jessie?"

"Umm, yes!" I stuttered, realising that, of course, he was right.

"Yes! Of course!" Arkley replied. "I will take it to the Egyptian Bellas. They have been working with gold and gold leaf for thousands of years. I think they could find a way of integrating gold into the fabric and still leave it light enough to float."

"Oh wow!" I exclaimed. "It's going to look so beautiful!" Then my face dropped. "It's such a shame that lightning will destroy it."

Arkley turned to me and said sternly, "Do you think anything could be more beautiful than the lives it will save?"

I felt awkward and stupid again. I did agree with Arkley, but I also felt a bit sorry for myself. Had they forgotten what I had been through and the reality I now faced?

I left the workshop on my own, and by the time I had made my way back to my bedroom, I was quite angry at them all. I lay on my bed and stared out of the window. The night was cold and clear and the cloud cover was below Bluebell Wood. Glaring up at the stars, I began to feel lonely and scared. I hadn't asked for any of this. Yes, it had been my own behaviour that had brought me here, but had I really deserved all this?

As I continued staring into space and struggling to calm down my fiery thoughts, the silhouette of Leanndi's petite head appeared at the window. I didn't say anything, and nor did she as she quietly climbed through. I shut my eyes and then could feel her whole body fit neatly on the pillow next to me. Her soft paw clasped my ear. It felt warm and comforting and reminded me of Tansy's silky presence beside me on the many occasions we had lain amongst the bluebells together. After a few minutes, I felt myself drifting off a bit, until I must have given way entirely as it wasn't long before I was fast asleep.

***

I awoke the next morning at the sound of a high-pitched squeal. Sitting up sharply, I noticed instantly that Leanndi had gone. Apart from a little indentation in the pillow where her body had been, there was no sign of anyone. Then again, the squeal.

I knelt up on my bed and stared down to the clearing to see Bluebell sitting upright on Daniel. Before she saw me, she gave that same screech, but stopped short when she spotted me peering down at her. I shouted to her, dizzy from sitting bolt upright so quickly from my deep sleep, and worried that something awful had happened.

"Is everything okay?" I asked.

"Yes, fine, Jessie, but get your goggles on now. Leanndi and Oakleigh are leaving in the rainstorm the Weatherman told you about. Signal me when they land."

A thick mist lay heavily, and the bluebells that had been so apparent the day before were barely visible. This meant that Bluebell Wood was deep within a storm cloud. I pulled my goggles on and immediately a bright light appeared, then the image of Leanndi and Oakleigh free-falling from the river that ran off the edge of our Floating Land. This was it: I was seeing them in real time, embarking on their quest.

I had no concept of how small they were at this point until they pierced the skin of what appeared to be a raindrop the size of a football and sat inside.

"Can you hear me?" I asked, but they both just waved at me.

I noticed little bubbles were rising upwards from their nostrils, and realised that they were holding their breath. Like the air bubbles, they were both floating around the raindrop and gently being pushed off the inner sides and off one another.

By the time Earth approached, Leanndi and Oakleigh

were barely visible against the mass of air bubbles which were now stretching the raindrop to capacity. Just before impact, the raindrop burst, throwing the Bellas free and making a bubbly bed of air for them to land on, although they did still land with quite a bump. Checking that they got to their feet okay, I watched them shaking themselves and refilling their lungs with the damp air that awaited them. They seemed fine, my clever new friends, so I raised my goggles and ran to join Bluebell in the clearing.

Once more I was on the back of Daniel, steadying myself by gently holding Bluebell's waist. Unlike the day before, when I could see the magnificent rolling hills and the beautiful natural form of our surroundings, the storm cloud that engulfed us made it somewhat eerie unless you had my companions' keen sense of direction. I couldn't find my hand in front of my face. Daniel was nevertheless in full stride and hitting the stone paths which appeared every now and then. We became a ghostly image, cutting the mist in two, then instantly being suffocated by it again.

We soon came to the river. The spray covered my face, but this time it was not refreshing but icy cold, stabbing at my already numb cheeks. I knew we would soon be at the water's edge. I could hear the wonderful music playing as soon as Bluebell pulled Daniel out of his gallop and into a slow walk.

Arkley was standing with the group of musicians with his finished kite. Still on horseback, I stared down onto its wingspan, cut perfectly to depict the shape of an eagle. Its feathers were brought to life by woven gold, thicker in places, giving it texture and the illusion that it was truly a golden eagle. The craftsmanship and detail that had gone into the kite overnight were breathtaking. The mist became patchy and a ray of sunlight filtered through, shimmering off the wingspan and bringing it to life.

I dismounted, and saw the little wicker basket under the kite. Inside stood Willoughby. He peered over the edge, then walked from side to side. He looked pensive until he was joined by Bluebell, whom he helped gently in with the use of his sturdy arm. They both now stood and stared up at me and Arkley.

Bluebell spoke. "Jessie, take Daniel." She laughed. "Well, actually *he'll* take *you* back."

"Yes, of course."

Daniel nudged my shoulder with his nose, at which point I realised with some trepidation that I was meant to ride him back on my own.

"Well, get on him, then," Bluebell said. "I only wanted you to see the kite. You do have work to do, and I am sure Grandad will be waiting for you."

Not wanting to disappoint her, I clambered onto Daniel's back and, before I was settled, he had turned and we were off. Once out of the river, he picked up speed again and I clung onto his neck, sliding from side to side, my eyes squinting, as we thundered home. Once back into the clearing, I slid my rigid body off the horse and stumbled onto the ground, catching my breath for the first time since I had left the kite. I didn't even have a thought for the tiny little Bella who appeared and proceeded to lead Daniel away, totally ignoring me as she did so.

CHAPTER 10

The Near Miss

Bluebell was right. Grandad was waiting for me in the watchtower. He had already laid a map of the village of Upper Chine out on the table and smiled at me as I walked in.

"What did you think of the kite, then?" he asked.

"It's magnificent."

I was already placing my goggles on top of my head, as if I had done this job a thousand times before. I knew I had to get to work, but before I placed the lenses over my eyes, Grandad stopped me and pointed to the map.

"Oakleigh and Leanndi will need to find their way to the village shop – here," he said, indicating a cross he had marked along a street labelled 'High Street'. "Once inside, they must look for the ledger the shopkeeper owns, which keeps records of deliveries of newspapers. Hopefully, the family from Rosemary Cottage will be amongst them. You are to direct Oakleigh and Leanndi, Jessie."

I took a deep breath and pulled down the goggles. As

before, the bright light appeared, and then our two rain-soaked Bellas walking in the long grass by the roadside. The downpour was relentless as they pushed on through the long, wet grass, parkas fastened tightly. Occasionally, they fell on the uneven ground. They passed the sign that welcomed them to Upper Chine and then the one saying 'High Street'. I spoke briefly to them both, explaining my intentions, finding it terribly hard to be so matter-of-fact when water was running down their small, wet faces and their eyes blinked furiously as the oversized raindrops splashed, one after the other, onto them. But they knew their task better than anyone, so they just pushed forward. As I had expected, soon enough they came across the village shop amongst a row of Victorian cottages. The door was open and they casually strolled in. Being at this point only an inch or two high, it was very unlikely that anyone would see them.

Behind the counter stood a plump, middle-aged lady: a real countrywoman, with rosy cheeks, strong hands and practical clothes. As I watched her, I noticed that the lenses of my goggles had tinted to a slightly yellowy colour. I blinked my eyes and shook my head, but the yellow sheen remained.

Oakleigh whispered to Leanndi, who then scampered to the front of the counter and edged around to the side. Oakleigh moved back to the door, and pushed on it with all his might. Amazingly, it started to swing until it gently whooshed shut. The woman didn't even appear to notice, her gaze fixed out of the window at the street.

I could see from Oakleigh's face that he thought this was a little odd. He scampered to the shelves of tinned foods, and heaved at a couple until they crashed onto the floor. He peered out from behind the remaining tins, but the woman still didn't move.

"Leanndi, look for it now!" Oakleigh shouted. His eyes widened at the clarity of her image. "She's a resident."

Startled at this news, Leanndi grew to her full height and shot up the side and onto the top of the counter, only to find writing paper, books of stamps, a stapler and a half-eaten rock cake.

"There's nothing here."

The shop door flew open with an almighty bang; the wind from outside had carried it forward. Leanndi reduced in size and slipped into a tiny crack between the counter and the drawer that hung slightly ajar. A customer stood in the entrance. She shook her umbrella, closed it and turned to face the young woman who had appeared from the stockroom to serve her. The shopkeeper from many years ago had now disappeared, as did the yellow tint in my goggles. Now I saw only the young woman and the customer exchanging pleasantries for a short time, before the customer asked to pay her outstanding paper bill. The shop assistant skimmed her milky soft hands over the counter, opened the drawer and pulled from it the ledger – with Leanndi upon it. Leanndi leapt from the ledger onto the shopkeeper's deep green mohair cardigan, nestled in, and watched her turn the pages. Within two or three turns the words 'Rosemary Cottage, Old Vicarage Road' shone like a beacon off the page.

Leanndi made her way around the lady's cardigan. Occasionally, her boots caught on the deep wool, so she loosened them, slipped them off and deftly tied them around her neck. Once safely at the hem of the cardigan, Leanndi floated to the floor. Being now so small it took her quite some time to reach Oakleigh at the door.

Once clear of the shop, they resumed a sensible size and took cover under a hedge to talk to me.

"Jessie, can you tell Grandad that the first lady in the shop was a resident and she appeared to us very clearly."

"Yes, of course," I replied, not thinking that a building with a resident in it was unusual at all.

"Grandad," I said when I joined him, "there was a resident in the shop who appeared very clearly." But after seeing Grandad's startled face, I realised that maybe it meant something different from what I had first presumed. "What is it, Grandad?"

"It's a ghost, Jessie. It may mean nothing, but that's highly unlikely," he replied, nervously touching the bottom of his chin. "We just have to be more vigilant. But not another word of this for the moment. We have work to do. Did they get the address?"

"Yes, yes. Rosemary Cottage, Old Vicarage Road."

Grandad and I soon directed them to the house. The rain had stopped for the time being. Oakleigh and Leanndi climbed onto a tree close to the cottage, and perched themselves on an overhanging branch, which just brushed against the thatched roof.

Meanwhile, Willoughby and Bluebell had just started their descent off the edge of the river and were gliding gently down to Earth in a circular motion, very gradually losing height. They broke through the rain clouds, dropping suddenly in pockets of air and being thrust upwards, then down, by strong currents of wind. The kite looked as powerful as a bird of prey. Willoughby and Bluebell tilted the wings from side to side, to ensure the direction was as near to the village of Upper Chine as possible.

"Have they left, Jessie?" Oakleigh asked.

"Yes, they are through the rain cloud."

In unison, Leanndi and Oakleigh gave a high-pitched shrill, the same as the one Bluebell had startled me with that morning.

I focused on the kite. Bluebell and Willoughby instantly reacted to the shrill from Earth and steered themselves to their final destination. Leanndi and Oakleigh continued the squeal, increasing in pitch when their friends came into view. The sun was now breaking through the clouds and cast a shadow from the kite. The birds, who had just started to sing again after the rain, fled the area for fear of this spectacular bird of prey. When they reached a hundred feet or so from the roof of the cottage, Bluebell and Willoughby saw Leanndi and Oakleigh waving madly. They pulled the copper rope. Just as Arkley had designed it, the kite folded its wings and transformed itself into a golden balloon. It jolted upwards at first, held still, and then gently descended towards the cottage. Once they were close enough, Willoughby threw a copper rope to Oakleigh, and he and Leanndi pulled them down to rest.

Bluebell and Willoughby hopped out onto the thatched roof whilst Oakleigh and Leanndi separated the copper wires. Oakleigh fastened one to a branch of a tree on the left side of the house. Leanndi fastened the other to a tree on the right, and once she had got the tension right, the balloon floated free above the house.

The four of them gathered on the front lawn to decide where they would view the balloon and the events of the next hour or so from. They decided first on a birdhouse which had a perfect view of both the cottage and the balloon, but then realised it was already occupied by its intended inhabitants, and thought it best not to frighten them away. They agreed instead on a Christmas tree. It must have been planted quite some time ago, presumably on the off-chance that it would grow, after it had brought its intended magic to this young family's Christmas.

The four of them sat high in the tree and awaited the lightning strike. The sunlight had lost its battle to shine. As night began to fall, it brought with it a thick black rolling cover of cloud which roared its anger in the guise of thunder and bullied its way around the sky. Sheet lightning fuelled its engine as it waited to strike its victim. I thought how tiny the four Bellas appeared, pitting their wits against this opponent that filled the sky above.

The family arrived home at around eight o'clock. Once parked, the mother unfastened the sleeping child from the rear seat and carried her straight upstairs. The father locked the car, rebolted the front gate which had swung free, and followed them in. The wind began to swirl, and it shook the Christmas tree furiously. Moving closer to the trunk, the Bellas settled once more, still perched high but sitting on a thicker branch. They watched the family move about and, just as I had foreseen, the father was now in the study and the mother was putting her child to bed. We knew that the lightning would strike at any moment, as soon as the mother turned the child's light out to make her way downstairs.

I could see the golden balloon floating helplessly above the cottage when the sheet lightning lit the sky. I felt sorry for it, moving from side to side, tied to the trees, sacrificing its short existence to such an abrupt end. But there it was, perfectly poised and ready to trick the lightning away from its intended target.

It is horrible waiting for something to happen. It is odd that you instinctively hold your breath. That's what I was doing, and I could feel Grandad doing the same. I could see the four little Bellas holding theirs. When I saw the woman turn the child's light out and the hall light on, I closed my eyes, tightened my shoulders and awaited the lightning strike. But nothing happened.

I opened my eyes again and saw my four little ones, heads down and eyes shut tight. I turned my vision to the balloon.

As before, I was flung backwards across the library. The bolt of lightning disintegrated the fabric, channelling its power down the copper wire into the trees either side of the cottage, desperately trying to strike at something but being foiled to Earth. It flashed at the trees, briefly catching them alight, before the thunder roared its anger and the torrential rain began to fall. The woman had barely started her descent down the stairs. She instinctively turned on her toes and ran to bring the child to safety. The four Bellas watched on. Although the family were clearly distressed, they knew as I did that, in a day or two, they would be discussing how lucky they were that the lightning had fallen just feet away from their house. They would think how, on that night, someone or something must have been looking out for them.

I felt exuberant. Everything had come together beautifully. As the image faded and the bright light appeared in my goggles, I slid them back away from my eyes and, for the first time in my life, I felt that I was part of something really special.

"You did well, Jessie," Grandad said, patting me on my back. "Let's tidy up and have some tea, and then you must get some sleep. It will all start again tomorrow."

CHAPTER 11

The Mystery of the Monk

The next morning when I awoke, the sun was bursting through my window. I felt so well rested that, for a few seconds, I wasn't sure if it had all been a dream. But reaching the reality that we had saved that small family filled me with an overpowering sense of well-being. I sprang out of bed, hurriedly put my clothes on, slung my goggles round my neck and ran, unbelievably, down the spiral staircase, which just yesterday had scared me so. I slowed up slightly through the tunnel, but hurtled through the little door into the clearing. I would have been happy to see any of the Bellas and to find them all well but, as had happened before, the clearing was empty. Or so I thought, until I heard a gentle female voice.

Moving closer to the noise, I squatted down and saw twenty or so young Bellas. Each of them held a magnifying glass and peered with a confused concentration at the grown-up Bella who continued with a gentle patience. "Okay, that's not too bad, now try again," she said using her arms to symbolise air being pulled into her lungs. "But this time visualise your clothes and boots as part of you; that way you won't leave them behind." She closed her eyes as she said this, then blinked them open again to see her eager charges breathing vigorously out and disappearing. Several of them left behind a pile of clothes on top of their boots, which made the teacher smile. "And now breathe in, and fill your lungs with the power to grow," she continued.

And in that instance, like popcorn, they all appeared.

At least eleven of them returned to their full height, though only partly clothed, while the rest found themselves in all different sizes, either standing next to or on top of their individual garments.

I couldn't help but laugh, as indeed did the young Bellas, who were clearly finding their lesson very amusing.

"How do they go so small like that and then come back?" I wondered out loud. It was something I had been fascinated by since that first time when Willoughby rose from the cluster of bluebells and then Oakleigh appeared from the floor of the log cabin with that fateful crystal telescope.

"Stardust," the teacher said, looking up to me whilst placing some Bellas back on their individual piles of clothes. "It's everywhere. There isn't a place in the world that isn't covered in it or in some part made from it."

"Really?" I exclaimed. Did things like stardust really exist? Mind you, now that I'd got my head round being on a Floating Land, I realised that truly anything was possible.

The teacher then stopped what she was doing. "Now, I shouldn't do this," she said, looking mischievously at me, "but put your goggles on and look at me."

Slipping my goggles over my eyes, I watched as she breathed out and her body slowly fragmented into trillions of glitter particles. I gasped in delight as the glitter filled my vision, and she was gone. I continued watching only to see the particles pull back together and she was standing once more in front of me.

"Thank you so much!" I said, knowing that I had witnessed something extraordinary.

"You're very welcome, Jessie," she said with a conspiratorial glint in her eye. "But, of course, that was in slow motion, just for your eyes." She then breathed deeply and said, "So if you want to grow bigger, pull in stardust and if you want to go small again, push it out in a billionth of a second." Still smiling, she turned to face the young Bellas. "Isn't that right, children?"

I wanted to ask why the younger ones held magnifying glasses, but I felt I had taken enough of her time. I said my goodbyes and walked on into my tranquil surroundings.

I had no concept of time, but nature itself told me that it was very early: the sun warmed the plants and flowers as they stretched, with open petals and leaves, drying themselves in another beautiful day.

I called for Grandad and headed to the orchard to find him sitting upon the bench. His eyes were closed, as was his mouth, and he was taking deep breaths of the refreshing morning air through his nose.

We spoke of many things and laughed a lot. I found myself already becoming very close to him. He reminded me of my own now-departed grandfather: wise and steady, with a sense of humour that broke through at unexpected moments.

All the Bellas safely returned home later that day on invisible thermals of rising air. I was really pleased to see them: it was the best reunion I had ever had.

But it was all short-lived, as we were quickly back to work on another mission.

***

As the months passed, bringing with them challenge after challenge, we responded to potential disasters, from railway crashes and rivers breaching their banks and wiping communities away, to lost pets and bullied children. Grandad took a back seat. Bluebell spent time with me in the watchtower more frequently. Her clear thinking was invaluable, and her experience priceless. My technique improved, and I must admit that I was getting a bit blasé as every mission became a success.

Summer passed and winter drew in. Although Bluebell Wood never lost any of its beauty, it did become very, very cold, and the darker and colder it got up there, the more missions seemed to come in, making Bluebell fully occupied with me. Even Grandad came back frequently.

But Grandad never seemed to use his own telescope any more, until this one bitterly cold afternoon, I opened the door of the watchtower to find him and Bluebell already at work. They both looked uneasy. That was the first time I had ever truly felt that from either of them.

"Everything okay?" I asked, raising my goggles to my head, ready for work.

"No, I don't think it is. You had better have a look," Grandad replied.

I pulled my goggles over my eyes, the room went black, and the images started moving towards me, fewer than normal. They made way for one in particular: a monk standing on a church tower. I struggled to keep him in view as he murmured to himself and faded in and out of sight against the grey stone tower.

Grandad viewed the same image through his telescope, and said, "An image from the past. That is not good at all."

I fixed my concentration back on the monk as his image became clear. He moved closer to the edge of the tower, called out "God help me!" and let himself drop.

I screamed out and tried to raise my arms to help him but the image faded from view. I pulled my goggles off and turned to Grandad. "That was strange, Grandad, wasn't it?" I pulled my fringe from my eyes, as my goggles had pinned my dank hair to my forehead.

"Yes, very," Grandad replied, squinting. He thought for a while. "Have you and Bluebell seen many other visions from the past?"

Scenes from the past were something that the goggles occasionally offered up. You could tell they were past events because of a certain tint to the images as they appeared before your eyes, as both Grandad and Bluebell had taught me.

"Well, yes, we have, actually. But they offered very little, so I brushed them aside."

I could see by Grandad's concern that I shouldn't have. He then explained their significance: that they were a warning that the past was returning to affect our present time. I went on to relay the other visions from the past that we had witnessed, from a young boy on the railway line, to a big grey cat who had called us when he was stuck in a chimney. Oh, and also a homeless man who had been caught in an abandoned warehouse when it was set ablaze. There had been reports of several residents just the previous week in Ireland; and, of course, there was the shopkeeper from my first quest.

"Okay." Grandad paused, glaring quite hard at Bluebell, who shuffled awkwardly in her boots. "But is this the first of them to speak?"

I quickly scanned my memory and each individual event, amazed at how I remembered every detail so clearly.

"Yes, definitely. This is the only one to speak, apart from the cat meowing."

"Right, then we must go to the monk and relieve him of his burden."

"But, in the past, Grandad? It has already happened. Or is he reappearing in the present as a ghost?"

Bluebell had already scampered up the bookcase. She threw down onto the table some books marked 'Legends', 'Myths', 'Abbeys' and 'Monasteries'. "Jessie, look under 'Legends' for any old tales of ghosts which fit the image," she said to my puzzled face.

Over the next few hours we worked our way through the magnificent old books, my question hanging over us all the while. Whenever I began to ask it again, though, both Grandad and Bluebell shushed me in that way that they did, which was infuriating but something I was getting very used to.

The aged books clearly hadn't been required for an awfully long time, as they were covered in dust. Their pages were fragile, which slowed our progress and, even though all three of us worked tirelessly, it was ten o'clock at night before we came across anything that resembled the monk and his fall.

It seemed that there was a myth which had grown through the years in the city of St Albans. Close to the abbey there was an old fir tree which had stood for as long as the abbey itself, and if you ran around this tree a thousand times on the stroke of midnight, you would witness the monk falling to his death from the church spire. But there was nothing about why the monk had killed himself.

Bluebell leant out of the window and gave that high-pitched squeal. I had heard it many times since that first quest, but it still made me jump. Just seconds after her call, Willoughby, Oakleigh and Leanndi appeared at the window and clambered in. The time was now twenty past ten, so if the four of them were to get to the abbey for midnight, it gave us all an impossible task. We had always allowed a fair amount of travelling time from leaving the Island to locating the area. All six of us knew the dilemma, but how to get round it?

Then the idea came to me.

"Listen, everybody," I said. "What if we were to use the air cannons to shoot you onto a passing plane? I have noticed that Luton Airport and London Heathrow are not too far from the city of St Albans. One of these planes that we divert from our Island must head that way, so you could drop off over St Albans."

"What fun," Leanndi said, clapping. "What a good idea!"

Then Grandad joined in with Leanndi's enthusiasm. "You know, Jessie, that really could work. Bluebell, get yourself and the others to the Cannon Masters as quickly as possible and, on your way, call Boomer the Plane Spotter to hurry up here."

Bluebell scrambled out of the window, with the other three trailing behind. She knew the quickest way to the cannons was on horseback, and that meant Daniel in full stride.

Boomer the Plane Spotter arrived at the window shortly after. He clambered in and fell to the floor, catching his foot on the inside of his parka, which was clearly too big for him.

He wore binoculars around his neck, and a pair of glasses so thick that I was sure they would magnify as well as any telescope. His hair was curly and flattened on top in a poor attempt to give himself a side parting.

"Planes, Grandad, you need to know about planes?"

"Hello, Boomer," Grandad said, smiling because Boomer's enthusiasm for aviation had made him skip his manners, even to the point of forgetting to say hello.

Boomer paused and blinked his lovely eyes behind those shockingly thick lenses. Still he said nothing, but just stared at me. "Planes," he said quietly.

"Yes, please, Boomer," I replied, as Grandad laughed and began to explain the plan and our destination of St Albans.

"That's easy," Boomer replied. "I know every plane there is to know and every plane's destination."

He pulled out a handbook from the inside of his parka, stared up at the clock, and skimmed through the pages. He reached high and slammed the open book on the table. "Any of these will do. They all pass every ten minutes, in the order they are written, between now and eleven o'clock."

Grandad pondered the times.

I had a quick progress report. My four Bellas and Daniel had arrived at the cannons and were dismounting Daniel by sliding down his nose, which he had kindly dropped forward to make easy access from his ears to the ground. Leanndi led the way up some rickety wooden steps which brought them out at the top of the turret. They were greeted by two Cannon Masters. These hardy Bellas wore little to keep them separate from the elements. No parkas, just chain mail tunics over fine cotton vests, with kilts to their lower halves. But still the big boots were the favourites for their feet.

The Cannon Masters seemed somewhat bemused to see visitors on their isolated work station, but it didn't interrupt them from pumping air into a huge wooden cannon, ready for the next turbulence shot to a passing aircraft. Each hugged a wooden arm of something I can only liken to a large set of bellows. This, in turn, pumped air into the base of the cannon, building up the pressure to such a degree that, when the two arms were locked fast with a wooden latch, it bowed under the strain.

Bluebell walked forward and pulled their kind but not-too-intelligent faces towards her own.

"Now listen, this is very important. You are going to shoot me, and these three, onto a plane. The plane in question, I will tell you of very soon, but when I do, you cannot miss. Do you understand?"

They both nodded their heads back at her, not understanding at all why this was happening, but more afraid of Bluebell's assertive tone.

Now I was back with Boomer and Grandad, who were still in conference over the gridded map. Boomer tried to explain the relative speed of the time in each square and how fast the plane would travel, giving us the optimum moment that they should leave the plane and hit St Albans perfectly. Sadly, neither Grandad nor I could grasp Boomer's mathematical trail and, in no time at all, he had got fed up with us both, pulled a little toy plane out of his pocket and told me that they'd best hit the next plane and he would do the rest.

I pulled my goggles on and gave them the go-ahead, and in turn they dropped into the barrel of the cannon. The four of them nestled in the bottom of the barrel awaiting lift-off. I was surprised to see them take their boots off and use the laces to tie them around their waists, and I smiled as I did whenever I saw how small their feet were in comparison to their big boots. I had asked Grandad why their boots were so large, and the reason was quite simple. They had been, at first, discarded children's shoes and, through the years, the fashion or style had stayed with them. They just liked big boots.

I continued to watch as one of the Cannon Masters turned a wrench attached to a wooden cog, which started a complex sequence of mechanical engineering, all of which was made of wood. The other Cannon Master sat on a little chair at the base of the cannon and fixed his concentration on the sight that ran along its length.

Willoughby, Bluebell, Oakleigh and Leanndi raised their hoods over their heads and fastened their parkas from top to bottom, until all that was visible were their tiny, paw-like hands, their not-so-big feet, and little noses. The speed of the aircraft approaching our Floating Land gave the Cannon Masters almost no time to aim and fire, but the sound of the aircraft gave them warning time for composure. And then, as if from nowhere, the thunderous noise of the jet engine shattered the night sky and burst through the sparse protection of clouds, which seemed to move out of the metal monster's way. Within a split second, the cannon was fired with a power equal to that of the jet, and our brave little Bellas were flung out of sight. They hit the side of the aircraft at such a furious speed that even I, knowing their capabilities now, found it hard to comprehend that anyone could survive that impact.

Willoughby, Oakleigh and Bluebell stuck to the side of the plane using their small paws and feet, spreading their fingers and toes wide apart and using their tips as tiny suction pads. I hadn't seen Bellas use this method before. I have to admit that there was still much at this stage I had to learn about them and their world. But I did now understand why they had taken their boots off.

Leanndi had overshot the other three and landed, star-shaped, on a passenger's window. Her face pushed hard against the glass and she became distracted by the passenger who sat just feet away. She studied the man as he sipped a glass of red wine and then steadied his food on the tray in front of him. Then the plane was hit with another turbulence shock from the Cannon Masters, this time pushing it a safe distance from our Land. Willoughby glanced upwards and slipped his cane between Leanndi's toes, which instinctively clasped the cane, and he wrenched her off the window and squeezed her between himself and the aircraft.

"How are they doing, Jessie?" Grandad asked.

"They seem fine," I replied, with some relief. "They are all on the side of the plane and ready to go."

Boomer, meanwhile, was steadily pushing his toy plane across the map. He spoke in a whisper, but at a speed that was barely audible as he worked out his equations. Then he slowed in tempo and, from ten, counted downwards.

"Follow my lead," he said, and from five I communicated the countdown to the four of them on the plane.

Five, four, three, two…

On 'one' Willoughby dropped first, turning and pulling Leanndi over his head and onto his back as he floated. Then Oakleigh dropped, twisting his back towards Bluebell, who dropped onto him in the same position she would have used to mount Daniel. Willoughby and Oakleigh pulled their arms back to their sides and tucked their hands into their parka sleeves. Bluebell and Leanndi held on tight to their friends, and pushed their feet into Willoughby and Oakleigh's pockets. They leant forward, hands in sleeves, and wrapped their arms around the two now missile-shaped Bellas as all four sped through the air towards the abbey of St Albans.

CHAPTER 12

A New Friend in Archie

The sky curved from one horizon to the other, placing St Albans in its own magical dome. Like small dots of darkness falling to the ground, silhouetted by the stars above, the Bellas' fast descent to Earth was slowed by a reduction in their size. The four of them now floated quite gently over the frozen parklands of St Albans. Leanndi and Bluebell leant their bodies back as they drifted down, still holding firmly onto Oakleigh and Willoughby, gazing at the dark-reaching trees and the crooked lines of rooftops that formed the city.

The landing was a little chaotic. They would have preferred frozen grass, but it moved beneath them, to be replaced by the ice of the lake, which they hit with a speedy bump. The local inhabitants – geese and ducks – made a slippery dash to safety on land. Bluebell and Leanndi wrenched hard on Willoughby and Oakleigh's necks as they slid helplessly across the lake, hitting the bank hard on the far side, which brought them to a sudden stop.

They lay in a heap upon one another for a second or two

and slowly untangled themselves, groaning as they did so. Bluebell was up first and offered a hand to Oakleigh.

"Bloody hell, Bluebell," Oakleigh said, "I am not a horse!" He rubbed his paw down his left leg, which had taken the brunt of the impact on the ice.

"No, you most certainly are not. Daniel would have handled that so much better than you," Bluebell replied sharply, pulling him to his feet.

Leanndi was already putting on her boots, still stretched across Willoughby's back and laughing at Bluebell's somewhat unsympathetic response to Oakleigh.

"Will you get off me, Leanndi?" Willoughby said, rather wearily, as if he had found carrying her harder than the landing itself, despite his wincing expression.

"Sorry, Willoughby," she replied as she dismounted.

The four of them shook themselves down, adjusted their parkas and, with boots back in place, turned to face the abbey. It stood magnificently upon a hill in the far distance. It was bitterly cold with no clouds to darken their path. The moon was bright and the stars that had watched them fall to Earth added a welcome touch of magic to the imposing view.

"We must hurry," Willoughby said with frozen breath, setting off in a steady trot, with his hat in place and his cane under his arm.

I took my goggles off and left the four brave, gallant Bellas to make their way to the abbey.

Boomer had departed, and Grandad had cleared the table.

Then he just stared into space.

"What's wrong, Grandad?" I asked. He looked very despondent.

"It is just that I feel so tired. It's been a long time since a vision from the past has shown itself to us quite like this. The last time, I had my youth on my side to deal with it, but now I just wish it hadn't happened."

I could see and feel Grandad's pain, but I had few words of comfort for him. What could I possibly tell him from my limited experience? He was the expert in these things, not me. Still, I had to try.

"Don't worry, Grandad," I said, resting my hand on his shoulder, "we'll get through it together." It was a line my father had used occasionally when things had gone wrong. It had always felt so solid and certain when he'd said it.

Grandad jerked with a look of surprise and then smiled at me, but his eyes didn't. I felt a little awkward. I suspected I hadn't been very convincing. "Some tea, Grandad," I offered. "Let's have some tea."

He nodded and smiled again. Tea here in our Floating Land seemed to have an almost magical quality, much like it did back in England on Earth.

***

After a short rest, I resumed my watch. On Earth below the little Bellas had reached the large conifer which mushroomed out above them, blocking the moonlight and casting an eerie shadow. The trunk was huge and it took them fifty paces to walk its circumference.

"And we have to run around this a thousand times before the stroke of midnight, which is not that far away at all, is it?" Oakleigh said. He adjusted his little bag of tools and commenced a full-speed charge around the tree.

The other three stood back as, in seconds, he was round

once, then twice, and then, in almost no time at all, he had reached one hundred.

"I think we have a problem," Oakleigh panted, as he circumnavigated the tree for the one hundred and eighth time and spun off course into a nearby flowerbed.

"Take over, Leanndi," Willoughby said, striding over to Oakleigh, who was trying to get to his feet, like an unfortunate woodlouse on its back.

Willoughby and Oakleigh burst out laughing as Willoughby tried to steady Oakleigh.

"Bit dizzy, are we?" Willoughby asked, as Oakleigh fell out of his grip back onto the frozen soil.

"Just a bit," Oakleigh replied, as he rolled helplessly around. "I'll be all right in a minute."

Meanwhile, Leanndi was picking up the pace. Her ponytail flew from side to side and her stride became bigger – so big that it was more of a leap from foot to foot. She smiled at the others as she appeared around the tree but, as Oakleigh had done, after about a hundred or so circuits, she flew off course. Oakleigh took over again.

Willoughby agreed with Bluebell that she would scout around to see what she could find at the base of the abbey, whilst Willoughby would make his way to the top of the tower and wait for the monk to appear.

He approached the huge wooden arched door and looked skyward at the tower that stretched into the cold night, hundreds of feet above him. I could tell from the look on his face that he was thinking 'That's a long way up', as his breath froze, giving him the illusion of mist hovering around the top of the tower, making it an even more uncomfortable place for him to be alone. I knew that it was not so much that he felt afraid, because I knew how brave Willoughby was. It was rather that Bellas really don't like being alone.

But he had little time to waste, so he reduced in size and walked through the tiny gap under the door. Once on the other side, he became full height and walked along the cold stone floor towards the steps. Although Bellas, like cats and dogs, can see better in the dark than humans, this was terribly black.

How my skill as a Relayer had grown! All my senses now travelled with my vision. I was feeling, smelling and breathing alongside the Bellas. Willoughby moved more cautiously than usual. All I could sense with him was the sound of his big boots hitting the uneven stone floor, and the musty smell of hundreds of years of damp embedded into the abbey structure. This must be as solitary as Willoughby had felt in years.

He began his climb up the stone steps, which were mercifully shallow. They had been worn in the centre just by human traffic. Willoughby feared very little, but he was not without fear altogether, and he relied upon it for his good judgement. Even in this dark tower he smiled to himself as the sound of Leanndi and Oakleigh padding around the tree below followed him and his own steps forward.

I turned my attention to Bluebell, who, sadly, was out of sight and sound of her companions when she came across the construction site on the left flank of the abbey – not directly by it, but near enough for Bluebell to become inquisitive. It was surrounded by a gridded metal fence with a variety of warning signs. 'HARD HATS MUST BE WORN', 'DANGER – CONSTRUCTION UNDERWAY' and a big sign reading 'BEWARE OF DOG'.

Bluebell scampered over the fence in a flash, leapt from the top to the other side, and landed on a big metal drum of diesel. A thud rang around the site, and within seconds she was confronted by the snarling face of a German shepherd. It leered at her, pushing its dripping black nose ever closer to her. The two of them locked eyes and the German shepherd pulled its face upwards and showed its huge fangs. Growling ferociously as saliva ran free, its hackles rose from top to tail as it lunged and snapped madly at Bluebell. She jumped back, moving left then right, narrowly avoiding the fangs and saliva that surrounded her. The dog reared up, put its two front paws as leverage on the top of the drum, and pushed its huge head towards Bluebell. Taken aback by the ferocity of the attack, she dropped down to her hands and knees and rolled across the top of the drum, steering herself away from the relentlessly snapping mouth.

As she reached the edge, she reduced in size and rolled off. The animal continued snapping at thin air, and then paused to sniff the top of the drum where Bluebell had stood. Opening and closing his nostrils frantically, he edged towards the side and followed the drum down to the ground where Bluebell was, the big black nose filling her vision. Loud and aggressive as a steam train hurtling out of a tunnel, his snorting sped up the closer he came to Bluebell, who was now standing no more than half an inch high.

She stared up at him. His nostrils flared and his lip curled with the scent of his prey tempting and tightening his jaw. Bluebell angrily twitched and exploded into full height, catching the dog with the top of her head. She had flattened her fine hat down her face, but had hit his under-jaw so hard that he wobbled where he stood.

"You stupid dog!" she shouted as she removed her hat and examined the damage. "What on earth were you thinking?"

Bluebell continued reshaping the feathers as the German shepherd edged back with ears flat to his head. She replaced her hat whilst shooting such a displeased stare at the animal that he cowered down towards the ground.

"Honestly!"

Bluebell tightened her gloves to her little paws and marched off to explore. I had to give it to her as I witnessed this through my goggles – she was one hell of a valiant Bella, that was for sure. This was certainly a harsh place for a Bella to be walking in, between the variety of machinery, diggers and dumper trucks towering high above her. The outstretched arm of an earthmover hovered just short of its last dig. The mud stuck to its metal teeth like flesh caught in the fangs of a hungry wolf, resting for now, until once more its hunger would penetrate the ground and rip at the soft tissue of earth.

She continued forward, walking upon the frozen mud and the tiny pools of icy water that had formed in the wheel tracks and human footprints. Her boots twisted her ankles on this awkward terrain, making her quite irritable. But even more annoying was the German shepherd behind her, sniffing her every move. She turned sharply to the dog and frowned, locking eyes once more with him. The dog now stared back inquisitively.

"What is your name?" Bluebell asked, impatiently running her little gloved paw around the leather choker until she found his brass name tag. "Let's have a look."

She turned the engraved side to the moonlight, and there, clearly, was the name, 'Archie'.

"Archie," Bluebell said aloud. "Archie? That's not a very ferocious name for a big dog like you."

Archie, hearing his name spoken, picked his head up and his ears sprang forward. He tilted his head from side to side and stared directly into Bluebell's eyes. But this time he looked more like a playful puppy than the aggressive creature he had been a few minutes ago.

"Well, Archie," Bluebell continued, pushing her little paws into the deep fur around his neck and enjoying the warmth that was locked safely away, "your big furry feet certainly seem quite at home on the uneven ground."

She leant down and gently patted the tops of them to feel the matted fur which had attracted the hard-frozen mud.

Archie sniffed the top of Bluebell's head as she did so, and she breathed his warm breath upon the back of her neck.

Bluebell stood and smiled, stroking the fine soft fur on his snout. She pulled herself up and around to sit upon the nape of his neck. Archie stood fast, then gently walked on with Bluebell's compassionate voice whispering in his ears, which fell flat to his head in comfort at her words.

Bluebell's dislike for this place had eased. Now she was on Archie's back she could view her surroundings with a little less agitation. Archie had all but forgotten his purpose of being a guard dog. The night was now one of interest with a companion to remove the loneliness he would normally have had to endure.

They rose up on a large mound of excavated soil, and Archie slid a little on their descent and leapt clear of the frozen water that lay at the bottom, bringing them opposite the site office. Bluebell dismounted, and Archie sat down on his thick, bushy tail. He yawned and watched Bluebell disappear under the weatherboard of the door. He sniffed the ground where she had stood and settled down to await her return.

There was little light in the Portakabin, but the moon produced just enough for Bluebell to recognise the outlines of various drawings and plans of the forthcoming building project. She hopped onto the desk and moved to one side so as not to block the moonlight that shone clearly onto the top corner of one of these plans. She quietly read to herself, muttering the words, which were slightly too small for me to make out through my lenses 'Easyway Construction Project… Museum… Client: Dr Brostoff.'

Once she had sifted through several documents, Bluebell relayed her findings to Grandad and me, but at this stage they explained very little. She asked if Oakleigh could assist her as she had befriended a dog and would be grateful if he could open the gate for them. And we would need to find a nice home for her new friend. Of course, I did as she requested.

When I next brought her into view, she was throwing paperwork out of the filing cabinet and expressing her uneasy feeling about Dr Brostoff and her need to find out more about this man.

With Oakleigh hurrying off to help Bluebell, Leanndi was left to do the final laps of the tree on her own. The pace of her charge increased, as did the bounce of her ponytail, and she laughed out loud as her imbalance weakened her speedy legs and turned her stomach as she panted, "Nearly there."

CHAPTER 13

Dr Brostoff, the Monk and the Written Truth

I focused my goggles on Willoughby, who was wearily climbing the last few steps up the tower. I could hear him tapping each of them with his cane before continuing, as the light was so poor. But his face slowly became clear as he got higher, where the moonlight leaked under the door which led to the roof of the tower. He reduced in size and appeared on the other side, standing alone and small, top hat tilted to one side, and his cane out in front of him supporting his body while he caught his breath. Once settled, he moved to the staggered wall and pulled himself up to perch on it. He peered down at Leanndi, who was just about to finish her final lap. Dropping back down off the wall, he faced the small wooden door of the tower. He pulled his pocket watch out and stared at the hands just as they hit twelve o'clock.

"Are you there, Jessie?" he asked softly.

"I'm here, Willoughby," I replied, wishing that I was truly by his side.

"Let's see what this monk has to say for himself, then."

Willoughby stood tall and brave. He straightened his top hat, put his cane under his arm, placed his pocket watch back and fixed his eyes firmly on the door.

The night was deadly still, apart from the sound of Leanndi shuffling around impatiently hundreds of feet below. Willoughby stood alone and the cold air stabbed his face, freezing his breath before it even left his mouth. He twitched his nose and pushed his ears forward. His breath, that had been so apparent, now stopped, and he leant forward as he heard the first sound of someone approaching up the dark, twisting stairwell.

The footsteps were slow, and we could hear a man's voice murmuring to himself. The wooden door creaked open and there stood a hooded monk. His face was not visible as he held his head downwards, with his robe hanging loose to his ankles. His feet were pointing inwards, reflecting his immense burden: his whole appearance was that of a crushed man. He staggered a couple of steps towards Willoughby, unaware of the little Bella's presence. He spoke aloud, then stared to the heavens, and the hood of his robe fell back. Tears ran down his gaunt face, leaving his desperate eyes staring hopelessly up at the stars.

"Please forgive us!" he cried. "You know they came to us for help, hundreds of your children, and we locked them away. We thought only of ourselves when it took us with them anyway. My punishment is to be the last, but I have written the truth in my own blood. Please forgive us. There is nobody left and I have made this confession for you, Lord, alone, so

I have laid it beneath the Roman bricks which support your wonderful home."

He lurched closer to Willoughby, who stood fast. The monk leant towards him as he stared down over the wall of the tower. "God help me!" he cried out.

Then he let himself drop. Willoughby turned quickly and watched the monk's descent as he hit the ground, feet away from Leanndi. His body lay twisted and broken, and blood ran out of his ears and trickled down the side of his neck. Leanndi moved closer and stared over him as he slowly vanished. Willoughby turned his face away, and frozen air left his mouth.

"Right, Jessie, get onto this. 'The truth lies under the Roman bricks which hold your wonderful home.'"

"Yes, of course, Willoughby," I replied.

I slid my goggles off to find myself sweating and shaking. What I had seen had looked so real, which it had been, but not now, not in my time.

I relayed the almost riddle-like message to Grandad, and we got to work on the history of the abbey. We stood side by side as we scoured through the many books which we had laid out on the table in front of us. Forty or so minutes soon passed.

Then I found a slight clue. The Normans had used bricks from the Roman city of Verulamium, by then fallen into ruins, to add to their abbey, in particular the round arches. This must be where the monk had hidden his manuscript of the truth. This was where the Bellas must start.

"What do you think, Grandad?"

"Yes, it is as good a place as any, but I must say I don't know how or where he could have hidden it. These round arches are very well constructed. They really wouldn't have a loose stone in them and, if they did, it would be unlikely that one man could remove it and then replace it. Unless, of course, the manuscript is buried under them. Maybe a passage that runs under the abbey. I am sure there must be many secret passages for escape or just hiding in. Jessie, get the four of them back together. But first, this Dr Brostoff – I think we need to stop the work being done on his site for a day or two. Get Oakleigh to dismantle the diggers. We need time."

"Yes, of course," I replied, knowing that since I had been a Relayer, my instincts had improved tenfold and, like Grandad, I had a bad feeling about this Dr Brostoff's site.

I quickly passed the message to Bluebell and Oakleigh and then moved to Willoughby and Leanndi. Willoughby had just made his way back to the large conifer where Leanndi stood. She flung her arms around him and buried her head in his chest. The sight of the monk's awful death had shaken her badly, and she held onto Willoughby like a child greeting her father home from war. Willoughby gently stroked the side of her head and then held her face in his hands.

"Leanndi," he said softly, "he is at peace now. He is free of his burden."

Her tear-filled eyes blinked at Willoughby and her little nose twitched from side to side.

"I know, Willoughby, but it was just so awful."

I felt terrible interrupting the two of them, upset as they were, but time was short. We had two major things to work on: Dr Brostoff, and 'the written truth'.

"Willoughby, Leanndi, I'm so sorry, but can you make your way to Bluebell and Oakleigh? They are on the left-hand side of the abbey, on the construction site."

Leanndi pulled away from Willoughby, wiping her little face with her paws, and sniffled. "Yes, of course."

Willoughby straightened his posture and, with cane first, marched forward. The two of them made their way through the open fence of the site where a chain and padlock lay abandoned on the ground. Oakleigh's trail of destruction had begun: digger buckets swung loose, parts of engines were strewn around, and shovels and forks lay sharply broken in two.

"Oakleigh, Bluebell, are you there?" Willoughby called, but there was no answer.

Leanndi, who had taken the lead, let out her familiar squeal, instantly making Willoughby's shoulders tighten as it ran through him. Within seconds, Oakleigh appeared, pushing open the exhaust flap of one of the diggers.

"Hello," he said, grinning from ear to ear, "everything okay?"

"Yes, fine," Willoughby laughingly replied. "I take it that everything was in working order when you arrived?"

"Yes! A few minor adjustments, then we will be there." Oakleigh giggled, holding his grin fast.

Bluebell responded to Leanndi's squeal with her own, and Willoughby and Leanndi made their way to the Portakabin. Archie, still waiting patiently outside, was somewhat confused at the sound of these unusual squeals. His head spun round when he heard the footsteps of Willoughby and Leanndi breaking the frozen edges of the mud and the small layers of ice.

"Don't mind him – that's Archie," Bluebell said from the other side of the door, recognising the sound of her friends' footsteps.

Willoughby pulled Leanndi, who was about to go off in full flight to say hello to Archie, to his left side. He held his cane out to Archie, who gave it a big sniff. Then the two Bellas reduced in size, continued past Archie, and joined Bluebell inside the Portakabin. Bluebell was now back on the table, walking up and down, and holding her head in deep thought. She didn't acknowledge her friends as they joined her. "Jessie, are you there?" she asked.

"Yes, Bluebell. What else have you found?"

"Well, first I have to know in turn what each of us has found. Willoughby, what about the monk?"

"Well," Willoughby replied, "he said that the truth lies under the Roman bricks that hold his Lord's wonderful home, and that he had written the truth and hidden it there."

"How about you and Grandad, Jessie?" Bluebell continued.

"Well, the round arches were built of Roman brick from the city of Verulamium," I replied.

"Okay," she said. She let her hands fall away from her face, leaving the moonlight to spring off her eyes as she continued without catching her breath. "Easyway Construction have built supporting columns in the walkway under the round arches. With money kindly donated by Dr Brostoff. In return, the wastelands that were owned by the church have had planning permission passed to build a museum." She paused, and then said, "Now this is the really interesting bit. This museum is going to be built with money donated by the very same Dr Brostoff."

She picked up the relevant information from the desk. "It is going to house works of art that Dr Brostoff has promised to source from around the world, some of which have been lost for many hundreds and, in some cases, thousands of years."

"How wonderful," I said, not digesting Bluebell's words at all.

"Well, it would be, Jessie, but looking through this list, the majority of the artefacts are in the hands of our own curators upon the four Floating Lands. Each Land, including ours, contains several of these priceless pieces. In the past years, we have removed from Earth works of art that have been thought so precious that the world below was too irresponsible to care for them."

"Oh, I see." I paused, embarrassed on behalf of the human race. "But the name Brostoff still has no relevance to us, Bluebell."

The door of the Portakabin crashed to the floor with an almighty bang. Oakleigh had loosened the hinges in his final touch of demolition.

"Well then," he said, smiling. He stood proudly in the empty frame, placing his tools neatly back into his little bag. I had not yet come to understand how such small pieces of equipment could cut, saw and destroy quite so easily. I had to actively close my gaping mouth.

"I think we need to pay Dr Brostoff a visit," Oakleigh announced.

"Do we know where he is, Bluebell?" I asked.

"Oh yes," she replied, and walked over to the edge of the table where she had neatly placed the relevant pile, far away from all the other documents that now lay strewn across the office floor, chairs and any other surface that cared to house them. "I have two known addresses for him. One is in St Albans itself, and the other is in Scotland. So, Jessie, if you can guide us from here to number 37 Elms Drive, we will be travelling by dog, or rather, Archie."

Willoughby, Oakleigh and Leanndi reduced in size and

nestled themselves in Archie's thick fur, which was soft and warm – a welcome break from the cold night air that had been biting at them for the past few hours. Bluebell stayed just big enough to gently guide Archie around the streets of St Albans, and Archie powered forward, enjoying his newfound freedom. There was not a sound around, only litter from the market that lay still, just briefly moving as Archie ran by. His body warmth increased and, hiding in the fur, Leanndi was soon asleep, with Willoughby looking after her by holding her ponytail to ensure that she didn't wake with a bump on the cold cobbled streets.

⁂

They arrived at Dr Brostoff's house, which was situated halfway down Elms Drive. It was a 1930s semi-detached house, with bay windows top and bottom, separated by pebble-dash. The front door was panelled, with a small arched window and traditional leaded glass, and was in need of some maintenance. There was a garage to the right, its doors held shut by two pieces of wood wedged under each of them. The front garden was overgrown, and stood out by its lack of care against the other prim and proper gardens in this sought-after area. Dr Brostoff was clearly a man of some wealth, but either he hid behind eccentricity or was preoccupied by other things.

Willoughby gently pulled on Leanndi's hair to wake her from her deep sleep, and she did so by stretching both arms and legs and giving a squeaky type of yawn. They dismounted, and the cold night air rapidly engulfed them. Fastening their parkas tightly, they made their way to the front door.

In turn they entered through a small gap between the

frame and door, created by years of bowing out of shape, and which would have caused a very unpleasant draught to the occupants. The four of them now stood in the hallway on a mountain of unopened mail. Although it had been cold outside, there it had felt clean and unthreatening. But in this unpleasant house the cold felt intrusive to body and mind. Bluebell moved forward, sliding uneasily on the letter pile, and the other three followed.

"I don't think he can be at home tonight if all this post is here. In fact, I wonder if he's been here at all in the last few months – it feels somewhat abandoned and awful. And what is that smell – it's terrible! There is definitely something amiss here."

The others agreed. There was a scent coming through above everything else, as if evil itself had settled within these walls. Oakleigh sprang forward and scampered up onto a small table which housed the telephone and a reading lamp. The receiver of the telephone hung loose and dangled off the edge. He stretched up and flicked the switch of the lamp, blinking furiously as he stared directly up at the bulb, which instantly gave light and life to this dingy hallway. Oakleigh left the table and landed with a bump on his backside, still rubbing and blinking his eyes.

"Well, I am glad he managed to pay his electricity bills. This would be so much harder in the dark!" he said as Leanndi and Willoughby helped him to his feet.

The layout of the hall was now clear, with a staircase to the right and three doors downstairs, one of which was open and led to a tiny kitchen directly in front of them. The other two doors were slightly ajar, allowing the Bellas' imaginations to run wild.

Willoughby leant over and gently nudged the door immediately to his left with his cane. It creaked open, just enough for the light of the lamp to sneak in. The four of them tentatively moved forward and peered around the door.

"Jessie, can you see this?" Willoughby's shocked voice called.

"No, no, I can't, it's just too dark."

Oakleigh angrily kicked the door wide open and the first of Dr Brostoff's surprises appeared.

The room, which was now clear for me to see, was identical to our very own watchtower. The tables, the books, the chairs, and even our telescope facing outwards to the window. I immediately called Grandad to view this and he gasped with horror that anyone could know our secret space apart from the Bellas and Relayers. His hands trembled as he tried to hold his telescope steady.

"Who is this Brostoff?" he asked. "Who is this man who knows so much about us, and who is causing such unrest with the poor departed and their past?" I gently moved Grandad's hands off the telescope and he steadied himself with the table.

"You said, Grandad, that only Bellas or Relayers know of this place, and Dr Brostoff is clearly not a Bella. So, was he once a Relayer?" I asked, looking into Grandad's face.

He slowly shook his head from side to side. "It is possible, I suppose," he said after a while, "that my predecessor William Wilson failed to die – though that's just too awful!" He slammed his hands on the table.

"But he was a good man," he continued, confronting himself with the worst of thoughts and then throwing them out before they took root.

I held my gaze at Grandad and took a deep breath. I knew

what I would say next would not make Grandad happy. "But I can't think of anyone else. Can you? Who else could do this?"

He didn't answer.

"Who else, Grandad?" I repeated. "Can you think of anyone else?"

Grandad's head spun round to face me and I was expecting an angry response, but instead he spoke to me with the heaviest of hearts and explained his deepest fears. He told me for the first time about William Wilson.

"My predecessor, William, was a Relayer from the age of twenty – one of the youngest ever. He joined the Bellas in 1820 and returned to Earth in 1930. Old, I know, but that is due to living here."

"But Grandad, we are in 2006. That would make him two hundred and six years old. That's not possible, is it, Grandad?" I paused. "Is it?"

"Jessie, look around you. The Bellas don't really alter, do they? Some are hundreds of years old; some are thousands of years old. They have a gift within them which keeps them alive. Unless they fail in a quest or they fall prey to a Malissol, they cannot die. Everything on Earth is exempt from this gift, to give value to life. If humans were to live forever, they would not care for their time on Earth, and without that, you remove compassion, and without caring, there is no love. Bellas are different. Their whole purpose in life is to keep the balance on Earth. Do you understand?"

"Yes, Grandad. But Dr Brostoff isn't a Bella."

"No, Jessie, but if he had taken a Bella's blood, it would be possible for him to live without fear of death – not as a Bella, but nevertheless to have the everlife."

102

I understood the enormity of what Grandad was telling me.

I pulled Willoughby and the others back into view.

They all sat on the table in a row looking very concerned.

"Listen," I said to them, "William Wilson." I paused. "Could he be Dr Brostoff?"

"No, Jessie," Oakleigh said, jumping to the floor. "William Wilson left us years ago. He was a great man who served us well."

"Please just look around."

"I won't have that, Jessie." Oakleigh angrily stamped his foot.

"I am sorry, Jessie, it's absurd," Willoughby said, joining him on the floor.

Bluebell had moved to the corner of the room as Oakleigh and Willoughby started to argue in defence of their former Relayer and friend.

She pulled a small picture off the bookcase and stared at it. Her face took on a look of shock followed by extreme sadness. She glanced at the others then gazed at the photo again. "It's true, you know," she said quietly.

When the other Bellas didn't respond, she turned to face them and raised her voice. "I said, it's true." She looked crestfallen.

"What's true?" Leanndi asked nervously, still sitting on the table and not enjoying the commotion at all.

"It's him, William Wilson," Bluebell replied, throwing the picture towards Oakleigh and Willoughby. They were stunned into silence as they studied the picture that lay now in a broken frame on the floor.

Leanndi, who was sitting on her hands, gawped at the

others, clearly hating the uncomfortable silence and the fact that her companions were so upset. She herself was too young to remember William Wilson.

"So, he was good and now he may be bad," she said. "I think we have all seen that before. Shouldn't we remember why we are here and just find the written truth?"

The other three glared at her. Then Willoughby's sadness turned to anger.

"Let's tear this place apart," he said, and the four of them jumped into action.

I watched on.

Willoughby, Oakleigh and Bluebell were full of purpose in their destruction.

But Leanndi seemed to be aimlessly throwing pieces of paper into the air and enjoying them fluttering down around her. She levered a draw open and climbed in. She soon returned and held aloft a Bella Roman uniform, terribly torn. There was little pride to be salvaged from this once-honoured garment.

"Look at this," she said, quite proud of her find.

Willoughby rushed to examine it, and was soon joined by Bluebell and Oakleigh. "This is Doggett's coat of arms," Willoughby said softly, running his fingers gently across it.

I didn't need to ask if this was significant. I could see and feel the sorrow being replaced by fear on the Bellas' little faces. I wanted them out of there as soon as possible.

"Please can we find the written truth?" I said, not hiding my urgency, as I hated this replica room. Its gloom seeped through my vision and I feared it would poison our own.

Bluebell turned first and scampered up the bookcase, opened her little arms wide, clasped the whole top shelf of documents and tumbled backwards. The documents hit the table, sliding them alphabetically in front of the others. Willoughby rushed forward to the letter T and began sifting through them.

"'Time... the creation of...', no," he said, throwing it over his shoulder. "'Treasure... another's heart...' no," – again tossing it over his shoulder. And then, twenty or so documents over the shoulder later, he held it fast in his hand. "Got it!" he yelled. "The written Truth."

They all moved closer and stared at the table as Willoughby laid this fragile paper in front of him.

Bluebell composed herself, then walked across the table and stood over the paper. Her boot held one side in place, because a draught entered the room from beyond the front door on this unusually cold night, moving the paper away from the table before it settled back in place.

"What's it say, then, Bluebell?" Leanndi impatiently asked.

"Wait," Bluebell snapped. "It is very faint." She leant closer and began.

"'I have written this before God and before I take my own life to be damned in Hell for my sin. Not for forgiveness but in the face of what we have done that we may be remembered for one thing only and that is in the way we have treated our fellow man.

"'On the day that hundreds of men, women and children came to us for help, for comfort against this awful black curse we call the plague, we led them not to safety and love but into the dark dungeons that lay deep within our abbey walls. There we sealed their poor souls away, never to be resumed, in the prayer that the plague would die with them.'

"That's all there is," Bluebell said, stepping off the edge of the paper and letting the next draught take it gently to the floor.

Grandad had joined me in listening to Bluebell reading the monk's words, and turned to me. His bright eyes grew in size as he realised that Dr Brostoff's intended building works would soon strike the hollowed tomb and let out the plague that had lain dormant with the memory of its victims.

"It's all in the footings, Jessie. Intentionally or not, he is going to release the plague."

"No, Grandad! Not on purpose, surely not? Why would he do such a thing?"

"I don't know, Jessie. I am not even sure if he does, but we have to stop work on that site for good. Maybe with history itself. With artefacts, or an archaeological dig – anything at all."

Grandad calmed himself and his thoughts returned to the job in hand.

"Jessie, get the four of them to 125 Spencer Street. It is a safe house for Bellas. They need food and rest. Tell them to leave Archie there. He will be well cared for."

I relayed the message and guided them back through the streets of St Albans.

It was strange, but in my short time as a Relayer, our Bellas had only been gone for a day or two, and I'd had no idea that there were safe houses in almost every town and city. In fact, until this moment, I'd had no idea how big the network of the Bellas' world really was.

CHAPTER 14

Sweet Little Arthur Fatelli

On arrival at 125 Spencer Street, Willoughby dismounted from Archie, rose to his fullest height and tapped three times with his cane on the door.

"Cat flap!" a voice from the other side shouted. "Use the cat flap."

Willoughby removed his top hat, bent a little and crawled through. Archie watched intently, cocked his head from side to side and his rear flopped down on the cold cobbled path. This caused Leanndi and Oakleigh to bounce out of his thick, warm fur and roll down his back to the tip of his tail. Bluebell sat fast in her riding stance, ignoring her friends' sudden awakening into this incredibly chilly night. She just murmured to herself, "Cat flap, use the cat flap – how very undignified."

But before her dismount was complete, the door was flung open and there, standing on a stool, was Arthur Fatelli. He was, without question, the smallest human man I had ever seen. His face was very round and his ears were unfortunately big for the size of his head. His clothes were clearly made by himself or a friend whose work with a needle left much to be desired. The jumper he wore was thick wool. The left sleeve covered his hand, but the right sleeve barely made it past his elbow. His trousers had been badly altered, finished off at the bottom by one black and one brown shoe. He had the loveliest big smile, but his amazingly uneven teeth detracted from it. I could only imagine what life on Earth might be like for such a tiny, odd-looking man. If I had suffered from my modest height and quirky ways, how much more must this man have endured, if he was still interacting with humans, that is.

"Come in, come in," he said, climbing down from the stool, and then beckoning them forward with his flopping sleeve. "Come on, Bluebell. Ah, you are just as beautiful as I remember you. Sorry it took so long to open the door. I couldn't reach the handle, hence the stool."

Bluebell walked forward, followed by Leanndi and Oakleigh, who tussled for second place.

"You do look very familiar," Bluebell said. "But I am not sure where I know you from." She concentrated her stare deep into his eyes.

"It's me, Arthur Fatelli. Don't you remember me, Bluebell? You were my invisible friend through my youngest years."

"Arthur!" Bluebell squealed, stunning her companions by her uncharacteristically childlike enthusiasm. "But that must be over forty years ago." She reached up to hold his little hand. "Oh Arthur, have you been well? I can see that you haven't grown so very much since you were little. Has life been okay to you?"

"Oh yes, Bluebell," Arthur joyfully replied. "Life has been so very wonderful since you went. I didn't fit in at school, I had no friends apart from you, and my parents left me at a bus stop. I was too much of a 'freak' for them, apparently. It was either put me in the circus – except that, thankfully, nobody does that any more – or just abandon me. They chose the latter. You can ask Grandad; he knows all about it."

Bluebell's jaw dropped open and she frowned hard. "Arthur, that sounds just awful, not at all wonderful. And you say Grandad knew all about this?"

"Yes, yes, he does. It was when he took you back that the angels took me in and I have worked with them ever since. I have seen so much wonder and beauty that I am blessed to be different. The Bellas I have seen, helped and cared for are so amazing; I just knew that one day you would arrive, and here you are."

Bluebell's eyes filled up, and Arthur's, too, as they stared at one another. But the moment was broken as Oakleigh squeezed passed them, asking, "Did you say the food is ready to eat now, Arthur?"

"I didn't, but in fact – yes, it is. Sorry, I forgot myself. Come in, settle by the fire and a feast will be served in the smallest of moments."

Arthur shut the door and with it the biting air was left outside. What a safe, warm feeling this small cottage had. Although it was sparse, with only the light of the fire to settle them in, it felt as a home should. Willoughby was already thawing out by the hearth, sitting on an old church pew which was cushioned by kneeling pads. His silhouette looked proud as he sat with his cane in one hand and his top hat in the other. The other three joined him on the pew and they all looked very tiny, enjoying this moment of heat and safety. Archie flopped to the floor in front of them and instantly gave out his most contented sigh. Arthur, struggling with the weight of some logs, rolled them out of his arms and jumped back, unsteadily placing them in the centre of the fire. Cinders landed freely around the room, but the flames crackled and jumped within the new wood.

"That's better," he said. "Would you like to eat where you are sitting or come through to the kitchen?"

"Oh, I think we would like to stay put, Arthur, if you don't mind," Bluebell replied, and her companions nodded in agreement.

Arthur disappeared, not through the door but through a black velvet curtain that separated the two rooms.

He quickly returned with two bowls, one with chopped liver and one with water, both of which he placed in front of Archie. Archie's nose twitched and he raised his head, eyes still half-closed, and then gently took small pieces of liver. He glanced up occasionally for reassurance that this food was indeed for him.

Arthur next brought four trays, balancing two on each arm, and passed them in order down the pew. The trays were piled high with freshly made bread, cheese and an abundance of fruit, all chopped into tiny segments, just the right size for the weary Bellas. They in turn thanked Arthur and for the next few moments the only sounds were of the fizzing blaze and of eating.

Arthur went to the corner of the room and pushed a small leather chair, its feet screeching across the floorboards. He raised his voice and asked, "So, how long will you be staying for? I hope it's a while." The four of them glanced over their shoulders towards him. Archie, too, raised his head and sleepily stared under the pew. "I suppose you'll know more tomorrow," Arthur continued, still oblivious to the awful screeching. He came to a halt just short of the pew and climbed on, smiling brightly at his guests.

"So, something big is happening. I am not surprised. My house has had the pleasure of some residents, an old man and woman. They peer around the velvet curtain at me. I just knew you would turn up soon. Don't get me wrong, I had the usual traffic of Bellas, but no one of your stature here. You are quite famous, you know."

"Really?" Leanndi jumped forward. "Even me? Am I famous too?"

"Yes, Leanndi, you have quite a following amongst the younger Bellas," Arthur replied, clasping his hands in delight as Leanndi spun round on one foot and gave a sarcastic curtsy to her fellow Bellas, who laughed aloud.

This lightened the mood, and for an hour or so they all forgot about the day's events.

The fire roared through the night as they settled down to sleep. Arthur offered them sleeping quarters which consisted of tiny little bunk beds. The linen was clean and the corner of each blanket was perfectly folded back. There were twenty or so beds in the room, which could quite easily have housed more as each bed was only a foot square or two.

But Willoughby, though thankful for Arthur's offer, said they would stay where they were. Leanndi and Oakleigh had nestled down with Archie, using their parkas as pillows, and Bluebell had rested her head in Willoughby's arms and was fast asleep. Willoughby himself stared at the flames for a time, and then dropped his head forward into Bluebell's neck and drifted off. Arthur battled with one more log and curled up in the chair, ready for slumber.

Meanwhile, Grandad and I worked on the history of St Albans and its connection with the Romans.

We were joined in the night, to my great surprise, by a Roman Bella named Claudius. It took my breath away that this little Bella was an original Roman, as were the clothes he wore. He was disciplined in his mannerisms and powerful in his stance. His uniform was beautiful and I analysed every detail: white tunic with purple bands, red cloak fastened with an intricate brooch, white kilt with yellow tassels, and grey breastplate with yellow decorations and white sashes. He was every bit a Roman soldier, but still evident were the big leather boots. If I'm honest, they did ruin the visual impact. He didn't have traditional headwear, but instead his hair was fashioned into a bright red crest.

On greeting me he clasped my fingers and I noticed how rough his little hands were and, behind the fine fur on his face, his skin was hard and weathered, indicating that times were tougher than ever for our little ones.

Grandad and I agreed that to stop work on Mr Wilson's site for good, the builders would have to come across something quite spectacular, and he explained it all to Claudius and what we proposed to do.

"In one night, which will be this forthcoming night, we need to excavate the soil and lay an original Roman mosaic floor. This will stop work on that land for good. I know we have the mosaic artists amongst us and the materials to do it, but we need your leadership and your units of soldiers, your legions, as I really do not know what awaits us down there."

Claudius frowned and walked a little around the room.

"I have no doubt we can achieve what you propose to do," he said, "but sending so many Bellas off the Island at once leaves our Floating Land vulnerable. If we were to fail in our quest, it would be the biggest loss of life from Bluebell Wood ever. Wouldn't Mr Wilson see us coming?"

"I'm really not sure," I answered, quite ashamedly, glancing at Grandad. He nodded with a reassuring tilt of his head.

"What about the Bellas on the other Floating Lands?" I stammered out, the idea suddenly springing into my head. I knew that travel between the Lands was pretty challenging, though not impossible.

Claudius paused for a moment, then shook his head. "It's impossible, I'm afraid. There's simply far too little time for that. I wish that were not so."

He then turned sharply on his heels. "So be it," he declared, to my surprise. "I will organise the Romans. You just get us there."

What with watching the Bellas below, and working with Grandad, the night was flying by, but it was most exciting. The Bellas' world was certainly full of magical surprises.

I took a moment to view my sweet ones as morning broke at Spencer Street. Light shone through the gap in the curtain. It moved slowly around the room, touching them individually, and gently waking them from their sleep.

Arthur was no longer on his chair, but he soon appeared with five cups of tea.

"I hope you all slept well," he said, as he placed the tray of tea down and began turning the fire. He clasped some bellows and frantically began pumping them in the direction of what was now quite a limp effort, causing a plume of soot to fill the room. Bluebell tutted loudly and coughed. "Honestly, Arthur, that's not the way."

But Arthur was oblivious to the commotion and seemed quite pleased with himself when the flames did eventually appear. He happily wiped the soot from his eyes and settled down with his tea.

"So, can you tell me what it is yet?" he asked.

"Yes," Willoughby answered. "It's all about Mr Wilson, who's now calling himself Dr Brostoff."

And before Willoughby could continue, Arthur shouted, "Dr Brostoff! I know him. He is often around. I don't let him in, but he stares through my front window and through my letterbox. He always asks to come in and speak with me, but Daisy Dreamer told me never to talk to him. He does scare me – he is so very tall. His shadow from outside seems to fill my whole room, but I sometimes shout 'Just go away' whilst standing on the stool to make myself look big, or I simply hide."

"Oh, poor Arthur," Bluebell said, whilst holding her arms out, allowing Arthur to nestle in, much to Leanndi and Oakleigh's amusement as Bluebell would most certainly be left with a great deal of soot on her unbelievably clean clothes.

"Do you know Daisy Dreamer?" Arthur asked.

"Oh yes, yes, I know her," Willoughby answered softly, raising his eyebrows to Oakleigh and Leanndi. "That was an awful incident she was involved in. It almost destroyed Grandad."

Arthur stared at Willoughby, obviously hoping that he would tell more, but silence fell awkwardly within the room, so he spoke.

"She is often around and talks about you, so I thought that you did know her, but I was just checking. That's how I knew that one day soon you would arrive."

"I like Daisy Dreamer very much," Leanndi said, now gently pulling on Archie's left ear, awakening him for a short time and then stroking him to put him back to sleep.

"Any more tea?" Oakleigh asked, gazing at Bluebell as she patted soot from her beautiful dress. "I think today could be a very long one." He chuckled.

Not knowing who they were talking about, I left them as Bluebell Wood became a hive of activity. From nowhere, hundreds, if not thousands, of Roman Bellas made their way to the clearing and formed ranks. Claudius stood on the high ground watching his strictly disciplined troops slam their shields. The eagle-headed standard was raised, and this ruthless war machine was poised to relive history through their quest.

The mosaic artists appeared from beyond the high ground where Claudius stood and he briefly spoke to them. They seemed smaller than most, especially alongside Claudius, but they were held in great esteem amongst their fellow Bellas. Next to pride in their Roman army, they considered art and architecture as the foundation of their society. The soldiers continued to slam their shields, and the noise grew, bouncing off the trees that surrounded the clearing, replicating an amphitheatre.

Bellas from every era lined the fields from Bluebell Wood all the way to the snaking river and beyond to the open lake. I had had no idea that so many inhabited Bluebell Wood. As far as the eye could see, they became full height and lined the path to cheer on this wonderful Roman machine. A carnival atmosphere was distracting me from the purpose of the mass exodus, and Grandad pulled me back to the watchtower.

Once inside, the thunderous noise of the shields was muffled and Grandad turned to me.

"I think Claudius may be right. This is a massive decision to send so many on a mission and to leave us so vulnerable."

"Grandad, I know. Are our Romans here to protect Bluebell Wood, or have they ever fought a battle on Earth before? And what could be waiting for them that could challenge so many?"

"Remember, Jessie, when I spoke with you about darkness entering a Bella to create in its own form an evil counterpart known as the Malissols?"

"Yes, of course," I replied.

"Well, I have read this, and also been told, that in the years from AD 789 to 850 the Vikings were the most fearsome fighting force known to man down on Earth. They were brutal in their attacks and looted everything in their paths. In response to the Viking brutality, Bellas went on multiple quests to try to bring healing and peace, but many of those quests failed, meaning many Bellas were left whose spirits had departed. In time, the fall in Bella numbers was such that the Malissols formed their own barbarian force which fought and pillaged alongside the Vikings, unbeknown to the Vikings themselves. Although our own Roman army were from a time hundreds of years previously, they had mastered the fighting and organisational skills of their human Romans and were the only force fit to confront these poor souls who had been consumed by evil. They fought with double-edged swords, spears and arrows, but their favourite weapon was the battle-axe.

"Claudius himself led the Bella Roman army with his second-in-command. One of the finest soldiers to ever grace the field of battle. Doggett. His name was Doggett."

"Oh," I said, fearing what was to come next. "Not the

Doggett whose Roman uniform was found in Mr Wilson's home?"

"Yes, Jessie. You see, when the Romans did eventually defeat the Malissols, and I say eventually, Doggett was so badly affected by war that he returned from the army and spent many hundreds of years as an invisible friend. Eventually he failed in a quest, and I thought his spirit had left. Now I'm not so sure. Doggett would never have prevented himself from dying – he knew that was his fate – but many Bellas have done in the past, which means it could well happen again in the future."

"I didn't realise they could stop themselves from dying, Grandad – how do they do that?" I asked. I still had so much to learn.

Grandad didn't reply. In fact, he seemed terribly troubled and it scared me. I wished to say that I was in full agreement with the quest in hand, but I wasn't.

I pulled myself onto the edge of the table and sat with my legs swinging freely. I stared at my bare feet and wiggled my toes. I hadn't thought of myself much since my arrival here and it was nice to focus on a part of me, but in truth I was shutting out the problem in hand and choosing not to speak.

"Come on, Jessie." Grandad's voice rose and he slammed his hand on the table. "You were sent here for a reason. Now help me do the right thing."

"No, Grandad. That's wrong, to ask that of me," my voice spiked back at him. "How do I know what is right? You knew Mr Wilson, not me. If you want the answers, ask him."

"That's it, Jessie! We will do just that. But in the meantime, let the Romans return to St Albans." His mood was erratic, not like Grandad at all, and I glared at him.

"What, Jessie? Why do you stare at me?" he asked, changing his mood from agitated to deep and inquisitive. He moved close to me, too close. I didn't like his gaze at all. His customary bright blue eyes were tinted with darkness.

"What's going on, Grandad?" I asked, sliding off the table and stepping away.

"Take control, Jessie. You really must take control," he answered, turning away from me and supporting his body by holding the table. Seeing him from behind he looked once again old and unthreatening, and I moved close and put my arms around his waist.

"You are tired, Grandad. That's all, you are just tired."

He loosened my grip and turned to me.

"Oh, my dearest Jessie, how you have taken to this place and everything it stands for. It is said that people find their greatest strength when they only have themselves to turn to. I knew soon a quest would arise that would challenge you, but this, I feel, is too much for you alone."

"But why would I be alone? I have you, Grandad." I swallowed hard, fearing that I no longer would have. "I do, Grandad." I paused, pulling at his cardigan. "I do, don't I? I do have you."

"My dear Jessie, I have to go now. I have no choice," he said.

"But why, Grandad? Just last night we were normal. You can't just go."

My lips trembled as he clasped my shoulders and stared lovingly down at me. His beautiful blue eyes returned, and then glazed over, and tears ran free.

"I will never leave you, and I will send somebody to guide you as I would guide you. Please focus, Jessie, on the quest. I love you, Jessie."

"I love you too, Grandad," I replied, as we held each other for a few seconds.

"Now go, Jessie. Go to Arkley. You have the Romans to deal with."

"But please, Grandad, please tell me why you're leaving me."

"Jessie, I am not leaving you, I just have to go. Please trust that it is for the best."

He gently held my face then pulled away.

I cried after him, "Please don't leave me!" but he didn't turn back, and he was gone.

CHAPTER 15

Daisy Dreamer

M y world had been turned upside down all over again.
The closest adult to me had left me, just as my
parents had disappeared on that plane. But this time it was
intentional, and he wouldn't tell me why. I couldn't shake
the intense unease I felt at the way Grandad had just acted
– there was something very wrong going on, but I didn't
know what.

I shook myself down and took a long, deep breath. I had
to focus: I had to start somewhere. So I left the watchtower
and scurried down the winding stairs, making my way to the
workshop and Arkley.

The Romans continued to raise the level of noise,
enthused to be marching once more. With frequent
turbulence shots from the Cannon Masters, it was hard to
think, so I was pleased to enter the workshop deep within the
heart of Bluebell Wood. I now enjoyed the dampness that on
my first visit here had made me feel uncomfortable. I held my
hand against the rock wall, letting the moisture build between

my fingers, and within seconds it pooled and then ran free, trickling down my skin.

The workshop itself was empty. Like the rest of the inhabitants of the Floating Land, the tradesmen and women had joined the farewell above me. I glanced around for Arkley and walked slowly amongst the individual workstations. The tiny tools were neatly laid out, regimentally placed across the surfaces. Each station was creating something to enhance the travellers' chance of success in their chosen missions. Little parkas hung in their hundreds at the far side, and angels' robes rippled, catching a breeze that only they could find. There were little wooden scooters, tiny parachutes, hang-gliders, balloons; and blankets, boots and socks, all small and sweet. I took one of the tiny parkas off the rail and held it up in front of me. I loved my little friends so much that it was tearing me apart. I felt empty inside, and so alone. It was the very same feeling I'd had when my parents hadn't returned. Tears poured from me as I buried my face into the little garment.

"Jessie, Jessie," a voice called softly.

I didn't acknowledge it. I just kept crying for a minute or two. Then I felt my hair being brushed away from my forehead and beautifully soft fingertips stroking me. I pulled the little parka away from my face to see a human girl standing before me. I blinked hard, trying to find vision through my tears, but I couldn't. Within this girl's presence, I felt consumed by the desire to let my emotions out. I fell into her arms. Although she looked about my age, she felt secure and held me just as a mother would have done. She didn't feel at all like a stranger, but familiar. She held me tight within one arm and stroked my hair with the other.

"I am sorry to cry into you. I don't even know who you

are," I said, pulling away and staring into her deep brown eyes.

Her pupils glittered like a kaleidoscope, concentrating on my mouth.

"My name is Daisy – Daisy Dreamer in full. I have come to help you." Then she drew my head back into her and hugged me firmly. I recognised her name from the Bellas' conversation at Spencer Street. "We are all so proud of you, Jessie. You have adapted yourself so bravely, without any thought of your own future in all of this. You have a selfless heart, a quality few can boast."

I liked what she said about me and I nodded my head in agreement, still with my face buried. I was making her jumper very wet with my tears.

"Your jumper is so soft. I like it very much," I said.

But Daisy didn't answer. I pulled away from her.

"It is an unusual jumper, isn't it?" I now looked directly at her.

"Oh, you like my jersey," she said, and smiled at me. "It was once everything a girl of my age would hope to own. It is mohair, fine wool. We wore them oversized. Often we would wear boys' ones."

She talked just like a girl exchanging fashion tips. I stepped back and stared at her from top to toe. Her hair was dark and naturally curly, crunched high behind an Alice band. Her skin was olive and her eyes big and brown. She looked at me kindly, encouraging my next words but not demanding them. She was taller than me, but then most other girls were. Her trousers were bright orange and tight down her leg, finishing short of the ankle. On her feet was a simple pair of white plimsolls and she wore no socks.

"I like the way you dress," I said, smiling, enjoying her company.

"Thank you, Jessie." Daisy gave a smile and a very sweet chuckle. "It's the fashion of the late 1950s. They were such good times. But hey, let's get the Romans back to St Albans, and then I'm sure the future holds in store many such times of equal innocence for the world, once we restore the balance."

"Yes, let's do that," I agreed, full of a newfound confidence with Daisy here with me. "But Daisy, I know I have learned to accept almost anything since I have been here and not to question too much, but how did you get here? And how did you know about the Romans and all that?"

"I came here by request."

"But whose request?"

"Well, mostly yours, Jessie," she replied, gently holding my hand.

"But Daisy, I couldn't request your assistance. I hadn't even met you until now."

Daisy was still holding my hand. "Dear Jessie, you don't have to know me to want me near. Think of me as a human-like Bella if that helps."

I guess it did help a little, though I did also allow myself to be slightly confused. I liked Daisy so much, though, that I was happy just to have her with me. So, once again, I bit my inquisitive tongue. Daisy looked with purpose around the workshop, so I looked too, hoping to find what she was looking for.

"There he is. Arkley!" Daisy said, as Arkley appeared, balancing two rolls of fabric which rested heavily on each shoulder.

"Daisy Dreamer!" Arkley rolled the fabrics one at a time

onto a workstation. "How wonderful to see you! I take it you have come to give our lovely young Jessie a hand in Grandad's absence?"

"Yes, just a little help," Daisy said, fondly brushing my hair back behind my ears. "I really don't think she will need it, but it does help to have someone else with you."

I smiled at Daisy. Then it dawned on me that Arkley, too, knew of Grandad's unwelcome departure.

"How did you know Grandad had gone away?" I snapped, leaning towards Arkley and giving him one of my most forbidding stares. I could see my reaction startled him, and he stammered whilst waving his arms, as if batting my words away before they got too close.

"Well... well... Daisy's here. That normally means Grandad had to go away – that's all, Jessie. I have never asked any more than that."

"I see. Well then," I answered firmly, as if I had just solved the mystery with my cunning questioning, but in truth I was even more confused.

"So, Jessie," Arkley continued, "I take it you have come down here for a reason and not just to pass the time of day with me, as nice as that would be."

I could see I had upset him by my abrupt manner. His tone was somewhat sarcastic, but I ignored it.

"Um, yes, I did come to see you, Arkley, but I am not sure in what capacity I need your skilful mind yet. You see, the Romans move as a unit. So I need to land them neatly as one, which means not in raindrops or from the Cannon Masters."

Arkley smoothed the beautiful fabric onto the table. It was material for the angels' garments. He took a pair of scissors from his side. They looked as if they were made not from steel but of glass or crystal.

"Well, Jessie, you could take them there yourself."

He touched the edge of the cloth with the tip of the scissors and guided them forward. I had heard what he had said, but I was distracted by the way the fabric floated free, lighting up for a split second as it melted apart.

"I'm sorry, Arkley, what did you say?" I said, clasping my own dress and stepping excitedly around.

"You could take them yourself in your plane," he continued with a wry smile.

"My plane? Does it work?" I shouted. "My wonderful old de Havilland?"

"Oh yes, Jessie. That was fixed almost as soon as it was broken." Arkley laughed.

"But why didn't anyone tell me it was fixed?"

"Why would anyone answer a question that wasn't asked?" Arkley grinned, not wanting to dampen this happy moment.

"Will you come with me, Daisy? Will you, please?" I asked, holding her hand and clasping it tightly.

"Yes, Jessie, but then who will relay messages from here while you're gone?"

Daisy's question stopped me dead, and the excitement fell out of me and slammed onto the damp, earthy floor. I stood very still, my hands beginning to tingle, my breath stalled as if my body had decided to press pause.

I touched my goggles that hung round my neck, as they often did, turned, and ran out of the workshop. Instead of going back to the watchtower, I went up just one level and through the tunnel where I had first met my beautiful Leanndi. I didn't slow as the darkness engulfed me, as I now knew the smooth wood so well. I burst through the door at the other end.

The tail end of the Roman army and the Bellas, who had rejoiced in their coming together, had all but passed. The bluebells, each perfectly intact, swayed gently in the breeze. Although the sun was out, it felt cold, and my bare feet were soon quite painful as the morning dew brushed onto them while I clumsily flattened the grass, leaving only my footprints. There was no trace at all of the Roman army or the hundreds of well-wishers who had just gone by.

I had no idea why I had rushed into the clearing, but I needed air. My breathing was back but now fast and shallow and my sweaty hands had clenched tight. Grandad's words to me, that I should take control, filled me with rage. How dare he say such words, with all that I had accepted here!

I picked a twig from the ground and snapped it furiously into tiny pieces. I found another and snapped it, too, snarling as it fell down around my feet. I did this again and again until my anger had subsided. Turning to walk away, I stamped heavily on one of the many fragments of wood that I had surrounded myself with, and it splintered into my big toe.

I yelped, clutched my foot, not daring to look, and screwed up my face. I held my balance on my other leg precariously, but soon fell to my side. I rolled, still with my foot in my hand. I hated the thought of blood, especially my own, and especially out of the one area of my body that I was particularly fond of. Even when I had loathed my small frame at times in my younger years, my dainty feet were a thing apart.

The rest of me was now like my feet – cold and wet. I contemplated why, as a Relayer, I hadn't foreseen this. It was somewhat embarrassing as I lay soaked in the morning dew with my goggles still prominently dangling from my neck.

To be a Relayer isn't much of a gift, is it, I thought. Especially if I can't even see myself hurting my foot.

I knew it was childish to think this way, but I couldn't help it. Although the pain was awful, I was quite happy to lie there. I felt little and frail and very cold and wet. But stay put I did, having now settled on my side.

I opened my eyes and watched the cold sun squeeze its way through the fir trees that surrounded me. It made no attempt to warm or dry Bluebell Wood. Winter was here and the sun's job, for now, was to give us light.

I let my thoughts roam through my head, closing my eyes again as the sun found me. A realisation was dawning on me: If I was a Relayer, that meant that I could have seen this happening, but that was all; I wouldn't ever have seen what the outcome would be. We only ever saw an image of an act of evil or impending disaster, or sometimes an image from the past.

That was it. Never did we see the outcome. The rest was relaying routes or information to the travellers in the field.

This quest had all arisen from one vision from the past: the monk. We had seen nothing more.

I knew that the watchtower was the overall eye to the events and that I shouldn't leave it, but I had no choice, I realised. I would take the Romans to Earth myself, and we would, by our own desire, complete the quest that Grandad and I had created in the early hours of that morning. Mr Wilson would have seen an image too, but, just like us, he would have only seen the one, and what it was no longer concerned me. He was no more able than I to change the outcome of whatever he had seen.

As for new callings coming through to the watchtower, the other three Islands around the world would cover me, I was sure. Over the months, Grandad and I had received messages from other continents through our lenses and helped out when extra Relayers were needed. They would have a Relayer who could watch and direct our Bellas from where they were if they had to. That was the beauty and magic of the lenses in our telescopes – or goggles, in my case. I was still in awe of how the whole system worked. Bellas really were the most wonderful creatures.

So, I was decided, and happy with my decision. I was very unhappy, however, with the pain in my foot, which was now throbbing in time with my heart. I still hadn't looked at my wound and, for the moment, I was glad not to, when the smallest of voices said, "That's not so bad, is it? I used to get all sorts stuck into my feet before I had my boots."

A few months ago, a voice from nowhere would have startled me, but no longer. I didn't even look for the owner of it.

I replied, "Is it not that bad, then?"

"No, definitely not. I can even fix that myself."

And then she appeared, standing at the top of my thigh, her closest viewpoint to where I held my foot. I only saw the back of her at first, but by her ponytail and the way she excitedly moved from foot to foot, almost dancing, she reminded me of Leanndi. She spun her head round. I was slightly startled, as her face was greatly enlarged by the magnifying glass the size of her head that she held out in front of her.

"Hello," she said, "my name is Poppy." Blinking her eyes, she moved the glass to and fro from her little face, trying to get me into perfect focus. Her face bowed and curved as she did so and I couldn't help but laugh.

"It is funny, isn't it?" She smiled, making me laugh again as her tiny little face circled around the glass. "This was my big sister's. She gave it to me when her eyes had finished growing."

"Oh yes?" I smiled. "And do I know your sister?"

I felt quite sure of who it was anyway.

"Yes, yes, yes," she quickly replied, hopping easily from boot to boot. "It is Leanndi."

"Ah yes, I can see that."

"Really?" she said, holding the magnifying glass for the first time quite still, giving me a larger-than-normal look at her face.

"Uh-huh, you really do look so similar."

"How exciting!" she replied, jumping up high then back down onto my leg. "I haven't had a really good look at myself. Even with the glass, it is a little hard. But only another year or so, and then my eyes will have done all their growing."

"Is that the same for all young Bellas?"

Poppy steadied herself and her focus through the glass, once again making her face entirely disproportionate to her body.

"Yes," she answered, deepening her voice, just as Leanndi would when she didn't like the question. "I'll have you know I am perfectly normal for my age."

"Of course, Poppy, I can see that," I replied hastily. "It's just that I saw a class of young Bellas a while back who had magnifying glasses and I wondered why. But now it makes perfect sense."

Poppy then flashed me a hugely exaggerated smile and zoomed her face purposefully in and out of focus, making us both laugh.

"You said you could fix me, Poppy?"

"And I shall," she replied, jumping onto the ground and pulling a bluebell towards her face. Once in line, she lowered the magnifying glass and snapped at the petals with her teeth and began chewing.

"Is that good for you, Poppy, to eat a bluebell?"

She put her tongue out and answered me but her words were quite inaudible.

"Sorry, Poppy, I didn't get any of that."

But this time she made no attempt to answer. She concentrated her gaze on my foot, clasped the fragment of wood with her right hand and spat the pulp-like mixture out of her mouth onto the wound. She then focused once more on my face, studying my response. I did wince a little, but on the whole it was quite painless, the splinter was gone, and my foot now felt fine.

Poppy's face waited eagerly, eyes wide, not blinking, and mouth open, not breathing. She held her gaze.

"Thank you, Poppy," I said, desperately wanting her to change her expression, as she looked quite stuck.

"That's okay. Bluebells work in all sorts of ways once they have been in a Bella's mouth."

I was thrilled with Poppy's nursing skills, but before I could thank her properly a high-pitched squeal came from beyond the trees and she scurried off towards it.

"Bye then," she said as she disappeared, "and good luck."

I touched the pulp on my toe to find it had already dried hard. I rose to my feet and marched, full of purpose, back through the passageway and down to the workshop where Daisy and Arkley awaited my return.

"I shall leave Bluebell Wood and take the Romans to Earth," I announced.

I realised as the words left my mouth that Bluebell Wood had truly become my home, and my stomach turned at the thought of leaving. But I was full of excitement too.

Daisy Dreamer gave me a smile and, walking towards me, held out her hand and clasped mine.

"How would you like me to help? Shall I still be coming with you?"

"Oh definitely, Daisy, I would like you there very much. And as for helping me – I don't know." I paused. "Do you know Bluebell Wood very well, and all the little ones who live here?"

"Oh, my dear Jessie, I know Bluebell Wood like no other place, and yes, I know all of the inhabitants too."

Her answer made me curious but, as before, I put the question out of my mind.

"Well, Daisy, help me, then. I need the Weatherman, the Plane Spotter, Claudius and one of the Cannon Masters, all in the watchtower in half an hour."

"Okay," she replied, and pulled me close, held me tight, then went happily on her way.

I turned and stared at her as she left. Her walk reflected her personality. She seemed to glide across the floor. Her posture was perfect, but her hair bounced freely behind her Alice band, giving her a slightly rebellious look. I turned back towards Arkley, who was poised and ready for work.

"Arkley, I need to change my clothes, and of course, I need footwear. Nothing fancy, just an image of a Bella, boots and all."

Arkley smiled. "It will be a pleasure."

"Best get a parka and some boots for Daisy Dreamer too. It will be cold out there. Oh, and could you also do us both some gloves or mittens, the ones with the string attached to them? I have always had such a habit of losing them and I really don't like my hands getting cold. I think that's all for now."

"Okay," Arkley said, as the door swung open and his little workforce returned full of high spirits and chatting excitedly amongst themselves.

"Come now!" Arkley raised his voice. "We have work to do."

The chatter quietened as the little tradesfolk returned to their work.

CHAPTER 16

Turbulence Shocks Punching Hard

I made my way back to the watchtower. I so wished to find Grandad leaning enthusiastically over a chart or manuscript. I longed for his smile and that excited glint in his eye. But it was not to be. Instead the tower was quiet and cold. The manuscripts that we had so tirelessly studied the night before still lay open on the table; our teacups were as we had left them both, half full – we had not stopped long enough to drink.

I hated it here without Grandad, and was very relieved when the sound of Daisy Dreamer's voice returned up the stairs. She entered the room as requested with Claudius. Second to follow was the Weatherman, then Boomer the Plane Spotter, and finally a very confused-looking Cannon Master called Bertrum.

I couldn't help but feel sorry for the Cannon Masters. They were very skilled in their precision-shooting of air, but away from their work they looked rather dim, almost as if they were seconds behind the rest of us. But I knew that could not be true, as their talent relied on lightning reflexes. Nevertheless, I leant down and picked Bertrum up and placed him on the table. He very quietly mumbled, "Thank you," and smiled at me. His eyes were dark. The pupils were huge from focusing his gaze for hour upon hour at the night sky, not daring to miss the next perfectly aimed turbulence shock. His chain mail tunic sparkled as he slowly moved his torso, staring nervously around the room and at his fellow Bellas.

"Don't worry," I said, "we won't be here long."

He just nodded his response.

I turned and faced the Weatherman and, as they had on our first encounter, his eyes flared open and went from silver-blue to totally silver. His presence made me feel a little uncomfortable, like the last time. He coughed deeply, so I patted him on his tiny back, and then he spoke.

"What can I do for you, Jessie?"

"Well, sir," I said, not wanting to refer to him as the Weatherman, but neither did I want to let on that in all my time here I still hadn't learned his name. I continued very politely. "As I am sure you are aware, the Romans are to return to Earth."

"Yes, of course."

"Well, yes, of course you are. I need to know the very best time for me to fly from Bluebell Wood."

"Today," he said, coughing the word out. "Right now… or early evening?" He paused and held his pendant. He began gently turning it, twisting the chain that held it around his neck, making it rise to his throat and then turning it the other way until it settled back at the centre of his chest. He stared out of the window and then rolled his fingers around his forehead.

Boomer looked hard at him through his thick glasses, which magnified his lovely eyes, and made the contrast with the Weatherman's cold silver ones even more apparent. Bertrum's face stayed completely emotionless. Daisy stood back a little behind me and I could feel her holding her breath, awaiting the Weatherman's response. But nothing was said.

I became impatient and asked him, "Well, what do you think would be the best time?"

"Best, or when can you go? They are two totally different questions. The best time would be in summer when the skies are blue and the wind is light. But going today – well, that will be all down to the Cannon Master, I would think."

Hearing his job title spoken, the Cannon Master sat fast.

"Why?" I asked. "Why is it down to him?"

"Well," the Weatherman answered, "our Floating Land is soon to sit lower to Earth for the winter months. As I am sure you are aware, the nearer we are to Earth the warmer it is for us, thus preserving the nature upon our Land. But unfortunately for flying, by late afternoon this position will also put us deep within a snow cloud which is due to stay for a time."

"How long is 'a time'?" I asked, understanding only too well my plight if I were to try to leave within a snow cloud.

"This period of time will be twenty-eight days, making returning difficult to achieve as well."

I lowered my head and my hair fell around my face. I glanced instinctively to my left towards Grandad, but, of course, he wasn't there.

"I am sorry, Jessie," the Weatherman continued. "The weather is how you wish to feel it. If it were Christmas you would long for snow, but on this day, it is your nemesis. The weather can hinder you or help you." He coughed and cleared his throat once more.

I found myself staring at my feet as I often did, a strange comfort habit, when the Weatherman appeared staring up at me. His eyes widened almost as big as his face, and within his silver gaze I could see my own reflection. He repeated, "The weather can hinder or help you. It is how you wish to see it." He reached upwards and touched my hand with his own shockingly cold little fingers and glanced down at my bare feet. "They must be cold," he said, the first words I had heard him say that weren't directly related to the matter at hand.

"Yes," I answered softly, "yes, they are."

He turned and walked to the door.

"You will be fine, Jessie. You'll work it out."

Claudius stepped forward, his stomps sounding heavily on the solid wood floor, and stood fast.

"My army awaits your command, Jessie. The snow that the Weatherman speaks of does not trouble my legionnaires, but it is in their best interests to set up camp or shelter in your flying ship."

"Yes, of course, Claudius," I replied, still speaking with care, but aware that I must leave before this night arrived. "Get your men to shrink down in size and have them take shelter beneath the cockpit and the rear seat of the flying ship. We will be leaving today."

Claudius bowed his head sharply towards me, accepting my request without any question or hint of doubt.

He believed in me. Not that he had said so, but in his actions towards me, which in turn helped me believe in myself. Just the positivity in his body language lifted my spirits as I turned to timid little Boomer the Plane Spotter and sturdy Bertrum.

"Boomer, can you guide us to St Albans whatever the conditions?"

"Oh yes, that's quite easy for me. I can show you your route right now on one of your many charts." He turned and walked to the leather sleeves in the bookcase that housed hundreds of such booklets. His oversized parka trailed around him and he stumbled on it with almost every other step. His little hands appeared and disappeared as his arms rose to run his fingers along the spines of the charts and then back down. They disappeared as he dropped his arms to another row below him.

"Okay, Boomer, sort out our route but don't trouble me with it, just guide me from take-off," I said, seeing it might take him some time.

Boomer spun back towards me. His eyes, already large behind his thick glasses, grew to their very maximum.

"From take-off?" he asked, and rotated his sleeves to simulate propellers.

"Yes, of course, Boomer. You are to come with us," I said, misreading his response as excitement.

"But no," he said, "I can't go in a plane. I would not like that at all. It would scare me terribly."

"Scare you?" I said, now totally bemused. Even Bertrum's expressionless face gave a hint of shock as he raised his eyebrows slightly. "But we thought you loved planes, Boomer."

"No, no, no. I have always watched them because I am afraid of them."

He was now limply holding his arms to his sides. He looked totally helpless and somewhat pathetic as he slowly shuffled across the floor. His glasses, parka and boots all seemed bigger than ever as he seemed to shrink within them.

Daisy Dreamer knelt down and picked Boomer up from his sad shuffle across the room and placed him on the table next to Bertrum, who turned and stared at Boomer, still holding his eyebrows high in an expression of disbelief.

"Is it okay if Boomer sits with me in the plane, Jessie? Maybe after he's directed you at the beginning?" she said. "I think we will be fine together."

"Yes, Daisy, that's fine. I just want to get there. I haven't even worked out how to leave Bluebell Wood yet."

I turned to Bertrum, knowing that he would be key to our flight, though how, I wasn't sure. He had lowered his eyebrows and again stared blankly at me.

"I am sorry to keep you. It's just I'm not sure of how I need you. I need time to think. Do you have to go back to your cannon or can you wait a while longer?"

He mumbled his response, which I couldn't understand.

"I am sorry, what was that?" I asked.

Once again, he mumbled at me.

"It's okay, Jessie," Boomer said. "I have spent a long time with the Cannon Masters and it takes a while to understand with ease what they say. But he said he would like to stay a while longer as he likes your company and the watchtower."

Bertrum then mumbled again. This time his mumbling was at great speed and became more of a murmur. I seemed to get caught up with him and began speaking rather quickly myself, asking Boomer, "What did he say? What did he say?"

"He said the Weatherman talks about snow. Your plane needs to slide across Bluebell Wood and take to the skies. Shocks of air can power you away."

I walked to the window as the first snowflakes, as foreseen, began to flutter down.

"Yes, of course, I understand perfectly," I said, smiling as I watched Poppy and some of her little friends appear from within the bluebells, magnifying glasses in hand. They ran excitedly into the clearing and followed the flakes down, laughing and screaming out loud as they peered upwards as the snowdrops landed, suddenly oversized, onto the magnifying glasses. The tiny Bellas spun round and round and gazed longingly up to the blanket of white that now covered our Floating Land, giggling as they bumped off one another and landed softly on the foliage that was receiving its first covering of snow.

I watched the flakes fall onto the branches of the tree whose firm grip held our watchtower. The first lot melted away, having fallen alone without others to quickly maintain the cold. But within minutes I could barely see Poppy and her friends, although their laughter continued. I didn't like losing sight of them and was relieved to hear them being called to cover by an elder.

I closed the window and felt my stomach turn slightly. Not at all in a bad way, but looking around the watchtower, and at Daisy and the two little Bellas sitting on the table, filled me with a loving, warm feeling.

"I think we should have a cup of tea," I said, and the tiniest of smiles appeared on Bertrum's face.

We spoke for a short time, all enjoying our tea. Boomer explained why planes scared him so much. As a youngster he had climbed a tree, only to find himself caught up there when a jet plane which had been missed by the turbulence shock had screamed over him and made him fall to the ground. He had not been hurt physically but he was very upset emotionally. He had never forgiven the jet plane, and had kept his eyes on them ever since. I have to say we did chuckle a bit, especially at how so many of us had totally misunderstood his enthusiasm for aviation. This even brought laughter out of Bertrum. Although it did sound like a car struggling to start on a cold winter's morning, I was sure he would get the hang of it.

We finished our tea, and it was time to pay Arkley another visit. The four of us made our way down the winding stairs that led to the workshop. Very carefully, of course. By now snow was beginning to crunch underfoot, causing us to stay in single file close to the trunk of the tree, holding the deep bark as we circled round it, not once moving across to the opposite side for fear of slipping and plummeting downwards to what would most certainly have been our deaths. Boomer and Bertrum followed our every move, which was very sweet, as the fears that concerned Daisy and me really did not apply to them.

We soon entered the workshop to the sound of the tradesfolk busy at work at their individual stations. Arkley stood amongst them facing the door, almost pre-empting our arrival.

"Just in time," he said with a broad smile. "Your clothes are ready and awaiting approval."

"Excellent, my feet are frozen," I replied, staring down at my toes, wiggling them to improve circulation, and admiring Poppy's nursing skills again.

Daisy was first to try on her parka, and it fitted beautifully. It was oversized slightly, but that was just like the Bellas' parkas, so in truth it was perfect. Daisy was positively thrilled with it and even more so with her boots, which were also authentic and oversized, so much so that they fitted over her plimsolls. She tried her mittens on last, then held them to her face and closed her eyes. She smiled and said how very wonderfully soft they were, and then brushed them at my cheeks for me to experience it.

Arkley showed me behind a wooden dressing screen that he had erected just for my own fitting, as my whole attire was to be changed. I placed the goggles from around my neck onto the corner of the screen and slipped my dress down to the floor. My new clothes were folded in order of dressing on a small table and my new boots were in front of that. My first garment was a white cotton vest top, long-sleeved and the opposite of attractive. Once over my head, it fell down my slim frame, finishing just above my knees. It was gorgeously warm and soft. So was the next item, a pair of socks cut from the same cotton, and they felt very snug on my poor neglected feet. The cotton seemed to hold its own warmth, and my skin relished each fibre as it tingled from top to toe. I was to be grateful for my larger-than-large vest top, as the fabric of my next item of clothing, my dungarees, was thick, rough and, I was sure, impenetrable. It felt unnecessarily coarse, leaving only the vest to save my exposed skin. I tugged the vest down as far as it could go and pulled my socks higher than they were designed for until the two met.

Once I had covered my body with the lovely cotton, the dungarees were not at all objectionable. They felt remarkably light, although, for now, they fitted like cardboard. I liked them. I liked the way they finished just below my knees, just as Leanndi's did. And after I had got my boots on, I couldn't help but do that little Leanndi shuffle from foot to foot.

I laughed out loud and sprang from behind the screen and continued the dance. Daisy thudded her mittens together.

"You look wonderful, Jessie," she said, "like a truly wonderful little Bella."

"Thank you very much," I replied, turning to Arkley. "Do you have my parka?"

I was desperate to finish my transformation.

"Yes, I do," he said, looking quite emotional. "Kneel down, Jessie, and let me place it upon you."

I followed his wishes and noticed that all the tradesfolk had collectively stopped work to watch the proceedings. I felt a little embarrassed as it all got quite formal. Even Boomer and Bertrum stepped closer for a better view. But thankfully everything relaxed as, true to form, Boomer stumbled upon his parka, giving Bertrum an opportunity to show his lightning reflexes. He clasped Boomer's parka and held him horizontal to the ground. It was funny to see Bertrum purposely raise his eyebrows and roll his eyes and smile at me. Boomer hung there like a kitten in its mother's jaws, holding his glasses with his index finger and patiently awaiting his return to a vertical footing.

I returned to my feet, reborn as an honorary Bella. I found that, just like a favourite party dress, my new clothes made me feel special. I placed my goggles on the top of my head and thanked Arkley and the room very much.

In the distance Bertrum's fellow Cannon Masters had become busy, as the snow cloud had brought unwanted air traffic close to our island, and the turbulence shocks were punching hard into the air above our snowy white Land.

CHAPTER 17

Evil at the Window

Daisy and I left the workshop, now fully protected from the elements in our glorious new parkas. The snow was very deep on the steps that led us back around the tree, and the wind had picked up, lashing the once gentle flakes hard around us. It was exciting to try our new clothes in such harsh conditions, and we stood upon the first step, heads downwards to allow our overhanging hoods to fully protect our faces. Just to tease the snow further, I dropped my hands out of my sleeves, as I knew they were safely wrapped in the most tightly knitted wool. I turned to Daisy and pulled her head to mine so that the rims of our hoods joined, leaving the snow and cold battling outside. Our breath on one another's faces instantly warmed the fabric cavern. I wanted to talk with Daisy, but there was no light. She chuckled as our noses touched. We pulled apart, held hands and crunched the fresh snow on each step.

I heard the workshop door shut behind us, and Bertrum and Boomer appeared. Bertrum was totally unfazed by the harsh conditions, but Boomer buried himself deep within his parka and stood quite still. I do believe, had Daisy not picked him up, there he would have stayed, creating his own little snowman. We enjoyed battling up the steps until we entered the passage. Now, although we were safe and warm in our boastfully tough clothing, it was nice to hear the sound of the wind soften, and step inside.

Daisy put Boomer down and he shook the snow off himself, like a dog, and pushed his thick glasses back to their correct position on his little nose. Bertrum stood back a little, as steady as stone, not shaking or shivering as the snow turned to water and ran away from his chain mail tunic.

"Do you remember, Claudius referred to my plane as a flying ship, and the Weatherman said it is down to the Cannon Masters to help us?" I asked Daisy. "We could easily sail from this Island using the power of the air cannons, as Bertrum suggested. So, we need to fit a sail, don't we?"

Bertrum raised his finger, halting Daisy's reply. He mumbled, breathed, and mumbled again.

Boomer interpreted for him. "He said that it would tear your plane apart, although in theory it is a good idea."

Daisy now answered the question. "What if we were to have lots of sails? Could they lessen the impact by moving independently?"

All eyes turned to Bertrum. His pupils decreased then spread open again while he focused on our expressions and ideas. He mumbled, and Boomer translated.

"He said two warning shots and then one hit and you shall be flying."

Daisy and I patted our mittens together, and Boomer tried to share our enthusiasm, but I think it scared him terribly. I was so happy with Bertrum, I couldn't help but kneel down and hold him tight. He relaxed into me and managed a little smile. He looked into my eyes and mumbled some more. Then he gave two very loud, high-pitched squeals, inches away from my face, shaking me and causing me to stumble backwards. Boomer and Daisy laughed aloud and Boomer continued to translate.

"He said the signal you shall give, via him, is – " and then Boomer repeated the high-pitched squeals.

"Shall I return to the workshop and discuss this with Arkley?" Daisy said, still laughing.

"Yes please, Daisy," I replied, now staring uneasily at Bertrum, "and please ask him to replace the wheels with skis." Daisy turned on her heels and, unlike earlier when we had both trodden our way carefully around the stairs, she flew down them at great speed, knocking into the tree and sliding off every other step. Her parka flew behind her like wings as she skidded to a halt and slowly entered the workshop.

Boomer and I thanked Bertrum, and he continued through the passageway as we turned back onto the precarious steps. We made our way steadily to the watchtower, this time to re-contact my gallant four.

I was excited as I placed the goggles over my eyes, instantly bringing the bright light, followed by the beautiful clear image of Willoughby, Oakleigh, Leanndi, Bluebell, Arthur and, of course, Archie. I watched the room for a short time. It felt like an age since I had set eyes on them all, and it was lovely. The fire was roaring, with Archie still lying stretched out on his side, absorbing the heat through his thick fur. Leanndi and Oakleigh stood, much reduced in size, on Archie's side. They were taking turns to drop, face first, holding their arms and legs out in a star shape. Arthur, back in the chair that he had dragged screeching and squawking across the floorboards the night before, was using a huge brass alarm clock to time their attempts at being buried head-first in Archie's fur. Leanndi's efforts were being thwarted around the thirty-second mark, as her tiny body would start to shake and she would lift her face, gasping for air as tears of laughter ran from her beautiful brown eyes. Oakleigh would manage a minute or so, and then Leanndi would sit on his back and pull his head free from the fur and demand that Arthur stop the clock. The pew that had been adjacent to the fire through the night had now been moved to the window. The curtain was open a little, and Willoughby and Bluebell were watching passers-by. The snowfall that had covered Bluebell Wood also coated Spencer Street. Children's voices rejoiced in the snow, but elderly people cursed it as they challenged the now-hazardous cobbled street.

"Hello all," I said, and the four Bellas responded. Arthur looked aimlessly around the room. Archie stayed fast asleep as Leanndi and Oakleigh slid around his tummy and joined Willoughby and Bluebell on the pew. Arthur joined them, too, not to be left out, as he found the whole visit tremendously exciting. Although he was unable to hear me, he could hear the responses and would have his own interpretation of events. I didn't mention Grandad's disappearance, but I did talk of Daisy Dreamer, and they seemed to be thrilled that she was with me, which made me relieved that they endorsed my feelings for her. I was sure that the four of them would have come to the same conclusion I had done, following the monk's words and fears, that Mr Wilson's interest in the abbey was indeed the plague. But I reiterated it anyway, along with our proposed objective of laying a perfectly original Roman mosaic floor overnight, and stopping all building works for good. They seemed shocked that I was sending the Roman legions alongside the mosaic artists, even as a precaution, but they had to trust my judgement, especially now. I told them that I would be leaving Bluebell Wood just before dark. Although at this stage I hadn't worked out the final details, I asked for help deciding where to land close to the abbey.

I was about to continue when the four of them, and Arthur, a second behind, dropped off the pew and hit the floor. The door to 125 Spencer Street rocked on its hinges and a man spoke.

"Come out here, Arthur Fatelli, you disgusting little creature. I know you are in there. Open this door. Or shall I open it myself and show you to the world where the children play happily in the snow, unaware that a freak like you lives in their street?"

The man's voice wasn't loud. It was shaky and whispery. It travelled through the door, spitting its venomous insults in the kind of tone that licks the inside of your ears before slashing you. Arthur grabbed his large overhanging sleeve and wrapped it around his head, trying in vain to cover his ears. He shook as tears squeezed through his tightly closed eyes. He turned to the others.

"Help me, please help me," he said, before hiding his face once more.

Archie arose, hackles high, and sneered as thunder roared in his chest. Bluebell and Leanndi moved either side of Arthur and held him.

Bluebell spoke softly. "No harm will come to you; I promise no harm."

Oakleigh moved to Archie and tried to silence him. "Shh, Archie, good boy, shh now." Archie sat back and stared at the door.

"I think he may have gone," Willoughby said, standing on the pew and pulling the curtain aside with his cane for a better view of the front door. "Yes, he's not there."

He leant further forward, steadying himself on the windowsill. His breath froze on the glass as he tried to see down the other side of the street, when the man's face appeared, pushing hard against the glass. Willoughby flew back. "Bloody hell!" he gasped as his hands slipped, leaving his big boots on the pew and sending the rest of him onto the floor.

Archie flew at the window, pushing the pew to its side. How ferocious he was as he let the thunder rise from his chest! He unleashed it inches away from the man's face. The man pulled back, allowing Oakleigh, who stood alone, to see for certain his old Relayer, and once good friend. I knew Oakleigh would remember his face, but now many years had withered it as the breakdown of tissue behind the skin left it gaunt and worn. The eyes that had once danced with life and glowed with compassion had not faded, but now they were sharp and cutting. As bright blue as Grandad's, they held their colour, but had lost their soul. Wilson smiled through the glass at Archie and ran one finger down the pane, teasing him, baiting him, pushing him into a frenzy. He held his hands open either side of the glass and pushed his face hard against the frozen pane. His fingers were long with swollen joints and skin so thin it was stretched to breaking, waiting for his bones to squeeze free. His thin white hair was pushed back away from his face, accentuating his high, scaly forehead.

His teasing smile showed teeth that were few and gums that had receded, curling away from the decaying stems. But his clothes were still smart. He wore a crisp white immaculately pressed shirt with silver cufflinks and a black tie held tightly to his chest with a tiepin. Over this was a black Crombie-style coat. Studying his face, Oakleigh saw, as I did, a man alive but with death's decay in his body. Oakleigh decreased in size, and Mr Wilson's cutting glare scanned the room beyond Archie.

"I prefer a night call," he whispered through the glass. "Don't you, Arthur? Do you prefer me coming round at night?"

He continued smiling sarcastically at Archie, then slammed his hands onto the glass and left.

"Oh Arthur," Bluebell said. "You poor thing. How terrible he is to you." She continued unwrapping his woolly sleeve from around his head.

Arthur wiped his eyes and nose with the front of his jumper and steadied his shaking body.

"He would have come in if it hadn't been for Archie, you know. Archie is fantastic! He really is fantastic." Then instantly forgetting his terrible ordeal he threw his arms around Archie's neck. "You shall stay with me for ever and ever, Archie."

Arthur then ran through the velvet curtain and returned with a packet of biscuits, which he fed by the handful to a very willing Archie. Willoughby picked himself off the floor and brushed his hat down before placing it back on his ruffled head.

"Are you okay, Willoughby?" Leanndi said, smiling from cheek to cheek, and glancing towards Oakleigh, who was itching to laugh because Willoughby's panicky slip had amused him so much.

"Laugh it up, you two," Willoughby said, not making eye contact with either of them, but knowing full well that he must have looked very undignified.

Bluebell was now standing on the windowsill. She touched with her little gloved paw the same pane of glass where Mr Wilson had placed his face. She looked sad, and she sighed as she ran her finger around the outline that remained in the glass.

Oakleigh moved forward and looked up at her. "I am sorry to laugh," he said.

"That's okay," she replied, still running her finger around the outline.

"It really wasn't the man that we knew. I think in truth he died many years ago," Oakleigh continued.

"I know. I know it wasn't, but how sad it is for us all. His knowledge of us is his power, and that worries me greatly," she answered, wiping his outline clear from the glass. "Are you there, Jessie?"

"Yes, I am," I replied, knowing that during a quest we didn't have the luxury to ponder events. Time had to move on and we had to move with it.

Bluebell continued, this time full of purpose, "The best place to land is near the lake. We shall await your arrival. God speed, Jessie." She jumped from the windowsill, patting Willoughby on the back as she landed.

I removed my goggles and placed them back on the top of my head. "Okay, Boomer, are you ready to go flying?"

Boomer didn't answer. He just stared at me through his big glasses. He then held out his arms like a child and I leant down and picked him up.

"Do you have your charts, Boomer?" I asked, as I prepared

to open the door and face the snow and wind that waited to jump and dance around us.

He answered me softly by whispering into my ear.

"Yes, I have them, but I am sure I would know our route anyway."

"Good, Boomer," I answered, not meaning to talk to him as if he were a child, but I couldn't help myself. I held him close, and opened the door to the harsh winter's day.

Daisy met us halfway around the tree, and we sheltered just within the opening of the tunnel to hear her words.

"Well," I asked, "is everything sorted?"

"Yes and no," Daisy replied, slipping her hood back and wiping her nose with her snow-covered mittens, making her face very cold and wet.

"Whoops," she said, and then with the dry side of her glove she warmed and patted her face. "Arkley can fulfil your request, but not today. It is too much work in too little time."

I knew I had always given Arkley short notice, but he had never failed me before, so I had presumed that he never would. It didn't stop me feeling let down and I asked sharply, "Well, what *can* he do today?"

Daisy replied swiftly, having already anticipated the question, "Replace the wheels with skis."

I pulled my hood over my head.

"Come, we need to go," I said.

I passed Boomer to Daisy. I struggled with the little door that led to the clearing, as the snow had settled heavily against it, and the three of us squeezed through.

It was like entering another world. Although this Floating Land was normally familiar to me, I had never seen it laden with snow. The wind picked the light flakes from the drifts and tossed the snow like confetti into the air, spinning it hard, then gently, dancing around us slowly, then fast, weaving its light-footed steps. I felt that we had entered a winter ball without an invitation, and were soon to be put out in the cold. We passed through the clearing and for half an hour or so we made our way across the open fields. It was hard going. Hand in hand, or mitten in mitten, Daisy and I dragged each other towards the torchlight and the activity around my plane.

Boomer had reduced in size and was sitting snugly in Daisy's parka pocket, occasionally raising his head out for a quick peek on our progress, but just as quickly his head would disappear. The snow was hitting us like waves, but we were warm in our new clothes. It was the deep drifts that slowed us.

But in time the light grew and we arrived at my wonderful de Havilland. The tradesfolk had all but finished replacing the wheels with skis, and the Roman legions had set up camp, some, as requested, within the plane. But some, as they were trained and disciplined to do, had posted sentries upon the wings.

Claudius greeted us, but it was hard to communicate with the wind howling around us. I beckoned him forward to follow me around the plane as it was slightly sheltered. I shouted in his little ear to reduce in size and step onto my hand. He followed my request without question and I put him in the overhanging fabric of my hood. He stood inches away from my face and I could see only his silhouette, but my hood made a fine fabric shelter and we were free to talk. I explained what we would have to do, but looking at the sentries on the wings of the plane also gave me an idea. I remembered how Willoughby and the others had removed their boots and how well their feet had stuck to a plane at high speed.

"Claudius, could I have some of your fine soldiers line the wings of the plane? Could their shields harness the power from the Cannon Masters' shocks of air?"

I turned my head to the wings to give Claudius time to digest my idea whilst he was looking at the sentries already upon them.

"Your thought patterns are inventive, Jessie," he replied, pacing my hood. "And that is what makes a Roman army. New, brave ideas. I shall choose my strongest men and we shall await your call. Is that all for now, Jessie?"

"Yes, Claudius, and thank you," I said. I loved his positive actions.

I joined Daisy just as she was putting a full-sized Boomer into the front seat, where he would join me for the first part of the flight, and briefly explained by the light of a lantern what the Romans would do. She climbed into the back.

"How exciting this is, Jessie, isn't it?" she shouted, her face full of eager anticipation. She looked like a young girl for the first time on a fairground ride awaiting that first jolt as the cogs engaged. I smiled back at her.

Boomer mumbled, "I so wish I could enjoy your enthusiasm."

But Daisy couldn't hear as she had pulled her hood tight around her face, awaiting departure.

CHAPTER 18

Hidden in the Shadows

I settled myself with Boomer sitting on my lap. Every so often he turned to me and stared longingly through his thick glasses, and I would give him a reassuring cuddle. Claudius, meanwhile, was upon the wings, with forty centurions abreast from one tip of the wing to the other. For their feet to hold the wings fast they had removed their big boots and tied them around their necks with the laces. The warmth still held in their feet soon melted the settled snow and so gave them a firm grip. Shields held tight and strong in front of them, they stood at an angle to the rear of the plane. Claudius, with a powerful command, spun the centurions as one, with shields aloft and square to the tail fin. With his second command they held fast.

"I think we are ready," I said into the ear of the little one sitting on my lap.

"Are you sure?" he replied, turning and staring up at me again.

"Yes, Boomer, I am sure. Now give the signal."

Boomer pressed his little paws into my thighs and let out his two high-pitched squeals. They cut through the snow and wind, challenging them for supremacy and silencing all around, leaving just the booming sound of the cannons as they marked our territory in the air, knocking the intruding planes bumping and shaking away.

Bertrum, as promised, calmly finished his shots into the sky, and with the help of his fellow Cannon Master he turned the mighty wooden barrel towards the de Havilland, which now felt small and fragile. The turret, which was normally visible from the flatlands where we sat, was almost impossible to see through the snow. How Bertrum, from such a distance, could make that shot without hitting us too hard and ripping my beautiful plane apart, and us with it, I really didn't know.

But I was soon to find out as his first practice shot whistled overhead, turning the fluttering snow in its path into a Catherine wheel of ice. The sound of it approaching, screeching its way towards us, was terrifying. And Boomer, forgetting all his attempts at bravery, tried to scramble out and make a dash for freedom. I held him fast as the second practice shot screeched above, this time shaking the plane and everybody on it before crashing into the trees.

Claudius's voice rained down upon his men. "Hold fast! Hold your line!"

The shields slammed together, locking as one above us.

The winds suddenly dropped and a silence fell. The snow that had felt harsh and threatening fell once more, but softly, almost as if trying to make its peace with us.

Then the pump of the cannon and that awful screeching broke the air into pieces for a third time, and this time it did not finish in the trees, but whipped us forward, propelling us at high speed across the snow. I had one aim: to hold the plane steady as we parted the snow, spreading it high either side of us, as in seconds we left Bluebell Wood and the Floating Land behind us.

The propeller spun and the engine choked and spluttered and coughed, then glided into song, and we were in flight. I let out a scream of excitement and Daisy followed suit. Oh, how magical it was to be flying again, dropping the nose of the plane forward and heading down to Earth! Boomer lost all fear and gave a squeal that sounded more like a howl, and he drummed on my legs and flung his arms up high, embracing the freezing air and flakes that hit us hard. With my goggles over my eyes, I thought of the Bellas awaiting our arrival. Seconds later, they appeared before me through my lenses.

"How long, Boomer?" I asked.

"Fifty-five minutes, maybe one hour." He slid off my lap, carefully avoiding treading on his fellow Bellas, and opened the charts.

"Willoughby!" I shouted. "We are in flight. Maybe an hour till we hit the lakes."

"One hour, Jessie," Willoughby replied, shocked that I had not contacted him before, but I'd had no idea of my departure time myself. "Okay, Jessie, we will be there."

I returned my thoughts back to flying.

My sight returned, but not without my inner sight for my Bellas. Lately I had discovered that even without thinking of them, and now sometimes even without my goggles, I did really feel their experiences. Later, when they told me the details of what had happened, I felt that I had drifted beside them through it all.

Willoughby was organising. "Arthur, I feel we must take

Archie as he will be our quickest mode of transport back to the abbey and the lake and surrounding parklands."

Arthur, who was sitting on the floor with Archie, feeding him the last biscuits, instantly broke into floods of tears.

"No, no!" he cried, staring at Willoughby, "please don't take him. There are other ways. Please, I will show you."

Bluebell instantly came to Arthur's defence.

"No, this is where Archie stays," she said, comforting Arthur.

Leanndi and Oakleigh stood together. They knew that the quest was all-important and that nothing should interfere with it, but it was awful to see Arthur so very upset.

"Quick, follow me," he said, and he took the four of them through the velvet curtain into the sleeping quarters. He stopped, pushed a bed aside and pulled his large sleeve past his elbow and knelt down on the floor. He blew hard, and years of dust and grime floated aside to show a floor ring attached to a hatch, which he pulled. At first it didn't move. Then Oakleigh jumped forward to help, and it creaked ever so slightly open. To begin with, it was too dark to see anything. Although there was a window in the room, it had been boarded over, and the only light came from the main room, just sneaking past the velvet curtain. Archie, not wanting to be left out, made his way to the hatch and sniffed hard into the open darkness.

Arthur jumped back and asked for patience, then fetched a small candle. It made little difference in lighting the room, but it was enough to light the first few feet and show concrete steps. Arthur jumped down the first of them, both feet at a time. He knelt down and peered at the underside of the floor and unhooked a lamp. Opening its glass door, he put his little candle inside. The lamp was tremendously bright and showed the way clearly. Leanndi, who always wanted to be first, jumped clear of the first steps and landed alongside Arthur. Bluebell firmly told Archie to stay, as the steps were steep and spiralled so tightly it made for little foot room. Of course, he listened to Bluebell and sat sulkily back on his tail and peered down through the hatch at them, Willoughby making his way down carefully last. Archie let out the smallest of barks and pricked his ears sharply forward as the five of them spiralled out of sight.

Arthur, with Leanndi by his side, stopped on the second-to-last step and held his lantern high. It shone brightly against the whitewashed walls and ceiling, giving shadows to the many spiders' webs, some new, but most old and clumped under years of dust.

Arthur shivered. "Ugh!" he said. "I don't like cobwebs one little bit." Then he crouched low and whispered. "Now look at this. You must tread carefully."

The light from the lantern crept across the floor, exposing a treasure trove of Bellas' transport throughout the ages: chariots, carts, scooters from the sixties based boldly on the Italian Lambrettas and Vespas, and all, apart from the dust, still in showroom condition.

"Oh, how wonderful!" Leanndi gasped, and jumped forward. "Look at these scooters, Oakleigh! What fun!"

Oakleigh appeared at her side within a moment. "Yes, I had all but forgotten about these scooters. They're really great. I remember I felt quite fashionable speeding around on one of these, out of sight of prying eyes."

"Oakleigh, teach me how to drive this very instant!" Leanndi demanded, but sweetly. She was now perched upon a little red scooter, moving the handlebars from side to side.

Bluebell and Willoughby had strong memories of the scooters themselves, and Bluebell sat on a particularly nice one, black with all-chrome trims. She sat as she would have done on her trusty Daniel, side-saddle.

"I never much cared for these," she joined in, looking around for Willoughby, who had walked straight past the scooters to the centre of the cellar.

There was a sheet covering something quite large, and Willoughby pulled up a corner of it with his cane.

"Just as I thought," he breathed with great excitement. "Look at this, Bluebell." Like a magician, he pulled the sheet aloft, exposing the most beautiful car.

"How brilliant!" Bluebell gasped, and Oakleigh and Leanndi stopped still with mouths open.

There, sparkling in the lamplight, was a Bella-sized replica Rolls Royce, based on the 1926 car named the Silver Ghost. It was, like its name, silver in colour with chrome wherever chrome could be. Chrome headlights, chrome radiator, chrome trims, even a chrome horn. The windscreen was highly polished glass with chrome surrounds. The huge hubcaps were chrome with gold insets.

Willoughby opened the door and led Bluebell forward, up on the silver running board and gently onto the green, studded-leather back seat. These seats would have looked at home in the finest of houses opposite a gentleman's writing desk. The leather was soft, and Bluebell sat with elegance. This car suited her, and the others loved to see her in it. Leanndi gave her the broadest smile and prodded Oakleigh in the back, demanding his attention. Willoughby offered his arm to help Bluebell back out.

"They were good days, weren't they, Bluebell?"

She nodded. "The very best," she said.

The two of them walked around the car, gently stroking it as if it were alive and in need of some tender care.

"I told you there was another way," Arthur said, pleased with their response.

"Yes, Arthur, this is certainly a fine collection, but it is still daylight and we need to leave this minute. Although the light is fading fast, we would still be quite visible," Bluebell answered, showing Arthur a great deal more patience than she would to almost anybody else.

"No," Arthur replied. "Look, look, look."

He shone his lantern low against the wall and it illuminated a small arch, no more than a foot high and maybe six inches wide. Above it, chiselled into the brick, was the word 'North'. "And look," he said, "there is the same on each of the four walls with 'South', 'East' and 'West'. All of these lead under the city. Know your direction, and off you go. I know the abbey is east because I can see the sunrise above its magnificent roofline every morning."

"Let us go then!" Leanndi shouted, now glaring at Oakleigh as his tuition would not be quick enough for her to take charge of the scooter that she had claimed for herself.

"Leanndi, you ride with me," Bluebell said sternly, realising that she was beyond listening to Oakleigh. Excitement had taken her far away.

Leanndi sulkily slid back on her seat and Bluebell sat in front.

"Don't worry, Leanndi," Bluebell said, backing into her, "you will be fine to ride it later."

She thanked Arthur by blowing him a kiss, and let the throttle out.

Willoughby jumped on the silver scooter and Oakleigh on a bright red one, following quickly. The scooters made very little noise, apart from the whirring of the fans as they spun with the scooters' motion, filling a leather bag under the seat of each. Once full, the throttles would release another jet of air which would push the scooters forward, repeating the process over and over. So quickly would the bags fill that the ride would be smooth and without noise. Once in motion, the headlights shone brightly, using, as a pushbike did, the dynamo system.

The three scooters formed an arrow shape, with Bluebell and Leanndi in front. At first the tunnel was clean and tidy. The floor was of smooth concrete, and the walls that carried around to the arched ceiling were covered by highly polished tiles, opal green, reflecting the light of the scooters and giving the impression that they were gliding through deep, dark waters. But this ended abruptly as the fine workmanship came to a halt and they were left with the bare skin of the tunnel. Damp wood replaced the smooth concrete floor, and mud and wood joists the splendid tiling.

The three drivers struggled to hold their lines as the scooters began to slide about, battling to keep traction on the rotten floor and sliding on the soft mud. They continued deep below the city before the direction veered slightly to the right and they began to climb. Occasionally, there were small passageways left and right of them, spreading into the tunnel network beneath the city of St Albans. The light of the scooters brought unwanted shadows cast by the wooden supports that stood proud of the muddy clay walls.

Leanndi, free to watch the shadows grow then disappear, suddenly squeezed Bluebell tight.

"Stop!" she screamed.

Bluebell released the throttle and pulled hard on the brake, causing the scooter to travel for a distance side-on before snaking to a halt.

This shocked Willoughby and Oakleigh into doing their own emergency stops, which Willoughby managed to do with the help of the gradient. But Oakleigh was not so fortunate. He clipped a wooden support, forcing the scooter to tilt slightly, pushing his head firmly against the mud wall, and using his poor little face as a brake. He sat still until Leanndi jumped to his assistance and pulled his face free. He coughed mud from his mouth and wiped his eyes.

"Not the best way to stop," he said, scooping little lumps of gooey clay from his right ear.

"Shush," Leanndi whispered. "I saw something."

"Where?" Willoughby whispered back, peering hard into the blackness behind them.

"Hiding behind one of those wooden posts." She stepped slowly back into the darkness. "There. Did you hear that?" She stopped dead.

Water dripped from the rotting joist above them. They all stood quite still, and listened.

"Everybody, come to me," Willoughby demanded, and they felt for comfort in each other's hands. A crow's squawk echoed within the darkness and rolled along the tunnel towards them. Then another, and another. Then the sound of a dozen boots running hard on the wooden surface, metal upon metal, and blood-curdling screams fell upon them.

"Malissols!" Bluebell gasped. "Hurry, go, go!"

Panicking, they clambered onto the scooters.

"It won't start!" Oakleigh shouted. He tried to push the machine free of the mud, but it slipped to the floor.

Willoughby appeared like a whirlwind behind him, knelt down and scooped Oakleigh under his arm.

Bluebell and Willoughby's wheels spun on the wet floor as they set off to the sound of the screams of the oncoming Malissols echoing around them.

The wind of a battle-axe skimmed Leanndi's ponytail as the scooters found their speed and flew away. She was frightened, and rightly so. She buried her face in Bluebell's back and held it there even as they entered into the dusk of the night.

They left the tunnel at great speed through a hollowed gargoyle, one of a pair either side of a small doorway at basement level on the west side of the abbey.

How welcoming the fresh white snow was and, although dusk was upon them, the rising moon made it light compared to the awful blackness of the tunnel.

They continued at some speed to the lake, where they pulled their scooters to a gentle halt. Leanndi took some prising free from Bluebell. It was her first encounter with Malissols and she was terrified. Although the others had come across them before, it was never a pleasant experience and they all breathed heavy sighs of relief now they were clear of them.

They stared at the sky, awaiting me and the Roman army. It looked heavy and full of snow. It bore down on them as they waited, reduced in size, on one of the scooter seats, as always neatly in a row.

CHAPTER 19

The Romans Return to St Albans

I had now started my descent. Boomer had navigated brilliantly and loved every second of our wonderful journey. Approaching the parkland next to the lake, I cut my engines and glided. The snow that had settled upon St Albans reflected pure white, lighting the darkness of the night that had now drawn in. The small gap in the snow cloud let the moonshine through, reflecting off the silvery rooftops and the heavily laden trees, giving them a shroud of glitter. The night was bitterly cold, which thankfully kept everybody away from the park and lake. The swans had settled safely in the small island in the centre, and ducks still slipped their way across the frozen, icy water. Rocks and bricks sat out of place on the ice, failed attempts from over-boisterous children to break their way through.

The high-pitched squeals from my four little ones awaiting our arrival made my stomach jump with excitement and gave me clarity on where to circle and land my plane. The squeals continued, and I followed the volume as it guided me down.

I felt like a bat using sound as a radar, as my ears had tuned into the high frequency.

It had only been a short time since my Bellas' departure, but I loved to see them. As it had done on our take-off, the snow sprayed high above us as the skis cut their way through. Claudius had once more placed his men on the wings and they used their shields, this time catching the air and enabling us to stop.

Willoughby, Bluebell, Leanndi and Oakleigh stood full-size, side by side. They looked quite forbidding from a distance. A strong little unit, stylish in their clothes and stances.

"It is good to see you, Jessie, and you, Daisy," Willoughby said, as we rushed as best we could towards them upon the thick covering on the grass.

But before we could answer, Leanndi broke ranks and jumped forward into my arms. She threw herself around my neck and grabbed my face with her little hands. Her eyes were wider than I had ever seen them and the moon shone like a spotlight upon her concerned face. I already knew what she would say.

"They tried to really hurt us – they did, Jessie! They tried to chop me up, they did!"

"Who, Leanndi? Who would want to hurt you?"

"The Malissols! They tried to hurt us in the dark tunnel." She related every detail, at great speed, from the cellar to leaving the gargoyles.

Bluebell stepped forward. "Come, Leanndi, let Jessie settle. We need to get the plane covered before we talk."

Oakleigh and Willoughby were now speaking to Daisy, who knelt down to them and gently stroked their faces. They smiled at her, as a child would at their mother, clearly very fond of her. I felt quite jealous for a time, but Daisy did have such a beautiful way about her. Who wouldn't love her? But I did allow myself one of my harshest glances, then let her be.

Daisy and I, my gallant four, and now the Roman army, who were quickly organised into ranks of precise marching lines, started around the lake and onwards to the abbey. The sound of us all marching forward drum-rolled upon the snow. Claudius and I marched along, with Bluebell and Willoughby beside us, describing the attack by the Malissols. Claudius was a fighting man, but only for peace. He knew that a war with the Malissols would bring a great loss of life.

"St Albans is historically a Roman town," he said. "If we were to lose to the Malissols on our homeland, it would send signals around the globe that Malissols truly do have the upper hand over the Bellas and the good upon the Earth."

He ordered his men into a quick march then continued talking to me. "Jessie, we will take one step at a time. First, the mosaic floor."

In his inimitable way, he calmed my inner fears and we all quickly paced forward.

The snow cloud had closed the gap within the sky, and snow began to flutter down again. Oakleigh and Leanndi had gone ahead on Oakleigh's single scooter. Leanndi's eagerness to drive it had been dampened by her ordeal in the tunnel and for now she was happy to hold on tight. Oakleigh swiftly made access for us into the construction site using his little bag of tools.

Daisy followed behind me, but I had noticed that, unless I was upset or requested her assistance, she always watched me from a few paces back. I turned and faced her. "Are you okay, Daisy?" I said, seized with a pang of guilt about my envious thoughts towards her earlier, almost as if she would know.

Her look was tranquil as she peered out of her fastened hood back at me. "Yes, I am very happy." Her answer didn't really suit the situation, but she did look happy, and really, why not? We were involved in something amazing and I excitedly grabbed her mitten-covered hand with my own.

"Oh, where is Boomer?" I asked. I had completely forgotten about him. I felt terrible!

A quiet little voice came from within Daisy's parka pocket. "I will be staying in here for the time being."

"Very well. It is a good place to be on such a night."

On our arrival at the site we found that the disruption that Oakleigh had caused the previous night had all but been cleared or mended. The site had now been floodlit as a security precaution, but no guard dog had replaced Archie. The snow was now heavy, the flakes the size of a child's palm, creating our very own snow globe in the glow of the floodlights.

Claudius, conscious of the Malissols' presence, placed many guards around the perimeter fence. The army, a thousand strong, began excavating the frozen earth. Each legionnaire carried with him a bundle, which lay heavy on his shoulder. Within this were all manner of digging tools which would be used usually to dig defences, but on this occasion their operators worked as a chain gang, hitting and clearing the earth like a machine. As Claudius checked the lines, I was concerned that under the lights they were visible, but my fears were soon laid to rest. On his second inspection Claudius bellowed, "Lightning speed, men!", and they fell out of sight.

"Daisy," I said anxiously, clasping her hand, "where are they? Where have they gone?"

Daisy didn't answer. She freed her hand from my own and removed her mitten. "Look, do this," she said, opening her fingers wide in front of her face and moving her hand steadily from side to side. "Do you see them? Do you see them now?"

I followed her with my own hand, and yes, how marvellous, they appeared as they had been, but moving like a picture book or a very old motion picture. I pulled my hand away and they went with it. Although I could still hear them and see the earth forming banks around the edges, they were too quick for my eyes.

"Can all Bellas move that quickly?" I asked, shaking my hand in front of my face again. I knew that they could reduce and increase in size within seconds, but I didn't realise they could do it continuously like this.

"Only if they have been trained for many hundreds of years by Claudius. It takes great effort. What they are doing is reducing back to size and then to big again, over and over, which takes a lot of concentration and energy."

"How clever!"

Claudius moved towards me, appearing to move slowly in comparison to his legionnaires in front of us.

"You have no need to stay in the cold, Jessie. I know what needs to be done and I promise it shall be finished by first light. I will take my army to the tunnel that Willoughby and Bluebell spoke of earlier. I know these from many years ago. I sense that we shall meet the Malissols there, as they would have butchered Willoughby and the others for sure if they had so wished. They must have held back so that they could meet us here. They are hungry for a battle, I fear. I shall not let them thwart us, though. And take comfort, Jessie, that our artist shall please you and honour you in the mosaic."

"I thank you so much, Claudius. You are a truly brave soldier and a loyal friend," I said, and continued holding his rough little paw. "Please take care, and I will look forward to seeing you at first light in front of a warm fire."

He nodded his agreement and turned back to his men. He stood fast for a second as the Malissols began crowing in every quarter. The soldiers stopped briefly, too, and came back to size. Though they looked strong, they must have felt the dark eeriness too.

Willoughby, Bluebell, Oakleigh and Leanndi appeared in a line beside me.

Willoughby pulled Leanndi in front of him and laid his cane across her chest. "Stay close," he whispered in her ear, but he needn't have said it, as she was already nestling into him.

Daisy stood ever so close to me. She held my wrist and I could feel my pulse increase.

"What is that awful sound?" I asked, staring at her, knowing the answer but still not wanting to believe it.

"I can't hear it, Jessie, but I feel fear and evil all too well."

"It's the first time I've heard Malissols for real. Do you think there are lots of them?"

"Yes, I am sure they are all around us. How many I don't know, but even a handful is cause for concern."

I stared at Daisy's beautiful brown eyes and pulled her hood back away from her head.

"Daisy, please forgive me for asking, but you can't hear me, can you, or anything at all?"

"No," she said, smiling. "Not a thing. I feel every vibration. It is a language of its own, and of course it helps if I can see your mouth too." Then she laughed.

"Why didn't you say, Daisy?"

"Oh, but my sweet Jessie, would it have made any difference? You subconsciously knew anyway. Think back: you always made eye contact with me."

How strange, I thought. I did do that.

Then Bluebell pulled at my arm.

"We should go," she said, gazing up at me. "Arthur Fatelli is frightened, I can feel it."

"Come then, reduce in size and travel in my pocket," I replied.

"No," she said firmly, then she looked at Willoughby, Oakleigh and Leanndi. "We must stand tall, at least until we are clear of the abbey. No sign of weakness or fear shall be shown."

As we left the construction site and the floodlights, although the snow made this awful dark corner a little brighter, it was still gloomy and unwelcoming. The squawking followed us into the trees and the wild hedgerow, causing the snow to shake free from the branches. There was a path that ran through the centre of the graveyard. It was covered by snow, but the space between the headstones showed clearly enough where it should lead. My four walked side by side with Oakleigh one end and Willoughby the other. They were full height and walked proudly, sure-footed, not even acknowledging the sounds from around us.

I was so joyful to be part of this new world. I dressed like them and thought as they did. I had a friend in Daisy, and together I felt we were invincible. My fear had subsided. Soon enough, so did the Malissols' squawking as we left the grounds of the abbey through a short passageway named Boot Alley, and marched onto one of the cobbled roads and into the welcome light of the street lamps.

The four of them reduced in size and were happy, for now, to travel in my parka pockets and Daisy's, joining a slightly put-out Boomer who had been enjoying his cosy cocoon-for-one. I had pretty well forgotten about him again, he had been so quiet.

What a beautiful street we arrived at: Tudor buildings stood precariously on shallow foundations, defying age, crooked and frail, quaint to us now but in reality badly built. Even so, they made a perfect backdrop for the snow to show, just for a short time, that it could enhance a man-made structure. The kerbstones were high, still in place for the height of a horse-drawn carriage, but now cars parked alongside them, drivers struggling to open their doors, knocking them time and time again and cursing as they did so. But thankfully, St Albans had kept its history intact, and it was wonderful to be wandering around its streets.

Willoughby occasionally poked his head out from within my pocket to give directions, and we turned into another alleyway which was sheltered from the elements. It was particularly dark, making it difficult to avoid the broken bottles that lay underfoot. I accidentally kicked an empty bottle, and it bounced in front of us and shattered. The sound echoed around the alley and for an instant I felt rebellious. If anyone was lurking in the darkness, it sent a sign out that we were just as at home as they might be.

But soon we left it behind, and walked back into the light from a Tudor drinking inn. We passed the entrance as four men, around their late teens, were leaving. They were loud and boisterous and began taunting me and Daisy, laughing at our clothes.

One in particular was invading our space. He was tall, much taller than me, and much taller than Daisy. He was heavy in build and, although it was freezing cold, he wore only a casual shirt hanging loose over the top of his trousers.

"Is there a fancy-dress party we should know about?" He smirked, as his friends laughed raucously.

We didn't answer. I took Daisy's hand and pulled her forward, but she stood fast. The smallest one of the group clearly liked himself. His hairstyle was studiedly scruffy and, judging by his mannerisms, he expected any girl to give him the time which he had so obviously given himself. He walked towards me. I instinctively stepped back and shuddered a little. I was only fourteen, could he not see that? I didn't want a strange man coming near me or Daisy. He smiled, though it wasn't a warm expression but one that looked, frankly, evil – just a movement of his mouth to manipulate people with. His mannerisms were not natural, but had been worked on, and his hair, which was undoubtedly the latest style, looked ridiculous. Wasn't there more he could have done with his time than adore his looks, which would soon fade, as the next generation produced yet another model just like him?

"Come on, girls, you must need warming up," he said, holding his arms open as if we should both jump into them.

I felt Leanndi's head pop out of my left pocket. She laughed nervously as Bluebell appeared from Daisy's pocket, shaking her head. They looked at one another and then at us. "Take care, girls. These people don't look nice."

The men, of course, didn't see them. They circled us as if we were their prey. I felt my chest tighten.

The tall one pulled Daisy's hood back, and her usually beautiful face contorted with rage. She took the man's hand. I saw fear in his eyes as she stared up at him. She held fast, and pain ravaged the man's face. Tears filled his eyes as his body twisted and he fell onto his knees in the snow. The small man held out his hand and tried to touch my face. Daisy let the tall man fall and then she grabbed the small man's hair. She pulled him hard backwards and he screamed out. She dragged him along the whitened cobbled street as the others watched. He screamed and wriggled in pain and shame as she turned him and pushed his face into the dirty slush by the drain.

"You have no right!" she screamed. "You have no right!"

She turned to me, and I could see not rage within her but sadness. She didn't look as if she had been in a confrontation, more as if she had lost someone dear. She let go of the man, and stood over him.

"Are these men of whom we should be proud, or gutter rats that are serving no purpose but to teach others to have no value for anyone or anything?"

I was troubled. Had Daisy overreacted or were these men bullies who needed to be taught a lesson?

I walked over to her. "Come, Daisy, we must go."

She took my hand and we left. As we did, the men shouted insults before leaving hastily in the other direction.

We approached the clock tower and sat on the wall at the base. We chose the side where the street had no lights, and I put my arm around Daisy. Bluebell and Willoughby got out and sat alongside us, whilst Leanndi climbed into Daisy's parka pocket to be with Oakleigh, who had been very quiet for him. Maybe he had been asleep, I guessed. I was right, as I heard Leanndi telling him that he should wake up as he had missed Daisy throwing some horrible men around the street, and how she would have liked to have done the same to them.

Daisy spoke. "I know you think I was harsh on them," she said to me, "but I wasn't. I hope tomorrow in daylight you can see for yourself what I saw in them."

Bluebell urged us to move along, as she was concerned for Arthur Fatelli. We met no one else on our route. The snow had now stopped, but the temperature had also plummeted and, even in my Bella clothes, it was cold.

CHAPTER 20

Claudius and His Old Friend, Doggett

On arrival at Arthur's, you could see the glow of the fire flickering its warmth and light through the raggedy old curtains. Archie barked even before we knocked on the door, as he heard our crunching footsteps. As before, it took Arthur a time to open up, needing to clamber on a chair to reach the handle.

"Oh my word," he said, "come in, come in."

He wobbled on his chair, fighting for stability. Archie moaned and groaned his hellos, sniffing excitedly at our parka pockets, soaking all the Bellas' faces as they tried to scramble free.

Arthur pushed the door shut and, still wobbling up high, held Daisy's waist.

"How wonderful to see you! How truly lovely to have you with me again." He spoke these words with unbridled compassion and joy, such a contrast to the men we had encountered earlier.

He suddenly loosened his hold around Daisy, but still steadied himself with the front of her parka, pulling it crooked upon her frame.

"And what a great honour, Jessie, to have you in my house," he said, smiling and waving his long sleeve at me. Even with everything I had seen recently, Arthur's unusual looks hit me when meeting him in the flesh. He was like no human I had ever seen before. But it wasn't just that. It was more his warmth and the misty white glow he had around him.

It was dark in the cottage apart from the light of the fire in this cosy front room, yet I could see his outline quite clearly. I found myself staring at him just as I would stare at my feet or at almost anything I didn't understand. I think I would have been happily transfixed by him, had his waggling sleeve not brushed the tip of my nose, snapping me out of my gaze.

"Oh yes, Arthur," I said, embarrassed, "it is so very wonderful to finally meet you too. And your home feels so, so welcoming."

"Thank you," he replied, hopping onto the floor, smiling. "You can have my chair," he said, pushing the small armchair closer to the fire. "And Daisy, would you like to help me make some tea?" He was already pulling her by the hand through the black velvet curtain.

A tiny voice from Daisy's pocket called out, "I like tea!", which startled Arthur somewhat.

"Oh, sorry, Arthur – this is Boomer," said Daisy, tapping her pocket to encourage Boomer to poke his head out, which he duly did, before diving back in again.

Bluebell and Willoughby took up positions on the pew as before, now back in front of the fire. Oakleigh and Leanndi were on the floor with Archie, who lay happily on his side soaking up the warmth. I sat on Arthur's chair and removed my big boots. I wiggled my toes within my cotton socks, and the heat from the nearby flames soon warmed them. I took my parka off and hung it on the backrest. Remembering that my cotton vest finished just above my knees and it would double as a cosy nightdress, I slipped my dungarees off, sat on the smooth leather, tucked my feet under myself, and felt content, safe and warm.

Daisy and Arthur returned with the most delicious cups of tea and, to great excitement, Arthur's homemade fudge. He explained that it could have done with a while longer to set, so its consistency was more like a chewy toffee. But curled up and comfy as I was, I found Arthur's fudge, which I scooped from the plate, sent my taste buds dancing with joy. I didn't think I had ever been so cosy.

I thought of Claudius and his mighty army, and the artists who were now honing their skills back in St Albans after so many hundreds of years. The contrast between the way I felt tonight within this warm cottage and the cold construction site made me feel quite guilty. I watched the flames dance and listened to the crackling wood. It was so cold outside that it had a quietness all of its own. As the flames battled against the chill as it tried to gain access to our snug room, it dawned on me that everything was a battle. Cold and warmth, dark and light, noise and peace, even movement and remaining still. It was the balance between them that was all-important. If it was tipped too far one way or the other, we would soon forget the natural meeting point of the two forces and adjust to our new surroundings, soon forgetting where we should be placed in the world in its intended state. We adjust too easily to evil, I realised. But not me, not now.

"Are you okay, Jessie?" Daisy asked, finishing the last of her fudge and running her finger around the rim of the plate.

"Yes," I replied. "I am very happy, just deep in thought, that's all."

Bluebell turned to Arthur, who had joined Archie on the floor, gently stroking Archie's face. How wonderfully they had bonded. Arthur's eyes filled up with happy tears when Archie opened his eyes and gave his hand a thankful lick.

"I was sure, Arthur," she said, "that you were distressed tonight. Did Mr Wilson return?"

"Oh yes," Arthur said, spinning to face her, but not breaking contact with Archie. "He stared once again through the window but quickly left. It was most strange."

"But you are fine?" she asked in her uncharacteristic mother-voice that she seemed to save solely for Arthur.

"Oh yes," Arthur bravely replied, straightening his back and pushing his chest out. "Me and Archie are not afraid of anything. Are we, Archie?"

Archie gave a big comfy sigh.

I, like Archie, snuggled down. But, still anxious for Claudius, I placed my goggles to my eyes. But it was hopeless – the sleep that I had denied myself could be kept at bay no longer. My eyes grew heavy and unable to focus, and I drifted and dreamt, with my thoughts of Claudius absorbed into the lenses within my goggles.

Before too long, I found myself within the graveyard of the abbey. Quite clearly, I could see our footsteps in the snow from before, and felt the cold penetrate me. For a minute or two I thought I was actually there outside the abbey, but then realised this was a vision. My thoughts were outside in the chill, yet still my own, but my body was left in the safety of Spencer Street. The cold I felt was not in my own body.

In fact, when I looked down at myself, I discovered I was now inhabiting the flesh of an old and tall man, experiencing pain so torturous in every joint that it was a challenge to stand at all.

I slid the snow off the heads of each gravestone. As I did so, I felt only the leather gloves that I wore to protect my thin skin, which otherwise would easily have split in the bitter air away from my swollen joints. My eyes peered beneath a black trilby hat as I approached the edge of the construction site and removed one glove. Peeling it from my right hand, I stretched my long taloned fingers in front of my host's face and moved my hand from side to side. I felt a smile grow and I pushed my tongue against my few teeth, forcing the tip clear, and wiggled it, like a lizard tasting my surroundings.

Then I heard a voice as my host's body spoke.

"I can see you, Claudius," the man's voice whispered as we peered through our fingers. "I can see you."

I watched from my host's eyes as Claudius moved in normal time and approached the fence.

"Leave this place, Wilson," Claudius demanded, "or I shall strike you down." He moved his right hand to the sword that hung off his left hip.

We slowly squatted down, clasping the metal of the fence, and again we smiled through at Claudius.

"Old friend," we whispered, "dear old friend, I mean you no harm, but come close because I do know somebody who might."

Claudius held his sword tight and pulled his left foot

back, supporting his body for attack. We pulled our body upright and turned as if to walk away.

Then we pushed our hand into the coat pocket and spun back towards Claudius, pulling a Malissol free and hurling him towards the fence.

By the time the Malissol hit the fence, it was full height, and it swung its battle-axe hard against it. It screamed as it shook the fence, and Claudius stepped back.

"Doggett!"

Claudius's voice rose, but this soulless Doggett had nothing left of the Bella whom Claudius had befriended and relied on for many years. He was wearing rough hessian, a kilt, and a cloak tied around his neck with a simple cord. The fine fur that nature had intended for Bellas was all but gone. His muscular, scarred little body was heavily covered with tattoos, each one symbolising the death of an innocent Bella. His eyes were as black as coal. His teeth were sharp, and with them he pulled at the fence.

"Fight me," he snarled.

Both Claudius and Doggett were keen for this fight and the fence between them became invisible to them as they clashed sword against axe upon it. They hit hard for a second or two then both pulled away. Claudius spoke calmly. "I shall meet you in battle and send your body to hell and truly free your soul." He placed his sword back in its sheath.

Doggett's venom still oozed from his mouth, leaving his spittle upon the fence. "I shall turn you dark," he screamed, "and take your light for good. That I promise."

Claudius stood back, as my host – like a playground bully – enjoyed stirring trouble between two old friends. Claudius knew that his friends from his past had long gone. Only their bodies remained, and even they had changed terribly.

I walked in Wilson's body, with Doggett by my side, back through the graveyard. The trees and hedgerows were alive with the crowing of Malissols, but the sound and movements steadily faded away alongside us. Doggett turned once more to face Claudius in the distance, and slammed his battle-axe against a headstone. It hit with such force that sparks flew high and Claudius flinched.

I left that awful body, and my vision returned to be with Claudius as he watched his once true friend Doggett fading into the distance. The metal fence showed where the two of them had clashed: the metal cleanly cut by their weapons.

Claudius whispered to himself. "Doggett is strong, maybe stronger than me. Pure evil now runs through his veins and he is blind to his senses. How many Malissols do we face? How many with such venom? I have won many battles by strategy, but only in open space. I know that my army could beat the Malissols. But if we are surprised in an ambush, we will almost definitely be defeated."

The night was passing and the temperature dropping. The snow cloud had gently moved along and stars now filled the sky. Claudius left the construction site and walked slowly around the abbey. He passed alongside Doggett's footprints and mumbled memories of their conversations, remembering his friend's face as it had been, and spoke quietly to himself.

"He was hard and battle-worn, but kind. His face was lined through laughing and smiling at all eventualities. His eyes were once as green as the fields that rolled upon our Floating Land and they sparkled as brightly as the stars that now fill this sky."

He stared at the abbey, the size and strength of it, and spoke now in a raised voice.

"How many wars and evil acts has this sacred ground witnessed? Do the happy and loving times outweigh them? Is this just another battle and loss of life, to be overseen by it and embedded into its stone? Doggett once said that if a solid structure suddenly moved, wouldn't it surprise you? Stand fast and attack at the last, and surprise will be your victory. And so it shall be."

He looked up and spoke quietly once again.

"And so it shall be."

My dreaming vision stayed with Claudius as dawn crept in and the floodlights switched themselves off. Claudius, on his return, called a halt to work, and all the Bellas returned to their normal size. The Roman army stood high on the banks of the excavated earth and stared down at the artists as they placed their final pieces. The sun rose upon the Tudor rooftops, casting its first shadow of the day. It was good to see the back of that night and to welcome the sun and the light it brought, although it struggled to warm the earth, with such a defiant icy covering upon it. The glittering snow and the reflecting white felt safe. All stood waiting for the sun to rise a little more and to shine its rays of life upon the artists' work.

The light crept along in search of this new wonder of art. It lit the gold of an angel. She lay within the arms of a young girl who was sitting on deep grass, damp with the dew of a new day. The girl was looking at the angel with peace and love, with no sadness at death. The angel's wings lay flat by her side, and she rested her heavenly face upon her hands, settled within the young girl's lap. The girl leant her body over the angel, protecting her. The angel had handed all trust to the girl and she was free to sleep. Demons were trying to attack the angel, but the young girl absorbed the blows. But the demons were dark above them, a contrast to the life that the artists had created around the two girls.

In a corner of the mosaic was a scene of bluebells. It was framed separately from the rest of the work, a little picture in its own right.

Claudius knelt at the corner of the mosaic and held his strong arm out to Garius, the chief artist.

"Your work is truly magnificent, Garius," Claudius said, pulling the frail artist to his side. "You have the magic of gods within your hands."

"Thank you, Claudius, for your words, but I fear this is a prophecy that I have created and it is one that I do not have the answer for." Garius looked down at his work. It was beautiful and fitting that the sun shone upon it, welcoming it to the world. "Her wings," Garius said, pointing and reworking them as he held his finger out. "I have never felt so sad as this night when I made them lie flat to her side. It was as if I were creating something perfectly new that was already losing life."

Claudius clasped Garius's wrist and pulled it back to his side. "You have created a prophecy and your work is done. It is now down to Jessie and the gods to prevent the sadness that consumes you from coming to fruition."

Hearing my name, even in this dream state, made me jump, as Claudius continued speaking.

"There is one question, Garius. Why are the bluebells separate from the rest of the mosaic?"

"I don't know," he answered, slowly shaking his head as he stared at them. "Maybe a separate piece of art, maybe nothing."

Claudius spoke softly. "Go and rest, and thank you."

He called his men to lightning speed to cover the mosaic, leaving only a corner open to human eyes. Time was now against them. As the mighty Roman army made its way to the hollowed gargoyle that would lead them to the tunnels and to certain battle, Claudius knew too well that it was not a perfect fighting ground, if it were to be one. But he was ready and his strategy was planned. He knew the tunnels well and so did Doggett, but he also knew by the rage that Doggett had shown earlier that on his part it would not be a battle of carefully laid out manoeuvres but a full onslaught of brutality and power.

CHAPTER 21

Cream Teas While We Wait

My thoughts left Claudius and fluttered for a time before I wearily opened my eyes. I was greeted by the sunlight sneaking through the curtains. All were asleep, apart from Daisy, who welcomed me to this new day with a broad smile.

"Morning, sweet Jessie. You sleep as an angel would, if indeed they sleep at all."

"Morning, Daisy," I replied, stretching my arms upwards, already questioning if angels would have to sleep. Then I remembered Claudius.

"Oh Daisy," I squealed, "Claudius has not arrived to meet us. And what about the mosaic?"

I panicked, jumping off my chair and stumbling as I pulled my dungarees on, catching my left foot and toppling back onto my side. "I had the strangest night's sleep," I said, lying there disorientated.

"Calm down, Jessie," Daisy said, as the room awoke, all now jumping and panicking. Even Archie barked at the sudden commotion.

She laughed. "You all look so funny, half asleep. How wonderful! What a lovely memory to store."

Leanndi, not one to miss a chance to chuckle at her friends, quickly scampered up on Daisy's side and settled in her arms to face them all and laughed as loudly as she possibly could. Bluebell stood fast, straightening her back and with it her slightly crumpled dress. She corrected her hat, and then poured her attention onto Willoughby, who yawned heavily at her and blinked his puffy eyes. She smartened him up and turned to Oakleigh, who had woken up but then settled on his side to go back to sleep. She sharply kicked his backside, apologised insincerely, stepped over him and caught him again with her foot.

"I'm so sorry, Oakleigh, I must be sleepy. I didn't see you there."

"Yeah, right you didn't," Oakleigh replied, sitting upright, with his curly hair messed around him, defying gravity, doubling the size of his head. "One thing you wouldn't miss would be me trying to sleep," he grumpily mumbled to himself.

Boomer had ventured out of Daisy's pocket and onto the pew to lie down for the night, though was now standing bolt upright and alert, an anxious expression on his face.

Arthur was sitting wide awake with Archie, just as I had last seen them before I nodded off.

"Who fancies breakfast?" Daisy asked, and like children we all responded: "Hooray!"

"Upstairs Downstairs," Arthur said joyfully.

"What do you mean?" I asked.

"Upstairs Downstairs – it's a very nice coffee and tea room on the hill opposite the construction site. They do breakfast, too – full English, the sign said. I have never been in there. It is very upmarket."

"That sounds just perfect." I smiled at Arthur, and asked Daisy, "Shouldn't Claudius be back, though? I still haven't told you yet about my night's visions."

"He is fine at present, Jessie, and I will know if his situation changes." She opened the door, not allowing me to tell.

So, in single file, Archie barging past with Arthur attached to him with a length of rope as a temporary lead, we all left 125 Spencer Street.

Willoughby and Bluebell travelled in my pocket, Boomer in Daisy's, but Leanndi and Oakleigh chose to travel upon Archie, deep within his fur, where they loved to be. Oakleigh saw this as another opportunity to have a little nap out of sight of Bluebell, his disciplinarian.

The streets were busy, a total contrast to the night before. The morning rush was upon them and the townsfolk slipped and bumped their way along. People stepped aside for us. Although we were in love with our clothes, they looked scruffy against everyone else's. I liked the way people looked at us. I liked my purpose. Smartly dressed businessmen and women, whom I would once have been taught to look up to, had no respect from me. Mothers pushing and driving their children to nursery and school had no care for their fellow parents. One thing mattered and that was their offspring. There was no community. No support. No structure.

The route that we had taken the night before looked very different in daylight. St Albans was a pretty place, as it was at night, but now, with the bustle of people, it was alive and vibrant. Designer shops, fitted out to the highest specifications, stood at the base of historic buildings. Mannequins draped to tease in the latest winter fashions, restaurants and bars now taking prime locations where once banks would have stood, keeping their features and frontages as reminders of the past. Even the library, which was central to the town, had fallen foul of the pressure of the leisure industry, and the only thing that remained of its once true purpose, before progress had made it obsolete, was a drinking house named 'The Library'. Coffee shops were in abundance, and the warm smell of freshly ground beans filled the cold morning air.

We passed back through Boot Alley, past the abbey and to 'Upstairs Downstairs' on the hill opposite the construction site. Arthur was a few steps in front with Archie almost pulling him along, slipping and sliding upon the snow, and occasionally Arthur would hit the ground with a bump and circle round before rising to his feet again.

"Well," Daisy said, "did you see it?"

"See what?" I replied.

"What I hoped you would see around humans now," Daisy answered, stopping me dead. "Look at that group of passengers leaving the bus."

"What about them?" I asked, and then, as clear as Daisy was to me, I saw a fine mist around their silhouettes.

There were six people walking towards us, all struggling with the snow on the gradient of the hill. Two boys and a girl led the group, smartly dressed in their school uniforms. They spoke excitedly about the snowfall and how maybe they would have to leave school early if it were to fall heavily again. They brushed past us, each in turn stroking Archie's head as they did so, and each remarking on how beautiful he was, making Arthur stand proudly as he agreed heartily with their comments. Each of the children had a white glow around them. It was not a sharp white, but comforting and protective with a creamy soft depth to it.

Behind them an elderly gentleman stood still on the flake-laden gradient, afraid to move for fear of falling. A very pretty lady passed next to him. She smiled at the traffic that stood at a standstill on the road and waved at friends she knew in an oncoming car. She was lovely to watch, as she was so happy on this cold morning. But, unlike the children and the old man, she had not a white glow around her but a grey one, as dark grey as charcoal.

The elderly gentleman's voice was weak and frightened. "Could you help me a little?"

She hesitated slightly and shifted her eyes towards him. The friendly face dropped as she moved along. I noticed that as she brushed past him, the gentleman's white glow drew a little grey into it, but it soon left as a very gruff-looking man with a hard face and a physique to match gently held the man's arm.

"Come on, old boy, let's get you up the hill."

"You are so kind," the elderly man replied, and smiled.

I looked at the old man's face. He was so secure in this stranger's care. He felt the stranger's strong white glow and he knew that he was safe within his hands.

"You see it now, don't you, Jessie?"

Daisy slipped her arm into mine and we walked forward.

"That lady wasn't very nice, was she?" I said, feeling angry towards her and wanting to slide her back down the hill in front of the traffic. She showed, all too eagerly, her outer self, which was nothing like a true reflection of her real personality. I wondered then how my own glow would be, having such awful thoughts, and I stared hard into a shop window at my reflection as we passed.

"Unfortunately, you cannot see your own glow, Jessie," Daisy said, laughing at me, "but I can assure you that yours is perfectly fine."

We reached the tea room and scrambled in. It is strange when you have a dog with you, as any doorway or small passage becomes hard to negotiate, especially with a hound the size of Archie. You can't help it, but it all becomes a commotion. So, our entrance was less than dignified and the pompous-looking waiter couldn't wait to tell us that dogs were not allowed, until Daisy, who was equally sharp in response, said that her friend Arthur had poor sight and of course he couldn't leave his guide dog out in the cold. The waiter looked us up and down and seated us in a corner, away from his other customers. Luckily for us, it was an excellent viewpoint for the construction site.

We watched as the first of the workmen arrived. They talked and joked amongst themselves, unaware of what they were soon to discover. We couldn't hear what they were saying, but Daisy could catch enough words from reading their lip movements.

One of them said that the earth looked freshly turned.

Another one replied, "It's not a bloody allotment. Do you think fairies are doing your work for you?"

She relayed these words, then added, "How funny. It wasn't fairies, it was Bellas." She laughed, enjoying her own little joke.

"Have they found it, Daisy?" I asked excitedly.

"No. Not yet."

She paused. "But they have now." She smiled and clapped her hands. "Look, see them all running over. Cream teas all round!" she squealed.

The three of us clapped our hands, causing more concern to our fellow customers. Archie joined in with a groan and Arthur patted his head, but looked straight ahead, remembering for now that he could not see all that well.

The workmen hovered around, a dozen or so, not knowing what to do next. But, like us, one of them had the bright idea of putting the kettle on and waiting until the boss arrived.

Our waiter returned to our table.

"What can I get you?" he asked, holding pen and pad in front of him, not once making eye contact with any of us, and shuffling to his side as Archie sniffed at his leg, leaving, to our amusement, a wet patch on his black trousers where his nose had touched. There were three women working the other tables, but he chose to deal with us himself in order to spare them. I couldn't really blame him, having looked at Daisy's reflection and mine in the mirror that hung on the wall opposite. Arthur's appearance was still hard to absorb, even having spent time with him. I especially looked as if I had just returned from many months in the wilderness. My hair was very long and fine, but dank and somewhat greasy. My face was dirty: not a little, but very dirty. Around my eyes was the cleanest. This was from hour upon hour of wearing my goggles, relaying messages and, of course, flying. I hadn't properly seen myself for months and, in truth, for the first time in my life, I could see myself as a pretty young lady. My eyes were ever so big and green and, although my ears protruded a little due to my dirty hair now being stuck to my head, I liked them, almost as much as I liked my feet. I looked even smaller than I could remember, but now, living my life around such small creatures and witnessing their amazing feats, I wished I was a similar size to a Bella. I stared at Daisy in the mirror. If I was pretty, I thought, she was truly beautiful. Her face, like mine, was dirty, but her hair shone, reflecting every light. The colouring was deep and soft, and the volume waved against her Alice band. Each of her eyebrows was shaped by an artist, and so, too, were her teeth, except one on the front centre top row. It twisted slightly, making her smile even more appealing.

"Well?" the waiter asked impatiently.

I glared at him, and Daisy answered. "Seven cream teas, please."

"Seven?" the waiter replied, staring over his pad at the three of us.

A little voice spoke from Daisy's coat. "Eight."

Daisy coughed. "Oh, sorry, my mistake. Can you make that eight?"

He stared suspiciously at us and murmured to himself as he walked uneasily away.

We were beginning to realise that tea was the key to luring Boomer out from hiding. Though he was missing Bluebell Wood and preferring not to socialise, a cup of tea, particularly if it was accompanied by scones or cake, was just too tempting to resist.

The women who were waiting on the other tables were splendidly dressed. They wore maids' outfits, traditional, as they would have done in Victorian times. Looking around at the many old pictures, it seemed the place had been open as a tea room for all those years. There was a doorway to the left-hand side of a most beautiful fireplace. The fire was no longer in use, and dried flowers lay upon the hearth. The door was tiny. It had had no need to be grand, as people were generally smaller in the times when the doorway had first been constructed. I thought that I would have fitted in quite nicely. I might have been considered tall, but I doubted it.

The latch of the door lifted and a little maid appeared. Her face was very pale and she looked undernourished. She had even got the footwear of the period perfectly and she moved with the tiniest of steps towards us. She looked downwards and seemed very sad. On reaching the table she spoke sweetly to us.

"May I help?"

"No, we are fine," I replied. "We've ordered. Thank you anyway."

But she didn't move. She kept her head down and spoke again.

"May I help you, Daisy?" she said, still with her hands clasped in front of her and head nervously down.

"Who is she?" I leant forward and mouthed to Daisy.

"Just a minute," Daisy said, signalling patience to me. She held her arms to the maid and she shuffled forward.

"Thank you, my sweet girl, for coming to me. But you must go. Everything will be fine." Daisy held her for a few seconds and the girl melted away.

"My word!" I gasped. "That is the first resident I have seen – well, witnessed – close at hand. Could you feel her, Daisy, when you held her?"

"Oh yes, as well as I can feel any living person or any creature. I feel the pain and sadness within her that she has not yet moved on, but still some of them wish to help us. Don't you find that remarkable?"

"Yes, I guess so," I replied. Then I thought a little and asked, "How could she help you, Daisy? What do you think she knows?"

For the first time I could see a slight look of doubt on Daisy's face. "That was a warning to me, Jessie, that I must be careful. But anyway, I have all of you with me, so I am sure I have nothing to fear."

"Yes, of course, Daisy. We would never let anything happen to you. That I promise."

I really meant those words. Although I had only known Daisy for the shortest time, she was everything to me, and I felt quite angry at the little maid's ghost for bringing any concern to her, even if she were trying to help her.

Our eight cream teas arrived, much to the waiter's bemusement and annoyance. He glared at each of us whilst placing them onto the table, just about squeezing the eighth one on.

"I have to ask, will there be anything else?" he said rudely.

"No, that will do for starters, thank you," I answered, but he had turned away with his own importance, to seat another customer as far away from us as possible.

Willoughby and Bluebell left my parka pocket and now sat on my lap. Oakleigh and Leanndi crawled from within Archie's fur, and Boomer from Daisy's pocket, and sat on her lap.

Arthur had no interest in anything but Archie, and he whispered his conversation into Archie's alert ears. Everywhere Archie looked, Arthur would start a conversation about his viewing. If Archie stared at a person, Arthur would say, "No, I don't like the look of them either," or if Archie flopped to the floor, Arthur would agree that it was tiring being the best dog in the world.

Daisy and I played mum, and prepared the scones with mountains of cream and jam.

Each cream tea came with its own little jug of milk which we emptied into one of the teacups, to make five little jugs of tea, and passed them under the table to the happy breakfast guests upon our laps. Arthur did manage to turn his attention to the table, but only to make sure that Archie received just the same as himself.

The sound and movement of Willoughby and Bluebell on my lap as they tucked into their cream teas was so sweet. The scones were almost their size. I looked down at them eating away happily and chatting to one another in between massive mouthfuls. The cream and the jam that we had piled high were tricky for them to negotiate, but Willoughby and Bluebell managed sufficiently, unlike Oakleigh and Leanndi, who made no effort at all to avoid getting it around their faces and on their clothes. You could barely tell the two of them apart as the cream spread evenly around their mouths, making them look almost ready to shave. Even Boomer had forgotten himself, his mouth smeared with strawberry conserve, his expression more relaxed than I had seen it since we had flown down to Earth. Oh, how I wished it could remain so despite the evil nearby us threatening to rain down on our valiant Roman army.

CHAPTER 22

Fearful Prophecy

I had just finished my last mouthful and washed it down with my remaining tea, when Arthur's eyes grew to the size of the plate that he held between his legs, and the colour left his face. "There, look," he said, "in with the builders."

I turned to the construction site and saw the back of a very smartly dressed elderly man.

"That's Mr Wilson," Arthur said, swallowing hard and moving closer, if possible, to Archie.

"Right," I said, wiping my hands with my napkin and standing up sharply, dropping Willoughby and Bluebell to the floor, along with their make-do teacups. "It is time I had a chat with him."

It felt surprisingly easy to just get up and go to talk to Wilson, despite his history or what he was trying to achieve, or indeed the idea that this man could be a threat to humanity. I marched across the tea room to confront him as if he had struck my dog or reversed his car carelessly into mine.

But our awful waiter lunged for the door and held it shut.

"Don't you think you should pay your bill before leaving?"

He was short of breath and red in the face. The stress of our presence there had upset him greatly. I felt he would have sacrificed his life for the price of our cream teas. Not liking him at all, although the mist around him was a good white, I wanted to hurl him out of my way, but he did have a point. I had no money and I was not at all sure if Daisy or Arthur did, when they arrived behind me.

"I'll get this," Arthur said, staring directly at the waiter.

The waiter snapped, "I thought that dog was a guide dog?" and then trembled with his responsibility to the tea room.

"Do you want my money or not?" Arthur replied, pulling from his pocket a huge bundle of twenty-pound notes.

The waiter stepped aside from the door, visibly relieved.

"Arthur, keep Archie this side of the road when you have paid. Daisy and I will come back for you."

Arthur nodded and paid the bill, doubling the amount for a tip.

"Where on earth did Arthur get that much money?" I asked Daisy as we held hands to cross over.

"I gave it to him. He also has a lot of gold which he looks after for me," she said, smiling cheekily at me.

I was just about to ask why when she shook my hand.

"I will tell you later, I promise," she said.

We entered the construction site to a man's loud voice, "Sorry, girls, you can't come in here."

"But I must see Mr Wilson," I shouted, making sure that Wilson could hear me well.

Wilson didn't move, except for raising his arm. "Let them through," he whispered, his voice menacingly quiet.

His back was still turned on us as he looked down upon the mosaic. The workmen had cleared the soil, although they should have waited for archaeologists, but it was well constructed: not just beautiful, but strong. I stood alongside Mr Wilson and stared down at the craftsmanship. I gasped at how the gold shimmered in the sunlight and at the remarkable detail. How, in a few hours of work within the cold night, could art such as this have been created? I had seen them do it myself in my night-time vision, yet it was still flabbergasting.

Wilson spoke. "Anyone we know?" he asked, still looking downwards at the mosaic.

I knew, as soon as my eyes settled against the glare of the gold, that the lady holding the angel was me and, to my suppressed pain, the angel whom I held was very similar to Daisy.

He laughed quietly to himself and looked past me towards Daisy. "It looks as if you haven't got a great deal to look forward to, doesn't it, Daisy?"

I arched my neck and glared up at his face. I had no fear of this man, he looked so very ill. Death had ravaged his body, but not taken him.

"Whatever you see in this mosaic, Wilson," I growled, "the outcome will be interpreted in the way I choose. Do you understand?" I felt so protective of Daisy that however evil this man was, I knew I could be strong against him.

"You must be Jessie," he said, with a wry smile. "I thought you would turn up." He laughed, showing the few teeth, which moved upon their dangling roots, sticking to his top lip as it pulled away. "Take a walk with me." He stared at Daisy, paused and continued. "Alone, if you don't mind."

Daisy shook her head, and two little voices came from

within my parka pocket. Willoughby and Bluebell had scampered back in there after being rudely dropped onto the floor at the start of my purposeful march.

"Don't go with him!" Bluebell screamed her annoyance.

"I would recognise that voice anywhere. That has to be my sweet little Bluebell," Wilson remarked, as if he were just greeting an old friend.

"I am no longer your friend," Bluebell added, glaring up at him and squeezing her angry little head out of my pocket.

"Come, you stay with Daisy. You have nothing to worry about. Isn't that right, Mr Wilson?" I said these words as if for some reason I should trust this man.

"Nothing on this day," he replied.

CHAPTER 23

Wilson's Story

So, walk with Wilson I did. We walked side by side, past the abbey and down to the lake. We didn't say a word to each other until we stopped by the lake and sat upon a wooden bench. Everything was quiet and still. All evidence of our arrival the night before had now been covered by the snowfall. Had I been sitting with anyone else but Mr Wilson I would have enjoyed this moment. The sun shone brightly against the snow, yet emitting only a weak warmth, meaning the frozen lands would stay for now as they were. Snowfall has a way of muffling the human race. Movements upon it are hushed, so peace and tranquillity can embrace nature. Rarely without the noise of man is there sound at all: apart from birdsong and the rustle of wind through the trees.

I didn't turn to Wilson to talk. I just stared at my surroundings and asked, "Why?"

"Why what?" he whispered.

"Why would you want to hurt us all? Why is there darkness around you?"

I felt him stare down at me as the rasp of his breath brushed my face. His voice remained quiet, but it shook now.

"Shall I tell you something about angels, goodness and your Floating Land? You and I have been used," he said, and I wanted to listen to him.

"I gave my life to looking after the Bellas and all creatures, but mostly the human kind. I watched as we battled and battled to ensure that the balance of good against evil remained as it should, but humankind are never thankful for what they have so close to them. The love of one another is but a sentence within a book. Greed is now all that matters. Kindness was once a recognised strength, but now it is taken as weakness. They follow not the example of good acts, but swim in the pleasure of using each other to get to the top of the ladder, only to find that nothing awaits them but equally selfish people."

I let him continue, as so far, his words had been true.

"When Grandad was ready to take my place, I was led to the steps. Have you heard of the steps, Jessie?"

"No," I replied, thinking that maybe I should have.

"Well, you have heard that there are steps to heaven?"

"Yes, of course, but not actual steps. I think they mean a righteous path."

He ignored my answer and continued.

"Well, there are invisible steps from all four of our Floating Lands, reaching down to Earth. They begin at the water's edge. In order to see them and follow them, you have to watch the rain falling onto them, or settling snow, or maybe just the way the sunlight bounces off them. It is hard to place each foot. Misread the signs, and you will fall. It can take days or weeks to walk down to Earth, but once followed as intended, the steps will bring you back to your birthplace. This is the Leading Angel's gift to you for a lifetime of service.

"So I did follow the steps, and on my arrival home, my house was as I had left it as a young man. Bellas and honorary members such as Arthur Fatelli had kept it in order, and I was grateful for that. But no one I knew was there or, come to that, even alive. The world had changed greatly and I was frightened. Memories faded by the day of Bluebell Wood, the Floating Land and, sadly, even of its inhabitants. Small events happened here on Earth, and I found myself arriving at them in hope of meeting a friendly Bella, just to talk, just to reassure me that I was not losing my mind. But if they had failed in a quest, I never found them. Sadly, they had hidden well and died.

"Until one day when I had taken the bus for my weekly shop. I sat alone and stared at people busying themselves in the high street. The day was dry but overcast, with nothing much to it. We pulled up at the next stop to let a young woman on with her child, a small boy. She was a regular on the bus, just like myself, but we never spoke. She, like me, was used to the route and chose to keep her head down as she stood in the aisle. The bus moved away and picked up speed. On leaving the town and passing the recreation ground to our right were some children playing football. I watched them and felt so envious of their youth. Behind me I could hear the young woman tell the child to just sit still, while she was trying to remove his coat. 'You won't feel the benefit outside if you leave it on,' she said, angry at the child's reluctance to help. A football jumped in front of the bus, and when the driver hit the brakes hard, the woman fell to the floor and lay motionless beside my seat. I had seen death so many times that I knew that life had left her. Her eyes were wide and they stared hard at me. She had broken her neck for sure, as death took her so quickly, leaving only a tear-sized trickle of blood from her mouth. Her poor child was shocked into silence. Then he murmured, 'Mummy, please, Mummy, get up. Are you okay?'

"I knew what I should have done was to help the child, but I didn't. The bus that just seconds ago felt empty was now full of confusion, sadness and panic. I left my seat and left the bus. A Bella had to be near, I could feel it. I walked along the pavement, leaving the mayhem well behind me.

"Houses stood to my left, with standard hedgerows, neatly cut above small walls. Most had waist-high, cast-iron gates, which I peered over to look under the hedges. I was so sure that a Bella had to be near. I felt like a cat hunting its prey. I listened for any sound of rustling foliage and stared hard for the smallest of movements. When pulling away to carry on my search further, I saw him. There, within the conifer hedge. A small area had been cut back too far, leaving it bare and easy for me to peer through at my find. Doggett, reduced in size to five or six inches, face downwards and limp across a couple of small branches. I just knew it was him. I was filled with compassion for my little friend, a feeling that has long since left me. I am now thankfully void of such feelings, but then, as I was, I was consumed by it and I couldn't let my old friend leave me. I gently took him in my hand and wrapped him within my scarf and hurried home.

"That night, as I struggled to keep Doggett alive, I failed to see his spirit weaken and darkness enter. When morning broke to a glorious sunny day, I threw the curtains open and turned to face my patient, who to my great joy sat upright upon the table.

"'Doggett!' I gasped. 'You are awake and well!'

"But his response was far from the one I had hoped for. He was not the friend I had once known. He was nothing now but full of anger, and his rage burnt at his body. He ripped away his parka and then his fine Roman uniform. He pulled at his fur, clasping handfuls and screaming at me.

"'You have sentenced me to live in hell. I feel the darkness in me, but you didn't let me die. My spirit is trapped next to this evil for eternity. How could you do this? I should strike you down!'

"But then, as if somebody had turned a switch, he calmed and stood still. He focused hard at nothing, then without any other movement, his now dark eyes shifted quickly from side to side and then stuck fast on me. 'What am I saying?' He spoke calmly. 'I should be so very grateful to you. Come close, William, and join me.'

"I didn't then know what he meant at all, but he held out his little paw-hand and I held my hand out to accept. He first took my thumb gently, then with the grip of a vice he pulled it hard to his mouth and bit. I screamed aloud, as the pain was like nothing I had felt before. I tried to pull it free, but that made my flesh rip, exposing the bone. He released it from his mouth and bit hard into his own, then placed the two pulsating flesh wounds together.

"I must have blacked out, as when I awoke, he stood still on the table, but had fashioned a kilt and cloak from a hessian sack from beneath my stair cupboard. At first, I felt alive, young and vibrant, but within an hour, feelings and memories of sweet, wonderful times turned to hatred for people and Bellas.

"But most of all I hated nature – the sound of it, the

look of it. My view on the world had reversed. Trees now just looked like roots, pathetically reaching for life, but always failing to grow high enough. Flowers and grass were just weeds, and sunlight was a light that burnt me and everything it touched. The same surroundings, but a different feeling. But to me now, this felt good. Doggett had let the darkness run free into my blood and opened my eyes to the evil truth."

Wilson moved closer.

"I hate your world, Jessie, and all it stands for. I shall return to Bluebell Wood, as I wish to destroy it and you. And the Bellas shall be the first to go."

We stared, inches away from each other. Why I didn't fear him, I don't know. I just wanted him to go. My adrenalin was high, pumping my heart hard against my chest. I knew he wished to harm me, but as Bluebell had said the night before, "We shall show no fear", and I didn't.

But I knew, just as time moved into slow motion, the truth of the words that I then spoke.

"I should not have walked with you."

He clasped the length of my hair and reached to bend my head back, exposing my throat, and then Doggett appeared at my front, swinging his battle-axe and moving at speed towards my neck. Doggett held my chin with his left hand and pulled back his axe. His boot pressed hard into my windpipe and I gasped for air. Wilson pulled again at my hair.

"Can you feel death, Jessie? Does it feel good to you?"

I tried to scream, but nothing came. Doggett's boot pushed harder and harder for leverage as he swung for his defining blow. I stared at the sky, and my vision blurred.

I was losing consciousness when his foot released my windpipe. I coughed and gasped for air. I looked down to my lap, and through my watery vision I saw Willoughby behind Doggett, pulling him backwards, his cane tight across the throat of this mad beast of a Malissol.

"Go, Jessie, go!" Willoughby shouted, as the two of them fell to the icy path.

Doggett still lay in front of Willoughby, his mouth foaming, and he let out the most awful high-pitched shriek, not of pain but pure rage. He wriggled madly, kicking his boot heels hard back into Willoughby. His battle-axe had fallen and caught on the edge of my parka pocket. Wilson still clasped my hair.

"I knew I couldn't trust a Granton!" he gasped, pulling my face with a jolt up to his own.

He was hurting me. How dare this horrible being lay his darkness upon me, I thought, and I felt down to the little axe and forced it hard into Wilson's bony old leg. It stuck fast just above his knee. He exhaled the putrid air that filled his thinning lungs, and loosened his grip.

Doggett had now overpowered my dear brave Willoughby, turning the poor Bella's own cane upon him. Willoughby ran forward kicking and punching, occasionally halting Doggett's onslaught for a stunned second before the brutal beating continued.

I pushed Wilson away and pulled the little battle-axe from his knee. Whatever strength Wilson had possessed had now left his old body and he lay weakened on the bench.

I stood and kicked with all my heart and power into this horrible Doggett who was hurting my friend, but it had little effect on him despite my superior height and size. It was as if he were made of rock. He moved slightly, but my kicks just enhanced his rage. He looked back to Willoughby, who lay bleeding on the snow.

Doggett raised the cane and hit Willoughby time and time again, so fast that I couldn't catch hold of it to wrest it from his hateful grasp.

I dropped down and placed my left hand on the back of Doggett's neck and, with all the power I had running through my body, slammed the battle-axe hard into the top of his head.

Time froze at this moment. Doggett, still facing away from me, dropped like a stone and lay face down in the snow.

I scooped my poor Willoughby into my arms, snatched his cane from Doggett's grip and ran faster than I had ever run before, back to Daisy. I sped past the abbey and approached the construction site. Daisy still stood staring over the mosaic.

"Daisy, Daisy!" I shouted, and the workmen turned and stared at me. But not Daisy. She kept her eyes fixed on the mosaic.

"Daisy!" I screamed, and one of the workmen held my arm as I passed him.

"Are you all right, love?" he asked.

It was quite clear that I was not. My eyes were wide and filled with tears. I was terribly distressed about my poor Willoughby, who now lay reduced again in my pocket, beaten and bleeding.

I snatched my arm back and replied, "Yes, yes, I am fine. It is just the cold; it gets into my eyes. It makes them run."

He wasn't convinced, but I didn't care. I moved along to Daisy and grabbed her hand.

She jumped a little and stared hard at me.

"So, he tried to hurt you, then?" she said, totally expressionless.

"Yes," I replied, confused by her blank face. "And we must go. Willoughby is terribly hurt."

"Come, then, let us take time at Spencer Street," Daisy replied, acting very, very strangely indeed.

We joined Arthur and Archie and rushed along the busy street. I had no time for people or anything in my way. I rudely barged past them and crossed the road, causing cars to slide and hoot their anger towards me. Daisy walked just behind me and said not a word. Poor Arthur slipped along, holding fast to Archie's rope as Archie instinctively tried to lead. In no time we reached Arthur's door and the little panting man, still praising Archie for being a good boy, fumbled with the front door key.

I turned and faced Daisy. "What the hell is wrong with you?"

I wanted to demand right away why she so obviously didn't care that Wilson had tried to take my life.

"Why didn't you call me when you were frightened?" she responded, with an equal amount of force.

"I called you on my return, but you can't hear me, can you, Daisy?"

Arthur flung the door open. "Put Willoughby on the pew," he said.

I turned my attention back to my injured little friend. His head was bleeding badly and his face and eyes were swollen from the repeated blows from that evil Doggett. His paws were swollen up and bleeding where he had landed some fine blows onto Doggett's iron frame, but to little avail. Bluebell now sat at Willoughby's side, sitting as she would ride, with both legs dangling to her right. Neither Oakleigh nor Leanndi had said a word about the attack. Daisy, too, had said nothing about it. They didn't need to express their sadness in words: the pain was clear in their big brown eyes.

Each looked transfixed by Willoughby. Boomer was also silent as his thick glasses magnified his blinks. Bluebell pulled a tiny silk handkerchief from under her cuff and gently wiped the wounds. Arthur had brought in a small bowl of warm water which she dabbed with her handkerchief before applying it.

"I am sorry I was so off with you, Jessie," Daisy said, pulling me close to the window. "It is just that I told you not to go. You must understand that evil, as Wilson now is, cannot and will not be reasoned with. He will take any opportunity to harm you, me or any of us. Our strength is in a unit. He knows that you are vulnerable without us, but your will is strong, and now you have witnessed his intention first-hand, I hope you can respect evil for your and our own survival."

"Trust me, Daisy, I do not want to go through that again, but as for calling you, how could you hear me?" I said. It was awkward for me to once more question Daisy's ability to hear, but I didn't understand her thoughts.

But again she smiled, and said, "Just think of me and I shall hear you."

"Do you think that Willoughby will be okay?" I asked. "Doggett was so awful." I was now sure that his injuries were my fault.

Then I continued, before Daisy could answer, "They are as open to harm as me, aren't they? If it is from a horrible Malissol?"

"Willoughby is strong. And yes, they are hurt as easily as you, if confronted by each other."

I sighed and then remembered. "Oh yes. I think I killed Doggett, though. I really put that disgusting battle-axe into him."

Daisy shook her head. "No, Jessie, I wish it had, but no.

You wouldn't have had enough effect on Doggett to finish his life."

"But I'm sure that he was terribly injured," I said, trying to justify to myself that something good had come out of my decision to walk with Wilson.

Daisy replied, but softly, with a distance to her thoughts. "If only it were that easy." She pulled the curtain aside and just a little of the sun beamed in. It moved like torchlight around the room and shone brightly onto Willoughby. Daisy moved the curtain again, controlling the ray of the sun until it covered Willoughby's little body alone. He sighed in the comfort of it and straightened himself.

"Thank you, Daisy," Bluebell said. "Thank you so much."

Daisy smiled at Bluebell. "I think our time here, Jessie, is running short. We must go."

"Go where?" I replied.

"Ireland."

"Ireland?" I said, bemused. What on earth did a trip to Ireland have to do with any of this? "I can't go anywhere, Daisy," I answered. "Not without everyone I arrived with. Especially Willoughby in his present condition."

"Willoughby will be okay now, that is why Bluebell thanked me. Jessie, please..." Daisy held her hands out to me. "The mosaic – you could see, as I did, the two of us."

"Just a likeness," I replied, knowing full well that it was us, without any question.

She clasped both my hands tight. "It was the picture in the corner of the mosaic of the bluebells. That is my favourite view of Bluebell Wood."

"And that means what, though, Daisy?" I asked.

"You can help me, Jessie." She held my hands and kissed

my fingers. "You see, I know little of my past, but I do know that I painted that picture before, and I know where it is."

"But it was a coincidence – Garius has certainly seen that view many times before," I said, trying to comfort her.

"No, Jessie, it hangs in St Bede's Orphanage. That is where I first remember life."

"I don't know, Daisy. It just doesn't feel right to leave now. If we go anywhere, it should be back to Bluebell Wood, especially as Wilson said he would like to destroy it, and us."

I could see my words made no difference to Daisy.

She just turned to Arthur and asked, "Some money and gold please, Arthur."

"But really, Daisy, I do not think we should go," I repeated louder than before, just one decibel below shouting.

"Jessie," Daisy said, sounding already full of adventure and with that little mischievous glint, "we thought that the plague was our quest, but no. It was the mosaic and what has been prophesied." She sighed deeply. "The outlook for me is not good. I think that is quite clear. But something within my picture will tell us more. Don't you see that it is all I knew of my life until the age I am now? It must be relevant or it would not be in the mosaic." She clasped my hand tightly again and whispered her emotional blackmail. "Didn't you say that you should determine the outcome of the prophecy?" She now had me, and the people in the room who were listening knew that too.

I felt Leanndi scamper up on me and, as I always had from our first encounter, I held her within one arm. Facing me, and looking hard into my eyes, she said, "I think you had best go. Willoughby is already recovering. I shall worry about you, though, being away from us."

I pulled Leanndi close, just to feel her tiny breath upon my neck. I held her and glanced at the others. This was my family and my life within this room. Clumsy but talented Oakleigh, beautiful Bluebell, brave Willoughby, Arthur who could write a book on positive thinking and love, his new companion Archie, Leanndi who could melt me with a simple look, and Daisy whom I looked to as a person I respected and loved. If only Claudius had been with us, I would have felt more complete.

I knew I had forgotten someone, when there was a tug on the tail of my parka and a voice said, "Shall I be navigating?"

"Oh yes, Boomer. You do come and go as you please, don't you?" I said, laughing with him as he smiled and blinked his excitement at flying again.

Arthur left the room for a short time and returned with yet another bundle of money and, to my shock, three bars of glimmering gold.

I gasped. "Where did they come from?"

Daisy laughed as loudly as I had ever heard her. "I really don't know. I have lots and lots of them in a number of places."

I was keen to ask, but, as I had learned to do in my recent life, I left the question for another time.

"Come, then," I said. "Shall we go?"

CHAPTER 24

Luchendoo's Desert of Dreams

After our farewells, and a special thank you to Willoughby, who had opened his eyes and seemed to be recovering quickly, we left a very upbeat Spencer Street. Daisy and I linked arms and marched, positively carefree, through the busy town and back to the parkland and to my beautiful but somewhat over-camouflaged de Havilland. Boomer sat fast in Daisy's pocket and only reappeared after the hard work of removing the branches and mountains of snow from the plane.

Although we had quite a distance of open parkland to elevate us away, it was still a very tricky thing to negotiate. My best chance of success was to coast us to the far right, just short of a small copse of trees. This gave us a gradient and some two hundred, maybe three hundred yards to leave the city of St Albans.

The din of my engine firing up split the muffled silence and for the first time I didn't enjoy the sound of it, neither did I like the smell. Although my de Havilland was a marvellous piece of engineering, I felt apologetic towards my surroundings. I hurried to take both noise and smell high into the sky. As we hurtled down the snowy gradient, skis cutting at the icy ground, I pushed the throttle hard, and left it until the very last to raise us into the sky. We passed low above the fragile buildings. The snow was still heavy upon them and the uneven rooflines began to dip and rise as we skimmed above the ocean of white.

All heads below turned and stared at the unusual spectacle. Would we fly high, or crash into the street? But fear turned to calm as we soared away.

Boomer sat on my lap. How this timid little Bella had transformed into a fearless airman! He had screamed with joy from the first motion of take-off and now he rocked from side to side on my lap, stretching his neck to peer down at St Albans. I knew where the sun had risen in the east, so west I headed, to follow the quest into Ireland and St Bede's Orphanage.

It was, of course, nice to be soaring through the sky, but horrible to be leaving without all on board. Boomer had dropped to the floor, pushing his few charts around. I don't really think he needed them as his life had been dedicated to aviation, but it was good to know he was so thorough. Although the sun shone brightly, it was bitterly cold. Both Daisy and I made full use of our new clothes, especially the parka hoods that formed little tents for our heads when we held our faces downwards. Boomer appreciated our hoods too, suddenly appearing at the opening of my mine, reducing in size and climbing in. Tapping the end of my nose and squeezing his little fingers into the tip, he said, "You can relax for a time, Jessie, and just stay on this course."

"Okay, Boomer," I whispered, avoiding the temptation

to shout above the noise of the craft as he was within kissing distance of my mouth.

I kept all thoughts of my gallant little ones at bay, as my goggles were now back on for their intended use to pilot the plane in. Although the vision of my Bellas would have been comforting, I had to focus on the job in hand.

I leant over and stared at the open land below. The snow had truly blanketed the fields so that even the hedgerows, that would have clearly defined them normally, had been covered by a crisp, white sheet. It was as dazzling as the brightness that appeared in my eyes before a vision from the present. I pulled my gaze back, but it remained white. I panicked and held the controls fast.

Then a voice said, "Hello, Jessie."

"Hello," I replied, still without seeing the stranger.

"Can you see me, Jessie?" he asked, talking now in broken English. "I can see you and how terribly cold it looks. I don't envy you at all."

And then he appeared: an African boy, I would guess around the same age as myself. He was slight in build with a smile that consumed his whole face. He stood alone with his back to a huge tree. Many birds and insects voiced their sounds of life around him, making Bluebell Wood seem quite unpopulated in comparison.

He lowered his hands and pointed to his toes, then touching his head, he said, "This is me. I am Luchendoo, the last at present of the Gallag family." He wore nothing but a highly coloured wrap, and his dark body glimmered silkily in the warmth that surrounded him.

"How do you see me without any goggles or a telescope?" I asked suspiciously.

"With this," and he pointed to his right eye. There, barely visible, was a monocle.

"That's very natty." I laughed.

"Yes, it is," he replied, and laughed so loudly that I couldn't help but giggle further with him. "Let me see you," he asked.

"Okay, but just for a second. It is freezing," I said, already just a little envious of his warmth.

I pulled my hood back, and my goggles down around my neck. I lost sight of him, of course, but took the opportunity to check the plane was still on course, which, thankfully, it was. Nudging Daisy to take over from me, I quickly pulled my hood and goggles back on.

"I know I am not looking my best," I joked.

"No, not at all. You are truly lovely, and what a lovely glow you have around you. But there is one thing."

"What is that?"

"Your nose is very red. You need the African sun on your face."

"What a wonderful thought. That would be nice. But where exactly are you?"

He smiled and opened his arms wide before replying, then shouted at the top of his voice, "This is my Floating Land – Desert of Dreams. Now look further, Jessie, and enjoy."

My vision moved back from Luchendoo with speed and I saw that he was standing on a platform many hundreds of feet above the jungle below. Just as Bluebell Wood was surrounded by open, lush green fields, his Land was surrounded by sun-kissed sandy plains. In the distance a lake quenched the thirst of the local wildlife and, just like Bluebell Wood's lake, this, too, was a welcome stop for migrating birds.

Luchendoo's Floating Land was very exotic, but it only made me feel more for Bluebell Wood. Maybe it was part of the whole scheme, that we were chosen to suit our Lands. Luchendoo was definitely as proud of the Desert of Dreams as I would have been to show Bluebell Wood to a newcomer.

"Thank you, Luchendoo. I am honoured," I said, keen to be polite and not give away how loyal I felt to my own Land.

Luchendoo smiled broadly. "I am glad you like my world, and I wish the warmth to travel to you," he said, pushing at the air in front of him.

It was probably just in my mind, but I was sure I did feel a lovely sensation upon my body: it felt for a second as if a hot water bottle had been placed within my clothes.

"Jessie, answering your quest is okay at present, but when do you think you will return? There is an uneasy feeling amongst my wildlife. Something in the balance between the four Floating Lands is amiss and I am afraid for Bluebell Wood."

"I understand, Luchendoo. Two days at the very most," I replied, knowing that I should have already gone back, but my longing to follow Daisy had overtaken me.

"You look worried, Jessie. I didn't mean to concern you. Everything is in hand. You go and follow your quest and I will look forward to talking to you soon."

Luchendoo was nice, and I was pleased to make his acquaintance. Before he left my vision, he asked if I had met Yazko from the Mountains of Peace – the Asian Floating Land – or Charlie Barrett from the Americanas. I said that I hadn't, and he seemed pleased to be the first of the other Relayers to pass time with me.

He left my vision.

Boomer appeared once more, standing too close for me to focus completely on him.

"You nearly lost me over the side when you pulled your hood back," he said, really quite upset with me.

"Oh Boomer, I am sorry," I replied, feeling awful, as he had been standing in my hood when I threw it back to show Luchendoo what I looked like. "Are you okay?"

"Yes, but only because of my lightning reactions."

"Oh, good." I hadn't witnessed anything lightning about him, but I had seen him grow in confidence, so I didn't question his new speedy reflexes.

CHAPTER 25

Remember Me, Sister Bernadette?

M y viewing with Luchendoo had taken quite a piece of our journey time, and when I gazed down below, I saw the ocean. I gasped with excitement. "How far, Boomer? How far to Ireland?"

"Look again and see the waves crash against the cliffs. I think we have arrived."

He was right. What a contrast to the snowy vision of the rooftops dipping and rising, simulating the sea. We now witnessed the might of the Irish ocean as it crashed against the ever-stubborn shoreline. The land here had missed the snowfall and it was a joy for our eyes to feast upon the rolling green around us. The sun shone brightly and, apart from the remaining cold, it was a glorious day.

"I know this landscape," Daisy shouted at the top of her voice. "I have flown it before. I remember it." She was excited, but also confused. She moved around in her seat, frantically peering from side to side. "It's not far, the orphanage, it's not far at all," she said, with the enthusiasm of a child returning home from a long summer term at boarding school. Her excitement continued as we zoomed further inland.

She then pushed me harder than intended in my back.

"We should land, Jessie. We should land in that field right there."

I turned the plane hard to my right. I circled low a couple of times, scaring the horses in a neighbouring field, causing them to kick and gallop, but thankfully they skidded to a halt at the dividing stone wall.

Boomer sat on my lap and pushed his little fingers hard into my thighs as his excitement grew like a small volcano inside him.

My intended landing site was a flat field that rose to quite a hill on the far side. From the air the grass looked flat enough, and I was sure it would hold enough moisture for the skis that had replaced the wheels as landing gear. Nevertheless, it was going to be bumpy.

I slowed the de Havilland as much as physically possible without it dropping from the sky, and we hit hard, and then slid at great speed. We rattled along, shaking so vigorously that all I could do through my blurred vision was to hold the plane straight. We could feel ourselves glide as we reached the hilly gradient at the far side, came to a gentle halt, and slid a little back.

I breathed deeply with Daisy and a very shaken Boomer, who still didn't fear flying. He loved it, even when it was undertaken so incorrectly.

I don't know if it was nerves or excitement, but I started to laugh, and then I couldn't stop. Daisy joined me, and then Boomer, and we just laughed and laughed, only stopping when I was so short of breath that it was beginning to hurt.

Even with my fears and concerns for us all, I remained happy. I felt fantastic.

We climbed from the plane, and Daisy beckoned us forward, marching so quickly through the damp grass that I, with Boomer within my pocket, had to do little spurts of running to keep up.

"Wait up, Daisy," I said as we reached the stone wall that divided the fields from a small track.

Daisy levered herself over in one leap, but the wall was much more of a challenge to someone of my height. With both hands I pulled myself onto my stomach and fell head first into the long grass the other side, to the yelps of an alarmed Boomer.

"Are you okay, Boomer?" I called, patting my pocket.

"Yes, but warn me next time, Jessie!" came his tiny voice in response.

"Here's your warning!" Daisy cried, as she picked me up by my hood and dragged me back to my feet. She held me high for a second, then gently lowered me until my boots, that were already walking, found the ground and I was off. She linked my arm with hers.

"I remember all of this, Jessie. It is so wonderful to find something of your childhood again."

I looked up at her wide eyes as they flicked around, remembering each tree that we passed, and each footstep upon the old tarmac that had failed many years ago, leaving it deep with potholes as nature reclaimed it. A wall rose to our right and a green-panelled rear gate stood within it.

Daisy pulled at the latch, which opened, but not the gate.

"It must be bolted from the other side," I said, stating the obvious, as Daisy then fixed her hands together and smiled.

221

"Come, then, give me your foot," she said, laughing as I steadied myself by pulling at her hair. "Brace yourself again, Boomer!"

Daisy was strong and she almost flew me over the top, but I steadied myself on my stomach on top of the wall.

"It is quite a drop, Daisy," I said, sliding off my stomach and dangling, not wanting to let go. But my strength left me and I landed, luckily on a deep bed of leaves. I lay still as I always had, mentally checking my body for damage, but all seemed well. "Okay, Boomer?" I asked. A slightly dishevelled face appeared out of my coat, nodding, so I jumped to my feet. I was a little annoyed when I realised I had to climb the gate once more to reach the bolt, but I freed it quite easily and we were all back together.

There was a small garden shed to our left and a pathway running through the nettles and bracken either side of us.

Daisy led once more, telling me to hold my hands high so as not to get stung by the leaves. We walked through a stone arch and onto a beautiful lawn that led to a magnificent mansion of reddish stone with a slate roof. It reminded me of Granton Manor, except that it felt more imposing than my home.

To the right, a section of lawn had been set aside for allotments. The nuns and young children who were working them had not yet noticed us within their grounds. But all children's minds wander. One little boy's head lifted and he stared at us.

"There's funny people over there, Sister." All heads turned and faced us.

A large nun ordered everybody to stay still as she approached us. She was a very big woman with the hardest of faces, but her glow was a welcoming white, so I ignored my longing to run for the gate.

"This is private property. I don't know how many times I have told you gypsies that."

She said these words not with anger, as her body language would suggest, but with the sweetest Irish accent.

Daisy stepped forward. "I am sorry to startle you, Sister, but we are not gypsies. We are on a journey and I really need to speak with Sister Bernadette or Sister Bridget."

The nun stopped a short distance before us.

"And what would you be wanting with them, may I ask?" She looked closely at Daisy's face. "I do indeed recognise you. Now, how would I know you?"

Daisy smiled. "I came here as a very small child, but that is all I know."

The nun stared a little longer at Daisy and then at me. She turned to her fellow sisters and the children who looked inquisitively on.

"Get back to your digging, there is nothing to see here," she called, but still softly, and then turned back to us. "You had best come with me, then. I can't be having you confusing my day like this. Mother Superior, that is Bernadette, will tell me if indeed you did attend St Bede's."

"Bernadette is Mother Superior now? How wonderful!" Daisy exclaimed, clapping her hands, and the nun briefly turned her head back to Daisy as we entered through a large open doorway.

This led us not into the front of the building, but down a large corridor. The ceilings were higher than I had ever seen, sitting upon Saxon-shaped arches made from beautiful carved wood. Apart from the rendered walls, it was as if a large ship had been turned upside down, and the hull was now the ceiling.

At the end we turned right and entered a small hall that had little light. The walls were now panelled wood, as were the stairs that led to a mezzanine floor which ran around the whole hall. Some children peered over the edge of the mezzanine, their chins barely reaching the dark wood. They tilted their heads to see us, straining their eyes to see below. They moved back when the nuns stared at them, but you could hear them giggling as they ducked quickly out of sight.

"Wait here," the nun said, and she knocked on a large studded wooden door, and then entered. Within seconds she returned. "Mother Superior will see you now," she said, holding the door open for us.

The entrance was wide enough for me and Daisy to enter together, and it felt as if I was back at school, being summoned to the headmistress's office for yet another dressing-down.

Mother Superior sat behind a large desk. She finished her reading, gently placed a bookmark, and slowly closed the pages. She rested both hands upon the cover of the book and tapped it, still deep in thought from her reading. She raised her head slightly and shifted her eyes towards us.

She had a gentleness in her fine face, and a kindness in her eyes, but still, whether or not because of her position here, I instantly felt that absolutely no nonsense would be tolerated.

I stared first at her and then up towards Daisy.

Daisy's face was alive. "Bernadette!" she gasped, then quickly corrected herself. "I'm sorry, I mean, Mother Superior."

"Well, you obviously know who I am," Mother Superior said with a concerned smile. "But when will I discover who you are?"

Daisy stepped forward, pushing the tops of her thighs against the desk. "It's me, Bernadette, it's Daisy. Don't you know me? It's me." Daisy threw her hands around her excited face, framing it, waiting for Mother Superior to acknowledge her and remember the young girl who had once lived here.

Mother Superior sat back in her chair. "My dear child, you do have the look of a particular young girl I knew, but that, for sure, would be ghostly, so it must be just a similarity."

"No, it's me." Daisy insisted that she be recognised.

Mother Superior stared at us both, then spoke. "You have a good, but somewhat unruly way to the pair of you. Now sit down, both of you, and explain to me your purpose here and who indeed you wish to be."

She had summed us up quite well, so I for one was happy to sit down and have a chat with her. Daisy flopped in the chair next to me and I couldn't help but feel sorry for her. This was the one part of her life she could remember yet the nun whom she so clearly knew didn't recognise her in return.

"That girl you said I have the look of, what was her name?" Daisy said, leaning forward and looking at Mother Superior with eyes wide and mouth open.

I couldn't help but giggle, as Daisy now looked to me like my dog, Tansy, waiting to be rewarded with her treat. Daisy's head spun round to me and she gave me a stern stare. Then she resumed her pose towards Mother Superior, waiting expectantly.

"Her name was indeed Daisy, but I feel out of turn talking of her, as she is regrettably no longer with us," Mother Superior replied, dipping her eyes downwards with sadness, then looking back towards Daisy. "So, my dear girl, you will have to enlighten me as to who you are."

I wished Daisy would let it lie, or at least her questioning about the poor deceased Daisy, but she wouldn't. "How did she die?"

Mother Superior fixed her gaze hard onto my friend, her fingers separated, and she slowly clawed the leather cover of the book.

"What is this interrogation from a girl I have never seen before?" she said, not shouting, but her lips were tight and she squeezed her words through clenched teeth.

"I am sorry if I have made you angry, but please tell me how she died."

"Enough." Mother Superior slammed her hands onto the desk and shot to her feet. The door flew open behind us and our escorting nun hurried in. Mother Superior marched around the desk. "Who are you, girl? State your purpose here this very instant or leave this second."

Daisy didn't rise. She instead took hold of the rosary around Mother Superior's waist. Her eyes filled with tears as she looked up towards her, and her shoulders dropped. "Please remember me, Bernadette. A mother wouldn't forget her child, and in my heart you were my mother. Why don't you know me?"

Daisy's pain froze me. How alone Daisy was, to hold someone so dear after such a short encounter.

Mother Superior's eyes glazed with imprisoned desire to recognise Daisy, but she felt for her loss and ran her fingers through Daisy's hair. She spoke so softly that her words left her mouth like song. "Who I am to you I am not, but who you wish me to be I am."

Daisy held Mother Superior's hand, tilted her head, and placed the side of her face within her palm. She closed her eyes and a tear left her long eyelashes and ran free, finding its end under the gold band upon Mother Superior's ring finger. Her eyelids fluttered, failing to hold the tears that now poured down her distraught face. She opened her eyes and stared at the floor. She looked at Mother Superior's tiny black shoes and followed the line of her black dress. She stopped at her waist and stared at the rosary that hung there, clasping it again and as she had all those years ago.

"Remember, Bernadette, I never let this go, and you were happy for me to be by your side?" Daisy stared up to her.

Mother Superior pulled her right hand sharply to her mouth and gasped.

"Now I remember! A pretty little girl who followed my every movement, holding the rosary like a lead, questioning life without taking a breath."

Daisy jumped in. "Remember the bluebells I painted with you by my side, and how the next day they appeared within the lawns just as I had imagined them? Remember the goodnight rhyme you would say, 'Take the best of today and bring it for tomorrow, and let the bad stay in the past with yesterday's sorrow'? These are all the things and the only things I remember of my life, so please tell me why I am me."

The room fell silent, but it no longer felt awkward. Daisy rose to her feet.

"When I hold you, feel beneath my skin and kiss the tears that run from my eyes."

Mother Superior kissed each of Daisy's eyes, and tears now fell from the little nun's face.

"Oh my dear child," she cried softly. "Welcome home, my dear girl."

They embraced like loved ones reunited. A glow of the purest white emanated between them, but not so bright that it hurt to see.

I turned to our escorting nun and held out my hand. For me, this was just part of a long list of events that were unanswered. I was carrying a little Bella in my pocket, after all, as if it were normal, so anything was possible. But this poor nun, who just a moment ago had been enjoying the fruits of her labour within the allotment, looked positively faint.

"What is your name?" I asked.

"It is Sister Helen," she replied, shuffling forward and squeezing my hand tight.

"It is nice to meet you, Sister Helen. This is a good moment, so don't be afraid," I said reassuringly.

I am sure she wanted to say more but her reply of "Okay" seemed just fine.

Mother Superior pulled away from Daisy, smiled and said, "My whole life has been focused upon trust and belief. You did indeed hold something precious within you, just as I witnessed, when at the age of six you painted that almost perfect picture of bluebells. I kept it our secret when the very next day you and I witnessed that they had appeared overnight, just as your painting had portrayed. Do you remember that the rest of the sisters and my predecessor, Mother Agnes, believed that we truly had a prodigy within our midst, and soon you were in all the papers?"

Daisy's mood had lightened and she relished Bernadette speaking about herself and her past. She looked back to me and Sister Helen nodding as if she were very important and, for now, the only one in the world to be spoken about. Her eyes sparkled as she laughed along with Bernadette when she remembered how funny little Daisy was with the flashing photography from the reporters.

"Yes, yes," Daisy joined in. "I thought it was lightning in their hands. I remember that so very well."

"Your painting still hangs within the main hall. Would you like to see it?" Mother Superior asked.

"Oh please, yes," I cried, no longer able to keep out of their reminiscing.

Mother Superior peered around Daisy towards me and asked tentatively, moving her hand in time with her words, "Are you a…?"

She paused.

"Am I what?" I asked, truly not knowing what she thought my form was.

"Are you the same as Daisy?"

"An orphan? No, my parents are dead, but I don't need looking after now."

Daisy laughed. "My sweet Jessie, haven't you worked it out yet?" she said.

I felt stupid that I had missed something obvious, but I had stopped trying to work anything obvious out the day I arrived at Bluebell Wood.

The two nuns and Daisy stared at me, and Daisy walked forward and held me so tightly that I thought I would burst. She whispered into my ear, "I am an angel, my sweet Jessie."

I tried to move to look at Daisy's face, but my body dropped within her arms. Her lips tingled on my cheeks as she pulled them round to my mouth. I wanted to feel her breath inside me and for my spirit to dance with hers. I had never felt this way before. I was bathed in desire to love and caress, to a point which I could only experience out of this body. She lessened her hold on me and my normal feeling returned. I pulled her back, wanting to feel that way again, but she just smiled and said, "Let us see the painting."

"An angel," I said under my breath. "An angel, how wonderful!" I paused. As usual, a question came to mind. "So definitely not a ghost, then?"

I wondered what the difference between the two was, and then instantly wondered if the question would be offensive.

"Crikey, no, Jessie. I have thoughts and feelings, and sadly ghosts mostly have neither. They have just failed to move on, at least until a message or forgiveness has rendered them free."

I stumbled after Daisy and the nuns as they headed for the painting. "An angel," I murmured, still stunned at the revelation, my shock rendering my limbs somewhat sluggish as I struggled to keep up. "An angel," I repeated, in awe, as my brain worked as slowly as my body to take in the news.

"But surely this changes everything?" I whispered.

CHAPTER 26

Daisy's Fate in a Little Black Box

On our way to the main hall, I saw the little faces peering over the banister at us again. This was their house and, like any other children, they were inquisitive about the strangers within it.

Daisy walked with Mother Superior, and Sister Helen had slowed down to walk with me. She was still in silent thought, for which I couldn't blame her. Every turn of this magnificent house brought memories rushing back to Daisy. She entered the main hall and onto a raised platform at one end. The wall to our right was dark panelled wood, as was the ceiling. The carving upon it was exquisite but simple. Entire flowers had been carved, including stems, leaves and petals. Others featured large petals alone.

It would have felt cold and harsh had it not been for the abundance of natural light that entered through large lattice windows running the length of the left-hand wall and the wall adjacent to us. Each of these windows rested in their own bay, creating wide sills that had been used for sitting on through many generations.

Daisy rushed to push her face hard against the glass. "I can see the small lake. I remember all too well being told, 'Don't go to the lake unsupervised, children'." Daisy laughed at the memory while repeating the instruction in a poor impression of an Irish accent. She sat on the sill. "This is where I sat, Bernadette, isn't it?"

Bernadette smiled at her. "It is indeed. And look, can you see your picture?"

Mother Superior spoke to her as almost all parents do, never realising that they have grown, but always seeing a small child in the teenager or adult's place.

But Daisy was that young child as she peered around the room. Between each window was a column which displayed with pride the finest art which St Bede's Orphanage had produced. Daisy got to her feet and rushed from column to column, stopping in the centre with a squeal.

"It's here, Bernadette, just as fresh as the day I painted it."

I hopped down from the platform and rushed to see.

"My word!" I gasped. It was truly breathtaking. The texture of the paint pulled you in to the tiny area of trees. Bluebells stretched and opened upon the light green grass. Their colour soft and sweet, they enjoyed the sunlight that played hide-and-seek through the trees, catching the occasional petal, giving it the illusion of being a different shade from the rest of the flower. The leaves in the trees pulled just a little to the right, expressing perfectly a gentle summer's breeze. As I stared, transfixed by their sway, I awaited that same breeze to stroke gently past my face. The painting was set in a bevel-edged frame, at the bottom of which was a small brass nameplate: 'Daisy Dreamer, aged six'.

"Daisy, you are a marvellous artist. To paint a picture this good at any age is remarkable, but at six years old! I can quite understand the fuss that was made of you," I exclaimed.

"Thank you, Jessie. Painting for me is not a task or something to be pored over. What I visualise appears. It is a purpose, and my whole being embellishes it."

"Why did I not know this before about you, Daisy? And why are there no more paintings?" I asked, longing to understand more of my friend through her work.

"I don't know," Daisy replied, and then she turned to Mother Superior. "Why aren't there any more, Bernadette?"

"Well, there may be, Daisy, but not here. You see, if you can remember, it was interest in you and your painting that caught the attention of Rupert Charles Granton."

"That's my great-grandad's name!" I shouted, shocked.

"Well, you should be very proud, as he was the loveliest of men. Such a gentleman, and a very generous donor to the orphanage."

"It's nice of you to say so, but I never met him. I thought he had died in the First World War," I said, again feeling utterly confused and a little disappointed, as now my own family history seemed to be entirely wrong.

"Isn't this terrific?" Daisy said, pulling at my sleeve. "Maybe we're related in some way." Her face looked full of joy and her eyes danced with delight. For Daisy, every piece of information or memory was a tiny section of a lost life placed back together. So I didn't want to spoil her joy. I smiled as widely as possible and joined in her happiness.

Mother Superior nodded. "That's right – he adopted you, Daisy. In fact, I still have the paper clippings of the day he came to collect you. Would you like to see?"

"Oh yes, please," Daisy and I replied as one.

I turned to Daisy. "So, you really are related to me. I can't believe it!"

Daisy grinned and squeezed my hand, before pulling me along to follow Mother Superior and Sister Helen once more through the house.

Children and nuns alike passed us and smiled. The children giggled at our appearance and the nuns stared in disbelief that two girls looking as scruffy and dirty as ourselves would walk with Mother Superior. The cleanliness of the building was clear. Not a speck of dust was present and not a footprint on the vinyl flooring. It made the corridor quite sterile, almost like I would imagine a Victorian hospital to be.

Our journey ended at the far side of the building. The whispering of the nuns and the secret laughter of children had passed. We approached two large doors, which Sister Helen opened together. They brushed the surface of the luxurious carpet that awaited us the other side. Daisy and I stared down at our big boots and then at each other.

"Would it be best if we were to remove these, Bernadette?" Daisy said.

"No, child," she answered. "I think that the mud off your feet has long displaced itself in the corridors."

Both Daisy and I peered back, and indeed the only prints you could see upon the vinyl were our own.

"Sorry," we said, ashamed.

Mother Superior and Sister Helen laughed. "I don't know about you, Jessie, but Daisy was always one for finding nature and bringing it back into our home," Mother Superior said, remembering the young Daisy whose eyes now filled up as she recognised her past.

"Yes, I was very much the same, and by the looks of things, I still am," I replied, chuckling.

The room that we entered must indeed, after the chapel, have been the most important to the residents. It was the grandest library I had ever seen. To my right, upon the dark red, deep-pile carpet, were the reading desks, maybe ten or so hand-polished teak tables which were each home to four chairs. In front of each chair was a brass reading lamp, highly polished, not a fingerprint in sight. They would only be used after sunset, as the room had been designed for natural light. Along the length of the wall facing us was glass set in stone arches, reaching up to the second-floor ceiling. Row upon row of bookcases started where the lavish carpet ended. They went full-height to the top of the ceiling and were built upon hardwood parquet flooring. Metal tracks for the ladders ran the length of them. A child, or indeed an adult, would have found it almost irresistible to climb to the very top rung and then be whisked along by a fellow student with equally high spirits.

Mother Superior asked us to sit down, so we did.

We waited in silence, as the room itself had ordered us to do so by its very ambience. She soon returned, holding a small black box and a newspaper.

"You made the front page, Daisy," she said, as she carefully and with some pride laid the paper out in front of us.

The headline boldly read:

The Weekly Chronicle
Daisy's Dreams Do Come True

"How exciting, Daisy," I said, then got to my feet and leant over her shoulder.

Daisy couldn't hear me, but she moved her hand across and tightly clasped my fingers. With her other hand she ran her index finger against the large black and white picture in the centre of the page, and then gently stroked the face of the little girl who stood next to a very smartly dressed man. I couldn't see his face as it was shadowed by the rim of his trilby hat. A short, heavy-set nun stood to the other side of the girl, and next to her was a very young Bernadette, who was quite recognisable by her slightly lopsided smile and slender build.

But what I recognised even more easily was my beautiful de Havilland, which made a perfect backdrop as it waited to fly this little Daisy away for her new life.

Daisy still stared hard at the little girl. "That is me, isn't it, Bernadette? I look very happy," she said.

Bernadette sat down and faced us. "You were always happy, Daisy," she said, and smiled sadly. "As the article said, you were the most fortunate little girl in the world to be adopted by one of the wealthiest and most revered families in England, and to be taken with Rupert Granton to Fairbanks in Alaska, where he was to lay claim to land for new gold-mining. There you would have private tuition and learn the family business first-hand. As I recall, when the two of you first met, it was just as if you already knew each other. You had no hesitation around Rupert, and you couldn't wait to fly away to your new life.

"But before you left, he asked if he could talk with me in private, as it was clear for all to see the bond that had developed between us. You still held fast to the rosary, believing that I was to join you in your new life. He said, 'It's clear, this young girl's skill as an artist, but is there anything else, anything that should remain between ourselves?' I was certain that I should not answer him, but his bright blue eyes pulled the secret from within me, and so I readily told him about the sudden growth of the bluebells in the garden. His eyes sparkled and his smile produced within me feelings towards this man that were truly improper. He thanked me for my natural judgement in my handling of this incident and of you. I promised that I would never speak of it again and I was left to explain to you that I must remain at the orphanage.

"Rupert wrote to me on your behalf and then, as you grew, you wrote yourself. You spoke of two magical places. One was Alaska, which you described beautifully, saying it was so fresh that you could still see the fingerprint of God on the land. And another place, which I thought at the time was a child's fantasy, called Bluebell Wood. You wrote so fondly of the creatures within the wood that I couldn't wait for your next letter, as I loved to hear about all of their adventures."

Mother Superior smiled with joy as Sister Helen sat alongside her.

"Tell me, is Bluebell Wood a real place?" she asked.

I guess I should have let Daisy answer, but I couldn't contain myself. "Oh, it is," I said, relishing the thought of it. "It is real and wonderful."

"And what about the Bellas: Oakleigh, Bluebell, and Willoughby, and that newborn, Leanndi?" Mother Superior asked, leaning forward, her face glowing, awaiting to unwrap the next truth.

"All true, all of it. But, of course, very secret," I continued, feeling positively mysterious, as I knew so much about a world many could only fantasise about.

Sister Helen agreed heartily, pledging her silence to me. "Oh yes, the secret's safe. Oh yes, indeed." Sister Helen was trying her best to understand, sweetly frowning and nodding in the correct places.

"Please tell me, do you know how and when I died?" Daisy asked these words calmly, but they still silenced us.

I rested my face into her neck and held her tightly. Although she had earlier shown herself in her true, beautiful light, to me she was a young, confused girl who wanted reason to come back into her existence.

"I don't even know how old I am to be," Daisy continued, slumping back into her chair. "The date on this paper is 1948 and I am six there. I should be sixty-four, which I am clearly not. So, do you know what happened, Bernadette?"

"Yes, Daisy," Mother Superior said, as she pulled the black box to herself and took from it a folded newspaper page. Her hands shook and tears filled the corners of her eyes. "You can quite understand why I did not believe that it was you earlier, when this paper had pictured your death, breaking my heart. Until today, when you have helped restore its well-being. But not that I shall ever feel joy for your life, as I did then, because your torment and sadness are, I fear, beyond any healing love that I can give."

Daisy slid the paper away from Mother Superior and fixed her eyes upon her. "Bernadette, you gave me love and the only memory I have of my life as a child. Nothing in my life will ever be purer or so clear. What this paper says is what I shall come to terms with and it will help me to understand my future."

The headline was as bold as the joyful one that had rejoiced in her good fortune, but this was in total contrast.

**Community Grieves for
Poor Little Daisy Dreamer**

Daisy's back straightened as she began to read aloud.

"'Local girl Daisy Dreamer Granton tragically died yesterday. Reliable sources say she was trapped alone when the mine she was in collapsed during blasting for its next stage of further excavation. Rescue workers dug for many hours, only to find their efforts to be futile as this beautiful young lady was brought to the surface, unmarked but for two small trickles of blood from each ear. It is believed that she died from dust inhalation when checking samples deep inside the mine. Explosive experts said that every check had been made and everyone who had signed the site book had been accounted for. It is a great sadness that human error on Daisy Dreamer Granton's part led to her death.'"

Daisy didn't flinch. Her posture remained the same, her hands steady, holding the page. "Friday the sixth of May 1958 this page is dated, and I had already been dead for one day. That would make me sixteen." She was calm and precise.

Sister Helen, Mother Superior and I didn't speak. What could we say? We let Daisy have her silence in peace and listened when she spoke.

"I did remember a blast," Daisy said, "but I had no idea where or when it happened. It is just the pain I felt in my ears that worried me." She laid the page flat to the table, but still fixed her eyes downward, remembering snippets as she creased her forehead and squinted. "I have roamed as an angel, returning to Bluebell Wood on occasions, and Bella safe houses across Europe, but one request rings in me and torments me. 'Don't show your gift even in death. It can and will be your demise.' Do you have a picture of Rupert Granton?" Daisy lifted her eyes. "His face is not at all clear in this one."

Mother Superior lifted the lid back off the black box and took from within it several pictures.

"All of these were taken on the day that you left, by our sweet departed Sister Stella," Mother Superior said, smiling as she shuffled through them and then passed them, one at a time, to Daisy.

I leant into Daisy's side again and inquisitively looked on. I, too, longed to see a better picture of my great-grandfather and more of that day. The first of the pictures were just like the one in the newspaper, taken at a slightly better angle. Then a very sweet one of Daisy and then, as she had been, Sister Bernadette. It was clear, in this black and white picture, the affection between the two of them, as little Daisy, holding onto the rosary around Bernadette's waist, stared up to her, head slightly tilted, smiling fondly. Bernadette looked at the little girl and held her loving hand out for Daisy to rest her little face upon. As Daisy took hold of the next picture, she giggled as she remembered.

"It was funny, I remember this man holding me and I kept knocking his hat to the floor."

"That man is Rupert Granton," Mother Superior said, smiling in fond memory of him.

I leant so hard into Daisy that she slid a little along the table. I gazed at the picture and the man holding this beautiful, giggling little girl and I did indeed recognise him, but not as a family member.

"That's Grandad! Our Grandad from Bluebell Wood!" I screamed, rudely snatching the picture from Daisy's hand, and staring closely at the man whom I had grown to love and trust in Bluebell Wood, only to be disappointed when he had vanished from my life. He was quite a bit younger, of course, but his eyes were the same: kind and loving.

"Did you know this was Grandad?" I questioned Daisy, holding the picture back in front of her.

"No. Since my death, I have never seen him again. I have communicated with the man you call Grandad, but sadly he has been invisible to me."

"But do you remember him as your adoptive father?"

Daisy replied tentatively. "I do. With every second, a little more returns."

I wasn't sure if it was hunger or my upset for Daisy, but I suddenly felt very ill at ease. My body felt frightened; the blood drained from my face. Daisy turned and stared up at me as I sloped like a dead weight into her side.

"I feel it too, Jessie," she said. "We need to go, Bernadette. I promise I shall return." Daisy held her hand out to Mother Superior, who, in turn, held it and kissed each of Daisy's fingers individually, and spoke tenderly. "I shall long for that day, my sweet child, and I shall pray for your soul to be forever in peace."

Daisy stood and held me. "Steady yourself, Jessie. You need to communicate with your Bellas."

I mumbled my goodbyes, holding myself up with Daisy. I felt awful. My head spun and my body was weak. I longed for the cold air to revive me. Daisy's arm held me fast and, not for the first time, I was pleased to be supported by her gentle strength.

"Just one second, Jessie," Daisy said to me as she turned back to Mother Superior. "Take this gold, Bernadette." She pulled from her parka one of the gold bars and handed it to her. Sister Helen choked at the sight, and Mother Superior struggled to keep the weight of the gold free from the table. This act of generosity silenced any further goodbyes, and

Daisy and I hurried through the corridors and burst into the garden.

I stopped and pulled the cold air into my lungs. It was now damp and heavy as the sun drew a curtain on the day. My senses returned fully as we made our way back to the plane. The stone wall that I had struggled to negotiate earlier became nothing but a small obstacle. In her stride, Daisy pulled me under her arm as she levered herself with one hand to the other side. She only put me back to my feet as we reached the de Havilland, and then perched me upon the wing.

"Well, I guess your great-grandad's goldmine in Alaska would explain the gold that I have in abundance, and the money." She paused, lost in thought. "I wonder if I have just kept helping myself to it over the years. I don't even remember." Daisy then pondered this, before she said kindly, "You must communicate now, Jessie."

I was indeed now all of a fluster and jumped when Boomer's little head appeared from my pocket and said, "Are we flying again?"

Yet again I had forgotten about Boomer, who seemed to have the remarkable ability to stay quiet during some of the most extraordinary events I had ever witnessed. For him, it was clearly preferable to remain absent from these episodes, making sure to only reappear when we were about to fly.

CHAPTER 27

Fading Life in Bluebell Wood

Daisy took Boomer, leaving me to put my goggles in place. The bright light shone and what a joyful sight as Willoughby appeared, sitting bolt upright upon the pew at 125 Spencer Street.

"Hello, Jessie, are you well?" he said, wincing a little as he smiled. His face was still quite swollen, but greatly improved.

"Oh Willoughby, what a brave chap you are. You saved my life! I feel just terrible for putting you in that situation."

He smiled again as Archie came into view and rested his massive head, groaning and moaning, affectionately across his lap.

"You did what you felt was right," Willoughby said, patting Archie's head. "I am sure that you learned a great deal from Wilson that you may not even realise until it comes into use."

Bluebell joined Willoughby on the pew and asked, "And what about Ireland?"

"So much to tell," I replied, excited at the thought of

sitting with them again, of course with a nice cup of tea, and explaining Daisy's wonderful past. "But that will have to wait for now. I had the most awful feeling that something was wrong. Where are Leanndi and Oakleigh?"

"They are downstairs playing with the modes of transport," Bluebell answered, laughing.

"But what about Claudius and the Roman army?" I asked. "Many hours have passed. Surely he should be with you now." I felt the pull to be in several different places at once.

Willoughby took his hat from his side and placed it, as always, tilted upon his head. "I do agree with you, Jessie," he said, "but the sound of battle would echo through the passageways like thunder, and it has been so very quiet."

"Nevertheless," I said, "I shall try and contact Claudius. Something is wrong."

I drew my vision away and thought of Claudius, but could make out nothing but blackness. My concentration for Claudius was clear, but he wouldn't appear.

Then a voice from within the darkness whispered, "Jessie, you are with me, but I fear I cannot talk."

"Claudius, are you okay? Just answer me that."

I realised that the blackness was the tunnel. He didn't answer, but I could hear the compressed breathing of thousands of soldiers waiting still for their command to fight. Water dripped like a heartbeat, counting in time for hell to be unleashed. Claudius spoke, but not to me, nor in a whisper. His voice was strong as he commanded, "Shields tight! Close unit."

Out of the eerie silence came a deafening crash as the shields locked together to create their fighting tortoise formation, covering their top and sides. I could feel Claudius's breath as if I were standing beside him, as he inhaled deeply to roar like a lion. Flames lit the gloom as fireballs slammed into his mighty army.

"Hold fast!" he screamed as the Malissols' venom filled the tunnel ahead, lit by their own flames, battle-axes swaying in a hurricane of speed and noise that locked in brutal combat with the Roman army.

The Malissols hit so hard that the first line of the Romans collapsed under their sheer power, only to be replaced by another. Claudius stood exposed as his army regrouped, and he screamed for Doggett to show himself, only to be set upon by several Malissols. His army once more encased him and he called for lightning speed. The Romans moved as a train, spears forward, choosing rapid movement to match the free-fighting storm of the Malissols. The Romans clashed with such ferocity that their train continued over the front line of the soldiers and rolled through, destroying all in its wake. It rocked through the tunnel like flooding water, burying the Malissols' attack underfoot, Claudius's perfect war machine impaling its enemy by spear and sword or slamming it with force. The Malissols were destroyed where they stood as if by volcanic lava, embedded now within the damp clay of the tunnel.

Claudius was now out of sight amongst the mayhem, but his voice spoke to me as if he were standing at the entrance of my ear.

"Jessie, there has been little resistance to our charge. This battle will be won, but I feel we have conquered only the smallest part of the Malissols. Tell Willoughby to secure the hatch to Spencer Street, as the handful that fled may be pushed towards it."

"Oh my word, Claudius," I replied. "I shall do that this very instant. Please be careful, Claudius."

My mind quickly returned to Spencer Street, not to the pew as I had expected, but to the cellar where my four little ones stood side by side staring, heads cocked, into the dark tunnel where the battle cries continued and the thunderous noise grew closer.

Leanndi, remembering her previous terror of the Malissols in the tunnel, said sweetly, "I think we should all sit upstairs. It is quite chilly down here."

Oakleigh agreed, giving a little shiver. Willoughby was clearly not ready for another fight. Bluebell, taking all the decision to move from the cellar onto herself, said to Willoughby, "These young Bellas really do feel the cold, don't they? Come, then, we'd best get back upstairs."

She held out her little gloved hand to Leanndi, and they all scampered quickly up the steps. I didn't have to tell Willoughby to secure the hatch as he and Oakleigh did it immediately on reaching the top.

Arthur awaited their return, with Archie nosily looking on.

"Good move!" he said, when the hatch was tightly shut down. "Shall we have some tea?"

I watched them, but didn't get involved. Instead I returned to Daisy and Boomer by removing my goggles.

"The best of news," I said, slightly short of breath, as my mind had just been within the heart of a battle. "Claudius has almost certainly defeated the Malissols within the tunnel." I was pleased with the way everything was panning out, but I still felt terribly shaky.

Something awful was beginning to turn my stomach, twisting at my insides. I doubled over, holding my chest.

"What's happening to me, Daisy?"

She rushed forward and steadied me.

"Be strong, Jessie. You are feeling pain from another source," she said, fighting with me to stand straight and place the goggles back onto my eyes. I thought her touch would lessen my pain, but not this time: she was rough with me as she pulled my goggles down.

Within that second the light appeared and my pain eased. Luchendoo stood as before with his monocle placed to his right eye, and spoke.

"I can see you now, Jessie, and by the look of you, I guess you have already felt it."

He didn't smile, as he had done so warmly before. In fact, he looked quite as shaken as I felt. The Desert of Dreams, in contrast to earlier, was totally silent. No birdsong, not a sound from the millions of insects, and the watering lake in the far distance was deserted.

"What happened, Luchendoo? What's wrong?" I asked, concerned that his island of beauty and life was so sad and still.

"Jessie, it is not the Desert of Dreams that is in trouble, but Bluebell Wood. I fear that it is fading as we speak, and the balance of the four Lands has been disconnected."

"I don't understand, Luchendoo. What do you mean, it's fading?" I asked, as my heartbeat raced and pushed the blood hard around my poor body that was already under so much stress.

Luchendoo's wide-eyed gaze stopped my racing heart, just momentarily, before it raced forward again.

"Your Land has for many years been vulnerable, as its core of life has been taken from it," he said.

"I don't understand. It's the most beautiful place. Nature is so at home there."

"But it has struggled to maintain its life since your Daughter of Nature was frightened away, Jessie," he continued.

I felt angry and frustrated.

"Please talk in words that mean something to me," I snapped.

Luchendoo held his hands out. "Please be calm and I will tell you," he said.

I bit hard into my lip and listened.

"The Mother of all Nature had four daughters whom she entrusted to the four Floating Lands. Each of these is to ensure that the world beneath them stays as it should. But as Mother Nature is volatile and short in temper, if the world disturbs her beauty, she unleashes her ferocity of power to remind all below that she can discipline the world in a way that mankind cannot match. The four Daughters have their mother's temperament, and can change the world with the stroke of a brush or the note of a song, but their real strength is the connection of the four of them around the world from the Floating Lands. Since the beginning of time, evil, as we call it, has longed to break this chain and to rest its hand on one of the Daughters. It was Mother Nature's volatile temperament that sent Bluebell Wood's Daughter away, and she has looked for her in the deepest of pain and regret ever since."

"Why would she send her away?" I asked, enjoying the idea of four Daughters of Nature.

"Greschen – that is Bluebell Wood's Daughter – was the last born and left quite alone to rejoice in everything she felt, touched, and laid her eyes on. She was so overwhelmed with the gift that she possessed that she would dance, sing and paint, never stopping or tiring of the beauty that she saw in every second."

"So why did Mother Nature send her away?" I asked again.

"Greschen had so much love for creating that she longed to share it, so she began sending her creativity to poets, composers and artists in the world below. Many of these men and women couldn't control their gift from her and they would become unbalanced and suffer greatly. It drove many insane and shortened their lives. In a moment of rage with Greschen, Mother Nature came down on her so hard that it frightened her, and she fled and has been looked for by good and evil ever since."

"So why today is the Land fading? And tell me what I can do to save it," I said, remembering not just the nature that was the Land, but the many wonderful young and old Bellas who loved it as their home.

Luchendoo shifted on his feet and took a deep breath before continuing.

"A darkness has dulled the light of Bluebell Wood and has all but extinguished it, and evil is making its home there. Yazko from the Asian Floating Land – Mountain of Peace – spoke of monstrous noises stirring in the mountains that create her Land. Charlie Barrett from the Americanas spoke of cracks the size of freeways stretching across his sandy plains. In your absence, and the absence of Greschen, your Land has been inhabited. I pray that the quest you have embarked upon is one of answers."

I felt my throat closing and the air that I breathed felt like dust. My eyes became gritty, causing me to close them tight. When I reopened them, tears ran down my face and my vision was blurred.

"It can do that, but you soon get used to it." A man spoke in a strong Texas drawl.

"What now?" I said, squinting to see who was within my vision.

"Now calm yourself, little lady, it is only your friendly neighbour, Charlie Barrett."

"Charlie Barrett, it is a pleasure to meet you, but my eyes appear to be struggling to see," I said, longing to remove my goggles and to rub them hard.

"Hold fast, little lady, they will soon adjust. You must have quite a connection to feel the sand in your eyes and mouth."

I coughed and agreed. I found this fine-looking man standing alone, gazing across the rugged terrain. He was dressed like the iconic figure of a Western cowboy, from his boots, denim trousers and shirt to his brown cowboy hat. He was indeed as rugged as the landscape he surveyed, but as handsome as the folklore of a gun-slinging hero.

"It would appear we have some rattlesnake sneaking around Bluebell Wood," he said.

"More of a herd of buffalo, I think." But it didn't sound right coming from my mouth. So I coughed politely and asked, "Do you know what I should do?"

He didn't answer, but he requested my company. "Walk with me, Jessie." He then climbed a small rock face and we looked out on mile upon mile of sandy plains that had been cracked like a shell, leaving a gaping canyon finding its way sharply across the land like lightning to earth.

"Is all this my fault?" I asked timidly. The scale of destruction and power was beyond words.

"No," he replied quietly, picking up a small rock from the ground.

"Not unless you created good and evil." He skimmed the rock into the never-ending canyon. "But first I think you need to get the Floating Land back. The balance is wrong and the Americanas are already drying out."

He pointed to his left where the vast plains continued. Across them were hundreds, if not thousands, of oil pumps, rocking and pumping, unaware of change, never stopping or slowing. Each one had a calm to it. Although they were magnificently large, they didn't intimidate: they were too busy minding their own purpose.

"Charlie?" I asked.

"Yes, little lady?"

"I am very surprised that you need to pump oil in your Land."

"So would I be," he said, laughing out loud. "It's not oil we drill for, but to the clouds below. It is just clear fresh water that is produced in these fields. It is a very different place to your Bluebell Wood."

It is, I thought, and that is what makes each Land so wonderfully special.

"Do you know the Daughter Greschen who is missing from Bluebell Wood?" I asked.

"Well, no, not personally, but I do know *of* her," Charlie replied.

"And do you know her sister who lives with you on your Land?"

Charlie laughed aloud again, pulled his cowboy hat to his thigh and slapped across it, bending forward as he did so.

"You make me laugh, little lady. Now that's a good thing. I would love to see her, but she is not for my eyes. That doesn't mean I don't feel her in the wind or taste her within the fresh stream."

"So, could I ever see Greschen if she was near me?"

"I guess if she chose it to be or if she was taken by surprise." I could see Charlie thinking about his reply. He placed his hat upon his head. "Now, you go and get that Land back and let me know if there is anything I can do."

I wanted to ask him to come with me, but I removed my goggles. When I saw Daisy's beautiful face looking down at me, I felt we were just fine as we were.

CHAPTER 28

Relaying the Worst of News

D aisy sat beside me on the wing of the plane and Boomer sat the other side. I relayed all that I had seen and all the words that had been spoken. Both Daisy and Boomer had heard the legend of the missing Greschen and both had longed for her return to Bluebell Wood, but neither Daisy nor Boomer understood how vulnerable Bluebell Wood had become.

If I had reflected on the decisions I'd made over the last forty-eight hours, I would have been so racked with guilt that I'd have lain on the ground beneath the wing and curled up and died for sure. But I was driven by one belief: that what I was doing in this quest would turn out to have a greater purpose than all the wrongs that seemed to be spiralling out of control.

I didn't need to think further than Wilson for the evil that had taken Bluebell Wood. How I hated him! I did, however, have some sympathy for the man when he had been left to walk the invisible steps from Bluebell Wood to his birthplace, to live the rest of his life with only fading memories for company. And that was something that I would certainly change for others returning to Earth in the future. But my concern now was for all on the Land and what was to become of them.

I tried in vain to contact many of them. Bertrum the Cannon Master, the Weatherman, Poppy and Arkley. I thought hard about all of my little friends, but not one appeared. Beads of sweat ran down my dirty, drained face as my pain for Bluebell Wood persisted.

I glanced at Daisy, whose expression was filled with rage, just like before with the men in the streets of St Albans.

"Please stay calm, Daisy. I really need you as I first met you. It is your kindness that gives me strength."

Daisy held my hand tightly. "You are so wise in your words, Jessie. Forgive my emotions." She smiled, pushing the anger away from her being.

My instinct was to fly, but not without a purpose. I knew I had to plan from here. Night had drawn in, but the sky was clear. I fastened my parka and placed my hands within my mittens. Rocking my feet under the wing, then holding them straight out in front of me until my stomach muscles hurt just a little, I began to understand my dilemma.

"One step at a time," I said out loud, tapping my big boots together.

"That's it!" I said, jumping from the wing and staring up at Daisy whilst holding her legs and swinging them excitedly. "Wilson said he chose to take the invisible steps back to his birthplace."

"Yes, and that means what?"

"Well, that must mean that I, too, have steps back to my birthplace. Which was…"

Daisy patted her mittens and in unison we both shouted: "Granton Manor!"

My heart started to beat a little faster at the thought of going home. It had been so many months now; I could hardly believe I was going back. My mind filled with comforting images of the woods and gardens, yet in the background was a slight anxiety about what I would find there. Would my plans for dispatching the staff have come off? I had executed such a careful plan, they surely would have all gone by now, wouldn't they? We wouldn't be back for long enough for the authorities to notice I was not exactly eighteen years old yet, or that my 'uncle' didn't actually exist, so it would be safe to go back, wouldn't it?

I resolved to put it out of my mind and face any challenges when I got there.

I pulled my goggles on, and what I saw made my heart rejoice again. Not only were my eyes greeted by my wonderful four, but the Roman army setting up camp in its entirety upon the pew and enjoying the warmth of Arthur's never-fading roaring fire at Spencer Street.

Arthur himself was busy feeding and fussing around his new guests, and Archie was chatting away to all who would listen, as he moaned and groaned his secret stories and caused havoc with his big bushy tail, knocking a weary legion of Romans off the pew to the floor.

"Hello. Can you all hear me?"

The room all but froze, apart from Arthur and Archie, who carried on as they were, until Bluebell gently pulled at Arthur's long sleeve. "Silence, Arthur," she said softly, and gave him the sweetest smile, the one that she saved solely for Arthur and Daniel.

Archie sat back heavily on his tail, sensing the sudden change, and flopped his big head heavily onto the pew, right in the centre of camp. This sent a sense of fun around the Roman army, as it was quite amusing to see some of their fellow soldiers crawling hurriedly away from their new, inquisitive – if not downright annoying – furry-faced friend.

"First," I said, "I would like to thank Garius and his wondrous artists for creating such a work of beauty within the shortest of nights. It will surely be revered and enjoyed for hundreds, if not thousands, of years. Second, my respect and praise to Claudius and his magnificent army who have won a great victory today. But alas, Claudius, some of your men were injured at the beginning, am I right? Are they okay? And I fear you were right to believe that the main might of the Malissols was elsewhere."

At my last words I could see frightened looks on their little faces, but still I had to tell them. "On this day our home and loved ones are in terrible danger, as Bluebell Wood is now…" I paused and my voice became shaky. "I believe it is under the evil hand of Mr Wilson and the strength of the Malissols."

I don't know what reaction I was expecting, but the silence became loud before it was terribly broken when Leanndi spoke.

"My sweet little Poppy!"

Then Bluebell. "What about Daniel?"

And then each of them, including all the Romans, naming their loved ones and voicing their rage and disbelief.

"Please, everybody," I said, raising my voice. "I am so very sorry that I did not understand fully the history and balance of the four Lands, but I have learned all of my knowledge within this quest."

Claudius stood strong and roared once again. "Silence!"

The room fell quiet. Even Archie slipped his head sheepishly off the pew and laid it out of sight.

Claudius rose to his full height and towered over his fellow Bellas. He walked to the fireplace and stood still. He stared at the flames and then turned to his side, glaring, transfixed by the moon that shone bright and cold through the gap in the curtains. His hair, cut and shaped in a crest upon his head, seemed to have grown in battle, and his splendid uniform, ripped and torn, showed all too well what he and his fellow soldiers had been through.

"Jessie," he said, gently, "our voices are not of blame, just concern. We know all too well that, to find a greater good, sacrifices and change have to occur. Just as the sun is at its most appreciated after a great storm, we trust your judgement to turn this darkness which lies heavily upon us into a magnificent new dawn."

I was pleased with Claudius's words, but somewhat lost about why they believed in me. If I'd had one ounce of that faith in myself, I would have been dancing barefoot upon any obstacle, but for now the expectation that lay solely with me grew heavier and heavier.

I liked the thought of the steps, invisible though they were, and I liked the thought that they would lead to Granton Manor. I now longed for home as much as I longed for Bluebell Wood. Although I had experienced great pain there, I had also experienced the warmth of love and safety. So, what better place to regroup? I stared around the silent room and smiled as I watched Archie grow restless at his motionless guests. He sniffed and pushed at them with his wet nose, trying to provoke the bustling as it had been before I joined them.

I thought for a little longer before announcing to the room that Granton Manor was to be our next point of call and that from there we would indeed take our beloved Land back. I knew Boomer could quite easily locate the position of Bluebell Wood in conjunction to the Earth. Below this point of the Wood, from the edge of the river, where many quests were launched, we should look and, I hoped, find our loved ones who would have fallen to Earth. My de Havilland had only a little fuel, maybe just enough to reach Granton Manor, but certainly not enough to pass via St Albans. Even if I had the fuel, I didn't think it would quite manage another couple of landings upon its skis.

"Bluebell, can you ask Arthur if he can drive?"

"Yes, of course. Arthur, can you drive a car?"

Arthur moved in relief, rocking a floorboard that squeaked loudly underfoot.

"I knew Jessie was there," he said, pleased with himself. "I have kept so very still, my feet hurt."

Bluebell walked over to him. He was stretching his quirky body and staring around the dark room in the belief that I would appear in view. "But can you, Arthur, can you drive?"

"No," he said sadly, continuing to look for me. "No one really wanted to teach me."

"Oh, my poor Arthur," Bluebell said, rushing her words, stumbling to show quickly how much she cared for him. She held his hand. "But you do know your way around buses and trains, don't you, Arthur?" She looked hard at him, longing for him to say yes, and not to feel awkward and defensive on his behalf again.

"Buses, trains," he said, confident and excited. "I was left at a bus stop, remember, by my parents."

"Stop it, Arthur," Bluebell said, pulling at his hand. "That is too sad for me to listen to again."

"No, Bluebell, I have told you it is the very best thing that could have happened to me," he said, smiling and rocking Bluebell's little gloved paw. "But why do you ask anyway?"

Bluebell in turn asked me. "Why is that anyway, Jessie?"

"Go and find a carrying device – a box or a holdall – because Arthur is going to take the Roman army back to Granton Manor."

Bluebell relayed this to Arthur and the room, which then continued with its bustle and its obvious concern for their loved ones.

Arthur rushed to Archie and held his face. Touching noses, he said, "We are going on an adventure, Archie. You, me, and the Romans, isn't that just wonderful?" Archie replied by flopping his huge pink tongue out and running it across Arthur's face. Arthur chuckled. "I must find something to pack the Romans in," he said.

I saw Claudius's head spin round and shake from side to side, as I am sure he didn't like being spoken of like an item of holiday clothing.

For myself, I had learned in my short time as a Relayer to think of the future and not to dwell on the past, just like a Bella. But pain connected with loved ones is not, if ever, brushed aside, and it jolted my heart when I focused on Leanndi crying, like the frightened child that she was, for her young sister, Poppy. Oakleigh pulled her close and held her fast, not speaking, but occasionally kissing her ear. Bluebell moved to Willoughby, who held her hand firmly. They felt between them every tear that Leanndi cried, but time and life had sadly taught them to suppress their own. Maybe it was to save the young from seeing that pain never lessens, but just takes its toll within the skin.

Is that all that ages us? I thought. Is it just that the longer we are around the more hurt we have to endure?

But, in fact, I had had the chance to learn and to embrace emotion and not to fear it. And I did somehow find myself discovering the positive within every situation, just like my little companions. And, just as Claudius had so perfectly placed his words a few moments ago by saying that the sun is at its most appreciated after the greatest storm, I knew that whatever faced us all, we should find the most perfect summer's day together. I let them out of my vision.

***

Later, I took the time to pull my goggles to my eyes to view all at Spencer Street in more comfort. Arthur was busy trying to find something to take with him on his journey.

"Now, what to take," he said, as he walked around the room and back and forth through the black velvet curtain. "I've found my bag." He came in once more through the curtain, draped a very old school satchel over his head, and rested it on his shoulder. It hung down too far so that he kicked it as he walked. "This was the school bag they left me with at the bus stop." He unfastened the toggles and peered into the all-but-empty satchel. "There was this bag and this ball of tin foil that my sandwiches were wrapped in."

"No school books, Arthur?" Bluebell asked.

"No, not for me. The teacher said that I was too stupid and wouldn't need them," he replied, oblivious to how awful the words were and how horrible the teacher must have been.

"But what really upset me was that I could never adjust the strap to my bag." He pulled at it, sending the satchel around his back and hitting him firmly on the head.

Oakleigh stepped forward. "Here, Arthur, let me look at that for you. How high would you like it to be?" He adjusted it back around to a sensible height at his waist.

"I think that feels okay, Oakleigh," Arthur replied, marching up and down the room, turning sharply and letting the satchel fly loosely away and back to its new position. "Yes, that feels just perfect. Thank you, Oakleigh. Will it move again, because I really like it like this? And Archie likes it, too, don't you, Archie?" Arthur showed it to Archie, who was happy to give it a welcome sniff.

"Yes, that will stay put now, Arthur," Oakleigh said, smiling at how pleased his friend was with his instant adjustment.

"Well, I'll grab some money, and then we can go if you like. So, hop in."

Arthur held the flap of the satchel open at the end of the pew to the Roman army, who paid him no attention.

"Not yet, Arthur. Let's wait until morning, and for Claudius to organise his troops," Bluebell said, patting clouds of affection around him in her sweet way.

"That's good," Arthur said, moving aimlessly back around the room, "because I haven't yet found anything to take with me on our journey."

He was looking for just one object that he could bag. But Arthur's life, just like all of ours in Bluebell Wood, was empty of most material things, though it was overwhelmed with emotions, good and bad.

Arthur settled down in time, having placed back into his

satchel the ball of silver foil that had once held his parting lunch from his wrong-headed parents. The room was silent and restful. The fire continued to crackle and, apart from Archie's contented deep sighs, there was peace for these little ones. No doubt each dreamed of loved ones and of their beautiful home, but for now they found comfort within each other as they slept, entrusting their safety in the breaths of those closest to each of them.

If only Bluebell Wood could have enjoyed its lovely natives, as this little cottage was doing.

Instead, I imagined, Wilson, Doggett and their evil Malissols had rampaged and torn at what had once been their home: Wilson occupying the library, with Doggett venting his rage as he stepped forward upon the table that had housed my kind and brave Bellas in a row, planning the quests, or just chatting fondly and laughing at one another over cups of tea. In my imaginings I saw Doggett swinging his axe, forcing it hard into the beautiful wood of the table. His rage had no boundaries or purpose other than deep-seated hatred for the world he had left behind.

I pictured Wilson holding Grandad's telescope, running his long, taloned fingers along it, pushing his right eye to the lens, and sniggering as future disasters came into view. I saw him flapping his remaining teeth with the tip of his tongue and blood trickling from the roots that held onto them like brittle string.

I envisaged him rejoicing as he clasped the telescope hard, wrapping his fingers around it, surprising his knuckles and forcing them to break free from the final layer of scaling skin.

Wilson, Doggett and the Malissols' purpose was just as determined as our own, but in total contrast to ours: to preserve human kindness and nature in its beautiful natural state. Theirs was to turn the world upside down and increase hurt and suffering. And who better to unleash this evil than the man who knew us, unfortunately, all too well?

I do believe if I could really have seen Wilson in the library and his evil playmates infecting Bluebell Wood with their callous presence, I would not have slept. I feel sure my emotions would have indeed taken away all rational thought, and my aircraft would have found itself lodged firmly in the side of the library, no doubt killing me and Wilson.

But the sleep I was embarking on was to turn out to enlighten my future and Daisy's forever.

Although we had planned to fly as soon as possible, I knew that leaving now would mean reaching Granton Manor before first light. Boomer could indeed navigate us there, but landing would be left to me. The Weatherman had suggested snow for the foreseeable future in the south-east of England, and he would be right. With a clear, cold night and the moonlight enjoying its own reflection in the snow-covered land, I could have attempted the landing, as I would have done those many months ago.

But not now. Patient with my thoughts, I would rest for the next few hours in Ireland and then, peppermint-fresh, make my return to Granton Manor by first light.

We could have returned to the orphanage to rest, or indeed a local inn, but we felt more comfortable within nature. The three of us sat facing each other under the wing and we spoke before tiredness overcame me.

"Do you feel tired, Daisy, as an angel?"

She smiled and yawned. "Do you know, I really do. I like to sleep, and within my dreams, I travel."

"Do you think that maybe you aren't dreaming when you travel?" I asked, staring closely at her eyes, not wanting her to sleep, just in case she left me.

"It is a thought, Jessie, and an interesting one. But come, let me lie with you and hold you close, so that if I travel, you shall be with me."

She unfastened her parka and I nestled into her. She laid it across me and I was warm and safe. I liked the way Daisy smelled: it was natural and becoming familiar to me. Her breath was cool and her body hot. Between them they produced a perfect temperature to let my mind and body release.

Boomer appeared. Jumping to his feet and standing on Daisy's taut parka, he stared down at us, and then sat upon us both.

"All this talk of travelling within a dream and without the plane is not making me feel so happy. So I shall stay awake and count to eighteen thousand to give five hours' rest, and happily we should leave, as we arrived, in the plane."

And off he went, counting, one, two, three and so on. His little voice was a nuisance, but it soon became part of my sleeping process and I think I left him at fifty-eight.

CHAPTER 29

Paris, 1866

Within Daisy's loving hold I dreamt of a wonderful time. We appeared in the heart of a passionate summer's evening in Paris. I could tell it was not present day by the shopfronts, the clothes people were wearing and the horse-drawn carriages bustling by. As we passed a newspaper kiosk, I gawped at the date emblazoned on the front pages: 1866. We were so far back in time! Night was closing in and the gas lamps had just been lit. We were walking beside the River Seine. The fashionable set were occupying the seating in front of the cafés where artists, famous and unknown alike, rejoiced in their own voices and their good fortune to be gifted enough to belong.

"My clothes are stifling hot, Daisy," I said, beginning to unfasten the tiny silk buttons on my heavy dress.

"Don't do that," Daisy said, pulling my hands down. "Not even a lady of the night would do that in public."

"But look at me, Daisy, I am just layer upon layer of fabric and my boots are tied up to my knees with laces so tight I have no blood in my feet."

"Yes, Jessie, and I am the same."

I pulled at Daisy's hand. "You look gorgeous, Daisy," I said, staring at her glamorous dress. It was deep green with bold, black stripes. It hung down to the cobbles, and she raised it slightly at the front so as not to tread on it when she walked. Her hair was fastened up and fixed under a small black hat, with flowers so beautifully made I couldn't tell if they were real or not. I instantly compared my own dress with hers.

"My dress is horrible. Look at it, Daisy. It is white and dirty. And who would put a mint green stripe down it? I felt my head and found a bonnet and a strap fastened under my chin. "I am dressed like a child, Daisy, while you look beautiful."

Daisy burst out laughing and held both my hands. "My sweet Jessie, I brought you along, but it is how you feel inside yourself that decides how you appear."

I smiled at Daisy and said, laughing, "Well, it's only a dream so it doesn't really matter."

"Well, you would think so," she said, turning to walk a little further, still holding my hand.

"What do you mean, Daisy? This surely is just a dream?" I asked, picking up the front of my dirty white dress – why, I don't know, as it looked as if it had been worn in a marathon around Paris.

"Well," she said, still strolling forward, "where I dream, I appear, and this is Paris in 1866, as much as that was Ireland in 2006 where we fell asleep."

"Surely not, Daisy," I said, realising that for a dream this did indeed have amazing clarity, with a smell rising from the river that was quite awful.

"Look, Jessie, if this were a dream, when I do this, wouldn't you wake up?"

"Do what?" I replied, looking Daisy quickly up and down, awaiting her move.

"This – " and she clasped my ear and twisted it very hard and very quickly and then burst out laughing.

I yelped in pain and covered both my ears for their protection. "Hell's bells, Daisy, that really hurt!"

"Yes," she said, still laughing, "I am sure it did. But you are still here."

We carried on walking, but I was sulky and refused to hold Daisy's hand until we negotiated the cobbled road which was chaotic and hectic, as horses and carriages charged their way in a never-ending blur of danger. As it was, my ear still throbbed, and I did now trust that I was truly in Paris on a summer's evening in 1866. I didn't want to test this by getting trampled by a horse and then squashed by the carriage that it pulled.

We waited for a small gap to appear and Daisy quickly dragged me like a doll between the snorting horses and the clattering carriages. By the time we reached the other side, my feet were off the ground and I waited patiently to be placed back down.

"Monsieur Monet, Monsieur Monet," Daisy's voice chimed in an exquisite French accent, and a small man rose to his feet from a crowded table. My French at school was not at all bad, so I could manage to follow a fair bit of the night's conversation.

"Daisy Dreamer!" he replied, rushing to greet her. "Where have you been, Daisy? You know my inspiration diminishes without your beauty to feast upon."

Daisy smiled shyly and held out her hand.

He gently kissed it, and said, "Skin as soft as moonlight which enjoys Paris on this summer's night," before insisting that we both join him. "My manners have escaped me, young lady. My name is Claude Monet – and you must be?"

"Jessie," I replied, "Jessie Granton." I didn't hold my hand out to him, but he took it anyway.

"You also are a beautiful young lady, but your beauty is playful and not yet quite settled," he said, studying me. "I shall enjoy your company. You have already inspired me to jump the light off my subject so as not to set them in a rigid state, which seems to be commonplace amongst my fellow artists." He said these words with such a wry smile as he looked back at his table and his acquaintances who occupied it. I wasn't sure if he liked them or not. To be honest, I wasn't sure if I liked him or not. Although the glow around Monet was good, it moved separately from him, sometimes letting in the dark of the night. His enthusiasm was clear enough, but he seemed to say so readily what he felt that I am sure he could only hear his own voice and thoughts, and wouldn't greatly care to listen to anyone else. But Daisy seemed to like him, so he surely must have been all right. He took us to another table, as he was so keen to keep us to himself. He spoke about his latest works and kept thanking Daisy for her inspiration. He asked her if she had painted recently.

She looked hard at him. "No, I feel my artistic side shall bring me harm at present."

Monet smiled. "Spoken like a true artist. I feel that is how creating can challenge the emotion and tear at the soul," he said, truly thinking that he understood her. In truth, I knew that Daisy meant that it really would bring her harm. But I didn't correct him as I felt that he and his fellow countrymen believed that suffering was almost as much a part of them as their choice of clothing. Speaking of which, despite how vibrant it was, the distinction between the classes was clear: the poor were very poor and the rich were clearly flaunting their status. The difference was silently understood.

Monet ordered red wine, and offered some to us. I was surprised to see Daisy accept and start to take dainty sips. Had she had wine before? I had had the odd taste from my parents' glasses but never liked it. I let him pour me a little, though, to appear polite. He leant forward and looked hard into my eyes.

"Your appearance is of a young girl, but your eyes tell me a different story." He sat back and sighed. "I do apologise, Jessie. I can be, how can I put it, a bit forceful in my appreciation of beauty. It's just that I find it so challenging and ever-changing. You don't have to warm to me, but I would find it quite stimulating if you could just humour me for the time."

I guess I hadn't hidden my feelings as much as I should have and, in truth, I didn't much care for Monet until he noticed that, and then I instantly felt a little sorry for him.

Daisy spoke before the silence between us got too heavy. "Oh Monet, you are sensitive. You mustn't think that everybody dislikes you. They love your work, and isn't that part of you?"

He stared into his glass, and slumped further into his seat. "If indeed my work is a part of me," he said.

Half of me wanted to giggle at this grown man taking his art so seriously, and seeming to want everyone to like him. The other half continued to empathise, feeling sad that a man so talented could look so unsure of himself.

Daisy was not slow in coming forward. She held his hand

and he raised his eyes to her. "Dear Monet, how many times have we had this conversation? It is a gift, but a gift that you are not squandering. Your work is beautiful and it is your hand that puts the brush to the canvas, is it not?"

His eyes looked downwards once more before the corners of his mouth rose and then he smiled, threw his head back and laughed. "What would I possibly do without you, Daisy Dreamer?" he shouted at the top of his voice.

He jumped to his feet. "Daisy, I have a gift for you. Both of you come with me, come at once."

Daisy took my hand as Monet took hers and we rushed through the bustling streets. Monet turned out to be a rather bad-mannered pedestrian. As we walked forward, he rudely took one line upon the cobbled streets, barging and knocking everybody in his path, outraging the gentlemen who challenged him instantly. But Monet didn't hear their cursing; he just marched forth, pulling us behind.

"My studio is here," he said, as he fumbled with his keys. "Top floor, of course. The only place to paint, with the light directly from heaven." He cursed as he sought the keyhole in the dark before the door flew open, making Daisy and me step back.

"Two hours, Monet, I have waited for you. Two hours of pay I shall require," said the young woman inside, covering her undernourished body with a white cotton sheet. Even with the slight light, which silhouetted her from the candles that shone in the corridor behind, it was clear that this poor lady was not of high standing. Even compared to my own smeared face and dank, greasy hair she was grubby. She had attempted to put her hair up, but it had fallen in parts, and the darkness beneath her eyes was prominent.

Monet stared at her, embarrassed, not by her appearance but that he had forgotten her. "I am so sorry, Joséphine," he said holding his hands out to her for forgiveness. "But my friends Daisy and Jessie turned the corner into my life, at a total surprise to myself."

She growled her annoyance through clenched teeth and slammed her foot hard to the floor before storming away shouting. "There is always something, Monet! There is always another reason why I am left waiting."

I liked her, and I could quite understand how Monet would try the patience of any woman.

Daisy held my hand tight and we looked at each other. She began to laugh, which I wished she hadn't because it convulsed me into such a nervous giggle that my body shook in trying to suppress it.

Daisy spoke. "Were you late for your dinner, Monet?"

I don't know why, but that set me laughing uncontrollably. Monet ignored Daisy's question. Instead, he took us straight upstairs where Joséphine cursed as she dressed behind a screen and continued to do so as she marched out of the room.

He did acknowledge her as she left. "So, tomorrow, Joséphine? I will see you tomorrow?"

She answered whilst waving her hand back at him. "Last chance, Monet. No more waiting around."

"You would think that *she* were the artist," Monet said as he viewed a painting of her. "But a subject with such an interesting look is in high demand at present. But you, Daisy, when will I have the honour of painting your beautiful face, instead of relying on my poor memory?"

"I should say, Monet, that I would never have the patience to sit for any length of time."

Monet laughed as he walked to a dresser and pulled from the top drawer the most exquisite silver box.

"This, Daisy, I have sourced for you." He held it very carefully in both hands and passed it to her gently.

"Oh, Monet, it's beautiful. Thank you so much."

"Open it, Daisy. It plays the prettiest tune," he said, staring at Daisy, mimicking her face as her mouth opened with delight.

Clearly, he did not know of Daisy's ability to lip-read and that a music box was not the best of gifts, but it was so pretty that I couldn't help but get a little tearful. Daisy so easily became a small child, and she looked at the box as I remembered staring at the Christmas tree back at home when the lights were ceremoniously put on.

Monet walked to Daisy and held the music box with her. "There is something secret in here," he said, sliding from the base a painting the size of a picture postcard. "Remember, Daisy, the very first painting I was recognised for, the one I finished just before you came into my life? Well, I have reproduced it for you, Daisy, as I know how much you love it."

"Oh Monet, it is so wonderful," Daisy said, sniffing in a failed attempt to prevent tears from falling.

I was emotional, too, but my inquisitive side could override any situation and I bounced forward to look. I recognised the scene instantly: a young lady standing alone within a wood of bluebells, her simple white dress gathered high as she danced barefoot, face down, as she carefully placed her steps so as not to harm a petal.

Although I could not see the girl's face, her posture and movement were just like Daisy's, and I asked, "Is that you, Daisy?"

I could tell, as Daisy held it close to her face, that she, too, felt that the girl had similarities to her, but she denied it quietly.

Monet said, "I painted it before we first met, and I have always believed, most certainly, that an angel sent me the scene and the movement in my brush. Never before had I painted with these strokes, nor had I ever painted a subject without a model such as Joséphine, or without first seeing the landscape with my own eyes."

I wondered, as I stared at Monet, who graciously credited his talent to an angel, whether he was one of the artists to whom Greschen had presented her gift. He was certainly a somewhat eccentric man, but if his raw talent had been nurtured by Greschen, I thought he was dealing with it admirably.

He walked over to me and started stroking my ear, which I found quite odd, and told me to wake up. I tried to flick his hand away, but the sensation and the voice continued.

"Wake up, Jessie, wake up."

I jolted in my sleep and then found myself safe and warm, cuddled ever so tightly into Daisy. I quickly pulled the saliva back into my mouth and checked Daisy's lovely soft jumper beneath my chin to see if I had dribbled on her in my sleep. Thankfully I hadn't, and I nestled back into her, just for a second, before Boomer's little hand stroked my ear once more as he whispered for me to wake up.

"Oh, it was you, Boomer, touching my ear. I thought it was Monet." Once again, I had fallen asleep with my goggles on, and once again I'd had the strangest dream.

"No, it was me," Boomer replied, in a small panicky voice. "I didn't get to eighteen thousand because the counting sent me to sleep too, so I am sorry, Jessie, but it looks as if dawn will soon be upon us."

"I had the most wonderful dream, it was in…".

And before I could finish, Daisy stretched and yawned and said, with a very sleepy voice, "Paris 1866."

"Yes," I said. "How strange that you would dream that too."

She smiled at me as she finished stretching, and fastened her parka up from where I lay, fumbling at the buttons through her mittens. I was going to ask more, but a light pink within the sky was leading the path for the sun to shine.

CHAPTER 30

Next Stop: Granton Manor

Under the cover of night, the finest dew had sneaked onto the landscape. By first light the greens were so varied that colour from a wildflower would have displaced the perfect harmony of it all. The grass was lush with a bright, light green, and in the distance the trees and the hedgerows were so deep in colour it looked as if the darkness of night were held within their leaves. It was a beautiful place. The land had a freshness that was not dissimilar to Bluebell Wood.

I breathed deeply and my lungs held the moist clean air, springing it around my body and jumping me to life. I would have liked to stay, but leave we must, and as soon as possible. The dew on the grass would be good for the skis, and the gradient which had helped us stop for our landing would now help us soar back to Granton Manor.

I had just one more look at my friends at Spencer Street. I watched with delight as Arthur was woken by Bluebell. He jumped up, excited about his journey and being out in public again with Archie. Claudius and his men had dismantled camp and were waiting for the off.

"Should everybody like a cup of tea before we go?" Arthur was, as always, being the perfect host. But everybody declined, to the relief of the Romans who had packed up their supplies long before. Departure was imminent.

Arthur knelt and placed his satchel next to the end of the pew and now, on Claudius's command, the Romans marched forward, reduced in size at the mouth of the satchel, and dropped in, out of sight.

Claudius was the last to enter and he looked up at Arthur. "This satchel will not leave your shoulder, will it, Arthur," he said, not as a question, but as a big reminder that he and his army were within Arthur's trust.

Before this, Claudius would never have trusted his life to the hands of another. If there had been one person, it would once have been his old friend Doggett, but most certainly not funny little Arthur. Although Claudius was following my wishes, he was clearly not happy about it.

Willoughby, Oakleigh, Bluebell and Leanndi jumped up on the pew and sighed slightly when Claudius entered the satchel and Arthur fastened the flap.

"He wasn't happy about that, was he, Oakleigh?"

Leanndi had said quite loudly what each of them thought, and Willoughby sharply shushed her quiet.

"Whoops, sorry," Leanndi said, laughing as Oakleigh pulled at her ponytail.

Arthur looked around his small front room and then placed the fireguard across the hearth. The fun had left his face, replaced by a terribly sad look.

"What's wrong, Arthur?" Willoughby asked. "You were so excited just a moment ago."

"I'm okay, truly. It's just that I cannot remember when I

276

have been away from here for any length of time and certainly not overnight. I just feel sorry for my home. It will miss me just as I will miss it. I don't want it to be lonely, as I myself was before these walls welcomed me and kept me safe."

Willoughby placed his hat crookedly, as ever, upon his head and said, "We all understand your attachment to your home. It is quite natural. But it will wait for you and embrace you with love and keep all those memories safe within its walls so that when you return you can enjoy them once more."

"I suppose so," Arthur replied, and turned to the window. "Do you think I should keep the curtains closed or open?"

Bluebell walked to Arthur and held his hand. "I think closed. Let your home sleep in your absence."

"Yes, that's a nice thought," Arthur said, now smiling again. "I think we can leave now I have money and my satchel, and, of course, you, Archie." He ruffled the fur on Archie's head.

"Come, then, let's go." Bluebell spoke in her busy, matter-of-fact tone, which helped bring everything back to normal again.

Arthur looked around one last time. "Sleep tight. I will see you soon with lots to say."

He slowly pulled the door closed, leaving the fire to die and the room to fall into darkness.

The cold that awaited them outside bit hard and numbed Arthur's face. "My word, I think this is colder than yesterday, Archie." He smiled down at Archie's magnificent form. Archie had caught a scent and pushed his nose deep into the snow, causing him to sneeze and pull his head sharply up. He licked his big black nose and looked instantly up to Arthur for reassurance. "Oh, my poor Archie, how horrible of the

277

snow to make your nose cold," Arthur said, wiping it dry with his oversized sleeve.

Bluebell's head appeared just below Archie's collar. "I really think we should move along, Arthur. Time is of the essence."

Arthur didn't reply, but looked indignant as he softly beckoned Archie forward. "Come on, Archie, some people don't have the patience that we possess."

Willoughby moved to join Bluebell at the front by Archie's collar as she occasionally popped her face out of the fur to check progress.

"Bluebell," Willoughby whispered.

"Yes, Willoughby, what's wrong?"

Willoughby took his hat down and placed it beside him. "I just want you to know that whatever happens when we get to Granton Manor, you and I will take the steps and bring Daniel back down to Earth to safety."

Bluebell moved to Willoughby and held him tight. "My dear Willoughby, you have already taken so many blows from that awful Doggett that I couldn't possibly let you run the risk for me and Daniel."

Willoughby didn't respond except to tighten his hold upon her and sigh deeply.

Leanndi appeared on her hands and knees, pushing the fur apart like thick grass.

"You dropped your hat, Willoughby," she said, tugging at his leg and proudly presenting it to him. She blinked hard at the two of them. "Do you think Poppy will be okay?"

Oakleigh appeared. "Don't worry about her, Leanndi. She is just like you, so they would have thrown her off first," he said, joking to lighten Leanndi's and his own fears.

"What a cheek!" Leanndi gasped, and threw herself crashing down on Oakleigh's thick mop of hair. The two of them laughed aloud as they rolled from Archie's collar to the clump of fur which rose slightly at the base of his tail.

Archie stopped still and shook vigorously. Leanndi and Oakleigh ceased their playful fighting instantly, and held onto Archie's fur. They were still laughing, but realised that Willoughby and Bluebell would not find their antics as amusing as they did, so they settled down and Archie moved along.

Whatever doubt I had in my heart, whether it be about my decision-making, or indeed about my purpose, I was refreshed now viewing my little ones, just as simply as water would have quenched my thirst. As uncertainty seeped in during that flight, I drew strength by checking their progress.

Arthur hopped from bus to bus and train to train throughout that morning. He was used to people staring at him: some because of his scruffy and odd appearance, others because they feared him, especially now with the formidable Archie alongside him. Children had no opinion. They just saw a small man with a very big fluffy dog who was very gentle and patient with everybody who approached him. But their parents were not so at ease and would hurry their child along without making eye contact with Arthur.

Arthur, however, was enjoying his time for now. He even stopped for hot dogs; one for himself, and one for Archie. He let it cool and tested its temperature with the tip of his tongue before presenting it to Archie, who devoured it in one gulp.

"Twenty minutes before the next bus, Archie, so let us sit on the bench for now," Arthur said, wiping the snow off the entire bench and climbing up at one end. "Come, Archie," and Archie too climbed up, then rested his head on Arthur's lap.

Arthur ran his hand through the fur on Archie's head, pushing it first one way so it stood high and then the other, so it was flat and neat again. "Scruffy Archie, smart Archie, scruffy Archie, smart Archie," he said, forgetting that the Romans were in his satchel and Bluebell and the others were in Archie's fur. "I can't decide which one is best, Archie, scruffy or smart." He held his face to Archie's head so his lips tingled on the fur. "Oh, but what am I saying, Archie, scruffy or smart, I don't care, you are the loveliest and the best dog in the world ever."

Every time Arthur held Archie close his eyes filled with the love that this odd little man longed to share. I think that they did, indeed, have a secret bond that neither was aware of, but both appreciated their new lives and were determined to stay with and look after each other.

That was the essence of this whole new world: the Bellas, Arthur, Archie, Daisy and me. It was just about simply caring and appreciating what was naturally ours to enjoy. It wasn't without fun. I had laughed more in my time with them all than I had at any stage of my life. It was just a simple and wonderful approach to love. Now I had found it, I wasn't going to let someone like Wilson or the Malissols take it away.

Anyway, I was weak with excitement that everybody was to converge on Granton Manor. So much so that any fears I had had about encountering Mrs Talbot – or any of the staff – had dispersed, replaced with a fierce resolve to protect my rightful home and my friends no matter what. High within the sky it was a beautiful day, but very cold. The sun shone brightly, but held little heat for us. The cliffs of Wales matched perfectly the snow which lay heavily on its surface. It reminded me of the Christmas cakes my mother would make, trowelling the white icing into a snow effect.

And for that moment I did spare a thought for my mother and father. Had they died or were they just missing? Maybe they were on another Floating Land? But I couldn't let my mind run there. It would only let the hurt that lay within my heart seep into my fragile body, and this was no time for self-indulgence. Granton Manor awaited, and the invisible steps.

Back to my journey. Over land we kept as low to the ground as possible. It was fun and a wonder for our eyes to fly deep into the valleys and alongside the mountainous terrain of Wales before making our way at full speed towards London, and to Kent which awaited us the other side.

The country was still covered by a blanket of white, until it faded into a damp grey as we flew over the capital city. There was little chance for the snow to linger any length of time there, as the persistent traffic and its unpleasant hurry wouldn't stand for even a short pause to let the flakes bring their magic. But we soon passed the grey and were back into the white on our homeward miles. My heart raced. Even under the snow I recognised each field, the woodlands and the odd scattering of homes.

"Marvellous, Boomer! Perfect navigation!" I shouted. "I'll take it from here. You enjoy the ride." He sat high on my lap and peered from side to side, clamping his glasses firmly to his head by pushing at his ears.

I was so full of joy, my stomach turned and fluttered. I swooped low at the last clump of trees and skimmed back down to Earth upon the perfect lawns of Granton Manor. Unfortunately for us, in my excitement I had overlooked my speed on the approach. Yet again, when and how we would stop was in the hands of the gods.

I, for one, was growing accustomed to my crash position. I grabbed Boomer and squashed him, for his own safety, under my stomach. I still held the controls, but pushed my head to my knees. I managed to keep the plane straight as we sped across the lawn, only to find ourselves charging into my favourite woodland, the very one where I had lain for hours enjoying my sweet Tansy's company. But on this occasion the strong and healthy trees welcomed us by dismantling my beautiful de Havilland and hurtling the three of us to a terribly bumpy, but thankfully harm-free, halt.

I was good at lying still after a shock to my body. It was the best way to mentally check myself before moving. Nothing really hurt, so I rolled onto my back and stared through the canopy of branches and at the sunlight flickering through them. I felt quite angry at these trees for ripping my plane apart. Not much of a welcome home, was it? And not the best way to welcome Daisy and Boomer to Granton Manor. Or to announce our presence to anyone there.

But, in truth, I was the only one of the three of us who could have come to any harm. I had instinctively held Boomer and covered him, as a mother would her child, and I still held him tight whilst I lay there contemplating rising to my feet.

"Did you mean to do that?" Daisy said, as she stood over me, blocking the sun which silhouetted the hood of her parka.

"Very funny," I replied, letting go of Boomer and pulling my body up.

Daisy held her hand out and hoisted me to my feet. She brushed the snow and mud from me as I stood quite still. She said, "All done," then pulled my hood back. "Look at your grubby little face, Jessie." She held my head still and ran her thumbs across my cheeks.

Daisy was the only one I didn't fuss with. In fact, I liked her giving me attention. I even liked the way she would carry me around like a doll. I stared hard at her, constantly studying her face, etching her beauty into my mind, making sure it would never leave me.

"Hello, is anyone there? Are you okay?" a man's voice shouted at the edge of the wood.

I froze. I didn't recognise the voice but I said nothing.

Boomer quickly reduced and scampered into my pocket.

"Hello?" the voice called again.

"Er, yes," I replied. "We are over here." Whoever he was could face me and Daisy together.

The sound of twigs breaking underfoot and crunching snow came ever closer.

"Who is that?" Daisy asked.

"I don't know."

"But you just told him we were over here. I thought you knew him."

"No, not at all," I said, moving tightly into Daisy as a giant of a man separated the falling branches and stood staring down at us.

"You're Jessie Granton," he said, in a voice so deep that the snow fell from the branches he was holding apart.

Hearing my name spoken in full and standing in the grounds of Granton Manor, I remembered my resolve and stepped forward.

"You are correct," I said pompously. I frowned hard at the man. "And you, mister, are on private property."

I don't think I would have been quite so forceful had Daisy not been with me, but the man had such a tough face. His nose had been broken in the past and he had two scars, one on the top of his right eye and the other, very deep, running from the side of his mouth to just below his ear. His dark brown hair was neat enough and his jeans and black T-shirt were not dirty, but his half-length waxed jacket had seen better days. He actually looked quite upset that I had been so blunt with him as he gazed at us the same way a child would stare at a disobedient puppy.

"I only came to see if you were okay," he said, not making eye contact.

I instantly felt awful and knew I should have looked at his glow, as it was as white as the flakes on the branches.

"Who are you, anyway?" I asked softly, trying to retract my aggressive tone.

"I'm sorry, I should have said. My name is Bo. Bo Wainwright. I have been looking after your house for you."

"Ah, okay, I guess. So, the staff have gone, then?"

"Oh yes," he replied, "months ago, as was requested."

"All of them?"

"Yes, all of them. All gone. The house is left until the legal side is sorted. There was talk of an uncle coming to take over. Everyone thinks you are dead, Jessie. In truth, so did I until, well, Grandad appeared."

"Grandad!" I gasped. "You mean Grandad from Bluebell Wood?"

Bo nodded and my mouth dropped open as I shook my head from side to side. I thought I would have been more shocked than anything, but anger became my most pressing emotion, and I shot my words out. "Grandad has been here –

whilst I have been attacked by Wilson, flown all over the place and generally having a nightmare!"

Bo pulled back. "I don't know, Jessie," he said quickly. "I don't really know about any of that." His voice had gone high and he started walking away.

Clearly Bo felt that I was blaming him, so I rushed forward and pulled at his arm. "Where is Grandad and how did you know it was me?"

"Jessie Granton," he said, laughing. "You have been in the paper for months, and, of course, there are a fair number of pictures of you in the house."

It suddenly dawned on me that my plan to reclaim Granton Manor had not been so cunning after all. People must have noticed it sitting empty and assumed I was dead. Dead!

"Oh," I replied. I was stumped for a moment, then remembered this new, shocking piece of information. "So, Grandad. Is he in the house?"

"Oh yes, I should think he is having lunch now. It is his time," Bo said, pushing the branches aside and walking back where he had come from.

I turned to Daisy with my mouth open. "What do you think to that?"

I didn't wait for her answer. Instead I turned and quickly stomped my way behind Bo. His long legs appeared to be carrying him slowly, but he covered a vast amount of ground in each stride and he was halfway across the large lawn before I reached his side.

"Now tell me, Bo, who employed you to look after my house?" I asked, staring up at him and running in between steps.

He looked down at me and laughed as he increased speed. "Absolutely no one."

"But Bo, somebody must have asked you to care for my lovely house," I pressed him, determined to keep up with his long legs.

He stopped dead and I, too, skidded to a halt.

"Little Jessie, no one has ever asked anything of me. To tell the truth, I read about your home and decided to burgle it."

"Burgle my home!" I shouted, hands on hips. I wiped my chin with my mittens, as I had spat a little in my shock and pure outrage at Bo's calm approach to his criminal plans.

"Calm down, Jessie," he said, smiling, as if he now found me quite amusing. I bent my neck back to see past his waist. "The main thing is that I didn't and won't. I care for your house and its contents. Your home is the closest that I have come to feeling that I belong."

I squeezed my eyes tightly and gave him my 'I'm not sure about you, mister' stare as Daisy joined us from behind.

"What's going on?" she asked.

"This man," I said, still squeezing my eyes at him, "was going to burgle my house, but now he says he likes it too much."

"Well, it is a very nice house, Jessie," Daisy replied, looking past us to the back of the house.

I gasped at Daisy's serene attitude. Unable to control myself, I slammed my big right boot to the ground so hard it rattled my whole body and it really did hurt. But, of course, I didn't let on. Instead I just marched forward without them. I shouted back, "Wait until I see Grandad!"

CHAPTER 31

I Need Answers

On reaching the house I threw the patio doors apart. But I calmed instantly, as the house and its contents were warm with memories, and a perfect fire was roaring its welcome. I had expected the furniture to be covered with dust sheets, but it was exposed and as clean as my mother's high standards would have demanded. Ornaments, rare china and silver were gleaming. My boots were dripping the melting snow onto the wooden floor that was polished like a mirror. Not a speck of dust was present. The house felt as it had done when I would return home with Tansy, not appreciating its standing or my loving parents within it.

"Grandad, are you there?" I shouted, not crudely, but quite sweetly, as the house had muffled my rage, and I found myself floating around the room. I had taken my mittens off and they hung loose beside my hands, on the string that Arkley had attached to them. I had rarely taken time to appreciate the fine works of art that the Grantons had accumulated through the years, let alone touch the figurines that were placed upon the mantle over the fire. I suddenly wondered if my mother and father had had favourites, as I gently held a young lady, moulded in white china, cradling a small child. The expression on the lady's face was perfectly formed. It showed the love she held in her heart for the child she supported in her hands. It was an expression I had witnessed many times in my new life with Daisy and the Bellas, and, of course, with Arthur and Archie.

"It's funny you should hold that piece," came a familiar voice from behind me. "I remember your mother holding that when she was a similar age to yourself, when she first started dating your father. Goodness, they were very young back then."

I didn't move. I just continued admiring the figurine.

"She, too, loved that piece. She would say that the lady must have cared for the child so much, to cradle it with such a love that it began to hurt her."

I hadn't noticed that in the lady's face, but now I saw that she did have pain within her. I turned my head to face the voice, knowing that it would be Grandad.

There he stood, tall and proud, as immaculately dressed as he had been in the photograph in *The Weekly Chronicle* in Ireland, the adoptive father to Daisy Dreamer. He wore a black suit with a crisp white shirt and a black silk tie with a silver tiepin. A smart trilby hat balanced on the end of his fingers. His whole demeanour was sharp, his silver hair greased to a perfect side parting, his black shoes matching the shine of the floor. This was not the Grandad I remembered from Bluebell Wood, the man who had worn the same tatty shirt and tired cords for days at a time, whether in the orchard or hard at work in the library. He had lost his softness, and the smooth edges that I loved had become formal. There was no doubt he looked every bit one of the elite, but I felt that his look betrayed us and I didn't like it.

I guess I should have asked, 'Why did you leave me?', or 'Why didn't you tell me you were my great-grandad?' Instead I just said, "Why the suit?"

The question was as bland as I felt, especially as for months now my emotions had been so high or low, but for that second they had left me and I couldn't raise any more.

Grandad stepped forward. The fine leather uppers of his shoes creaked and he looked down at them, embarrassed.

"I had to leave, Jessie, as I must every time Daisy returns."

I turned my body to face him fully and stared deep into his eyes. They were such a beautiful blue that focusing on them allowed me to talk to the Grandad I knew. But still I lost patience.

I shrugged my shoulders and flatly asked, "So tell me why."

Grandad was nervous, that was clear, and for now my compassion had disappeared, until his eyes glazed and he blinked them and swallowed hard.

"It's true, Jessie, there is so much I could, or maybe should, have told you," he said, looking at me, then back to his shoes. "But your arrival, well, it was a surprise to me. In truth, your father should have been the next Granton to relay from Bluebell Wood, but his disappearance was as much of a shock to me as it was to you."

I was disappointed to hear Grandad say these words, as a part of me clutched onto the hope that there would, one day, be a great reunion, that my parents were elsewhere being incredibly brave and saving parts of the world far from here.

But I had created enough emotion on behalf of my parents, so enough was enough, and I wanted to know why Grandad had not foreseen their disappearance.

He looked hard and lovingly into my eyes.

"You lost a father and a beautiful mother. I lost my grandson and his loving wife, and we both deserve answers. Why he was skipped, I don't know. First my own daughter. Then my grandson, your father. It is almost as if the need for you to arrive was not to be delayed. But it has been said that when the next in line is overlooked, they have lived a parallel life, never realising the change, but continuing to live with everything in a separate path. It is possible. Through the years it has been known for a new Relayer's soul and being to split, one jumping very slightly ahead and living a totally separate life from the one who is left to live his or her intended life."

I frowned and shook my head. It was a mind-boggling idea to get my head around. "So, Grandad, am I to believe that somewhere in this place, just ahead of time or behind time, my parents and I are living a life together?"

"It is possible, Jessie." Grandad smiled. "Every person you meet or action you leave is just a breeze shutting a door, or a vision from the past to another time. The world is small, and many lives and times share the same space. But for us Relayers, at the core of it all, our actions send ripples of good or bad to another place in life."

I looked around the room just as a breeze caught the patio doors, not slamming them, but gently pulling them to.

I shivered. "Do you think that may have been my mother or father?"

"Quite possibly," Grandad said. "Or you." He looked in the direction of the door.

"Do you know, Grandad, I like the thought of that. Just to think that they could be happy at Granton Manor."

"I am pleased, Jessie. It brings me great comfort too."

We looked at each other and our smiles grew at the same time. But they broke suddenly as the patio doors were moved again, not by the breeze but by a very shocked and disbelieving Daisy.

She stood on the steps just below the threshold of the door, which made her appear reduced in height. Her mittens hung loose behind her hands and the hood of her parka sat beneath her eye line, causing her to tilt her head back to see past the overhang. Daisy looked like the little girl who had appeared next to Mother Superior, Bernadette, and she looked as lost as she had then.

I rushed to bring her into the room and she took my hand without saying a word.

"Mind the step," I said, as her snow-covered boots flopped sadly onto the wooden floor.

All the time she fixed her eyes upon the man she thought had disappeared from her life forever. Grandad's hands began to shake, losing grip of the trilby, which dropped to his feet. His top lip trembled and his eyes closed and reopened behind a wall of tears. Daisy pulled the hood of her parka back, loosened her grip on my hand and rushed forward.

"Daddy, Daddy, it's you, Daddy, it's truly you!" she cried, and embraced Grandad. He stood, strong, to welcome his child within his arms.

"My sweet child, my beautiful, sweet Daisy. How I have longed to hold you again. Please forgive me," he cried, pushing his lips onto the top of Daisy's head. He spoke with relief to be holding the young girl he had grieved for so tirelessly.

Daisy pressed her cheek against Grandad's chest. "I never thought I would see you again. I looked so hard for you, Daddy, I never stopped, and there you were all the time. Why didn't you show yourself to me? Why would you do that?"

I, too, felt tears running down my face as I stared at my poor Daisy, her vulnerability and need for love so raw and tangible. Amongst the torrent of feelings I, too, wanted to know why Grandad had hidden himself from Daisy.

I took my parka off, sat down on the chaise longue and stared, transfixed by their embrace. I sat, perched, my hands on my knees, gazing at the scene in front of me. Snow was puddling around Daisy's boots as well as my own. My mother would have been quite beside herself if she knew I had worn shoes, let alone these big things, on her beautiful floor, and yet, of course, I wished desperately for her to be here.

My eyes followed the trail of water back to the patio door where Bo stood silently. For such a large man he made very little noise, but my glare at him was thunder itself and I asked quite rudely, "Why are you still here?"

If I had only taken note of his white glow, which was so strong, I would never have asked. But Granton Manor made me stupidly protective, and my behaviour was not that of the person I had become. Although Bo was a hard man, he clearly had a side to him that words hurt more than a physical attack ever could, and he looked very upset again.

"I actually thought that you would thank me," he said.

Grandad, still holding Daisy, turned to me and agreed.

"Jessie, without Bo looking after Granton Manor it would not be at all as it is for you now, so I think Bo deserves an apology."

"Apology," I said, jumping to my feet and catching a

glimpse of myself in the mirror that hung above the mantle. It was sparkling just like everything else, and here I stood, dressed as a Bella, face, hair and body dirty, but pure and clean inside. So, what was I doing to this man? I had learned so much, yet in five minutes of being home I was letting it go. I could see my face redden as my embarrassment at myself dawned. I quickly turned to Bo.

"Sorry, Bo. I *should* be thanking you. Please forgive me."

Bo's smile sadly looked more like a grimace in his scarred and battered face, but I now could see him as I should have done, and I quite liked it.

He was generous with his forgiveness. He rubbed his huge hands together, and with his deep, gruff voice asked, "Would anyone like tea?"

I felt every muscle in my body relax at the idea of tea, so replied for us all. "What a splendid idea, Bo!"

I resumed my position upon the chaise longue, while Grandad and Daisy joined me on the settee to my right.

Daisy's tears had dried, but she looked quite drained. She held Grandad's hand on her lap and nervously pulled at each of his fingers. The jubilation in their faces had passed and now a terribly awkward feeling had arrived, a feeling that some uncomfortable questions would need to be asked.

Grandad and Daisy spoke at the same time. Grandad quickly apologised and asked Daisy to continue.

"So why, Daddy, did you hide from me? There must be such a simple answer, something sweet and kind. What was it?" Daisy asked, longing for Grandad to answer in one sweeping sentence that would lighten the hurt and make her love him more.

But Grandad lowered his head and with anguish he

rubbed his eyes with his thumb and index finger, struggling to find the words. It was clear that whatever he was going to say would be painful, and he removed his hand from his face and looked directly at me, flicking his eyes sheepishly towards Daisy.

"First I shall speak of everything that I know, and please listen to every word," he said, looking in my direction but straight through me. His mind wandered, wanting to capture every word, and not to confuse or mislead us. He continued as a school teacher would, leading with facts that he was sure of.

"Each of the Lands was gifted a Daughter of Mother Nature. Greschen from Bluebell Wood, Angelina from the Americanas, Celeste from the Desert of Dreams and Evelyn from the Mountains of Peace. In return, and to restore the balance of good and evil, four men were to rise from the darkness and from each point of the globe. The beauty and charm of each matched that of the Daughters, in the hope of enticing the girls and wrapping them in a shroud of deceit. The evil Sons were no threats if the Daughters were safe within their Lands. But to be found roaming alone – without question these men could bring any opposite into their arms. Evil Himself knows too well the gift of a charming man and a solid frame in which to hold his prey. And within his four Sons he held no boundaries. They are the opposite of what an open field is to a charging horse. Mother Nature's only defence for her children was to let them see a person's aura, though you can still be aware that somebody has poor intentions. But with a charming man, love can be blind to all his imperfections, however cruel and dangerous. On realising that her daughter Greschen had left Bluebell Wood in fear of her, for sharing her creativity with the world below, Mother Nature sat heartbroken. She lashed out with severe storms and shook the Earth, longing for Greschen to fall back into her arms. And so the search began. It has continued for so many years." Grandad breathed deeply.

I sat spellbound. "Oh my word!" I said. "What do you think, Daisy?"

But she didn't answer. She was studying Grandad's mouth with eyes as wide as a frightened foal.

"Sorry, Grandad," I said. "Please continue."

And he did, almost as if he were speaking these words without emotional attachment and to an empty room.

"We all looked for a sign on Earth of a gifted child or an unusual occurrence in nature, but no sign of Greschen existed. Until that day when news of a little girl living in an orphanage in southern Ireland came to me. The art world was already rejoicing at this young prodigy, and when I first saw her work I was lost for words. Not only did it transport you, at the first glance, into her beautiful mind, but it showed a place few had set eyes upon, and that, of course, was Bluebell Wood." Grandad paused to let his words take root.

A couple of seconds passed before I realised what he was telling us and I swallowed hard and turned my head sharply to Daisy. Daisy's jaw dropped to match my own and I leant forward to grasp onto my knees. She then clasped Grandad's thumb tightly and shook it.

"You don't really mean me, do you, Grandad? You can't really believe that I am Greschen."

"It is true, Daisy. I just wish you could remember life before Daisy Dreamer."

I was flabbergasted. Not only was my new best friend an

angel, but a truly fabulous, important one at that. I began to rock, holding my knees tighter and tighter before I couldn't control myself any more and I jumped to my feet.

"Daisy, you are Greschen!" I cried. "And part of creation. Not a little part but a huge part."

I don't know why I was so excited about it. Nothing else which had astonished me had brought out this excitement. I think it was because I wanted the best for Daisy and I really did think this was the greatest of turns.

"Grandad, you haven't answered my question. The only one that matters to me," Daisy said, holding Grandad's thumb so tightly the exposed tip was now purple.

"Oh Daisy, I know my actions were strange and terribly cruel, but I wanted you to know or remember as little as possible of your past. It was the only thing that would keep you safe."

I could see Daisy's body language change as she straightened her back and let go of Grandad's thumb. She slapped her hands down upon her thighs and demanded, "So tell me why you hid from me."

Grandad's head dropped and he stared downwards. Holding his hands together he closed his eyes and mumbled to himself as if praying. Then he spoke softly. "Because it was I who set the explosives."

Daisy's body jolted. "I need to see you, Grandad."

Grandad's head turned to Daisy and he opened his eyes wide. Desperate for the questioning to end, he calmly said, "Oh Daisy, I knew you were in the mine and I knew when you were deep enough for no return, because it was I who detonated the device. It was I, your loving father, who killed you."

Grandad's eyes stayed wide as tears filled the lower lids and broke free onto his long lashes.

Daisy stood, trying to find support to steady her shaking body. She breathed deeply and quickly and stumbled backwards towards me.

"Yes," she said. "I remember that you asked me to check for samples. You smiled at me and said there was an unusual storm brewing and that I would be in the best place. I remember you calling me back. I can still remember your smell, as you had been working hard in the mine setting explosives. You held me so tightly, I thought I would burst. And it was you who said those words that have repeated in my head, echoing in my sleep and when I'm awake. It was you who said, 'Even in death your gift will harm you'. And because of that I have never painted or sung since. Never one brush stroke or one note."

Daisy continued to stumble backwards, knocking her legs on the chaise longue, where I had sat back down, shocked at the actions that Grandad had just laid claim to. Daisy fell next to me.

"My God, Grandad. But why?" I asked.

He answered me, but his eyes stayed fixed on Daisy, now blinking for forgiveness and releasing tears. "It was because they had found Daisy. More importantly, they had found Greschen."

"Who, Grandad? Who had found her?" I asked, standing once again and leaning forward, longing to know the reason.

"The four Sons," Grandad said, his voice rising as he stood to defend himself, and pointing to Daisy with his hand shaking. He cried, "They were going to hurt you, Daisy, beyond anything that you could have felt on Earth.

They were going to take you as their own. Please, Daisy! I killed you out of the greatest love. I couldn't protect you any more. The storm I spoke about was the Sons' arrival. It is the only time the winds blow from each point of the compass simultaneously. Your safety then was your demise."

Daisy sat crumpled, staring at her father, and she spoke not with words, but with the great sadness that possessed her beautiful eyes.

Grandad dropped his hands and stared like a child back at her, longing for understanding.

The room was silent but for our breathing and the steady, firm tick of an ornamental travel clock. Grandad sighed as he reached for a cushion to prop behind Daisy's sagging back, never once losing eye contact with her as he did so. I placed my arm firmly around Daisy's shoulders. How much more should my friend have to endure? Staring at the side of her beautiful face, I thought she looked so young. Never mind that she was an angel or Greschen, the daughter of Mother Nature. To me, and more importantly to herself, she was a young girl whose life at every turn was hitting a new struggle of confusion and pain. I wanted to take away the sadness that chased her existence and swallow it whole. But the clock ticking reminded me that time was forever moving. As I looked at Daisy, she turned her pale face to me. I kissed her cheek and pulled her into my neck. I am sure my heart stopped and time froze for us both. I felt her tears fall and trickle down my collarbone and her breathing slow as the room fell into darkness. My eyes became heavy with Daisy's and I could feel us drifting to sleep. But then I jumped awake as Bo re-entered the room.

"Nothing like a nice cup of tea," he said happily, carrying

a tray with my mother's finest china tea service upon it. He looked around at the three of us, noting the obvious upset, but didn't comment. With his huge hands he very gently stirred the tea in the pot and then poured.

Daisy sat upright as Bo passed her a cup and saucer. She sipped at it and pulled just a little away.

"That's a bit hot," she said, and blew gently across the top. She sipped again and then sat up, strong, with her big boots crossed at the ankles.

She then spoke. "I do forgive you, Daddy, and, what's more important, I do understand." She blew across her tea a second time and, just before sipping, raised her eyes to Grandad and smiled.

CHAPTER 32

The Gathering Darkness

The forgiveness had been so long in coming to Grandad – especially now it had arrived in no more than "Could you pass the biscuits?" or "This tea is nice" – that I could see that the relief he craved was a bit flat. But the forgiveness in Daisy's eyes and smile was substantial enough.

"You didn't do me any tea," said a little voice from my parka pocket. Boomer, as he was always doing lately, surprised me by his presence. But food, tea or a flight were sure to bring him to show himself. He rose to his full height and stood on the chaise longue next to me, pushing and correcting the position of his massively thick glasses. He walked without an apology across my legs, and then Daisy's, causing Daisy to quickly raise the cup and saucer high out of harm's way. Then, with one leap, he landed next to Grandad on the settee, pushed his glasses tight to his forehead, and blinked his magnified eyes at him.

"Nice to see you again, Grandad." He marched forth over Grandad's fragile legs and stood staring up to Bo sitting beside him. "Well. You haven't any tea for me."

I couldn't help but laugh as this huge and quite forbidding man leant his giant body as far as possible in the opposite direction to little Boomer, who stood with his big boots pushing into Bo's now exposed left buttock. Bo squeezed the tiny china handle of his teacup with his big fat fingertips, attempted to hold the cup daintily to his mouth and took a sip.

He then slowly moved the cup back a couple of inches from his mouth and, looking straight ahead, said, "Would somebody please tell me what the hell is this creature staring at me demanding tea?"

Boomer fixed his stare and blinked a couple more times and once again asked, separating his words in the belief that Bo might not have understood, "So... is... there... any... tea... for... me?"

It was cruel, but I really started laughing at Bo's reaction to meeting a Bella. Unfortunately for Bo, this first encounter was with Boomer who, once you got to know him, was very sweet and kind, but on first meeting had a way about him that was different to the others and slightly odd.

Grandad leant across Boomer, placed his hand on Bo's arm, pulled him back towards him and said, "This is one of the many Bellas I have been teaching you about. This is Boomer, the Plane Spotter."

"And Navigator," Boomer said, bending his head back to look up at Grandad.

"Yes, okay," Bo said, edging off the seat and shooting to his feet. "I'll just go and get another cup." Still not making eye contact with Boomer, he quickly left the room.

"He seems nice, Grandad," Boomer said, quite oblivious to Bo's total disbelief at seeing him.

Grandad brushed Boomer's little head, and gave that loving smile which perfectly expressed his spirit.

Daisy looked at Grandad as he did so, and there was no doubt that she still loved him.

Time passed, and Bo and Boomer got properly acquainted. Boomer told him stories of our heroic flight, which gave Daisy and me time to bring Grandad up to speed.

Daisy resumed her position next to Grandad on the settee, holding his hand and studying his mouth as he spoke. I couldn't wait to tell Grandad of my encounter with Mr Wilson and how he and Doggett had tried to bring me great harm. Indeed, had it not been for our brave Willoughby, who had suffered so terribly, I think they would easily have succeeded in ending my life on that park bench in St Albans.

I explained how awful Wilson looked these days. I also said that I felt it was terribly unjust that he had been left so alone, with the need to search for just a little of the life that he had left behind. I made it quite clear to Grandad that no such parting should or would ever happen between us. Grandad looked pleased that I was strong in this stand. He knew that he should in theory be leaving Bluebell Wood now I was settled in my role as a Relayer. And in fact I longed to confront whoever had decided such a ridiculous fate, after serving with one's life to come to such an ungrateful end. But for now I spoke, and Grandad listened intently, sometimes aghast at what I had witnessed and been through in such a short time. But life was like that now. Days and nights could be as if they had the time span of a year, and just as important to the memory. He was also very concerned about Willoughby and how severe his injuries were. I described them with great sorrow, but told him how Daisy had directed the sunlight onto him, and how with her guidance the beam had sought to heal him.

Grandad raised his eyebrows.

"And what else have you done, Daisy?"

"Nothing else major. I don't think so, anyway," Daisy replied, knowing that she might well have done, but for now couldn't think.

"And what about you, Jessie? Can you think of anything else that Daisy has done to help any of you?"

I paused before jumping in with "No", but I could see by Grandad's expression that it was in Daisy's best interest that, if there were anything, I should now speak of it. "Well, there was the little lady in the cafeteria. You know, Daisy. The resident or ghost," I said, brushing away the detail. "She warned you to be careful, didn't she, Daisy?"

"Okay," Grandad said, leaning forward. "Anything else?"

"Err…" I groaned, thinking hard. "There was the mosaic which, incidentally, is truly magnificent, if not a little upsetting."

"In what way upsetting?" Grandad asked.

"Because it is me, Daddy," Daisy answered. "It's me lying in Jessie's arms as demons try to harm me from above. Wilson saw my destiny only too well, and he laughed at me, enjoying the image that he saw. But as for me, my eyes were drawn to the scene of bluebells in the corner of the mosaic, which led us to Ireland and my earliest memories with Sister Bernadette."

Grandad placed his arm around Daisy's shoulders and pulled her into his neck. He kissed the top of her head and held her tight.

Daisy turned to me with a frightened little smile. "I think they are coming for me, Jessie. I remember now how I felt on that day in Alaska. I remember feeling cold. Not from the elements but a cold freezing me from within."

I moved next to Daisy, and Grandad and I sandwiched her. Instinctive, but quite futile, were our efforts to warm her. Daisy's eyes moved to the fire.

"Is it my fault that Wilson is in Bluebell Wood, Daddy?"

"No, my sweet child, there is not a part of this that you can take the blame for. You are just like any young being: your need to explore is part of your growth. I have quite successfully harvested from Bluebell Wood the new life that is nurtured in the orchard – all those flowers and plants – but, Wilson's attack is not a plan of any great magnitude. He and the Malissols are a black cloud directed by the evil arm of darkness."

"But aren't the Four Lands in terrible crisis, Grandad?" I asked. "And isn't Bluebell Wood's life fading without Greschen within it?" I continued, talking of Greschen still as if she were not Daisy at all.

"Thanks for that, Jessie." Daisy laughed through her saddened smile. "It had quite slipped my mind that I am a Daughter of Mother Nature."

Grandad stood and began to pace. His leather shoes creaked and squeaked as he did so, and my thoughts were easily taken to them as he stepped even numbers of paces back and forth.

Another question popped into my head as I watched his feet. "Grandad, why, if Daisy has been back at Bluebell Wood, has she not been embraced by her mother?"

Grandad's feet stopped and I watched them turn to face me.

"Because one of the greatest differences between

happiness and sadness is free will. Mother Nature would not, or could not, demand or even ask Daisy or Greschen to return. Greschen has to long for and feel a true desire to return, without fear and with a true understanding of her mother's strict hand." Grandad used his hands to accentuate his words. "And although Daisy has returned in body, her spirit as Greschen has not. She has slept in silence until this time. She has now allowed the Sons to glimpse her great but gentle power."

My gaze remained at Grandad's feet and I answered, thinking aloud. "How can Daisy want, or long for, a life she has no memory of? Even more than that, I am not so sure Daisy would like to be with anybody that strict, even if it were her mother." I brought my eyes to Grandad and spoke quite forcefully on Daisy's behalf. "No, I don't think that is the way forward for my friend. Besides, Daisy should like to stay with me." I took Daisy's hand and held it tight and spoke inches away from my beautiful friend. With eyes painfully wide I asked her, "You should stay with me. Don't you think so, Daisy?"

I was expecting her to agree readily, but instead she looked sad. Darkness had drawn under her eyes and the beautiful soul that radiated from within them had now withdrawn. She did smile at me, just as she had when first we met, but her breath, that had always calmed me, was very cold.

"I shall stay with you until the very end," she said.

This made my body drop as if I had lost any use for my feelings beyond this point. But Daisy had been through far too much and I had no right to fuss any longer around her. For my friend's sake, I would now follow the path that she wished to take, and I would not become a hindrance, but a strong and true cradle for her to lean upon and to rest her tired body.

I simply thanked her. Not for that moment, but for every wonderful second, and for giving me a love so pure I could feel it releasing for evermore with every beat of my heart.

CHAPTER 33

The Romans Arrive

It was late afternoon before the sweet sound of the snow crunching under a thousand pairs of marching boots grew. Arthur had laid his satchel down and the Roman army, led by Claudius, appeared from within it. Arthur, with Archie by his side, stood back and let Claudius lead his army down the drive to the warmth that waited to embrace them behind the huge entrance door.

Grandad and I, Daisy, Boomer and Bo, all stood upon the stone steps that formally led the way into Granton Manor, and we waved like royalty at our parading army.

Bo had thrown salt down the steps to melt the snow and ice beneath. I stared at a small groove that I had bevelled away with a piece of flint, when Tansy and I had sat for many hours, swapping our watch from the back of the house to the front, awaiting and longing for my parents' return, before I was unwillingly stolen by thoughtless adults to boarding school. But on this occasion the wanted people had arrived: what a joyful sight.

The sun, that had shone earlier and succeeded in battling the cold for a brief spell, had disappeared behind the dark snow clouds, letting an icy mist engulf the woodlands and the wild nature that circled to protect the perfection that was Granton Manor.

By the time Claudius reached us, the soldiers had disappeared from view within the watery haze, lagging somewhat behind, along with Arthur and Archie. I welcomed Claudius formally. But I did allow myself to give him a little cuddle, at which he looked quite bemused. For him and his powerful battle-worn body such affection was only for those he was to protect. But he didn't tighten his stance, and in fact I felt him quite lean into me and show, just for the briefest of seconds, a side of him that could long for gentle affection.

I had just released Claudius from my hold when Archie, like a husky free from his sledge, came bounding into view. He had no understanding of the ceremony and order of the Romans, so his bounds across the lawn, following his own line, were quite understandable. He couldn't wait to greet the people and the voices he recognised from his new life.

He moaned and groaned as he barged into us, unaware of his size, leaning like a bear on a tree trunk as he pushed his love upon us all. Even Bo got the full force of Archie's welcome, but that no longer surprised me. I reckoned Archie could understand the aura of people well, just as I now saw it too.

It took Arthur such a long time to reach us that his breath had all but left him on his arrival at the steps, so he steadied himself with both hands upon Archie's back. He still found enough breath, though, to explain that he had told Archie to go ahead say hello.

Archie hadn't met Grandad before, but he instantly stood

in front of him, flopped his rear end down and offered his right paw. His tail overhung the drive and swung from side to side, fanning the snow and the legionnaires who awaited orders to be at ease. His tail brushed and flicked against them, slowly then quickly, when Grandad took his paw and made his acquaintance.

"I taught him to say hello, you know," Arthur said, having caught his breath.

"Well, you are indeed a gifted trainer, and Archie is a gifted pupil," Grandad said, smiling at Arthur, and encouraging his confidence in the bond with life outside the world of the Bellas. "You look so enthused with life, Arthur. What a joy to see you again and to see you so happy." Grandad rested his hand on Arthur's shoulder.

Arthur waggled his long sleeve over Archie's floppy ears that rested flat to his head, then pricked forward to capture each word and tone that was spoken. "If I didn't tell everybody how happy Archie has made me, I think I would truly burst," Arthur said, his eyes filling as he pulled Archie's magnificent head up and kissed him.

Watching the two of them was lovely. Everybody would be taken with them, enjoying their friendship, just as one would enjoy watching a foal finding its first steps. It looks magical, but it can also make you smile with its clumsy control, as harmless and amusing falls are inevitable.

Still smiling at them, I asked, "Where are the others?"

"Oh, Bluebell, Willoughby, Oakleigh and Leanndi had a message for you, Jessie," Arthur said.

"Really? I was expecting you all to arrive together."

"Yes, yes, we did, but at the gates back there the four of them were keen to leave."

"Leave? So they got to Granton Manor but wanted to go again? Go where?" I asked, confused and upset that they were not with us all here. Remembering their conversation on Archie's back, I feared the worst.

"Well," Arthur continued, "I don't want to sound like a telltale, but it was Bluebell. I wouldn't normally talk about her, but I was concerned, as she was going to leave and bring Daniel back to safety on her own."

"And, of course, the other three had to go with her," I said, finishing Arthur's words.

I was angry with them, though I didn't show it to the others. Not because my Bellas had followed Bluebell on her quest, but because I so longed to see them at Granton Manor. But I wasn't going to put another cloud on them as dark as the one above, waiting to burst and drop its destructive weight of snow.

Instinctively, I raised my goggles to speak with them, but just before sliding them down to my eyes I knew that I could offer nothing at this moment. Bluebell was following her heart to go for Daniel and the other three were following their friend. I didn't even have to ask how they would get there and return, because I knew it would be the same way that Grandad had hidden from Daisy: by using the invisible steps. But how Daniel would navigate the steps was a concern. It sounded hard enough for humans.

I really wanted to know where the first step lay, so I asked Grandad later that night. When he told me, it was felt so obvious. Much to my comfort, it was where I had lain almost every dry day with Tansy's head on my lap, dreaming through my protection of leaves and branches. Maybe even then I was looking for Bluebell Wood, or maybe it had already found me.

Back inside the house I allowed the Romans to set up camp within the deep-pile carpet of the dining room. Nobody had requested it of them, but no doubt it would have pleased my mother when they all removed their boots. Even these hardened little soldiers enjoyed the plush carpet as they pulled at it with their bare toes and smiled happily to each other as they sat and lay upon it. Bo had lit the fire for them, and brought mountains of cheese and bread from the kitchen.

Arthur and Bo liked each other instantly, just as people do when they recognise the same hardships. Although hardships occur in different ways, the understanding of them is a silent recognition of being somewhat ousted by society. Both men rallied happily around the troops, moving with plates of food and cups of tea like synchronised swimmers, spinning gracefully past each other and around the fragile ornaments that adorned every table. They made a wonderfully quirky duo, one large and stocky, one small and eccentric, but the sight of them at work together was a joy.

That evening the dark snow cloud that had sat over us opened. The snow fell heavily, with flakes so large that they could quite easily settle in the palm of my hand. Layer after layer joined the already frozen snow that covered the unfortunate outside, and how I longed and wished my four Bellas had waited, even if it had only been till morning, to bring Daniel to safety.

Did they have a plan on reaching the top of the steps I wondered. Wouldn't the Malissols have blocked their entrance, with Wilson surely knowing the steps' whereabouts? So many questions I presented to myself, knowing that I wouldn't have the answers. Instead, terrible images came forth of my little gallant friends freezing, huddled together upon the steps, finding it too far to go down and too dangerous to go up. Or had one of them fallen and floated to another cold place to be left alone, scared and hungry? Or maybe they had reached the top only to be slain on the very last step by that awful, aggressive Doggett.

Each image made my eyes open a little more. Wider and wider they grew, as I lived their terrible fate with them in my head, until thankfully Archie poked my mouth with his runny, wet nose, snapping me out of my trance, and I fell backwards, quickly trying to wipe my tongue clear from Archie's mucus.

"Oh dear, Archie. That's disgusting."

I laughed, because Archie thought he had provoked a game: he placed his two paws upon the chaise longue between my knees, and moved his playful tongue around my face. I fell further back, trying to avoid his big fluffy face. I tried to push him clear, but my giggling had got the better of me and I flopped to my side, unable to defend myself against my furry adversary.

Daisy laughed loudly and, instead of pulling Archie away, she held me down and encouraged Archie back to my face by wiggling her fingers around my nose.

"Here, boy," she called, and Archie groaned louder and louder as I giggled more and more. He pushed his big wet nose at me, finding my face with ease as I tried in vain to hide it. I wriggled and giggled my way to the floor and there I sat red-faced and catching my breath. Archie, having ousted me from the chaise longue, now sat where I had been sitting. He dropped his tongue out and smiled contentedly around the room.

"What a cheek," I said, as I stared from the floor up to him. "All that to get my seat!"

He did push his paw into my head, but comfort had now taken over his mind, and his face became very grand. Slipping his tongue into his mouth he held his pose like a proud lion now that victory was his.

"I shall get you for that, Daisy," I joked, and smiled up to her as she sat fussing around Archie. But already the laughter had left her, and she snuggled into Archie's warmth to battle the cold from within.

I glanced across the room to Grandad, who stared into the darkness and at the closest snowflakes, which just caught the light that shone through the patio doors, boasting of our comfort to the chill outside.

Having Grandad with me was not the relief of duty I had thought it would be. Instead, it added to my responsibility, as I had surpassed him in decision-making, and I now knew that the only person I would listen to would be myself and the love within my heart. I rose to my feet and brushed a covering of Archie's fur from my dungarees and joined Grandad. I linked my arm through his and we both stared at the darkness of the snow and at each other's reflection.

"Is there anything we can do for Daisy?" I asked, still looking forward, and talking to Grandad's reflection.

"I fear not, Jessie. If a doctor were called, he would take her from us to hospital, but they would still find her there, you know." He paused and turned to me, knowing I knew full well who 'they' were.

I also knew the next words he was going to say, as the heart of Bluebell Wood was fading. I felt the pulse of the Wood allowing time to settle between each beat. So I listened to the man in the reflection, distancing myself from the truth.

"Daisy is dying with every step that brings closer the four Sons."

"How are they doing that, Grandad? How are they making her leave us?" I asked calmly, but inside I was screaming.

"It is not they, Jessie, who are actually shutting Daisy down, but Daisy herself."

"What!" I yelped, and then pushed my lips tightly together, in disbelief that she could be so selfish and hurtful to me. But again what I was pushing onto another was, in truth, my own selfishness without understanding why. "Why would she, Grandad?" I asked, staring back to Daisy, who now rested her face into Archie's back.

"She knows that the Sons cannot take her. She knows the consequence without understanding the action."

"And that means what, Grandad?" I asked in frustration.

"It means, Jessie, that Daisy knows that the power that she possesses as Greschen must be protected and cannot be taken by the Sons. With the gravity of a black hole, the sons wish to engulf Daisy and to re-emerge as a newborn: one entity, one mighty demon enslaving Greschen and her power forever."

"I will not let them have her, Grandad," I cried. "Like I did in the mosaic, I shall shield her with my life."

"The four Sons have extraordinary power, Jessie, but there is a part of me that believes you will do just that."

Grandad then put his arm around my shoulders and we stared for a while longer at the blackness outside, and ourselves appearing within it. We watched the large flakes settle high upon the beading that held each brittle pane of glass in place.

Although it was cosy inside, ice still formed on the interior of the glass, eventually frosting over completely, creeping into in the heart of Kent and into our safe, sheltered hideaway.

CHAPTER 34

Can We Dream Together Again?

I left the room and everybody there to enjoy the peace and quiet, and that heavy sleepy feeling that is enjoyed after a large, fine dinner. Bo kept both fires roaring, both ours and the one in the dining room for the Romans. He was helped by Arthur, who considered himself to be quite the expert on this subject. He followed Bo, prodding at the logs with a large poker that Bo had placed, moving them just an inch or so to give the fire that expert touch that he possessed. I smiled and quietly pulled the large oak door behind me to stand in the cold and grandeur of the main entrance hall. The chandelier that hung above me was magical, but it gave only a little light to a space such as this. As my big boots squeaked and scratched upon the staggered black and white floor tiles, I remembered this area feeling a little gloomy as a child.

When Christmas arrived, however, a tree big enough to camp in had been placed in the centre. Welcoming the season with a pine fragrance and dazzling tinsel, it had looked quite the most exciting place to be. I would sit and stare at the tree for days, mesmerised by its beauty, admiring it from the landing above and sitting on every stair, enjoying each view as if it were the first. But eventually the season had passed, leaving the branches dry and brown. It was then that I would promise myself that the following year I would insist that my parents spared the tree from certain death, and that they decorate the entrance hall without it. But I had never kept my promise. Instead, I had simply pleaded for a new tree from the middle of every November.

I do hope I can be more responsible with Bluebell Wood, I thought, as I sat on the second stair reminiscing.

Daisy had followed me out and sat next to me, with her arm around my waist and her head resting on my shoulder. Leaning my ear into the top of her head, I knew these final few hours with Daisy would be the last. There was not a sound. Even our breath was silent. If there were voices elsewhere in the house, they had not made their way through to us. We breathed as one and stared at the main entrance door, awaiting the arrival of the Sons.

I felt Daisy rummage in her parka pocket and I slid my head across her silky hair to discover what she felt for. She carefully placed onto my lap the very same music box I had dreamt of when she and I had enjoyed Paris. My dislike of Monet came flashing back to me, though I brushed it away.

"Does it play a pretty tune, Jessie?" Daisy asked, raising her head and looking at the box in my hands.

"Hell's bells, Daisy," I gasped, looking down and then to Daisy. "I thought that was all a dream. How did we do that?"

"Daisy Dreamer," she replied, smiling. "My name is Daisy Dreamer."

"Yes, but we were in Paris over a hundred years ago!"

"You are funny, Jessie. I love it so when you are excitedly shocked."

"Well, I am so very shocked now, Daisy. Can we go somewhere else?" I was aware that I sounded like a small child at a fairground, finding the most thrilling ride.

Daisy laughed again, with little energy, and softer than I had known her to do. "We have to sleep to travel, Jessie."

"Well, let us sleep, then," I said, closing my eyes tightly, but opening one again to see if Daisy had followed my lead. But, of course, she hadn't. She just smiled at me. "Is it a pretty tune?"

I lifted the lid and the music began. Its tinkle echoed high around the hall and then dropped onto the hard, tiled floor and vibrated before disappearing to start again. The melody provoked images of Bluebell Wood, each note kissing and brushing across the wildness as gently as the grass that swayed in the fresh breeze and tiptoed inside the new buds, easing their petals open, ending the fear of being alive.

"Oh, it is so very beautiful, Daisy. Monet knew you better than I gave him credit for. It is you, Daisy, becoming music itself. I wish you could hear it," I said thoughtlessly.

"I think I know what piece it would be. I do think that it was me who allowed it to escape from heaven."

"Do you know, Daisy, I think I could whistle this melody already. It sounds like nothing I have heard before, but the notes are ones that are placed so simply that I think I could never forget its pattern."

Daisy cupped my hand, which held the box. "I would like you to keep it, Jessie," she said, peering into my face.

"Oh Daisy, I couldn't possibly. Monet had waited for your return with such longing to present you with this gift. I would feel that I had stolen it from you."

"You are silly, Jessie," she said, pushing the box with a little more pressure into my lap. "Monet's gift was for my pleasure, and it couldn't give me any more joy than to know that you held it safe." She paused, looked away and then back to me. "I know!" she continued, having found a way of twisting my reluctance to accept it. "Think of it as a way of us being together. Whenever you open the box, think of the breeze as my breath, and fill your lungs, and your heart shall feed life into us both. That way we shall always be together."

She gazed at my profile and I thought about what she had said. Already I was afraid of closing the lid, afraid she would disappear. But I did like her idea very much.

"Okay," I said. "That sounds lovely. Thank you, Daisy, so very much. I shall treasure it forever."

Daisy embraced me, which was nice, but her hold was weak. So I squeezed her as tightly as possible just to let her know that I had strength enough for both of us. I closed the lid of the box, cautiously holding Daisy with one arm, making sure that she stayed put, and asked if she would like to look around Granton Manor with me. We walked hand in hand through the corridors and into the individual rooms.

Bo, in his time here, had removed all the dust sheets and, just as Grandad had pointed out, had kept the house perfectly. Each room induced a small tale from my past. In my bedroom Daisy found out more about me than I realised a person's room could tell. I had all but forgotten that as well as my beloved Tansy, I had loved and kept such a selection of stuffed toys and teddy bears.

Daisy sat on my bed and gazed around the room with eyes so playful that they sparkled, skipping from pictures of me when young to toys, which she, as a child, would never have had, until, of course, she was adopted.

"Did you have names for your toys?" she asked, and we laughed together as I remembered them easily. How funny they sounded now spoken aloud to somebody other than my parents.

"I like the littlest bear best," Daisy said, dangling it by its ear and staring hard into its dark brown plastic eyes. "His nose is sewn slightly wonky but his face is very sweet," she continued, examining him for injury. "What did you say his name was?"

"That's Topsy." I fought back tears as Daisy sat Topsy on her knee, stroked his head and gently pulled at his ears, waiting for a reaction. "I like his softness, especially his hands and feet." It was clear from Daisy's eyes, so full of excitement, that a room like this was something she could not comprehend. Perhaps for all his kindness, Grandad had not provided Daisy with the normal trappings of childhood out in Alaska. Or perhaps it was part of her memory loss of her past. Even the way she cared for Topsy and awaited a response: it was as if she found it hard to define the difference between the toy bear and a Bella.

I couldn't respond as tears were only seconds away from exploding down my face, especially when we left the room and Daisy carefully placed Topsy in her parka pocket and gently patted the flap shut. Time had passed and we had almost explored the whole house. It was wonderful but somewhat upsetting to consume so many memories in one go, but I was pleased I had shared them with Daisy.

We were making our way back down the stairs when Daisy stopped several steps from the bottom. "We haven't been in that room there, have we Jessie?" She pointed back up to a door just to the right.

"No, Daisy, I haven't been in there since my parents disappeared."

"Oh. Why not?"

"Well…" I paused. "I just couldn't face it."

"Best you face it with me, then," she said, taking my hand and marching me back up the stairs. We stopped and looked at each other.

"Come on, Jessie. It is your parents' room. There is nothing to fear," she said, putting my hand on the handle.

"Okay," I replied, as I eased the door open. I whispered, "My mother's perfume – it smells just as if she were here, after all this time."

The light from the landing crept across the bed and onto the nightclothes that were folded upon plumped pillows, still awaiting their return, but not in this time. I walked to the side of the table and switched the lamp on. I didn't want to startle the room with the glare of the main light, and the softness of the lamp eased me into the reality of the lonely belongings.

"I think this room is in need of some company, Jessie. Even belongings need attachments to their intended purpose," Daisy said, sitting heavily on the edge of the high bed and bouncing as she did so.

"What a strange thought," I said. But, of course, she was right. As soon as I stopped creeping around and whispering, the room felt as it had before, welcoming and not at all sad. I held my parents' clothes, remembering them within them, holding them to my face and enjoying their fragrances, which I rejoiced in, bringing their memory back clearly. Pictures of my first flying lesson with my father. Tansy sleeping as a pup within my arms as I slept, held safe and warm in my mother's embrace.

"This is such a wonderful moment, Daisy. I am so pleased you made me enjoy this time."

She smiled at me and took my mother's nightdress, holding it out as she stood. The silk unravelled, revealing a beautiful gown.

"My daddy is a naughty man, Jessie." She laughed.

"What, Grandad? Why is that?"

"This nightdress is angel cloth," she replied, pushing it softly above her as the purest white folded and turned, dancing its way back to Daisy's beckoning hands.

"How do you know it's from Grandad?" I asked.

"I can't think of any other way it could have got here, can you?"

I thought just for a second and agreed, liking the mischief that Grandad had allowed himself.

"This room is so cold, isn't it, Daisy?" I said, looking at the ice on the inside of the leaded windows. "I hope Wilson's nose has frozen off up there in Bluebell Wood and his nasty Malissols are so cold they all decide to run away back to wherever they came from."

Daisy laughed. "Wilson without a nose. I would like to see that very much." She laid my mother's nightdress out upon the bed.

"Should I light the fire for us, Daisy?" I asked, noticing our breath freezing as we spoke.

"No, Jessie. That won't be necessary. Shouldn't we join the others?" she continued, seeing that I was already quite cold.

"Well, in truth, Daisy, I would like it very much, if you

should need to rest, that you settle in here. Once the fire is lit it will soon be very toasty."

Daisy raised her eyebrows and asked, "Why, out of all these rooms, would you like me to settle in your parents'?" She plumped the pillow, already picturing her comfort, and then slipped her hand in between the sheets.

"Because this is my house now, so the room should be mine, as I am sure my parents would have intended it to be," I said, sitting at my mother's dresser and staring at Daisy within the mirror.

She stared back at me then flopped front-first onto the bed and rested her chin upon the backs of her hands. She looked young within the mirror, and free from any fate that was soon to confront her. She lay there smiling up at me, raising her eyes, focusing on my lips and whatever words I would speak next.

"Also, I think you should have the angel cloth next to your skin. It will help you rest," I said, sounding quite bossy for a second, rushing my words out sharply. "My mother would have offered you that garment if she were here."

I stood abruptly and walked to the fire, which was set and ready for lighting on my parents' homecoming.

Daisy pulled her knees under her body and sprang forward. "Please don't light it, Jessie," she said. "Not yet. The cold within is not so apparent when it is balanced with the air outside."

She leapt off the bed, moved across the room and pushed her nose a fraction away from the frozen glass in the window. Spreading her fingers and bringing them level with her face, she gently tapped each of them against the fine layer of frosted ice, jumping over the vertical lead that held each pane of glass in place.

"Do you know, Jessie," she said, still facing the glass, "the weaker I become, the clearer Bluebell Wood is to me? I don't even have to imagine it to see its beauty because within me I can feel it breathe."

"Come away, Daisy, please. You look so cold," I asked, walking towards her, knowing that she had not heard my words. I gently pulled at her arm and she spun round to face me. She turned so quickly that it made me jump back.

"I need to be alone, Jessie," she said, staring with such intensity into my eyes that I wobbled.

"Okay," I replied, concerned for Daisy and moving my hand to her cheek. "You will call me, won't you?" I asked, respecting her wishes as I had promised myself I would.

"Yes," she replied, with her mind already racing elsewhere. She followed me to the door, ushering me out, and closed it quickly behind me.

CHAPTER 35

Nowhere to Hide

The snow that had fluttered down before had now been caught by a strong wind, which began to howl around Granton Manor. I joined Grandad again and he admitted with a slightly pink face that he had asked Arkley to fashion the nightdress from angel cloth for my mother. I explained that Daisy should be resting in my parents' old room. Like me, Grandad longed to be with her, but we agreed she must continue in the way she felt fit.

This day had brought me nothing but longing, and fear of a greater loss in my life. Grandad and I spoke openly. Both of us were consumed by guilt that all that we had strived to do right had brought around us fear and pain to the ones we loved most dearly in the world.

I talked about the mosaic and the prophecy, which Wilson had seen as a clear sign to rejoice in Daisy's death, but I questioned that. Reading a picture is only bringing to life the pieces that are important to oneself. Wilson hadn't questioned what the new life in the corner was telling him, where the freshest bluebells stretched their stems and flowered on the same page as the demons inflicting their pain. Neither had he once mentioned that I was there to protect my sweet friend, with my heart that roared like a lion at the thought of these bullying Sons choosing to take Daisy for their evil gain.

Earlier I had tried in vain to contact Bluebell and the others, but the vision from my goggles had all but lost its power, fading, I feared, with Bluebell Wood.

Bo kept the fire stoked, leaving Arthur to sleep, using Archie as a pillow on the chaise longue. They breathed in time with each other with tiny snores. Arthur had done so well today, but the excitement and travelling had got the better of him and I wondered if he had ever slept so well and contentedly.

Archie on a night like this would have been chained outside in the past, on man's command, protecting yet another ugly building site. Again and again I was reminded that it is in the shortest space of time that the greatest love is forged and the best and most dramatic changes happen.

Grandad, too, his eyes shut, was dropping his head and resting just for a time. How he must have longed for this day, though he would also have dearly wanted to avoid telling Daisy the reason behind his disappearance. But for now his heart was full of Daisy's forgiveness, which this fragile man needed beyond life itself.

Bo busied himself in the kitchen, Boomer back with him, having exhausted the Romans with his tales of flying. I sat alone listening to the ticking clock and the vicious wind lashing at our protective walls.

"Jessie, Jessie – are you there, Jessie?"

I jumped to my feet and rushed quickly to the bottom of

the stairs, just as a mother would to her sick child. And there Daisy sat on the very top flight. She looked down at me and then stood up.

"What do you think?" she said.

"Oh Daisy, you truly look like all of the angel that you are," I replied.

My breath was wonderfully removed by this beauty in my mother's nightdress. The angel cloth flowed upon her, rippling across her skin. It silhouetted her body, curving with the arch of her back, and melting off her thighs as water shimmers on the ice before running free. The cloth and Daisy within it shone so white and so pure I rushed to embrace her.

"Quickly, Jessie, I need to show you this," she said as I reached her and threw my arms around my very own angel.

Reluctantly, I let her go and she pulled me by my hand into the bedroom. She flung her left arm to the window and pirouetted to my side.

"I have been so hard at work," she said.

"That is amazing, Daisy!" I gasped.

My eyes, in disbelief, feasted upon a work of art scratched into the ice on the large leaded windows. Even with the lead separating each frame it was a perfectly scaled picture of Bluebell Wood.

"It's beautiful, Daisy," I said, and then paused. "No, it's amazing, magical. It's just everything that Bluebell Wood is. How on earth did you do that?"

She sweetly held her index finger out with ice still under her nail. "It's a bit numb now," she said, placing it in her mouth to bring life back to the tip.

"Please, let me light the fire now, Daisy. These old windows do let the cold creep in," I said, as the wind found its way through, moving the heavy velvet curtains that hung either side. "You must be so cold, even more so with just that nightie to keep you warm."

Daisy had used the last of her precious energy scratching Bluebell Wood so perfectly into the ice. She had turned the freezing window's purpose, of making us shiver and duck for warmth under the bedclothes, into a magnificent landscape.

But quite suddenly her shoulders dropped and she steadied herself by resting her cold hand upon the back of my neck.

"Oh my, Jessie, I went quite dizzy. Maybe I was a little too excited and shouldn't have done that pirouette."

I put my arm around her waist to steady her, and thought how perfect the angel cloth felt in my hand, and Daisy within it.

"Come, Daisy, get into bed," I said, walking her slowly across the room – only for my heart to jump as I fought with my tears over my friend's sweetness, when I saw that Daisy had already placed Topsy the bear in the bed and tucked him in for the night. I didn't mention it. In fact, I couldn't mention anything for fear of showing my sadness. So I pulled the bed covers aside and laid them over my beautiful Daisy. I sat at her side and stroked the hair away from her face.

"If I light the fire and you become sleepy, couldn't you dream yourself to another place and time?"

Daisy slid down the bed and I pulled the covers neatly around her. I carried on stroking her hair.

"It is no longer possible for me to hide. They would find me, now they are sure of their intention," Daisy said. She gazed past me as she spoke, turning to her side, pulling her knees up and snuggling further down for her protection.

"Oh Daisy, please go home. I beg of you. Don't let the horrible men destroy you," I said, unable now to fight the tears that held my cries for help.

Daisy pulled her hands to her face, and as her tears ran free she cried as the child inside her thankfully came to her aid.

"I am so frightened, Jessie. More frightened than I could ever have imagined. I don't want to die. I want to stay safe in this bed. Why me, Jessie? Why am I Greschen?"

"Oh Daisy, please," I cried. "I love you so much. Please go back home."

Daisy pushed her knees tighter to her chest, trying to hide from the hurt and fear that tore at her stomach.

"I can't, Jessie. My mother doesn't love me. I can't go home. I have tried and tried to remember her, but she has no face for me." Daisy's sobs became muffled.

"That's not true, Daisy. Your mother has longed for your return with violent weather. Her anguish beats the world," I said, kneeling upon the floor and holding Daisy's pained face inches from my own. "It was to protect your own existence that memories of Greschen escaped you. But now, Daisy, now is the time to find them again."

Daisy blinked to release tears, pulled the covers tight and looked longingly at my mouth, trusting that I would unlock her past and find the key to take her home.

I spoke precisely and softly with words that trickled out upon breaths of emotion. I spoke of the feelings that had formed me in the grounds of Granton Manor. How I had grown with nature, embraced each growth of the new seed and buds, and celebrated the resting times when the leaves would fall, making way for the new life which waited its turn in the following months. Not once had I found sadness in the changing seasons, because each was complementary and as exhilarating as the next. And never, but never, had I felt alone within nature, because it enjoyed my company, keeping me warm in summer and fresh in winter, always reminding me to appreciate the following change.

Daisy settled and blinked again. Her tears had stopped and her mind wandered upon my words.

"You see, Daisy," I continued, "that was not my mother who gave me comfort and safety, teaching me how beautiful life and the changes within it are, but yours. That was Mother Nature with me, sharing her beauty, because I let her in and I trusted her to keep me safe."

I dried Daisy's face with the cuff of my sleeve and smiled. "You have looked for a face that is ever-changing, but it is the feeling that you must remember. Just think of the picture that Monet gave you in the music box, where you danced barefoot amongst the bluebells."

Daisy nodded, brushing her hair on the cotton pillowcase.

"Remember the warmth of the sun, and the cool grass in between the beautiful bluebells. Fill your lungs with the purest air and let your eyes be dazzled by the rainbow of colour that danced with you in every corner. Hold the feeling of safety and love, and return your memories to your mother's arms."

Daisy's face stayed still. She blinked a couple more times and the smallest of smiles grew to light her face.

"Do you believe that if I dream about everything you say I shall return to my mother?" she asked. She straightened her legs and sat upright, pushing back and adjusting the pillows behind her. "Do you, Jessie?"

"Yes, I am quite sure of it," I replied, clasping her hands

with my own. But how could I be sure? I began to doubt myself. Was I lying to my sweet friend to alleviate her fear? Or had I spoken the truth as I saw it? Because I really did believe in my words, and more importantly in nature, which I cherished even in my lowest times.

CHAPTER 36

The Sons Arrive

I faced the window and Daisy's wonderful landscape. The wind had suddenly stopped howling outside. And, as it did so, the temperature inside dropped terribly. Daisy crept down inside the covers and her eyes became large with fear.

"It is so cold, Jessie," she whispered, resting the blankets on her chin.

"Let me light the fire for you, Daisy. Please."

She pulled her head forward to see past the blanket and nodded in agreement. "Yes," she said as she lay back, "now is the time to remove the ice and evil from this place and our Land above."

I thought no more about the words Daisy had just spoken as I struck the match and, on all fours, held it against the knotted newspaper that had been built up with kindling wood and small, very dry logs. I watched the blue flame become yellow and jump from paper to paper. Already it gave me a little taste of the heat to come as I stood brushing my hands together.

"There we go," I said, gazing at the fire.

I turned to find Daisy sitting bolt upright on the end of the bed. Fear had taken her to an awful place and she stared up at me.

"They are here, Jessie, I can feel it. How can I sleep to dream now?" she cried.

"Oh Daisy, please trust me," I said, quickly moving across and squatting down in front of her. "I shall help you sleep. When you close your eyes, you won't hear a sound, and I promise, I truly promise, I shall hold you until you dream yourself from this room."

Daisy opened her mouth, but paused.

"The words you spoke before about the feelings you felt – they helped me find my own feelings. Except, I can't remember them now. Not at all."

Daisy began to cry. I put my hand around the back of her head and leant forward, pushing my lips against her ear. I mouthed slowly, without sound, "I shall be with you," and then faced her again. "What did I just say to you Daisy? Could you feel the words?"

She wiped her wet nose. "I think so," she sniffed. "You said, 'I shall be with you', didn't you?"

"Yes, Daisy." I smiled, and helped her wipe her face. "You don't even have to see my lips to feel my voice, do you?"

She shook her head. Once again, I settled my friend, when Grandad called up to me.

"Jessie," he said, sounding calm, "would you come down here for just a minute?"

"Let the fire warm you, Daisy, and I shall return in one moment."

I glanced back at Daisy, watching me like a child as I left

the room. I felt so strong inside, not at all helpless against the approaching Sons. This was my home and the people within it were my responsibility. I rushed down the broad stairway to Grandad, who waited, now wide awake and with eyes sparkling, alert and ready for the challenge ahead.

"They approach," he said, taking my hand and leading me to one of the narrow windows to the left of the main entrance door. "Look at the flakes, Jessie," he said, nervously whispering in my ear. "Do you see how the wind is making not a sound, and how it moves from each point of the compass, pushing only upwards when it meets?"

"Yes, yes," I said, wiping the frozen glass so my eyes could witness this extraordinary sight. The flakes shot to the sky like fountains of snow, sprung from every meeting of the Sons' warning breath. Flying high to the sky, the flakes disappeared for just a second as they attempted to settle, only to be caught sneaking to ground. In the far distance, at the Granton gates, two faint lights appeared. Their beams grew as they travelled, snaking on the lowered snow on the gravel drive.

"In a car, Grandad?" I asked, surprised. "Would they arrive in a car?"

"Oh yes. 1920s Rolls Royce, I think. That is how they appeared to me in Alaska," Grandad said, in a voice one would expect to hear when waiting for friends to arrive for a short stay or a fancy dinner party.

Bo appeared and stood behind me and Grandad. He wiped the higher panes of glass. Towering above us both, he leant forward.

"Are we to let them in, Grandad?" he asked.

"Yes, I am afraid so," Grandad replied.

"I don't think so," I said, angry at Grandad's acceptance

of the four Sons' arrival. I turned and faced up to Grandad and Bo. "This is my house and that door shall not be opened." My hands instinctively went to my hips, giving myself the pose I had adopted as a child when I was not to be argued with. Both men gazed at me, flicking their eyes to the approaching car and the sound of the snow crunching under the wheels. The headlamps shone brightly into the entrance hall and moved eerily across Bo and Grandad as the car moved to the steps.

I turned and peered through the window, wiping it clear, as the ice had already sneaked in whilst my back had been turned.

The figurine that adorned the elegant long bonnet was the trademark glimmering silver of the lady in the rippling gown. But this one was different to the rest. Instead of the Flying Lady with arms held back as she gracefully led the car in the joy of motion, this figurine was Greschen, standing with hands cupped as she peered to heaven in a final call to her mother.

"Come away from the window, Jessie," Grandad demanded, pulling gently at me.

But I couldn't. I watched as one man alone opened the passenger door, placed his highly expensive footwear upon the running board of the car and stood, holding his body in wonder at his own glory. His overcoat fell in perfectly stitched lines and his hat tilted forward, allowing me to see only his strong jawline, and lips that softly held a cigarette. His overcoat was dark, as too was his hat, but his suit was very light grey, made from the smoothest of cloth. It had a slight shine to it, with the trousers falling in wide legs from their high, pleated waist, turning up at the bottom but with plenty left to rest on his fancy black leather footwear. He wore a dark grey silk scarf around the collar of his coat, which served no purpose but to look rather dashing.

He took a little jump to the snow and walked to the figurine. Pulling the cigarette from his mouth, he flicked it away and the end extinguished instantly. Taking a handkerchief from his inside pocket, he wiped off the moisture that rolled upon the figurine's perfect form. He removed his hat, flicked his dark hair from his forehead, leant forward and kissed the figurine, pressing his full lips gently upon her head.

Shifting his eyes quickly to the window where I stood, gazing out like a bewildered child, he smiled knowingly at me, placed his hat to his head and raised it again in a polite greeting.

He was nothing like the Son I was expecting.

He began to walk towards the door.

Somehow, I no longer thought of stopping them from entering. I moved out of clear view, as a child would if caught spying on her parents' glamorous guests arriving in their finery. I peeped around the corner just as the other doors of the car opened, revealing his playful brothers. No capes or pointed hats, not one of them spitting fire and exposing talons as I had pictured, even though Grandad had quite clearly explained to me that their most wicked gift was perfectly presented in glamour, charm and, of course, stunning good looks. And why wouldn't they be, so as to match Daisy, who was by far the most wonderful person I had ever, or would ever meet? I ducked to the side, not daring to stare any longer. I stood flat to the wall as Bo waited like a giant to greet our unwelcome guests. My heart pounded as I looked up the stairs to where Daisy waited, frightened and alone.

"Bring them to the drawing room, Bo. We shall entertain our visitors there," Grandad calmly said, holding out his hand to escort me through.

"I can't, Grandad. I must go to Daisy just for a moment. I really must settle her."

"Okay," Grandad replied, but his next words were stopped by the tap, tap, tap on the hard wood of the door, as a cane was used to announce their arrival. "You must hurry back. They need to greet you and you must know the measure of these young men."

I was already moving across the tiled floor and bounding up the stairs, missing a number of steps, stretching my little adrenalin-pumped legs to find Daisy lying without covers on top of the bed. She had taken Topsy from the pillows and discarded them onto the floor. Facing the window, she didn't hear my entrance, but felt me there.

"I am so pleased you are back. I think I can sleep now the rain is to start," Daisy said, her voice soft and frightened.

I walked round the bed, and sat with Daisy curled horse-shoed around my lower back. She lay still, and her eyes blinked and closed just for a second, before she forced them open again, frightened by doubt at whether she was sleeping to die or to be home safe within her mother's love.

I stood, and then repositioned myself with Daisy's head on my lap. With my left hand I lifted her, enjoying just for that second Daisy's fine hair rolling down my bare forearm. The tap, tap of the cane echoed around the hall once more, finding its way, thankfully, to my ears alone.

But Daisy did know the boys were here as she bravely continued to shut down. If I could have given my life for Daisy on that night, I would have done, without question.

So I shouldn't have been so surprised that she was willing to do the same.

I stroked Daisy's hair and gently placed her head on a pillow. Moving out of her eyeline, I hurried to the landing, crouching down behind the spindles to hide (I hoped) my small body.

Eerily, as each entered, I mouthed their names: a voice within me knew them well.

Bo opened the door to the colourful voice of Fabion and his rude sarcasm. His hair was dark and greased so tightly to his head that it had a blue tint to it which matched his piercing eyes. He adjusted his turquoise cravat, which he displayed foremost from his white silk shirt, puffing his chest like an exotic bird of prey in search of its mate.

"For a giant of a man you must have very little ears, to take so long to open the door to guests," Fabion said as he squeezed past Bo, reached up and put a white trilby hat on top of Bo's head. "Keep it safe. I shall request it on my departure from this elaborate dwelling."

Bo snarled at him.

The next to enter was Nicholas, stylish in his cream Oxford bags and with white and brown leather uppers to his shoes. He wore a fine white cotton shirt with a brown sweater draped over his shoulders and tied with the arms at his front. He said nothing on entering but looked up to Bo from his ruffled blonde fringe.

Philip entered next, laughing as he placed in Bo's hands a fistful of snow.

"Be a good chap and warm this up for me," he said, continuing to snigger. He then placed a cigarette to his lips and pulled on it deeply, exhaling as he looked around the large entrance hall. "This place could do with a jolly good party. Don't you think so, chaps?" He then hopped from black tile to white tile in his white leather shoes, spinning round and round, dancing with himself. He removed his tweed jacket, resting it over his shoulder and continuing in his matching waistcoat to dazzle only himself, as the long brown mop of curly hair bounced free from his head.

First out of the car, but last to enter, the only one dressed for such a night was George. He passed Bo his cane and then removed his hat and coat. Bo placed them over his arm and reluctantly requested that they join Grandad in the drawing room.

Moving on all fours, I watched as the spaces between each spindle passed, showing my presence like a cat above. To be undetected I lay flat and looked through the open door of the drawing room at Grandad, standing by the fireplace and holding a large glass of whisky.

Following Bo, the men entered the room in the same order they had entered the house, Fabion first.

"Well, well, what a joy to see you, Mr Granton. If I remember correctly, when we last met, you delighted us all by ending the life of your sweet adopted Daisy," Fabion said with a wry smile. "We chuckled about that for quite some time."

Grandad didn't respond. He looked past Fabion and sipped his whisky.

Nicholas walked in.

"Don't look so serious, Granton," he said as he sat in the single leather chair closest to the fire. His puppy-eyes gazed through his tousled blonde locks as he requested in his most urbane voice, "Should we not be drinking some refreshing champagne? I feel quite parched after that awful drive."

Grandad nodded to Bo, who still held the door ajar, anticipating such a request and then duly disappearing.

Philip joined Nicholas and sat upon the arm of the chair. He pushed his mass of curls away from his face, smiling always, with no attempt to communicate except for that one gift.

George now stood alone in the doorway, serious and more purposeful than his brothers. "Hello again, Rupert."

"Hello, George," Grandad replied, rolling the whisky in his glass and then using it as a subtle pointer towards the decanter. "Help yourself if champagne is not your tipple." Grandad was not going to push his hospitality far enough to wait on them.

The four Sons' cigarette smoke in a short time turned the drawing room into a gentleman's club. As Fabion, Nicholas and Philip enjoyed their champagne, they laughed like children about their awful fake romantic conquests over women and men alike, and the cruelty they had unravelled in their twisted form of love. George, like Grandad, sipped his whisky. He now stood next to Grandad and drew close to the side of his face.

"You know there is one prize which we all desire," George said slowly, releasing cigarette smoke with each word. He baited Grandad. "Would you like to tell me what that is, Rupert?"

The moment froze. All become silent. The smoke from George's mouth lay flat in front of Grandad's face. Nicholas stared with his little-boy-lost expression up to them. Philip's smile was annoyingly out of place. Fabion smirked, enjoying Grandad's anguish. Grandad once more rolled his whisky, sending the remainder to the rim of the glass, leaving the bottom clear. He steadied his hand and watched as the fine golden liquid settled and, in its own time, not to be rushed, smoothly trickled to the bottom of the glass.

"Is Greschen all you require?" Grandad asked, moving his eyes from the glass and fixing his glare hard into George's deceptively kind-looking, big brown eyes.

George leant his face forward, a fraction away from Grandad's nose. He pushed his lips hard together and diverted his gaze from Grandad's eyes to begin studying his face.

"You have aged well, I think," George said, pulling away and stepping back to study Grandad as a whole. "It has not been a bad life for you, has it, Rupert? Your mentor, Mr Wilson, has gone quite mad, making you look almost dynamic."

Fabion laughed and sipped his champagne, almost choking with delight as he joined in. "Nothing like a bit of madness to make the less insane of us feel quite normal."

"How very perceptive of you, Fabion," Nicholas said quietly. Never sarcastic or cynical were Nicholas's words, and his expression was so submissive that you would almost have invited his company.

"And what say you, Philip?" George said, turning to face the large mop of hair which hid Philip's face.

"I say I am bored," Philip answered, pushing his hair free and exposing quite a solemn expression.

George pulled himself back, inches away from Grandad, lit another cigarette, drew hard on it and held it away from his soft lips, letting the smoke leave from his nostrils.

"I think I would look a bit withered around the edges if I had failed in the simplest task of looking after Bluebell Wood. Even more so if I had let Greschen slip, time and time again, through my fingers." George tilted his head. "But you didn't let her go, did you, Rupert?" he continued, raising his voice. "You thought that you could keep her safe, didn't you?" George pushed his forehead against Grandad's temple, applying pressure to hurt. "Either way, you silly old man, Bluebell Wood is dying and with it the other three Lands shall follow."

Grandad began to shake as his calm bravado had now ceased to protect him from the words that George spoke. George pushed harder, stepping forward and levering Grandad into the mantle.

"And if I am not mistaken, beautiful Greschen is dying, too, isn't she? You stupid old fool. How could you let your loved ones die twice in your own miserable lifetime?"

Grandad turned away from George and faced the mantle. "She is better dying a thousand times than letting you enter her life," he said, absorbing George's dark remarks and weakening under the weight of them.

George tutted and removed himself from Grandad and spoke facing his brothers. "We have no desire to take over a sickened Greschen. Weakness quite repulses us."

Grandad turned his head back to George. He tried to hold his stern exterior, but a single tear built and ran down the side of his nose. "Then you have no further business here."

Nicholas stood, brushing aside his foppish fringe.

"I would very much like to see Greschen, if that is possible," he asked with a chilling gentility, resting his head forward and raising his eyes.

"Yes, of course," Fabion agreed. "What a waste of a couple of hundred years if we did not at least rest our gaze upon her."

He removed the champagne from the cooler to pour himself, Nicholas and Philip yet another drink.

Grandad slowly shook his head and grimaced, his eyes squinting with the pain behind them.

"Please can you just let her be? Your presence here has produced not your desired outcome, but a devastating end to a beautiful life and spirit. So please just leave."

George frowned. "No." He paused. "I don't think that is really possible. The sadness within this house is quite revitalising. I should like to see Greschen right now."

Still spying through the spindles, these words each in turn punched the air from my body. Then they came again.

"I would like to see Greschen right now."

I stood, with no thought of my own detection, and ran to my sweet Daisy. Instinct for a loved one's safety took control and I gently covered her with my own body.

I knew that Grandad had waited for me in the drawing room, but nothing could or would have taken me from Daisy.

I held her cold ear to my mouth and spoke my words of nature. I felt Daisy's breathing slow down and her head rest heavy within my arms. She held Topsy close to her chest and breathed just past his ears. She no longer fought to open her eyes. The fight for the outcome had passed.

Now she sighed and slightly wriggled, loosened her grip upon the bear, and became silent.

I drew breath as I held my beautiful friend. I knew in that instant that she had left me. So openly I had loved Daisy and so freely I had let her travel away with my heart. The two of us had embraced in warmth, but not now. The chill in her body froze my veins and the tears that withdrew within my painful eyes. There was no beauty to be seen beyond the point of Daisy and no love to fill without my heart. But still I held her. So tightly I pulled Daisy into my chest, kissing the top of her head. She smelled sweet and gentle, perfect to me.

"I love you, Daisy. I truly love you," I whispered.

CHAPTER 37

Shadows to the Darkness

The footsteps that approached me upon the stairs meant nothing. The Sons and their evil road had ended at Granton Manor. Would there be fear to challenge me within the dark shadow that they cast?

I let Daisy rest upon my lap and stared down at her. The peace that had followed her always behind a closing door had now entered the room to find her there. A tangible calm accompanied it and suppressed and numbed my screams, as Daisy's body faded and simply vanished through my arms and away from my life.

"Daisy's dead, Grandad," I said quietly as he entered the room. "She left and just faded away. She was here, Grandad, in my arms and just simply faded. I don't know what to do, Grandad. Please tell me what to do."

Grandad joined me on the bed. He placed his arm around me and pulled me close, resting his jaw upon the top of my head. I could feel him tremble as Daisy had passed through his life yet again. The forgiveness that she had allowed him earlier, and the shortest time of happiness within which he had rejoiced, were once more replaced with guilt. His frail arms held me tight and I hid my face in his neck.

I began to cry. "She looked so beautiful. Far too beautiful to stop breathing," I whimpered. Grandad held me tighter. I pulled my head free and stared up to him.

"I told her all about my time in nature and the feeling I had experienced with her mother and she said that she would try so very hard to return home. But she stopped breathing and faded away." I drew hard for my own breath and pawed at my wet face and nose. "I am so sorry, Grandad, I really thought that she would go home. I really did."

Grandad gently took my hand from my face and wiped my tears with his rough old thumb. The four Sons walked in and stood, peering down at me within Grandad's arms. Fabion squatted and tried to catch my eye. I had no desire to look upon these men. I just wished them gone. I peered at him out of the corner of my eye, as he moved his head to catch my gaze, but I buried my face back within Grandad's neck.

"You're a sweet little thing, aren't you, Jessie?" he said murmuringly. "Quite delicious. I can see why Greschen would have cared for you."

I pushed my face harder into Grandad's neck and began humming the pretty tune from the music box to muffle his words. His three brothers squatted down beside him and their eyes began to burn into me. Nicholas lightly took my hand and moved it from Grandad's chest. His touch felt confusingly soft and kind, so gentle in fact that I found my face drawn to his, my hand resting in his firm, reassuring grip. I glanced at the others, but was captivated by Nicholas and the affection in his eyes.

"Let her be, Nicholas," Grandad demanded.

But he ignored his words and smiled sweetly to me.

"Now, Jessie," he said. "How can I put this?" He paused and looked to the floor. Then he looked back to me with his big blue eyes glimmering through his long blonde fringe. "Greschen – or Daisy, as you so sweetly call her," he said, running his thumb softly across the back of my hand. "Now, she must have loved you very much to keep sending such positive vibrations around the world about you. It made it quite simple to track her down." His thumb stopped and he squeezed my hand tighter, not to hurt, but to signal trust. I sniffed hard and wiped my nose with my other hand. "You see, Jessie," he continued, "the boys in the streets of St Albans, weren't they just awful?" I nodded in agreement. "And then Mr Wilson hurting you and Willoughby having to almost give his life for you. And he would have, wouldn't he, if it had not been for Greschen making him all better again?"

I sniffed again and with the tiniest voice said, "Yes. Willoughby was so very badly hurt. Daisy worked a miracle on him, I think."

"Yes, Jessie, that's what she did," he said, shaking my hand and speaking with enthusiasm. "A miracle to lead us to her." He then waited for my agreement.

"Come, Nicholas, this is pointless. Let Jessie be, I beg of you," Grandad repeated, pulling me hard towards him.

But Nicholas flicked his fringe and slowly blinked. His eyes reflected me alone within them.

"And do you remember what she did next, Jessie?"

I shook my head. "No."

"She saved you, when you should most certainly have died, when you crashed in the woods at Granton Manor.

347

And I bet she gifted you with the ability to see people's auras, didn't she?"

"Was that all Daisy?" I asked, understanding Nicholas's words to be true.

"Yes, Jessie," he said. "And that is what brought us to you and, of course, Greschen." He smiled broadly and placed his other hand on top of mine. He then pulled close and I watched his soft lips expose the lies within his next words. "So, my sweet child, she needs us to find her to help her. She has been calling for our help."

I moved my gaze from his lips and stared into his eyes. I now saw myself within the arms of Grandad, and the fear clearly on Grandad's face. I squinted and reopened my eyes to stare up at the darkness that stood behind the men. I saw the demons clearly and how the men were, in truth, shadows of the darkness around them, projecting to the world these beautiful Sons.

George became agitated. "Look at *us*!"

But I couldn't. I watched the darkness behind them move like a single tree, cold within the night. So dark was the truth. It played their beautiful image in total contrast to itself.

George barked, "What has caught your eye?" He stood and backed away, furious that he might be exposed to me.

I watched the figures of darkness grow, each towering above their projected image. "Nothing, nothing at all," I said quickly and gazed back into Nicholas's glistening eyes.

I knew at this point that I should not be able to see past the Sons' earthly forms at all, and judging by George's reaction, it was certainly the best pretence to keep.

Nicholas smiled graciously. "The problem that we have is that my brothers and I can sense Greschen and can quite enjoy her sweet fragrance, but it would appear that you have hidden her away from us."

I pulled my hand sharply away from Nicholas and snarled at him. "Why would you lie to me? Why would you do that? Daisy is dead and it is because of your intentions."

The kindness dropped from his face and he grabbed my wrist and twisted it. "How did you help her?" He pushed harder, gritting his teeth and curling his nose.

I screamed at him, "Let go of me! If she is alive, she has returned home."

Philip stood, throwing his thick tresses back. His annoying grin filled his face as he bent his neck and sniffed the air.

"No, Jessie," he said slowly. "I think she could be nearer than that."

"Jessie has told you what she can. Now please let her be," Grandad said, hopelessly trying to unfasten Nicholas's hold on my wrist.

"She is moving. She is moving now, I can feel it," Fabion said, jumping up.

"Yes, she is," George agreed and twisted his head to pick up the direction.

"You are really hurting me. Let me go. Let me go!" I screamed once more at Nicholas.

The blue of his eyes had turned from a kind tranquil sea to a dark raging storm. His irises flared open, lashing at the whites of his eyes. He gripped me tighter as he demanded to know. "You said to Grandad that you had told Greschen all about your time in nature and the feelings you had experienced with her mother."

"It was just talk, Nicholas," Grandad said.

"Shut up," Nicholas replied, twisting my arm further.

I screamed as my skin began to burn beneath his hand.

I cried at him, "I was just telling Daisy how I felt in the grounds of Granton Manor."

Nicholas opened his fingers and I pulled my arm back and hugged it, rubbing the redness where his hand had savaged me. "You are horrible!" I screamed at him, and then buried my face back into Grandad.

Nicholas laughed and stood straight.

"And you, sweet Jessie, had just talked Greschen to sleep and to dream of the grounds of Granton Manor." Standing, he closed his eyes and breathed deeply. "And my brothers are right. She has woken and by the feel of it is quite alive."

"No!" I cried, jumping from Grandad and running to the window, hopelessly trying to see into the darkness, and past the melting ice that trickled away at Daisy's drawing. I turned back as the Sons stumbled upon one another, laughing like merry hunters leaving to stalk their prey.

"What tremendous fun," Fabion said, departing the bedroom last. "I wonder," he continued, resting his well-manicured hand on George's shoulder, "if that ghastly-looking man Bebo…"

George chuckled and corrected him. "I think, Fabion, that was Bo."

"Yes, of course, quite right. Him, anyway," Fabion continued, "if he would do us a couple of hip flasks. Nothing like a shot of something fiery to help with a sport such as night-hunting, is there?"

I ran to follow them, but lost my footing as Granton Manor felt a great thunderclap and the sky above split in two. A second thunderclap shattered the clouds, sending them to Earth in a torrent of rain.

"It is Daisy's drawing on the ice, Grandad," I said, spinning to the window. "She said that she could sleep now the rain had started."

Grandad and I stared at the glass, watching the ice melt as water trickled from the lead, forging paths within Bluebell Wood and washing her creation away.

"There will be nothing left of Bluebell Wood, Grandad," I gasped as it disappeared from view.

Grandad stared forward. He looked painfully tired. I walked to the landing and watched the main entrance door swinging in the elements where evil, in its departure, had brushed against it.

Bo appeared and pulled the door shut. He stared up to me.

"Are you okay, Jessie?"

I paused before answering, feeling the atmosphere around me change. Panic had lessened and just the sound of the main door closing on the outside brought calm with it.

"I really don't know, Bo," I replied, and walked back to Grandad. He had laid himself down on the bed, still with his feet on the floor.

"Have they gone?" he asked.

"Yes."

"You tricked the Sons, Jessie," he whispered, looking to the ceiling without blinking.

I walked round the bed, pushed my knees into the side of it and stared down at Grandad.

"How did I do that, then?" I asked, not really wanting the answer or feeling that it mattered to me now.

"It is you," he said.

"What's me?" I replied.

351

"When you talked with Daisy and reminded her of the beauty of nature within the grounds of Granton Manor. You pictured her just as you had been as a child, walking free, and alive in your Eden. The breeze, whispering to her, and the branches above, towering to protect. Who could harm Daisy there, and how could she fail to remember her Mother Nature?"

I sat back next to Grandad and lay down beside him. He pulled me close and we both lay there staring at the blank ceiling which symbolised so simply how we felt.

"Why did they say Daisy was in the grounds of Granton Manor? Because she really isn't. Of that I am sure, Grandad."

Grandad laughed just a little through his nose.

"Because…" He paused and sat forward, resting his hand upon my head and gently stroking my hair. "What they felt wasn't a lie."

I swallowed hard and panicked. "What? She's alive?"

"No, no, you misunderstand, Jessie. What I meant to say is that she is very much alive in your heart, and you created her life so clearly within Granton's small woodland, I am sure that even I could hear her footsteps."

"Oh, I see," I said, sighing and closing my eyes to rest them.

"The Sons believed your power of desire to be quite true and will search for that illusion. For as long as you keep Daisy alive in your heart, they shall believe it."

I didn't say any more. I was tired and felt quite sick. I knew that Daisy would forever be alive within me, but I felt infiltrated to think that the Sons would feed off my love for her. I opened my eyes and stared at Grandad, and spoke softly.

"I shall grieve for Daisy, Grandad, but also I shall rejoice in her finding peace, because it found and covered her so gently."

Grandad smiled and lay back down beside me. There we lay in silence, the rain lashing against the windows. Time slowly passed and still we lay there, both too tired to talk and both content just to be still.

I could hear somebody slowly approaching up the stairs, stopping every couple of steps, unsure if they were welcome in this part of the house, but too inquisitive to stop. The creaking slowly continued. The bedroom door swung open as lightning filled the sky.

Then quickly around the bed it approached. I lay still as a heavy weight pushed upon the mattress, and there he was staring down at me with his big pink tongue dripping out past his wet black nose.

"Hello, Archie." Just hearing his name caused his body to move wholly side to side as his tail swayed his enthusiastic welcome. I held my hands to his lovely soft face and he pushed his wet nose down to me and groaned his playful talk. I had felt so empty, but just holding Archie and seeing that uncomplicated love in his eyes made my heart slowly come alive.

Grandad laughed and held his hand to Archie's face. Archie pulled at Grandad's hand gently with his powerful jaw, and sat back on the floor to give us both an impatient big bark.

"Archie, Archie!" called Arthur from downstairs.

"He is up here, Arthur," I shouted down, as Archie had already trotted around the bed to stare at Arthur from his high point on the landing.

"There you are, Archie. Did you go exploring?" Arthur said, bounding up the stairs.

I pulled myself upright. Grandad stood brushing Archie's ever-moulting fur from his fine suit. I stared at the window, seeing nothing of Daisy's creation and watching wave after wave of rain roll off the glass.

"Hell's bells, Grandad," I choked, jumping to my feet. "Willoughby and the others are up there on the steps while Bluebell Wood is being washed clean!"

CHAPTER 38

Together We Survive

Grandad and I peered through the window to the darkness that lay so deeply within the sky. Sheet lightning now flashed continuously upon the ocean of water that hurried in its turn to fall to Earth. I had never seen a storm so fierce nor lightning battle so tirelessly to break through the thick cover of cloud beneath it. How I wished that my sweet friends hadn't left, but I could quite understand why Bluebell would travel there for her wonderful Daniel. I just prayed that they had cleared the steps before the rainfall.

At that time, I was ignorant of their plight, as even my heightened senses for my little ones had faded with Bluebell Wood. I was just thankful that the Sons had left and that no harm had come to anyone else at Granton Manor. But even with the evil that had stood next to my bed, there was little desire in the demons that held their image to leave a trail of brutality behind them. Their hands were too soft to wield an axe. That would be left to the likes of Wilson and Doggett, to fight in the dirt for the pleasure of revenge and the blood that runs through it.

I sighed deeply and held my hands to the glass, sending my love to my sweet Bellas and all that remained good in Bluebell Wood. Knowing now, however, what my Bellas had gone through, it pains me to write the following.

If only I could have seen my friends' progress. I'm sure the deep fear within me would have cleared for a while. The Malissols' attempt to take cover in the main circle of Bluebell Wood had meant that my Bellas had managed to pass through the long grass of the meadow. That was now free of snow, as the rain fell in drops so big that a clear hit would knock them heavily into the mud that deepened with every step. Leanndi had marched forward, leading the way as usual, until her big boots sank as three raindrops hit her with precision, knocking her into the ground with a splash, splash, splash. Oakleigh pulled at Leanndi to free her, but was too weak with laughter. Seeing Leanndi being neatly squashed had amused him to the point of collapsing. Leanndi held her arms up to be rescued, as always awaiting one of the other three to hold her safe in times of misfortune.

Willoughby took charge, pushing Oakleigh aside and pulling Leanndi like a cork popping free from the mud. She held her arms around Willoughby's neck and couldn't wait to tell of her experience.

"That felt so funny," she said. "Really quite good fun," she chuckled.

Oakleigh still laughed until a large raindrop flattened him out of sight, bringing him to an abrupt silence.

"But not as funny as that," Leanndi giggled, pointing past Willoughby's shoulder to Oakleigh, who raised just his head, squelching free from the deep mulch.

Even Bluebell found a second to laugh at Oakleigh, who

slipped hopelessly in his determination to rise to his feet without assistance.

"Of course, I would help you, Oakleigh," Bluebell said, standing clear of him as he pulled himself vertical with the help of the strong meadow grass, "but you can quite understand that I don't wish to get any mud past my parka onto my fine dress."

Oakleigh moaned as his big boots slipped under him and he steadied himself and pulled his filthy hair away from his ears. "Everybody shush," he said, moving to his side, avoiding another forceful hit from the rain, which landed to his left, covering him with its mucky aftermath. He quickly wiped his face again and listened. "Can you hear anything?"

"Hear what?" Leanndi said, no longer laughing, as Oakleigh's face was unusually stern.

"I felt the ground rumble under my body when I lay in the dirt," Oakleigh said, kneeling back down and pushing his hands deep into the goo where his body had lain. "Yes, I can feel it like before. It is moving beneath us."

Willoughby pushed his cane past Oakleigh's hands and let it stand free. It shook vigorously, sinking further as it did. He pulled it back and dragged Oakleigh to his feet.

"Come, we must go," he said, pointing the direction with a nod of his hat and beating the long grass aside to clear a path.

They battled through the ever-rising mud, each in turn being buried by the raindrops that grew to an unforgiving size. They pulled at one another, never losing their grip, linked by a trust that would sink together or live to tell the tale. Their little bodies tired with their efforts and weakened as the mud began to move with a current, dragging at them to sink in the darkness and to give in to its increasing strength.

Willoughby pushed his cane hard into the solid ground that rose under the cover of a small copse of trees, and pulled, with his remaining strength, his little chain of friends onto the hard surface. The raindrops had torn at the branches and they lay strewn around, ripped to pieces by the very same rain that had shared its gentle drops to give them life.

The four of them crawled to the base of the largest tree and pushed hard into the trunk for the little shelter that the bark could give them, and to rest. The sheet lightning cracked above, giving them light to view their broken Land. They stared down to Bluebell Wood in the distance. They watched as the river that snaked, dividing the Land to their left, rose in its valley to form a lake in the sky. Raindrops fell, of uniform size, crashing with the power of rock, breaking the dry land and filling the wet. The waves grew in their new home, jumping high and curling back down, overspilling the valley to add weight to the slush that recruited everything in its path to creep forward with its destructive power.

The light in the library, where many Relayers had plotted their quest against evil, still shone high above Bluebell Wood. Had Wilson left or was he still unaware of the fate of this once-unrivalled Land?

All four stood, breathing deeply with their backs tight against the tree, each shaken to the core as they watched the beauty of the Land turn upon itself. The weight of the mudslide reached the edge of Bluebell Wood, felling the smaller trees, swallowing them up as they cracked in cries for help before being engulfed in its flow. The skyline of the woodland had changed forever and all that had stayed within it were taken beneath it.

Bluebell moved to face Willoughby. She didn't have to

say anything as he pulled her close. Her Daniel was stabled in the woods. As Willoughby held her tiny shivering body, he watched the light in the library fall into darkness. The thunder above built to a crescendo of power, spitting a burning white fork into the heart of the wood, and all was silenced by that downward stroke of its baton. The rain became fine and soft and the waves on the lake settled.

CHAPTER 39

Not For Glory Do We Die

For us on Earth in Granton Manor, the rain had cleared the snow and was now a fine drizzle. I stood at the patio doors and watched the silence fall on the grounds. Archie sat beside me, trying to see past his own reflection and nudging my hand with his big wet nose.

I turned to Grandad. "The rain has stopped."

He smiled, as the ticking of the ornamental travel clock became the most dominant, but gentle, sound.

The past couple of hours, and the loss that they held within them, had been beyond words. So, eerily, we just continued as if they had not happened.

I faced the room and it looked just as it had before the Sons' arrival. Arthur busied himself, helping Bo keep the fire, and Grandad sat with an unusually quiet Boomer, who had talked himself into silence.

Bo leant down to clear the delicate china cups from the table, but he stopped and held his large hand away from them as they began to rattle in their saucers.

"That's not me doing that," he said, opening his eyes wide for a clear view of the strange happenings.

We all looked on as the shaking became vigorous. The cups moved to the edge of the tray, gathering at one end, tipping over and shaking out the little tea that remained onto the tray. They were soon joined by the ornaments that began to dance across their surfaces, dropping to the floor, breaking and becoming a puzzle of pieces.

Not one of us moved. We stood or sat fast, holding onto ourselves as the room around us began to fall apart.

I then dared to move, as a noise, loud and unfamiliar, grew from the small woodland. I threw open the patio doors and watched the trees being crushed. The flowing mud and debris had followed the invisible steps, bringing its force down to Granton Manor. The clouds had parted from their source and the moon shone a light upon Bluebell Wood's open wound as it bled down upon us. The ground shook under the weight of the twisted trees and wave after wave of flowing mud. As it crashed into Earth it shot as high as a fountain, erupting onto the fine lawns.

The commotion had brought forward the Romans for battle. Led by Claudius, they hurried past us and formed ranks on the lawn.

"What are you doing, Claudius?" I screamed.

He ignored my words at first as he brought his men into line just short of the debris that had been spewed out from the heart of the impact. He raised his sword towards it and turned his head sharply to me.

"If Bluebell Wood has cleared herself of the evil that stood on her, they have fallen to Earth and onto our swords," Claudius said, filling his lungs to ignite his body ready for battle.

I didn't answer him. I just looked at the carnage within the sheer weight of the flying mud, and at how it had brushed aside the woodland. I couldn't believe that anything could survive in it.

The clouds, which had parted for that short time, closed again, and the flow drew still. Branches and twigs still continued to snap as the mud settled on them.

And then it started. That awful crowing that had followed us around the Abbey in St Albans.

One at first, soon to be joined by thousands, as the evil Malissols pulled themselves from the mush, crawling free like maggots upon rotting flesh. The Romans, in response to their battle cry, slammed their swords upon their shields.

Archie barked with hackles up, snarling into the darkness.

"Take him inside, Arthur," Grandad said. "This is beyond the strength of even Archie."

Arthur, of course, dragged Archie back – perish the thought of any harm coming to him – though he disagreed, saying under his breath that Archie could probably stand alone against the Malissols and still win.

A slight breeze ran gently across the Romans, rustling Claudius's hair that was still shaped back neatly into a crest. The mudslide had built high, giving the Malissols the advantage in military strategy. But Claudius knew that it had also buried the trees, making no hiding place for his enemies, leaving them no choice but to fight in open battle, which would surely be the advantage the Romans required.

As the crowing rose, I called to Claudius to bring his army back into Granton Manor. But my words had no sound to him as he ordered his magnificent army to move forward. I stared at the clouds, watching them again pulling apart, thinning just enough to let the moonlight show the mighty number that had risen from the mud, led by their unhinged Doggett, who screamed the rage of a thousand rabid dogs. He frothed at the mouth and laid his battle-axe into his own men, showing no mercy to anyone who stood between himself and Claudius.

I hated Doggett. To me he was even worse than the Sons, dumb in rage and blinded by his fury. He had no place on Earth, or on our Lands, but he knew that, and that was the seed that gave birth to his hate. The sweet soul that had once possessed him should have died to honour his failed quest. And it would have done, if it had not been for Wilson tampering with the outcome. But now, to evil's joy, these empty shells of Bellas were happily home to the darkness which challenged everything that we were.

The Malissols moved across the mud, gathering pace. No ranks, no order. Just a vastness to their number, their gurgling battle cry filling the air. The first wave hit hard into the waiting spears and swords that held close behind the military strength of the Roman shield.

Both the Bellas and Malissols fought the battle in their largest possible size. Each side was looking for the advantage which, for now, was given to the Roman legionaries in their organisation. For them the battle was being won by holding fast and trusting the hand of their fellow soldier. But I knew that this battle would only be won, in truth, by Claudius or Doggett. Whoever could stand as the other fell would bring forth the victory.

Claudius screamed, moving forward from his locked army.

"We will end this tonight, Doggett. On this night."

I am sure that Claudius knew that Doggett had greater power within him, as Doggett cut with his axe into the air, twisting it upon his head. Turning with the power of a tornado, it crashed into Claudius's shield, splitting it, and Claudius fell to his side. Doggett had no words for his former friend. His savagery could not be spoken as he drooled upon Claudius, wheeling his axe down, as Claudius blocked and pulled himself to his feet.

Wave after wave of Malissols rolled down the mud, breaking the locked shields of the Romans, only to have them push forward to lock once again and to drive their spears through the empty hearts of the Malissols.

And still Claudius held his sword in his strong hand, straining at every muscle in his arm, as Doggett's axe, with the weight of a mighty oak, crashed down.

I ran from the light of the patio doors. I picked up a garden fork and was eager to fight.

My anger replaced any fear. I ran past the rear of the Roman army. I felt Bo beside me and he swung his own axe.

"I wish that could stop Doggett," I shouted above the noise of battle. "But the blow has to come from the hands of a Bella."

Grandad, Boomer and Arthur joined us, the latter two ignoring Grandad's wishes, Arthur holding back a vicious Archie.

We stood side by side, a band of hope, willing to die in a fight for the good of creation as the rest of the world slept or awoke to a new day. The most unlikely heroes, as each of us in our way had found ourselves here protecting a society that didn't want us or we had failed to understand and fit into.

Grandad was old and frail, having given his life to the

Bellas. Arthur had been shunned by his parents and society. Bo, a good man who had never been given a chance. Archie, used and mistreated. And me, born to question and to lose my parents so I could stand here on this night. And, of course, little Boomer, fascinated by flight due to his fear of it, only to find himself to be a natural aviator, now without a plane.

I felt for Daisy's hands through instinct, but clasped the dark night instead. I quickly closed the door on my loss of her before it consumed my heart again.

We stepped forward with our garden tools. Me with my fork. Bo with his axe. And Grandad with his unfrightening hoe. We knew that our participation would have little impact, but to do nothing would most certainly have less.

Claudius had found his footing, bending his torso as Doggett's battle-axe scarred his body plate armour. Thrusting forward, he plunged his sword beneath Doggett's collarbone, cutting it in two as he pulled back with his blade. The severed bone broke free through the skin, halting Doggett just for that second as he twisted his neck right over to feed off the wound, holding his mouth open, catching the blood that poured freely out. Claudius swung again to catch Doggett off guard, but he had moved clear of Claudius's blade and swung his axe low, striking and embedding it into Claudius's thigh.

We gasped and I screamed as I saw Claudius drop. Doggett pulled at his axe, jarring the head from Claudius's thigh, exposing a large wound that had cut to the bone. He plunged his axe again into Claudius, who tried to defend himself as he lay wounded in the mud.

I ran forward to reach him, but the line that the Romans had formed to defeat the Malissols was preventing me from aiding my gallant friend. I screamed his name as I watched

Doggett plunge his axe downward. I pulled my garden fork back, using it as a spear. In desperation I hurled it towards Doggett. The centre forks passed either side of him, pinning him back against the mud from where he had crawled.

"Archie, no, Archie!" Arthur cried as he broke free from Arthur's hold. Leaping forward over the Romans, he snapped his huge white fangs hopelessly around Doggett's solid, impregnable body. Within seconds Archie was engulfed in the savagery of the Malissols.

I looked on in horror as he battled, snarling and biting, and then sank to the ground yelping as they tore at the soft flesh beneath his deep fur.

"Archie!" Arthur cried and jumped among the Romans to save his loving companion.

Grandad yelled to the Romans on his command to move forward. The war machine grunted with each step, moving like a dam against the wave of darkness, containing it and slicing at the heart of each Malissol that flowed in the current towards them. They moved up to Claudius and Archie and brought them back cocooned under their shields.

Doggett stood again, pulling at his vocal chords as his twisted screams penetrated through the heart of the legionaries. They marched to mow him down as he watched Claudius being dragged away from his wheeling axe. With ease he had removed himself and the fork from the mud, plunging the prongs of it into the line of shields that had taken Claudius.

The line broke and time slowed, exposing Claudius once more. He was standing, but with only enough strength left to stare his victor in the eyes as Doggett cut through his weakened sword arm, and continued that fatal blow into his heart.

I watched him drop, defeated and silent, never giving Doggett joy to hear him scream or to see fear. He fell back and lay in the soil of his final battle, eyes open, gazing to the sky where his home remained behind the dark clouds. One slight and final effort to raise his sword and then it fell to his side.

The strength in the Roman shields weakened as word ran like poison through the lines that Claudius, their great leader, had fallen.

Grandad called out. "Move forward! Hold fast! Make this a victory for ever in honour of Claudius!"

And on those words we ran without fear into the darkness and the outcome it held.

Doggett must fall, I knew too well. So think, Jessie, I punished myself, think now! I watched Boomer run at great speed beside Bo, dodging the large axe as it swung by Bo's side.

"Get on the axe," I shouted to Boomer, who jumped on the head as it swung like a pendulum towards him.

The battle now howled around me.

Arthur cradled Archie's large, brave head in his arms. His soft warm fur was now matted in blood. Bare flesh was cut deep where trophies of fur were ripped in clumps and his ears showed the puncture wounds of the feast that he would have become.

"You are so brave, Archie," Arthur sobbed. "So brave. Please get up, Archie. Come back inside."

If Archie could have moved from where he lay, he would have done. Just minutes ago we had all been enjoying the warmth and cosiness of Granton Manor, only to be pulled outside by evil and to lose Claudius and many of his fine legionaries. But for now, Archie's comfort would be within Arthur's arms and his familiar breath.

Time circled around me as repeated blows of sword and axe spiralled into carnage. I watched Doggett continue his feast of slaughter, ripping through the Roman lines. He was growing in strength as they fell before him, despite his collarbone jutting out and still dripping blood.

I slipped on the mud as I tried to keep up with Bo's long stride.

I shouted, "You can destroy Doggett, Bo. Make the fatal cut be Boomer's. Release the axe, Bo, and fly, Boomer. Fly for us all, Boomer!"

Bo never stopped. He neither turned to me nor reduced his stride as he pulled the axe back upon his shoulder. He twisted his upper body and screamed as the power inside him released into the axe. He fell forward as the axe stole his coordination and soared free from his large hand, invisible but for the sound of the metal blade turning, propelling itself across the field of battle, whirring forward in the hunt for its target.

The moon shone on this stage for Doggett, silhouetting his final scene. He opened his arms and howled to the sky. The axe brought down the curtain and buried its blade into his centre. It pushed on through his spine, which cracked just as the trees had done under the mud that had brought this evil army.

How one sound could rise above a thousand others, signalling the battle's end for the Malissols! They fell, weak, under Doggett's cracked spine. His pulse was the heartbeat of the army and those who didn't flee were taken from this field by the strike of a Roman's sword.

Boomer had closed his eyes on his flight and kept them so until he was removed from the chest of Doggett.

The breeze stroked my hair, just as it had brushed over Claudius before this battle, and that is the image I shall hold of him: Claudius, strong and brave, leading his army, not for glory, but for the good that it could uphold. I stood where he had fallen, but already his body had passed, just like the legionaries who had died alongside him. All invisible in death, as they were to the human eye in life. But not to all. Not for us. We have the honour of being part of this complicated struggle between good and evil and of knowing and holding dear to us the greatest of souls.

CHAPTER 40

The Mighty Hollow Oak

Although our night was drawing to a close as the battlefield was cleared, it was not so for my Bellas floating high above. This, I am told, is what unfolded for my poor little ones.

Bluebell had moved from Willoughby's hold, but was not ready to let go completely. She held his hand tightly as the four of them moved from the cover of the tree and stood upon a fallen branch. All that they had known had gone, and the fields that had once been nature's perfect hideaway were now churned and beaten by the rain that it had trusted to quench its thirst, only to have it fall upon its fragile and colourful landscape, drowning the friend it had enjoyed in Bluebell Wood.

"Do you think anyone got free of the Land before the Malissols found them?" Oakleigh asked, squatting down on the branch and pulling at the bark.

Bluebell tilted her head down towards the ground then raised it a little and peered past the rim of her hat towards

Oakleigh. "I have no doubt that many Bellas would have jumped free from Bluebell Wood, and those who stayed would have found hiding places. This storm and its ferocity, though..." Bluebell shook her head then continued, "It makes me question: was it Mother Nature who did this to her own Land? No one else has this power."

An eerie feeling fell between the four of them, which Willoughby quickly broke.

"It could have been Greschen," he said, giving a hint of a smile out of the corner of his mouth. "For sure." He paused, nodded his head slowly and then continued. "Greschen has the power; she wouldn't have let the Malissols settle upon her Land." He raised his cane and pointed out to the far horizon. "She could have guided the winds and the rain to wipe her fields clean from the poison that has walked upon them."

Leanndi looked at Willoughby and began to cry. "I still don't like what has happened even if it was Greschen getting rid of the Malissols because where are all the Bellas and Poppy?" She sniffed and wiped her nose on the back of her paw and again asked, "Where is my little sister?"

"Leanndi," Oakleigh said, springing to his feet to comfort her. "I'm sure Greschen or Mother Nature wouldn't have hurt them, in fact I'm certain of it. I was just being careless with my words." Oakleigh held her tiny head under his chin.

Willoughby knew, as he placed his hand on Oakleigh's shoulder, that uncomfortable as it was, the question of who had survived on Bluebell Wood was the only one that mattered now. Yet it would have to wait until safety was restored around them. The four of them were clearly numbed and lost for direction. The branch that they now sat upon became their escape. It raised them from the ground and was free of movement. They sat in a row as they had always done, big boots dangling free, swinging, as they were all lost in thought.

Silence was once a rare sound in Bluebell Wood, because in truth it never *was* silent. Every part had its own voice, from the noisiest oak swinging its mighty branches to the grass whispering as the breeze moved through it, telling a story to every blade. The river never slowed, tinkling its melody as it polished the pebbles that formed its bed. But now it truly was utterly silent.

It was not to remain so, however, as the sky that they sat within was shattered by three painfully loud claps sending shock waves, hitting hard what little there was left to be disturbed. The branch that they sat on trembled, shaking them to the ground.

"That's the cannons!" Bluebell shouted, quickly jumping to her feet and straightening her clothes. She no longer bothered to brush herself down, as the struggle through the mud had put them sadly beyond a simple overhaul.

Again the massive claps of three shook the air as Oakleigh ran to the tree that had so kindly sheltered them, and scampered up on the bark, using for footing the fresh splintered wood from where the branches had been torn away.

The others followed his lead and, just for that short second on reaching the top, they saw with delight, in the distance, the silhouette of the cannon turrets standing undisturbed by the movement of the Land or indeed by the Malissols, as even they would have known the significance and importance of the cannons to their intended stay upon this Land.

Bluebell's gaze was not on the turret. It was taken by the

mighty hollowed oak that now stood alone, as the young trees that had grown beside their great mentor hadn't survived the storm.

The cannons fired a third round, and then a fourth.

"I don't want to alarm anybody," Bluebell said calmly, "but I think that they may well have missed their target and I really don't want to be up this tree if that is the case."

"Oh no," Oakleigh said, sounding wearied. "I am so tired. Can't we just wait and see what happens?"

"No, we cannot," Bluebell snapped. She continued at Oakleigh as she pulled him from the top of the tree and they landed, big boots first, upon the mud below. "If a large plane flies across this Land, we will be picked into the sky by its turbulence and we will end up wherever, and most certainly separated."

Willoughby and Leanndi squelched down beside them as the shots of three became a consistent thud, and the sound of the jet engines became audible.

"We must hurry," Bluebell said, pushing them along.

"Hurry where, though?" Leanndi asked, turning nervously to the black sky and the noise of a hurricane being pushed through a needle's eye as the jet rocketed towards them.

"Follow me," Bluebell demanded, as they ran, leaping over the debris and using its trail to show them the firmer ground which had not been swallowed by the mud.

"To the oak tree!" Bluebell shouted, urging them forward away from the small copse of trees, pointing to the huge dark silhouette in the distance.

Leanndi picked the pace up, determined to lead again, running the route that they should follow.

"Stop, Leanndi!" Willoughby yelled, as the debris had

disappeared and all that lay between them and that mighty oak was flat and dark, tempting a careless foot forward.

"It's okay, I can see the way," Leanndi answered, as Willoughby dived at her back, only reaching her ponytail, and they fell together and disappeared out of sight. Oakleigh pulled at Bluebell's arm as they fell too, sliding to the edge of the once-vibrant field, though they stopped just short of being swallowed themselves.

"Oh my word, Oakleigh! We nearly went in too!" Bluebell gasped, struggling for her footing to continue after her precious friends. "We must find them and get them out!"

"Bluebell, no, it will take you too!" Oakleigh cried, pulling her back and firmly pushing her to the solid ground.

He moved quickly back to the fallen branches and returned holding one aloft. Standing on the thickest end, he lowered it like a drawbridge upon the layer of water that had been returned by the regurgitating mud.

"Hurry, Oakleigh. Please hurry," Bluebell said, shuffling her little gloved paws and begging her eyes to see just the tiniest movement.

Oakleigh reduced in size and scampered along the branch. Under its own weight it slowly submerged as Oakleigh lay flat upon it and pushed his arms, at full stretch, either side. He desperately felt for his friends and, believing that he had made contact, he became full-size to reach for a secure hold.

The cannons increased their shots and the jet engines, fed on the pure air, sucked their way ever closer. Oakleigh pulled his arms straight out to his side and raised from the mud Leanndi in his right hand and Willoughby in his left. Neither showed life as Oakleigh sank upon the branch in a frantic attempt to keep both on the surface.

Bluebell screamed and pulled at the bark, but the mud swallowed back its prey, unwilling to let them go free. The bark slipped through Bluebell's hands and ripped her gloves and delicate pads beneath, and she cried her high-pitched squeal, desperate for help to arrive. Again, the shriek left her mouth, beckoning any Bellas who might be near for immediate help. She left the safety of the solid ground and blindly walked into the mud, fixing her eyes upon the spot that had moved to cover any evidence that her friends were once there. The mud quickly rose around her, and sobbing, she pushed her hands in, stretching her little fingers, longing for the tips to touch her companions as she, too, was sucked further down.

She called out once more and stared forwards to the large oak, resting her body and no longer fighting. Bluebell remembered Daniel and Jessie hiding within that hollowed tree. She pictured her wonderful stallion charging forward as he had done on that day. And now the image was so vivid she smiled as she could almost hear his mighty stride powering in an unstoppable force. She blinked her eyes as the mud rose to her chin and Daniel's velvet nose pushed gently into her face.

"How lovely," Bluebell said, remembering his soft kiss, when Arkley dropped the reins upon her head, snapping Bluebell back to reality.

"Daniel!" she yelled, lifting her chin and mustering the strength to pull her arms free from the mud. She held onto the rein that dangled down so she could reach it. "Daniel!"

Arkley appeared between the horse's ears and stared down at her. "Hold tight, Bluebell," he said, unaware that she was the tip of the Bellas who lay in the mud beneath her. That moment of joy in finding Daniel was left on the surface as

Bluebell pushed herself back into the mud, sinking out of sight, but for her hand, aloft, tightly holding the rein.

Arkley waited. Then he looked on in disbelief when the rein became taut and Bluebell pulled herself back into view. Spitting the mud from her mouth, she softly and with little strength to her words asked Daniel to walk on. Instantly her faithful friend followed her command. Slowly, but with his controlled power, he pulled Bluebell and a chain of three Bella-shaped lumps of mud to the solid ground.

Arkley dismounted, flexed his muscular strength and placed two at a time upon Daniel. The jet plane cast its monstrous silhouette in the distance, and was soon over the cannon turret, as once more the race between horse and man-made machine was started by a final cannon shot.

Bluebell raised her head to peer along Daniel's mane and the target of the hollowed oak between his ears. She had no need for words as her wonderful steed had found her and was galloping her and the others to the safety that he knew lay in the tree.

How hard the charge must have been, even with the power that ran in Daniel's legs, as the mud pulled at each stride, sucking at his hooves and spitting up at his beautiful face. Snorting back his annoyance at the Land and at the jet that stole the air from his lungs, Daniel tucked his front legs under his chest as they rose from the mud and flew, just for that moment, as did the plane that bore down upon them. They were only just in time to enter the hollowed oak, as the turbulence tore at its roots and that awful smell of aviation fuel fell like a poisonous mist.

The heat from Daniel's body flattened his coat with sweat and he snorted to catch his breath. Shaking his head from side to side and with muscles twitching, he gave small whinnies as his body and mind slowly calmed.

"It's okay, everybody," Arkley said to the darkness inside the hollowed tree. "The Malissols have gone. I feel that we are safe to light a lamp now."

Hundreds of tiny voices chatted in the dark as the lamp was struck and the light grew to show the Bellas' colony within this trunk, quite safe and sound.

"Quickly, let's get them down," Arkley said, sliding Oakleigh, Willoughby, Leanndi and a very disorientated Bluebell from Daniel's broad back.

"Leanndi, is that you under that mud?" a very tiny voice said, moving forward and holding a magnifying glass up to her own face and then to Leanndi's.

Leanndi coughed. With eyes still tightly closed, she answered, "Is that you, Poppy?"

"Yes, it is, Leanndi. I missed you so much. Are you okay?" Poppy replied, holding the glass inches away from Leanndi's face and wiping the mud clear.

"I'm always okay, Poppy," Leanndi replied, stretching her little arms and legs and knocking her big boots together.

Poppy stared through the magnifying glass, inches away from her sister, waiting for Leanndi to open her eyes. Leanndi opened them slowly, blinked a couple of times and then jumped up as she focused on this huge face bearing down on her.

"Oh sorry, Leanndi, it's only me," Poppy said, pulling the magnifying glass quickly to the side of her face to show herself in true scale, and then back to see every moment of reaction from her sister.

Leanndi held her arms out and Poppy leant forward into them.

"I was so worried for you, Poppy," Leanndi said, knowing all too well how wonderful an embrace is to lessen fear and just to comfort.

"I was so worried too," Poppy replied, nestling into her big sister, enjoying the affection that is known to be there but not often shown between siblings.

As Willoughby, Oakleigh and a very silent but emotional Bluebell came further into the tree, their joy and relief at finding everybody there took their breath in the most perfect way. The mighty hollow oak stood strong to care for its thankful guests. It was a very decent surrogate home. The single lamp cast happy shadows of loved ones embracing each other joyfully.

CHAPTER 41

Downstairs to Earth

Dawn wiped away the darkness for us on Earth and for the Bellas above. I reflected on how awful it had been. The night was thankfully coming to its close. Although we had taken the Malissols apart, the losses had been great. Archie now lay on the chaise longue, which we had moved closer to the fire. Arthur comforted him while Grandad and I washed his wounds. Archie never fussed or whimpered, even though he must have been in the greatest of pain.

I couldn't help thinking how marvellous Archie's actions had been. What had driven him to close down from Arthur's wishes to stay by his side, and to lunge forward at Doggett? How hard humans find it to distinguish between good and evil, when animals see it all so clearly. And how very brave he was to offer himself to protect our great Claudius, with whom he had spent so little time. We thankfully found each wound and cleaned and bandaged them. A little relief came from our efforts, as Archie closed his eyes to sleep.

I watched dawn creep tentatively upon us, and nervously

it brought light to a landscape that was now new to my eyes. The mud had simply destroyed these fragile grounds and moved me from my past to a new beginning. I didn't feel the loss one would expect to feel when looking upon such ugliness. I felt a time for great change was dawning.

I placed my hand to feel for the music box that I had carelessly taken into battle, and my heart jumped for fear of its being damaged. I pulled it free and raised its lid to hear, to my relief, the beautiful melody welcoming this new day. I breathed deeply, feeling Daisy's breath within the air that opened my lungs, and my beating heart raced for us both. I looked to the sky and followed the muddy steps reaching through the clouds. If anyone was awake to see this sight, the steps looked like a trail of thick smoke spiralling up to choke the sky above.

Everyone down here who had made it through the night was now safe in Granton Manor and my thoughts jumped from good to bad and the fate of all my loved ones in Bluebell Wood. And, of course, my gallant four.

Still holding the music box, I listened to the tune dancing its way back to the Floating Land it was written for, and I pictured each note being plucked from the air to be stored in the heart of a new Bluebell Wood. I let the notes fly repeatedly from my hand, pollinating the mud that had brought such destruction, but would now be used for the bed of nature's survival.

Arkley, too, had watched the dawn rise, and he brought out of the tree everybody who had hidden safely within its secret hollow. This was their home that they were gazing at and which was now all but gone.

Bluebell led Daniel, still unsettled by the night's events,

but very thankful to have him by her side. She had wasted no time in cracking and shaking the dried mud from her clothes. On seeing Willoughby, Oakleigh and Leanndi appearing into the daylight, still laden with mud too, she shook herself again to encourage the same actions from her weary friends.

Poppy skipped forward, magnifying her little face as all the young did, as they looked in horror at the destruction of their Land. She peered up to Leanndi and asked the simple and only question.

"What now?"

Leanndi leant forward and stroked her sister's head.

"I think we should go and see Jessie," Leanndi said, sounding quite the adult.

"What, down there?" Poppy asked, finding a very big smile and raising her voice. "What, down the steps to Earth?" she continued, sharing her enthusiasm loudly with the rest of the colony, who started a whisper of expectation.

Willoughby turned his hat upon his right hand, spraying the dried mud free.

"I'm with Leanndi," he said, watching his hat wobble to a halt. He then placed it back on his head, adjusted it to its crooked style and tapped Bluebell with his cane. "Could Daniel make that journey across the field and take us all to Granton Manor?" he asked.

Bluebell pulled Daniel's head down and whispered in his ear. He raised his head high and nodded, running his left hoof into the hard ground, eager to make that charge.

The air of anticipation rose to high excitement as Bluebell, Willoughby, Oakleigh, Leanndi and the others reduced and found their spot upon their brave horse's back. Bluebell turned him twice and he leapt forward, charging once more with his perfect stride. They ran close to the newly formed lake and watched as it broke just a little of its bank to let the clear water run alongside Daniel, leading its way to wash the steps clean.

Back at Granton Manor, I called everybody to the patio doors, and together we watched the spectacle of the water running from the Land above. It trickled and rolled down the steps as rain falls upon a marble floor, gathering pace as each sheet of water fell to the next, until the flow became seamless. Gently, without sound, the water poured from the sky, striking the willing seeds that lay dormant to flower from nature's palette. A spot of white disturbed the water flow, growing in size as it spiralled down within the fall.

Grandad stood beside me and his firm grip rubbed his rough skin around my hand. He chuckled, and then laughed aloud. "If the ancient Greeks had the flying horse Pegasus, do you think that he might have taken these very steps that Daniel is treading to us?"

"Oh my word, Grandad!" I replied, barely squeezing my words past my elation. "It is, isn't it? It truly is Daniel."

I walked, quickly at first, and then broke into a run, leaning forward and using my hands to crawl up the steep bank of mud where its flow had halted. I reached the top and stood panting as Daniel pulled up and nudged his hellos, almost tumbling me back down the steep sludgy incline.

"Hello, Daniel," I said, steadying myself. "I can't tell you how pleased I am to see you." I dared to look past his ears to see Bluebell proudly back where she reigned completely, seated high upon her beloved horse.

"Hello, Bluebell. You are such a wonderful sight," I said,

holding tight to the reins. I was going to allow no more disappearing. Well, not for the foreseeable future anyway. Bluebell showed me such love in her smile that before I asked my next fearful question she spoke.

"It's okay, Jessie. We are all safe and well."

And at those words my tense muscles that held onto hope could now relax, lightening my body and allowing me to breathe with ease.

"Jessie!" Leanndi shouted, leapfrogging Bluebell, sliding down Daniel's nose and choking me as she threw her arms around my neck.

I let the rein go free and supported Leanndi as I had on our first meeting, resting her in my right arm and, just as it had then, her ponytail tickled my face as she spun her head to look at her fellow Bellas, who dismounted and became full-size.

Grandad called to them to join him. In an orderly manner, without rushing, but with an excitement in their busy little voices, they made their way to Granton Manor. Grandad welcomed each by name, speaking softly but reassuringly to all, just like a kind headmaster putting at ease the new pupils on their fearful first day of school.

I looked for Willoughby and Oakleigh and found them sitting sideways, dangling their big boots on Daniel's left flank. They rocked them and stared wide-eyed, bringing me back to that very first morning when they sat on my bed, speaking happily in riddles about my purpose. Bluebell moved from Daniel's mane and sat beside Willoughby. I kissed Leanndi and placed her next to Oakleigh, then looked at my four sweet companions. I lowered my head and swallowed hard, staring at my boots squelching in the awful mud.

"Daisy's gone," I said. "But not with the Sons."

I raised my head, seeing the sadness in each of their faces. Willoughby removed his hat. "We know, Jessie."

Again I swallowed, struggling to push my words forward. "She made the rain, to wash the evil away," I continued, without detail, as I hadn't the strength to explain.

"We thought it may have been Greschen," Willoughby said. "She almost decimated the place, I must say, but it will all return in time, I have no doubt." He paused and pushed his lips together. Brushing his cane along Daniel's fine coat, he continued quietly. "She had to be that brutal, didn't she? It was the only way."

And that was that. No more was said as I walked them back to Granton Manor, the reins in my hand. The water stopped flowing upon the steps, leaving them invisible and secret again.

Once settled, my wonderful four told me of their horrific experience on our Land above. I couldn't yet speak of mine, and our losses.

So it was much to my relief later that day that the snow fell heavily, and with its pure white covering it took from the forefront of our minds the events that had brought us all together at Granton Manor.

CHAPTER 42

Poppy's Secret

The run of the house was left for all to enjoy. The young Bellas were distracted from thoughts of Bluebell Wood, as this magnificent house had much to amuse them. All day long they played within the many rooms, as hide-and-seek for a Bella could be quite a challenge in a house of this size, particularly when they could reduce to the tiniest speck. The huge stairway, especially the banister, was certainly their favourite: sliding or bumping their way to the bottom never seemed to tire them. But inevitably night fell and with it their energy dropped to a yawn. With little resistance they were placed to bed in the airing cupboard, snuggled safe and warm between the towels.

I had, of course, offered many of the beds, but the airing cupboard had won the vote hands down.

Archie's recovery was slow but positive. Although he still lacked strength, the noise and playfulness of the young, and his popularity amongst them, took his mind off the pain. He smiled most of the day, dropping his big pink tongue out and licking at the little ones as they ran to greet him even before they charged into Bo, ready for breakfast, lunch, dinner and any number of snacks in between.

The night brought with it time for reflection, and I let the darkness rest with us. Bo and Arthur worked tirelessly keeping all fed and the fires roaring, which complemented the dark. We spoke each night of the future and our plans to return to Bluebell Wood. We never used the electricity, not once, as candlelight settled and calmed, creating an ambience for the most wonderful storytelling, led by Grandad, who began with a slight cough to bring everybody close to where he sat with a small glass of whisky and stared into the flames. Even after the young Bellas had gone to bed, the older ones stayed listening, mesmerised by his words.

It was during these times that I would leave to be alone in my parents' room. I sat where I had cradled Daisy's head in my lap and allowed myself to cry. I feel no shame for that. And I did also understand that I would never feel such love for anyone again. But that is how I wished it to be as I would rather hold onto my feelings for Daisy than confuse them in an attempt to love another.

I listened each night to the music box and studied the little painting that Monet had housed within it. Although he had painted it before he met Daisy, it was clear that she had gifted him the ability to create the images that he placed upon the canvas and fill them with life. How consumed he must have felt by the calling of Greschen, to feel her movements amongst the bluebells, and to paint her image without, at that time, having laid his eyes on her. I wasn't sure if the painting brought me comfort or pain. But I treasured it and the box beyond the seconds of my life, which ticked away in front of the thoughts that I now experienced alone.

One night I closed the box and the music tinkled gently away. The stairs creaked as someone with little weight stepped upon them. Still sitting on the bed, I turned and watched the door open very slowly.

"Hello," a tiny timid voice said, leading the way for the owner of it to peer around the door. "Hello, Jessie, are you there?"

I answered and smiled as Poppy's face magnified into view. "Come in, Poppy. It will be nice to have some company," I said, patting the bed.

She reached high and placed the magnifying glass upon the covers and pulled herself up after it.

"What are you doing up?" I asked, lifting her from the cover and placing her with a big cuddle onto my lap. She was lovely and warm, just like a small hot water bottle, and holding her there made me instantly sleepy.

Poppy leant her head back and blinked and squinted up to me. She held fast to her magnifying glass whilst it rested on my thigh.

"I know you might think that I am not telling the truth, but it has troubled me since we left Bluebell Wood," she said, with the tiniest voice.

"What's troubled you, Poppy?" I asked, squeezing her a little more for reassurance.

"It's troubled me that Daisy is alone in Bluebell Wood," she said, pulling the magnifying glass to her face to peer at my reaction.

I stared back at her in shock.

"What do you mean, Poppy? Why would you say that?"

Poppy's brown eyes grew in size and then she faced away from me.

"I know I can't see very much without my glass, but I saw Daisy just before we left Bluebell Wood."

"So, you didn't hold your glass to your face to see her, Poppy?" I asked, leaning close to her and whispering, as it was clear that she was very concerned.

"No, I didn't," she said. "But I didn't need to as she was so clear. The clearest I have ever seen anybody." Poppy began to speak quickly, desperate now to tell all as she continued. "I haven't spoken of it because Daisy smiled at me and held her finger to her mouth and hushed to keep me from telling. But I am worried that she is alone. Can we go and find her? Please, Jessie, can we?"

I held Poppy tight into my stomach and looked to the darkness being lit outside by the moon's reflection on the snow. Poppy's words had numbed me, as they carried with them such hope for Daisy's safe return to her mother and Bluebell Wood. But how could I rejoice in such news from this sighting, knowing of little Poppy's poor vision?

"Of course we shall return," I said, cradling the miniature Bella as I stood. "And don't worry, Daisy is not alone. She has her mother to care for her now."

Poppy smiled at my words and became heavy as she fell straight to sleep. I placed her back in the airing cupboard and stared at the little ones as they slept.

Her news was wonderful, if it was true. I had to find my goggles to try to find out. Did the lenses have sight again? Had Daisy returned to the heart of Bluebell Wood and back to her mother's embrace? If Daisy had found herself, had she found the memory of Greschen? In that case, were the Daughters complete, and with it the balance between the Lands back to its harmonious state?

I hesitated before placing the goggles on my eyes, then put them aside. I didn't need to know. Whatever the outcome, we were going back to Bluebell Wood and we would reclaim our Land.

I had survived with scant sleep in the past few nights, and this night was to be no exception. I returned downstairs to enjoy the enthusiastic silence as Grandad's story, as always, had captivated his audience. A big "Aaah" filled the room as Grandad finished his tale on a happy note and I walked to the fireplace.

"Listen, everybody," I said, clasping my hands together and rubbing them for no reason other than that my favourite teacher, Mrs Woods, had held that stance when addressing the class. The room fell silent and I continued.

"This may seem a little rash, but I think the time has come for us to return to Bluebell Wood. So please take the next hours ahead to sleep. We should leave before first light."

My news was welcomed with a total lack of response, making me feel quite awkward as so many little pairs of eyes held their gaze upon me, reflecting the fire and me in front of it. Not one of them blinked. They just stared and their lids slowly closed as they took my words so literally that they slept where they sat.

I turned to Grandad. How frail he had become, and how at home he looked, warming himself by the fire, enjoying the comforts of Granton Manor.

"It's up to you, Grandad. There are no rules," I said, looking down to this man whose eyes still sparkled with the blue of youth. But now his face could no longer lie for his slowing heart. He didn't answer.

"There is no need to leave Bluebell Wood for good as Wilson did. Never shall that be brought upon you. I promise that," I said, selfishly wanting him with me.

He sighed deeply and stared at the flames as they crackled and spat, and the logs folded and found a new place to lie.

"I am old, Jessie. Too old to be away from home," he said, staring back to me.

I swallowed hard and smiled. "I understand, Grandad."

"No, I don't think you do. I am too old not to be at home." He paused and sighed. "And my home will always be with my family in Bluebell Wood."

I couldn't help myself. I gave the strangest little yelp and leant down to squeeze Grandad so tightly I think it quite took his breath. I called Bo and Arthur to the kitchen.

"I am so sorry, Bo, for ever doubting you. You are a lesson to me and one I will never forget."

Bo smiled and placed his huge hand upon my shoulder.

"Please stay at Granton Manor, Bo. It needs you, as I needed you on the field of battle."

"Of course, Jessie," he replied. His actions were always going to be greater than his words.

I placed my hand around his big thumb now resting on my shoulder, and gave it a squeeze of thanks. Then I turned to Arthur.

"What about you and Archie? Will you stay with Bo or join us in Bluebell Wood?"

Arthur spun his oversized sleeve and peered at Bo, then at me.

"Do you think that I could stay at Granton Manor for now, as Bo would be very lonely, and Archie still needs his strength to return?"

Bo laughed and placed his other hand heavily on top of Arthur's head.

"That sounds just fine by me," Bo said, still laughing at Arthur's considerate nature.

"That's sorted, then," I said, relieved that Granton Manor was in such good hands, and that by their own wishes both had agreed to stay.

CHAPTER 43

Letting Go for Greschen

I think I may have slept a little that night, resting next to Grandad as the fire brought a glow to my cheeks. But I was awake and ready when, at four-thirty precisely the next morning, Bluebell waited on the lawn with Daniel. It was so cold outside it made our departure from Granton Manor even more questionable. The young were not woken, as Bo had wrapped them in the towel where they lay and placed them upon Daniel's back.

Archie knew by the apprehension that filled the air that we were to leave, and he braved the cold once more with Arthur by his side to say goodbye. I kissed his magnificent head and embraced Arthur and Bo. I promised to visit soon and made our goodbyes as brief as possible to lessen the inevitable tears. These two men and, of course, Archie were now my family and it seemed only fitting that they should be safe within the walls of my family home. I had made sure Grandad had packed some nice warm clothes and that he was dressed appropriately for the journey ahead.

With the Bellas reduced in size and Bluebell, Willoughby, Oakleigh and Leanndi all occupying the mane, with Bluebell at the lead, there was room for Grandad to travel upon Daniel. Boomer had emerged from a period of quietness following that fateful night with the Malissols, and was tucked snugly into my parka pocket. I was happy to hold the bridle as we began our walk across the frozen snow and onto the stairs that reached high to the moon and home to Bluebell Wood. Tentatively, I stepped up onto the first of many, and excitement tingled through me as they spiralled out and upwards in front of us. Each tread allowed six paces before a small rise and then six paces again. The steps became clear, with the moonlight picking out our path as we walked upon the glistening air. The cold tried to steal our heat as we rose into its bitter space and Daniel snorted it quickly out of his body. I pulled my hood up and fastened it around my face and enjoyed the snug warmth of my hands within my mittens.

***

As the moon slowly dropped away, our journey was nearing its end. In truth, my first experience upon the invisible steps had been undemanding compared to how it could have been. The mud and debris that had travelled upon them had left a milky sheen, allowing navigating each step thankfully easy. My stomach turned and jumped as Daniel and I placed our first returning footsteps onto Bluebell Wood. How long it had taken us to get there, I could not tell. I just knew that we were there, that we were home.

The mud that had wiped the Malissols free from our Land was now thankfully, as it was at Granton Manor, covered with crisp white snow, and the landscape that had looked so turned and twisted now looked settled. I gasped in wonder at the huge lake that had been formed to my right and looked down the frozen Land to the wood, now sparse, with the watchtower still high within the trees. The Land did look damaged and beaten, but it felt very much alive.

"We're home. We are all home," I said softly, partly for Daisy as well as the Bellas, who dismounted, shaking and shivering their little bodies to defy the cold.

With the waning moon, the sun rose, spraying orange and yellow across the canvas of sky which stood as a perfect backdrop to Bluebell Wood. The trees flexed and stretched their branches, touching one another for reassurance and comfort against the loss of the younger ones. And in doing so they reformed the shelter for the bluebells to grow once more. The Land's uncharacteristic silence was happily broken as we trudged through the snow, our spirits being lifted further as a flurry of birds made their return. They circled, uncertain of the changes and the magnificent new lake. They skimmed low with a slowing beat of their wings and settled down to rest.

As we moved forward, our many boots cleared the snow in our wake, revealing the rebirth of the wildflowers and grass. A vast catalogue of nature had occupied this Land, from the rarest wildflower to the butterflies that were now so seldom, if ever, seen on the world below.

Grandad and I walked together up the wooden steps that led us to the watchtower, and I felt almost too frightened to open the door. Not that I thought that Wilson might still be there, as I knew that evil had little courage. And in truth I knew in my heart that had he stayed with the Malissols, this mudslide and the rain would not have slowed until all was wiped without exception from this Land. I was afraid of the intrusion. Just the fact that he had laid his evil hands upon our library upset me.

I creaked the door open and peered in. I stared first at my bed, feeling very protective about my little nest. But, thankfully, it looked quite unruffled. I then peered around to the library.

Grandad nudged me gently in the back. "Well?" he said.

"It looks okay," I whispered.

"Let me see," he said, nudging me again.

And we walked in.

It is true that it was messy. No doubt, had Wilson had time to think before leaving, he would have done more to disrupt its order. But apart from shivering at the thought of him being there, it was lovely to be home. Grandad and I got straight on with the immediate tidying, and were soon joined by Leanndi, Oakleigh and Willoughby. Bluebell appeared a little later after finding temporary shelter for Daniel.

Within no time it was just as I had held it in my memory with Willoughby, Oakleigh, Leanndi and Bluebell back in a line upon the table and the six of us enjoying a lovely cup of tea.

Grandad came alive within this space, and that night I went to bed while he busied himself in the library. I felt Leanndi settle next to my head on the pillow, and through the night Oakleigh and Willoughby slept a little upon the bed too.

The next day I woke alone, with the sunlight shining brightly and calling me to rise and to join it for a private walk of our new Land.

From there on, each morning I would do the same,

and each day I would find the Land had been sculpted and brushed back together. The bluebells appeared with a simple stroke, thousands to house the Bellas, and with the coming of spring the landscape flowered its completion. In the months following, all of nature's creatures came back home.

The quests had returned, and calm between our Lands was for now settled. I spoke often to my fellow Relayers and we planned to meet that summer. Grandad and I shared the work in the watchtower, at Grandad's request, which gave me time to dream amongst the bluebells as I had done in my childhood with sweet Tansy. And it was in these semi-conscious states that I would spend time with Daisy.

I now lived and looked like a Bella, never out of my dungarees. But I did enjoy walking barefoot and cooling my body in the lake when the sun appeared to be too close. I liked to walk and enjoy every inch of the beauty, and I knew well the grass that stayed cool at its roots and the petals by their fragrance.

Peace covered me on those days. I let go of my mental image of Daisy in the woodland at Granton Manor. I allowed the Sons to leave my inner thoughts, and I replaced them with Greschen within our Land.

The End

The Truth Behind Us All

It was on one of the most glorious summer afternoons that Grandad's shadow fell over me as I lay with my mind in flight. He knelt beside me and gently stroked my hair. He then placed a picture in my hand and asked me to look at it away from the glare of the sun. We walked to the shade of the trees, and as I let my eyes adjust to the light, I looked upon a sepia picture of a beautiful young girl on a large horse. I turned the picture over and read the fine writing:

'Victoria Long, September 1918'.

I studied the picture again, as Grandad shared with me the truth that lay behind it, and the truth that lay behind us all at Bluebell Wood...

This book is printed on paper from sustainable sources managed under the Forest Stewardship Council (FSC) scheme.

It has been printed in the UK to reduce transportation miles and their impact upon the environment.

For every new title that Matador publishes, we plant a tree to offset CO_2, partnering with the More Trees scheme.

For more about how Matador offsets its environmental impact, see www.troubador.co.uk/about/